FIRST, DO NO HARM

FIRST, DO NO HARM

K. AVARD

Kurt S Avard

First Printing, 2020

ISBN 978-1-7354089-0-3 Print

ISBN 978-1-7354089-1-0 Ebook

Front and rear cover art by Alessandra Suppo.

What follows in this book is a work of fiction... somewhat. Though some names have been changed, and others condensed into a single persona, the tale that follows is anything but pure fiction.

Contents

Acknowledgement

With gratitude:
to Jim, without whom this would not have been inspired,
to Karoline, without whom this would not have been edited,
to Milan, without whom this would not have been read,
to Glenn, without whom this would not have been finished,
to Alex, without whom this would not have been published,
and to my parents and Karl, for the dozens of books placed into my
hands throughout my life.

I cherish you all.

O Du Lieber Augustin

O, you dear Augustin, Augustin, Augustin,
O, you dear Augustin, all is lost!

Even that rich town Vienna,
Broke is it like Augustin;
Shed tears with thoughts akin,
All is lost!

Every day was a feast,
Now we just have the plague!
Just a great corpse's feast,
That is the rest.

Augustin, Augustin,
Lie down in your grave!
O, you dear Augustin,
All is lost!

> - Excerpt from the ballad
> "O Du Lieber Augustin" c. 1679

I

A Thirteenth Chime

The light in my hand died along with him.

I was to blame for the death of the former, having failed to realize the smothering gloom as the wick had burnt lower and lower, the flame drowning softly in melted wax. Others in my profession would have preferred a torch, my more complex lantern too elegant for our evening patrols. But a torch to me has always meant impending destruction, the consumption of life. A lantern was more refined, and it was nearly the 18th century. How could we ever pretend to be anything but civil?

Such a concern was beyond the poor devil at my feet. I had discovered him before the darkness descended, a shambling form stumbling across the plaza to collapse on the steps of the Stephansdom herself. I felt her look down at his body with the acquired distaste of disdainful religion, but even in that cold glance I could sense her unease.

Or perhaps that was wishful thinking, a vain desire to not be alone with the disquiet that twisted my stomach into harsh knots.

I clutched at my pocket, my grasping hand going hungry for a moment before it found its quarry. Pulling a tallow candle out, I fumbled blindly in the cold dark, the pale glow from similarly starving streetlamps not enough to assist me in replacing the now-dead candle in my lantern. Shivering, I searched my other pocket for my trusted tinder-box, my matches for the evening having been exhausted an hour before when I indulged in my pipe.

I had nearly relit the candle when the bell sounded overhead, the sonorous boom tolling out the late hour. I heard it peal again and again, counting it along in the beats of my own heart, feeling my face twisting unconsciously when I counted thirteen rings where there should be twelve. The priest would have harsh words with the offender tomorrow, I was sure, but light was a more pressing matter than considering the inconsequential sin.

The flame sparked in hopefulness, the char cloth of my tinderbox carrying the smallest promise of heat. I blew it gently into larger life, holding it to the candle and whispering a soft prayer. I had already been alone in the dark with my unwelcome company for longer than I had intended, the cathedral's tolling distracting me from my role in the night.

Yet once I had coaxed the lantern into its fullness, I wished I had left the newly dead alone in the black. He was far from an attractive man in life, the thick, coarse hair of his face protruding in every direction; his clothes were in tatters, nowhere near enough to preserve him as summer gave way to fall. I gave his pockets a quick search, my skin crawling inexplicably as I felt the outside of his threadbare coat.

My search turned up nothing, not even a keepsake that spoke of any connection to another man, woman, or child. A poor man - from the countryside perhaps - another refugee fleeing the Ottomans. No one, it seemed, would miss him, his fate that of any other pauper.

But it was not his clothes nor his face, as ugly as it was, that had given me pause. In death his looks had decayed further, his skin taut in some places, falling away to reveal flensed flesh in others. Though it may have been a trick of the light, it seemed as if his veins bubbled underneath the patches of unravaged flesh, the thin red and blues lines shrinking from the revealing light of my lantern. His eyes stared into the shade, though I doubted he would see anything ever again.

My examination was blessedly stopped as I heard the doors to the cathedral creak open. A voice called out to me from behind. "Dietrich?" I stood, turning away from the corpse, eyes peering at the shadow that ghosted up to stand next to me.

In spite of my own roiling stomach, I managed a soft smile. "Max. How'd you know it was me?"

My friend smiled back, his wide shoulders shrugging expressively. "Lantern," he said, pointing vaguely at my hand. "You're one of the only watchmen in the city that bother using one of those things. A torch is better, you know. What brings you around these parts?" He looked tired, though that didn't diminish his light tone, nor the mischievous look in his eyes.

That look died as I pointed at the corpse at our feet. "*Mein Gott!* What the hell happened to him?" he asked, crossing himself furiously.

"Hell happened." I said simply. "More than that I can't say without looking at him further."

But I don't think Max heard me, the blood draining from his face until he looked half-dead himself. "Who does this to a man? What kind of demon would... could..."

I pulled the flask from my hip, extending it to him until I had it right in front of his face. "Drink." Waiting until he had fortified himself with a sip, I stayed silent, trying to make sense of the scene myself. Taking back the flask, I took a small swig myself, letting my body warm slightly as the corpse chilled further. "I really can't say. These are far from optimal conditions to even consider the body. I don't have any of my tools, nor do I have the right amount of light to look over all of his extremities.

"Help me get him into the Stephansdom," I said. "Perhaps we will learn more about him there."

I walked halfway to the cathedral door, setting down my lantern before returning to the body. Motioning to Max to move towards the feet - he went grudgingly - I took the body by the arms, my face twisting at the prospect of shifting the heavy burden towards the cathedral narthex.

Tugging sharply, I nearly fell as the body practically flew after me.

I dropped the body with a thump and a harsh curse. Snarling in exasperation, I was ready to scold Max for not warning me before I noticed him standing off to one side. "Are you ok?" he asked, his head tilting to the side in confusion.

I grunted in reply, peering back at the body. In my time with the night watch, I had been called upon to shift my share of bodies. Admittedly more than a few of these would wake up the next morning with a headache or several new bruises, but I was acquainted with the weight of the dead. Though I was nowhere near Max in terms of muscle, I was far from weak; and yet, I had nearly thrown this body about as if he were made of feathers.

What had happened to him to make him so light?

I brushed myself off, waving away Max's helping hand, instead covering the rest of the distance to the cathedral with the body in tow.

"What is the meaning of this! This is a house of God, not the drunkard!" I winced as the bishop stomped over to me, his vestments trailing along the ground behind him like some perverse marital train. I should have anticipated the objection from his eminence, but I had been too intent on finding the truth.

"Forgive me, your Excellency, but we have need of Stephansdom's narthex." I tried to bow my head in respect, but part of me bristled at the bishop's tone. Wasn't God God to rich and poor alike?

He waved away my reply imperiously, peering up at me through clouded spectacles. "I see that, but wouldn't this man be more comfortable somewhere else?" His lip curled in disgust. "One of the almshouses at the city's edge perhaps?"

I couldn't resist my reply. "No, your Excellency, I think a more appropriate place might be below the cathedral in the catacombs. He's quite dead, after all."

A smile came unbidden to my face as the revelation apparently stunned the bishop. Crossing himself several times, he asked, "What in God's name happened to him?"

"That is what I hope to find out, your Excellency." I knelt beside the body again, though I let my eyes drift back to the short clergyman. "Do you think you might manage to say a prayer for our departed brother here? I am not sure there are any others who might regret his passing besides us."

The venom drained from the bishop, a more contrite air coming over him as he crossed his hands again, this time in more silent contemplation. Making the sign of the cross, he smiled gravely. "Of course, my son. May I steal away your friend here as well? Young Max and I often pray the Mitans together, and as you might have heard, that hour has now come and gone. Though I would stay and assist you, perhaps it would be better to leave you alone and see if God might give this newest departed soul peace?"

I knew the bishop was uncomfortable, his shifting from foot to foot apparent even under his robes; it would be better for me to examine the body without other distractions anyway. "Of course, your Excellency. Might I ask for a few candles, perhaps even another lantern if you could spare it?" I waited until he nodded before asking further. "Your Excellency, you just said that the midnight hour has come and gone, yet I could not help before hearing thirteen rings of the cathedral bells?"

The bishop peered back at me, his eyes hidden behind their spectacles. "No, my son. I rang them myself. I let them toll exactly twelve times." He scoffed then, shaking his head in wonderment. "No man of God would ever let bells ring thirteen times! Judas was the thirteenth, and while we could thank him for his part in the Crucifixion, I would never invite such ill luck on this city by ringing his number." He strode away, surprise still in his voice as his back smiled at me. "Thirteen times! I would sooner let the Muslims or the Jews set up an altar in the cathedral!"

He had lapsed into silence by the time he had returned with my requested candles and another lit lantern, retreating again with Max in tow, the duo leaving to pray in mutual solitude. I had not spent the time idly, turning the body carefully over on his back and arranging my own lantern as best I could to look at the ruination beneath me. I had hoped the additional lantern would have shed more light on the matter, but the more I looked at the body, the more confused I became.

As I had already seen outside, his face was a tattered mess, in some places ostensibly human, in others so completely corrupted by gangrenous tissue that it was a miracle that I did not empty my stomach on the corpse there and then. I removed his clothing carefully, noting strange puncture marks on his chest, my eyes drawn all too easily to the blackened, dead flesh that covered the unfortunate victim in a patchwork blanket of death and misery. In some places the gangrene retreated in the face of severe swelling, most notably his knees, armpits, and groin. In these few, less defiled, locations, his veins stood out in stark contrast, a spider's web of failing health that made him less man than some demented nightmare.

I had to know more.

Though I was loath to do it, I pressed the back of my hand to the body's forehead, jerking away as my fingers brushed against frigid flesh. Even allowing for the passing of time since I had discovered him, there was no cause for him to be so glacially chilled, even in the face of the cooler evening. Even had his heart stopped pumping half a day ago, he should still have some warmth to him.

I leaned back on my heels, as much to retreat from the body as to have space to think. My mind rifled through my memory, throwing aside stacks of information piled high in the depths of my mind. The dead man was shattered by decay and desolation, his flesh unnaturally chilled despite having died only a short time ago. Was this some kind of sickness, a fever that burned away the body?

But coupled with the barely concealed spider's web of veins and the strange puncture marks about his nipple, what kind of illness could it even be? The gangrene I had seen in tobacco smokers, the engorged veins in those of greater weight, but along with chills, the lack of balance I had seen outside? Despite having studied the human body for years, I could not label the disease.

Clearly, there had to be an explanation - we were no longer the same scared species that scurried safe through the depraved Dark Ages - but I still could not identify what that might be. Some manner of infection? A curse from God? I peered again at the body, my hands tentatively probing at the puncture marks on his chest. They looked fresh, raw, but where they should have bled freely, there was nothing, save soft smears where someone must have dabbed with a cloth of some kind. Not a single drop of moisture. I opened his eyes next, staring into the glassy void. Not a drop there either. I felt the unravaged skin, unwilling to touch the blighted, dark flesh, my face twisting as his hide felt more like paper than tissue.

I had been determined to come up with an answer, but the longer I looked at the poor man lying there, the less I felt I understood.

In desperation, my mind flew to the stories I had heard as a child, vainly searching for an answer in the tales of night-mares that had filled me nightly with dread. I remembered the stories my maid had told me, of creatures who consumed the body from the outside even as the darkness devoured the soul within, of alps and marts that tormented those with filthy spirits. She had used those tales to cruelly terrify me into obedience then, unaware that the years passing since would do little to dull the painful memories generated from it.

But perhaps there was truth in her words? Perhaps there was some manner of creature stalking the streets of Vienna now, and I had merely stumbled across its first victim.

My rational mind banished these thoughts as idle fantasy. The time of ghouls and ghasts was over; they had died with witches and druids in the mists of human superstition. No, what I saw here tonight was something terrible, but myth had nothing to do with it.

This was illness, pure and simple. No, not simple, I realized with a rueful smile. I still had no idea what this truly was, though perhaps it might have been some new epidemic that had been blown our way by bad luck. I had heard tales of plagues coming out of the east for almost twenty years now; indeed, Sophie and I had lost our parents to the last one when we were yet children, and to see another now was an unsettling experience.

Nevertheless, if the corruption I saw now was any indication, I prayed that Vienna would endure the horror that had slipped unnoticed across her threshold and into every home.

II

A Pact Sealed

I opened my eyes to the sound of church bells again, this time so close to their ringing that I might have been heaving on the bell pull myself. After realizing that the noise was coming from somewhere outside of my pounding skull, I tried to stand up, failing the first time as weary muscles whined in quiet misery. Blinking my vision clear, I extended my hand out to Max as my friend came towards me with two mugs of what I hoped was ale.

My hope was rewarded when he extended one of them to me, pulling me upright with a gentle tug. "Morning," he said equitably, his usual genial smile in place. "How did you sleep?"

"Like the dead," I replied without thinking, a tight grimace washing over my face as I realized what I had said. Then again, I needn't have been concerned; Max and I had known one another a long enough time that he knew what I had meant. That I had been a little tasteless with my word choice wouldn't bother him, especially in the wake of the events of last evening.

His gentle shrug confirmed my thoughts. "Then you and our guest have something in common, then. Besides your unfortunate looks, I mean."

"You know, I know other people who might actually be insulted by that remark. But then, none of those poor, homely men have my sister's money to fall back on when times are tough. Besides, as long as I spend time with you, I'll always have my pick of the women you turn away!" It was true. Max's gentle nature and good humor attracted women in their dozens, the fairer sex seemingly drawn to the quiet humility of the big man. In truth, Max hated the attention, his head ducking low in embarrassment whenever some madam batted her eyelashes his way.

As it was, I was far from unattractive, but it was the game we played with one another. Sharing a laugh and a dull clunk of our mugs, I took a deep swallow of the bitter liquid within, my face screwing up in moderate disgust. "Max, where did you get this? It's horrible!"

He laughed back at me, rolling his eyes in mock dismay. "Well, it's what we poor people drink on a daily basis, and it was what the bishop gave me this morning. To be honest, it's good enough for me, and frankly should be good enough if you are as much a man of the people as you claim to be."

"Do I hear that my ale isn't good enough for your lordship?" Appearing as if by magic, the bishop crossed in front of the altar, crossed himself, and came to sit next to us in one of the pews. He was dressed far more ceremonially now, a simple green chasuble overtop a white cassock, his skullcap on his head. "Well, I must run out immediately and buy your lordship a much finer vintage, so as to better suit your needs!"

I felt another grin grow across my face. "But, excellency, you aren't even moving a muscle. Should we pray to God that he send an angel to fetch us this most holy water?" My fear that I had been too irreverent vanished when the older man chuckled softly. I continued more soberly, "Actually, I need to thank you for allowing us inside last evening. I realize that my... visit was less than welcome."

But he waved away my concerns, a hand coming out from beneath the chasuble, a small bladder cradled in it. After squirting a shot of the fruity liquid within into his mouth, he responded. "I admit that your timing was more a concern to me than the reason behind it. I admit that I can occasionally get caught up in the trappings of my office, and last evening was a reminder of my humanity."

It was a deft response, and I found myself wrong-footed at his gracious reply. He smirked as my own mouth gaped, clearly enjoying my awkwardness before he went on. "Max was telling me a little bit about you, my son. I admit I was confused as to who he was speaking about; I may not always be humble, but God blessed me with a perfect memory that I may tend to my flock." His tone was just barely on this side of reverent, though I could see the mischievous twinkle in his eye.

Regardless, my face burned in honest chagrin. "That is likely because I am not usually to be found among your other sheep. I admit that God and I are not on the closest of terms, bishop, a consequence of my childhood."

"And his family's money," cut in Max. "He may not come to Stephansdom, but the family does have a small chapel over at Michelerkirche."

I shot him a glare, though it had little effect on my larger friend. The bishop, meanwhile, grinned even more broadly. "Then, my son, allow me to more properly introduce myself. Wilderich von Waldendorff."

The name didn't spark any particular reaction from me, though he didn't seem to mind. "Well, your excellency-"

"Wilderich, please. I realize that to the world, I am a servant of God, but between us three here, let's forget other titles?" I felt my eyebrows soar in confusion. When we had crossed paths last evening, I had thought of him very differently, having pegged him as a more stiffnecked bishop than any man of the people.

Max easily read the expression on my face. "You know, Dietrich, if you came to mass a little more often, you might realize that he is something of a local celebrity."

"Oh?" I prompted, waiting for someone to tell me why the short man should be so popular.

The bishop - Wilderich, I supposed absently - obliged me a moment later. "It really isn't anything, but there are those who are impressed by my care and charity for the local poor. I try to deflect their praise, but as loudly as I ask them to stop, they continue all the louder and drown me out." The irreverence from before was gone, replaced with a quiet humility that embarrassed me yet again at my first assessment of the man.

Thankfully, he went on before I could attempt any kind of weak response. "In any case, I haven't come over here to puff out my chest or speak about my health. Quite the opposite, actually." He leaned in from his seat next to me. "How is the unfortunate man of last evening?"

I appreciated the change in topic. "Still quite dead, I'm sorry to say. I hope you did not mind, but I moved him to the rear of the cathedral, if for no other reason than to keep him out of the public eye."

Max looked at me, not understanding. "We've all seen dead bodies before, Dietrich."

"True," I nodded. "And I'd normally agree with you, but there is something different about this one. I've seen bodies die of old age, accidents, tavern fights, even the occasional illness, but there is something hideous about this one. I don't want to cause a panic yet."

Wilderich frowned. "Do you think there is a reason for panic?"

I felt my mouth twitch, a nervous tic I had failed to completely forget along with most of my childhood. "No," I said carefully, realizing that any misunderstanding had the potential to explode beyond what I intended. "At least, I should hope not, though can you blame me for being cautious?"

Neither man spoke, turning away from me, each reliving last night once more. Max was the first to face me again, tapping his hand uncomfortably against his mug. "No, I can't, though I don't think that we might keep this a secret for long. We're in the biggest church in all of Vienna, and I don't know about you, but have you ever heard of a secret that didn't get told to the entire world?"

"No, but then, no one would ever brag about that kind of thing, would I?" I said, earning an ironic chuckle from both the bishop and his sheep. The cathedral smelled different now, the musk of incense and history replaced by the gentle aroma of conspiracy. "Look at it this way. If this body is the only one we come across, then we risk nothing by keeping still for the common good. If it is not, then we have greater problems than a lie of omission.

"Besides, are we even sure what we're dealing with?" I stared down each in turn, letting Max grimace and the bishop shake his head gently before I continued. "Let me take the body back to my sister's estate and study it a bit more. If nothing else, we need to learn what might be coming our way."

Wilderich stood, clearly uneasy with my proposed vow of silence. Not even looking me in the face, he spoke, his voice taking on an otherworldly quality in the stillness of the cathedral. "'Do not participate in the deeds of darkness, instead strive to expose them...'"

"Were we living in the time of Paul, I would be inclined to agree with you, excellency. But given the situation, I imagine God might forgive us this secret." I knew he had asked us to speak to him by his Christian name, but with him quoting the Bible, it was difficult to think of him as anything less than a man of God.

"I am surprised, Dietrich," he replied, an almost heavenly ghost of a smile on his face. "Given Max's observation before, I did not anticipate you knowing the Bible so intimately. I don't know many who would be as quick as you."

I allowed my own thin-lipped grimace into existence. "Before they died, my mother and father believed that education came from God and man in equal measure. By the time I learned my letters, I was read the Bible nightly and have continued to study it ever since."

Wilderich nodded, satisfied. "I see that. I'm sure you aren't surprised to hear that I am... uneasy about remaining quiet about something that might be a grave threat to us." He looked to Max for support, but my friend merely shrugged, convinced, perhaps, by my perspective.

I stood, stretching out the muscles that whimpered again in half-remembered fatigue. "I understand that, which is why I need to ask something more of you. While Max and I will return to our lives out there," I said, pointing outside towards the slowly waking city, "I need you to remain here, keeping watch of a different sort."

"Where else would I be?" he asked, his hands spread wide. "My place is here, with my flock."

"Of course," I agreed hastily. "But your watch is even more important than ours. We can only watch for physical signs of sickness."

"I understand," he interjected, aware of where I was headed. "I will watch over our souls as best I can." He brushed his cassock as if the action could remove the dark thoughts infesting the corners of his mind. His gaze came up a moment later, his stare boring into me without remorse. "But I will not stay silent if I feel that the city is in danger, and there is nothing you will do to convince me otherwise of that. Are we clear on this?"

I waited for Max to nod acceptance before I followed suit, more to ensure that we were together in this than due to any caution on my own part. Though I had misjudged the bishop before, there was little doubt in my mind that he was a moral man, or at least more moral than most of the other members of the priesthood I had met in my three decades of life. There would, no doubt, be a time soon when he would object to keeping still, but if he remained silent for now, that was good enough.

None of us said anything for a time, perhaps debating with ourselves, perhaps steeling ourselves for what the road ahead might bring. In those few quiet moments, I heard the sound of the first carriages outside, the gentle, clip-clop of the shoed horses steady against the cobblestone roads.

I recalled when the rocky boulevards had first been installed, the expensive oyster-shell roads replaced by locally quarried stone in an effort to drive down costs; despite the financial benefits gained in lowered taxes, the decision had not been popular with the native Viennese. In an expression of solidarity not seen since the last Ottoman invasion, the rich and poor had united in their hatred of the drab, common rock, seeing in its use an assault on the otherwise beautiful city. That hatred had faded as the citizens had come to realize the benefits of the new roadways, no longer forced to pick out shards of sea-shell from their soles, no longer required to endure the salty stench of slowly decaying mollusks day-in and day-out.

I had been one of the few who had not despised the change from the get-go, my own pathological need for regularity soothed by the steady, mostly smooth streets that twisted around the Innerstadt. That I was forced to endure the occasional stumble seemed a worthwhile trade-off, my nose no longer under constant assault, my shoes whole and un-pierced.

Hearing the sound of the roads outside was a reminder that the city was waking up from her slumber. If I wanted to bring the dead man back to my sister's estate, I would need to leave soon, or else risk others discovering the grotesque sight. As it was, I couldn't exactly carry the corpse through the streets on my own, watchman or not, noble or not. No, I needed a more comfortable means of transporting the body.

"Bishop," I asked, "Wilderich, I mean - would you have any wagon or carriage that I could use to bring the dead man to my home for study?"

I winced, expecting some kind of outrage at the prospect of cutting apart the dead, but instead the shorter man gave a cursory nod. "I admit I am not pleased by the idea of having you carve up the body of some unfortunate, regardless of his anonymity, but under the circumstances I will allow you three days to examine the body, then I expect you to return it here, that we might give it back to the earth." He waited for me to nod my agreement before going on. "As to a means of moving him, I have donated most of the finer materials for the creation and maintenance of the poorhouses, but I believe we still have an ox-cart of some sort in the stable nearby. Let me speak to Johann about it," he said, standing up and turning to go.

"Johann?" I asked, confused. "Your servant?"

Wilderich turned back around, smiling broadly. "Though he is offi-cially an auxiliary bishop in the eyes of the Church and God, he has a great deal yet to learn, so for now... Yes, let's call him my servant." An impish glint came to his eye. "But I would never call him that to his face."

He went several steps before stopping again, coming back over to the two of us, the playful look gone, replaced instead with gravity. "Like the two of you, I cannot possibly imagine what the next days, perhaps weeks, might bring. In light of the terrible sight we all experienced last night, it seems appropriate to beseech God for his love and light to sustain us through all that might happen."

Wilderich turned to look me in the eye. "Normally in times like these, I pray in the chapel. I know Max is aware of its location, but maybe you would care to join us for a short moment of meditation? Whether you are one of my sheep or not, I would have your soul prepared as best as it might be to face the darkness to come."

I fought down my initial desire to laugh at the idea of a single prayer protecting me, but I was moved by the earnestness in his voice. "Lead on," I replied. "God may not know me by name, but if he is all-knowing, then he knows we might need him by our side soon enough."

III

An Uncomfortable Thought

Subject continues to decay physically.

I stared at the scribbled words, my clinical entry terrifying in its brevity, the complete lack of anything more definitive painfully apparent. Given the last several days of examination unearthing nothing new, I slowly had come to a single conclusion, one painful to accept given my persistent belief in inevitable success.

I was in over my head.

The realization had come slowly, creeping up as the hours passed fruitlessly, bludgeoning me over the head sometime late last night viciously as I attempted to learn about the manner of the newly dead. I had examined the dead man's clothes, going over them time and again, resorting to a microscope when my own eyes went blurry with the effort. There was nothing to be seen there, his jacket unremarkable, his shirt common but for several small tears about the region of his chest. I ended up setting them aside for the time being; fabric lasted longer than flesh.

His body told me little more, decay beginning to set in despite my attempts to preserve the body as naturally as possible. Were I less concerned with what fluids and flesh might have told me, I would have injected the man with the new chemicals that were being pumped into the newly departed, supposedly saving them for study for later. But given my limited understanding, those chemicals might also destroy crucial evidence, and I desperately needed to understand something, or anything.

Because of this, the guest cottage of the family estate played host to a slowly moldering corpse, the corrupted flesh filling the small, lavish place with a stench that I could still not accurately describe.

I heard a polite knock at the door, the delicate sound announcing another attempt by my sister to return me to the affairs of the living. She had come several times since the arrival of the body - each time I had turned her away to preserve her ignorance. It was not that I did not think she could withstand the sight of the body; she was one of the most formidable women I had ever met, having been the foundation of our small family since the death of our parents. Rather, I had hoped to keep her unaware, to keep her mind open and unaware in case I needed her for a sounding board later.

I should have realized that my attempt to keep her at arm's length would fail. If I was someone used to success, she was someone used to getting her way. As it was, I had been absent from the world for almost three days now, barely doing anything but peering over every square inch of the body for clues. She had a right to be concerned; even in my previous retreats from the world, I had never disappeared for so long.

Pulling myself into some vague semblance of respectability, I opened the door, smiling as if nothing at all were amiss. "Sister! What can I do for you?"

A perfectly manicured eyebrow arched imperiously. "Sister?" she asked in false confusion, though I heard a justifiable hint of irritation beneath her unruffled exterior. "I'm used to being an orphan of circumstance, but I've never thought that I'd also be an only child."

My smile became a rueful grin. "I'm sorry, really. I admit time has a way of passing when I find myself facing off against a new puzzle."

She waved away my apology. "No excuse. The children have been asking after their mad uncle, and after three days I've run out of fairy tales to tell them." I felt my cheeks heat in embarrassment; I had promised her when my first niece was born that I would be around more often than her usually absent husband. "I came to offer you some coffee and something to eat. That is, if you have not already had your fill of your little mystery." She peered over my shoulder towards the interior of the cottage. "What is it you're working on, anyway?"

"I'm not sure yet," I lied. "There was an incident near Stephansdom the other evening. Some refugee collapsed and the bishop there thought I should take a look at the body before he is buried."

My sister, always skeptical, fixed me with a look of complete disbelief. She was always the smarter of the two of us, her the brains while I dreamt and read. Though she always downplayed them, there was a great deal of truth in the rumors that she was the power behind her husband's good fortune. He was the face of the operation while she tugged the strings from behind the scenes. The face she wore now was the same one she wore whenever she considered the family's finances. "Dietrich... little brother. You should know by now that I have become very good at knowing when little children lie to me. Would you care to change your answer?"

The implicit threat in her voice sent a small shiver through me, another memory of the past I had thought forgotten. Suppressing it as best I could, I shrugged in surrender. "You caught me," I confessed. "There is more to the incident, perhaps, than I let on. I just don't want to worry you or..."

"Or pollute me when you want someone to bounce your ideas off of," she finished for me. Seeing my face, she went on. "Oh come, brother dear, at some point you should realize that you shouldn't try to hide anything from me. You remember that pretty little thing from your younger years." I did. "What was her name? Marie something?"

I knew that she knew my former lover's name; her mind only became foggy when she was making a point rhetorically. "Marianne," I sighed, knowing where she was going with this.

She snapped her fingers. "Marianne, exactly! You were beside yourself with her, and then you realized that I was never going to allow a marriage between the two of you. So what did you try to do?"

After being caught so recently in a lie, I had no desire to live in the past. Massaging the bridge of my nose, I asked plaintively, "Sophie, can we skip to the part where I come into the manor and eat something? I promise if you stop this trip down memory lane, I'll tell you everything."

My sister, ever the gracious victor, smiled. "Good. Shall we?" She extended an arm formally, as if we were at a state function and not simply strolling from the cottage to the manor house. Dutifully, I linked my arm with hers and we began the slow walk. "Speaking of former flames," she began.

I waved her off. "Don't push it, Sophie. I am in no mood for you to bring up my love life."

"Well you're practically an old man! When else will you find someone?" she exclaimed.

"Old man?" I repeated wearily. "At twenty-six? I think you're trying a little too hard to foist some poor woman off on me. Besides, I have-"

"-your work. I know. I've heard that answer for years now. Some days I wonder if your inclinations lie on the other side of the spectrum." I looked over to see her grin smugly, sighing at the inevitable comment. "You know, with all the time you spend with Max during your nights walking around the city..."

I had heard the same comment for years, not rising to the bait of my older sister. Still, I needed to respond in some way. "You know that I am out there for your sake as well as the city's." She patted my arm delicately, soothing me back to silence. My lips pursed thoughtfully. "I always thought Father would be proud that I volunteered for the city watch."

She nodded supportively. "He would have been. The same way Mother would have been proud of me for not letting my eventual husband control me. But then, we are not quite the norm in this city, are we?" That was certainly true. My family had managed to alienate most of our fellow nobles through somewhat liberal ideas of equality across both gender and economic lines. As a result, we tended to survive on the outskirts of social circles as well as the city itself, an existence that never seemed to bother Sophie. I certainly didn't care. "All the same, do you mind bowing slightly to social convention and maybe someday finding a wife?"

I was silent for a minute or two, feeling her hope as her back straightened almost imperceptibly. "Perhaps after I solve this puzzle," I said as we approached the manor house, the stones underfoot changing to the polished wood of the interior. She sighed, exasperated but determined to not let me know how much my bachelor life bothered her.

We had barely crossed the threshold of the dining room when my legs were assaulted by two squealing figures. "Onkel Dietrich!" one of the tiny figures shouted, its voice cracking halfway through the greeting. "You're back from the moon!"

I threw my sister an askance look, relishing the genuine flash of happiness that stole across her face. "That's what you decided to tell them?" I asked, her laughter my only response. Unlinking my arm from hers, I pried one of the children loose. "Knuddelbär!" I shouted back, kissing the giggling cheeks of my niece, her brother still clinging tightly to my legs. "How are you? Have you been behaving while I was away?"

My niece nodded vigorously. "Ja, Onkel, and I've been looking after Freddie, too!"

"Oh, have you?" I asked, looking down at the tiny grinning face that beamed up at me. "And have you been behaving?"

My nephew, as was his way, said nothing.

"Children? Go play. I need to talk to Onkel Dietrich and hear all about his trip, ok?"

Freddie scowled, his silent protest joining little Katarina's whine. "But Mama!"

"But nothing," said Sophie, my sister overriding the complaining with a sharp wave of her hand. I had been on the receiving end of that hand before, and I knew then and there that our privacy was assured. Both niece and nephew slunk off, though not without one final protest.

I found myself chuckling at their momentary defiance, though I also knew that it wouldn't benefit them at all; my sister ruled the family, and the easiest way forward was to bow before her wishes. Which I now found myself doing, I realized, pouring a small cup of coffee and pulling a several boiled eggs onto my plate. A couple small pieces of *speck* and bread joined them as my stomach protested.

Perhaps it was a good thing that Sophie had forced me to take a break. I couldn't remember the last true meal that I had had, too busy with the body slowly rotting in the house outside.

She left me alone for most of the next few minutes, doing little besides summoning one of the few house servants to refresh the coffee, dismissing the young woman back to the kitchen with a courteous nod. I appreciated the calm, the silence allowing me a chance to marshal my thoughts before the inevitable storm of questions. And she would ask them; her many questions came out of pure interest, one of the reasons we remained so close.

A polite cough during my second cup of coffee told me it was time to explain matters. "Yes?" I asked mildly, letting her push the issue.

"I left you alone before on the condition that you would tell me what was going on. Do I need to go back to asking about your love life?" There was a slight edge to her voice, equal parts concern and affection. "I can't think of the last time you holed up in the cottage for so long."

"True," I allowed. "I suppose I didn't want to come out until I had something more definitive to share with you."

"Please," she scoffed, her eyes rolling. "You've always been secretive. Usually it's part of your charm, especially to Freddie and Kat, but I'm not sure I really want to deal with it. I haven't seen that look in your eyes since that messy business several years ago."

"Which look?"

"The one that says you've seen Hell itself and you are trying to protect me from knowing what it looks like." she accused.

I shifted uneasily in my seat. "Being on the watch means sometimes I see things I would rather not speak about. Not everything about the city is beautiful, Soph, even though I wish it was."

Her chair creaked mildly as she slid it further from the table, leaning back to loop one arm over the back of the top rail of the seat. She was not a large woman, shorter than me by several inches, though she was far from the slight, wispy things that populated most of polite society in the city. "Well, by all means," she said. "Shock me. I know better than most that some 'incident' at Stephansdom wouldn't give you the haunted look you're wearing now."

"You're not wrong," I agreed. "There is more to the incident..." I launched into my memory, relaying everything as best as I could recall. I spoke about the body, about the way the flesh had fallen away from bone, about the ghastly images of the blued veins that had, if anything, gotten more stark since that night. I spoke about the strange ringing of the bells and the response of the bishop. I mentioned the strange weightlessness of the body, the pact newly made with Max and Wilderich.

At length I finished, taking a sip of coffee to soothe a sore throat, enjoying the bitter warmth while Sophie digested my story. If she were not my sister, I imagine I would have been terrified by how intense she seemed. Sophie had said nothing throughout my entire tale, her blue eyes taking on an expression disturbingly similar to the victim's, though I knew hers was one of deep contemplation, not death. It was this way whenever I came to her with a puzzle, her face always distant, her mind blocking out everything but the sound of my voice and the cold, hard facts of the situation.

"What do you think it is?" she asked me, her head jerking as if she were coming out of a trance.

I shook my head helplessly. "I've been looking at the body for three days and I have absolutely no idea. There are no answers in any books, at least not in any that I've been able to find."

"Hmm," she mused, waving away the servant that poked her head in to check on us. "That's a little unsettling."

I threw my hands in the air. "Well, that's helpful!"

"Well, what do you want me to say?" she asked. "You're the one who's spent the bulk of his life buried in medical textbooks!"

"I come to you for a sounding board! You are the person I turn to when things don't make sense!" I stood up, more than a little agitated.

"And I'm aware of that," she said calmly, clearly unfazed by my outburst. "So use me for that. I can't - and won't - help you if you just complain instead that I don't have answers."

I bit back the acidic words already on my tongue, swallowing them with more than a little effort as I realized the wisdom in her words. It wasn't her job to solve the mystery on her own. I had involved myself. It was my burden to bear.

I began to pace the length of the table as Sophie assumed her previous position of immobile consideration. "Let's rule out the most obvious possibilities first," I said, clasping my hands gently at the small of my back. "The cause of death was blood loss."

"How can you be so sure?"

I shrugged, the answer obvious to both of us. Sophie was asking so that we could officially cross off the most common afflictions. "The lightness of the body coupled with the relative existence of musculature. Despite the portions of the body that had more radically decayed, the body was more or less intact, which suggests the only missing element would be blood itself."

"Relatively intact," snorted Sophie softly. Raising her voice again, she asked, "Tell me about the decay again?"

I stopped, my mind recalling the macabre image. "His skin was severely cracked, in some places blackened as if he had thrust his hands into a fire. The flesh underneath these locations was exposed and looking similarly charred."

"Ok," she replied. "And the swelling. You mentioned some of that, as well."

"Yes, at the armpits and the groin, there were tumors, raised sections of flesh that were initially soft to the touch and have since hardened. I attempted to lance one of these sections: it bled yellow bile and blood freely. I have a sample that I've examined under the microscope you gave to me several years back. I have been confused since."

She ignored my admission of confusion. "Yellow bile," she repeated.

"Were his humors out of order? An overabundance of bile suggests a disease based on insomnia and wakefulness. Didn't you tell me that he was stumbling through the plaza in front of Stephansdom?"

I nodded, remembering the way that he had staggered this way and that. "I did. He seemed very much like a drunk. The bishop had thought him one before he noticed the corrupted flesh. If that's true, then maybe I need to look at Avicenna's treatise again. Perhaps there are some answers there."

"Our first clue, then." responded my sister. "Who knew the Muslims could be good for something besides death and destruction?"

"Oh, stop," I rebuked her gently. "The Ottomans aren't quite Muslims, are they?"

My sister came out of her thoughtful expression long enough to roll her eyes. "I'm sure the residents of Constantinople wouldn't label them as Christians."

"Istanbul," I corrected. "Constantinople hit the works."

She smiled, waving aside my response. "Istanbul, Constantinople... They are Muslims, in any case." Her lips pursed as she entertained a new thought. "Have we classified this as a particular malady, or could it be some kind of poison?"

I let the thought percolate in my mind. "You know, Soph, I had not even considered that angle. I haven't heard of anything, but that doesn't mean that such a thing doesn't exist. But who could I ask about that kind of thing? I can't imagine many of the *apothekes* in the city that carry a steady supply of poisons."

"Try the one on the northeast Ringstrasse, by the river."

"Isn't that the royal pharmacy?" I asked, surprised. "What are you doing over by there? I thought you hated court life?"

"I do," was her reply. "There are occasions, though I find it necessary to establish certain examples when competitors seek to horn in on my business." Seeing the shocked look on my face, she lifted her hands in surrender. "Don't worry, I haven't killed anyone... yet. Though that is liable to change if the Hausdorfs fail to take my warning to heart."

I shuddered unconsciously at the way her eyes flashed. I always forgot that my sister, so often doting and affectionate, was a lioness when someone crossed her. "Sophie," I began, leaning in carefully to kiss her on the top of her head. "Have I ever mentioned how shocking you can be when you want to be?"

She smiled as I pulled away from me. "Well, brother dear, make sure you never need to be the subject of my anger, then."

"Too late," I quipped, getting a small chuckle from her. "Since you seem to know it so well, should there be anyone in particular that I should speak to over at the *apotheke*?"

My sister was silent a moment; I could see the wheels of her mind turning as she considered and rejected one possibility after the next. "Abraham," she decided.

"A Jew in Vienna?" I asked, intrigued. "I thought they had all been deported? Isn't that why we have Leopoldstadt now? To pay homage to our brave emperor for forcing them out?" The contempt oozed freely in every syllable, my face twisting in derision.

It was Sophie's turn to shrug. "For the most part they have been, but Abraham is quite special. I'm convinced he's more mage than man; it's certainly impressive that he's survived the persecution that's claimed the rest of his people." She looked up at me. "Is his Jewishness a problem?"

"No more a problem than the Ottomans being Muslim. But then," I said, smiling. "I've always been the open-minded one of the family." I turned to walk away, stopping as I realized I was about to disappoint two very small hearts by leaving again so soon.

"Go," said Sophie, reading my mind. "But be back for dinner."

"I will," I promised. "But for now," I muttered, half to myself, half to the body in the cottage, "it's time for an answer or two.

IV

A Growing Conspiracy

"May I help you?"

"I should hope so," I replied, stepping over the threshold into the *apotheke*. "May I come in?"

The woman just inside nodded politely, setting aside her broom to step behind the counter, her hands wiping themselves relatively clean on the cloth about her waist. "What ails you, sir? You're looking a bit peaked."

"Thank you, but I am not looking for any cure for myself, but rather for a friend of mine." Half true, I supposed, but there was no need to tip my hand so soon. "Actually, I was hoping to speak to Abraham. I don't suppose he's in?"

Her eyebrows raised carefully, the motion too slow to be true surprise. "Abraham? I admit I've not seen him in quite some time." She scratched at her chin, the small hairs there yielding beneath her scraping fingers. "It has been several years in fact."

"Really?" I asked, skeptical. "I heard from a reliable source that I could find him here. I've heard he's a man of almost supernatural powers. You're sure that he's not here?" I let my eyes rove around the small room, taking in the dozens of jars littering the shelves, the small piece of parchment carefully affixed to the door leading back to the living space of the shop. "I find it hard to believe that a good Christian woman would keep a *mezuzah* in her shop, to say nothing of her even moving into a Jewish household before having a priest expel the demons from it."

The shopkeeper's eyes narrowed as she scanned me up and down. "Who sent you this way, sir?" she asked, a slight edge in her voice. "I want no trouble for me or my family."

I held up my hands, palms carefully tilted towards her to calm her. "And I'm not here to offer any, but my sister, *Gräfin* Sophie von Rohan, told me that no one would be able to help me with my problem except for Abraham."

The shopkeeper's posture immediately changed, her eyes widening in delight. "Sophie!" she exclaimed. "I haven't seen her in quite some time. How is she?"

I should have known to lead with my sister's name; though we were held in low esteem by the nobility, the common citizenry seemed to hold a special place in their heart for my family, especially as my sister continued the philanthropic work begun by our parents. It cost us little, but always seemed to pay dividends in the most unexpected of ways, as it did now. "She's well," I said, letting a smile of my own appear. "Busy with the household and other family matters, but she asked to be remembered to you."

My white lie only seemed to charm the shopkeeper further. "She is an inspiration to us all, your sister. Especially in trying times such as these, that she is willing to be our customer... It is a godsend." Another benefit of my sister; despite her disdain for politics, she was adept in creating a webwork of support wherever she went, the public adoring her for her lack of pretension and lavish patronage. Even if every other noble ignored them, she would always remain by their side.

The shopkeeper's pleasure faded slightly as she realized her earlier tone. "I'm sorry if I seemed... unwelcoming before, lord. You must understand that-"

I cut her off with a gentle wave. "It's more than understandable, Miss-"

She gave me a small curtsy. "Sarah, my lord."

"Dietrich, please," I said attempting, perhaps awkwardly, to seem as accessible as my sister. "I don't suppose this might change your answer about Abraham?"

Sarah nodded, appreciating my attempt at equality. "Now that I think about it, I may have seen my husband puttering around the back of the shop. Would you mind waiting here while I fetch him?"

"By all means, take your time. I'll browse in the interim." She nodded again, disappearing through the door, the parchment fluttering gently as she passed by into the living space beyond.

In her absence, I did my best to amuse myself by guessing at the contents of each jar, giving up soon after I discovered one that housed an entire collection of pickled eyeballs. Though they didn't seem human, I didn't want to find out, gingerly placing the jar back on the shelf and backing away slowly.

"No, they aren't human," came a voice behind me, its owner clearly reading my mind. "In fact, they aren't even eyeballs, but to keep some of my customers happy, I am forced to keep some odd things on hand."

I turned about to see Abraham for the first time, shocked by how... normal he looked. I admit to having met only a few Jews in my life, but every time I was always surprised by how unassuming each remained. If I listened to the stories told by fearmongers, I would have expected a beaked monster with horns, a devilish, vile disciple of an uncaring, inhuman god. I would be robbed blind, my soul stolen as quickly as my purse by the sticky-fingered man-thing that plagued the staunchly Catholic streets of the city.

To the more prejudiced of the city, then, Abraham was a disappointment, his kindly face without any deceit, his exterior perfectly average in every way. This commonality extended to his apparent age, though I guessed he was older than he looked, his telltale hairline beginning to recede the further he moved beyond middle age. He was a few inches shorter than me, but in the cramped space of the shop he was perfectly placed, skillfully maneuvering a small chair about the confined space.

Motioning me to it, he retreated behind the counter as his wife had. "It isn't often that a new face comes in asking for me. My people haven't been the most welcome in recent years. What can I do for you?"

I nodded understanding. "I am Dietrich-"

"-von Rohan. Yes, I know. Sarah is a great admirer of your sister, but I admit I am more impressed with you." I narrowed my eyes, peering carefully at him to find the hidden insult behind what seemed a compliment. Reading my expression, he chuckled. "I mean that. I appreciate her for her business here, but I admire your decision to remove yourself from the usual trappings of nobility and serve."

I shifted uneasily in my seat. "I'm not sure that's exactly true..."

The *apotheker* shrugged, his lips frowning a moment. "Perhaps not *all* of the benefits, but how many higher-born men serve on the city watch? You might think little of your efforts, but I can hardly think of anyone - Catholic, Jew, or Muslim - who isn't aware of you."

My face flushed in embarrassment. "Do you mind if I smoke?" I asked, trying to deflect.

"By all means, lord," he said, bowing slightly at the waist in mock deference. On anyone else, the motion might have come across as insulting, but Abraham made it seem somehow respectful, as if he and I were now equal. Strangely, I felt relieved at the idea, though I hid that relief behind the small puffs of smoke rising from my pipe.

He waited until I had taken several deep breaths before asking me the reason behind my visit. "Your sister coming by, I would understand, especially in the wake of her impending conflict with the other families, but I didn't think you were involved regularly in her business?"

I felt my eyebrow raise. Sophie hadn't mentioned anything to me about a trade conflict, but then why would she? "No, I'm still only a guest at the family house." I replied, coughing gently as I accidentally inhaled some tobacco smoke. "No, I'm here for information, and she thought that I might find some answers here."

Abraham's head tilted to the side. "Ok... I don't know exactly how I could help, but I will if I can. What kind of information are you looking for?" He looked back at the door to the rear of the shop. "Sarah mentioned that you were looking to cure a friend of yours. What ails them? Pneumonia? German measles?" he asked.

"I wish it were that simple," I shook my head, reaching into my pocket to draw out a small notebook. Though I had left my journal back at the estate, I had jotted down the major symptoms of the strange sickness. I passed them over to Abraham, feeling my face grow grave. "What I am about to tell you might prove unsettling, and I won't pretend that the details of it aren't terrifying in the extreme. But I have no idea what I am dealing with."

My host looked at the page, his eyes flashing back and forth before looking back at me. "That's terrifying, coming from a student of medicine."

Despite the circumstances, I felt myself smile. "My sister said much the same." Pulling my pipe from my mouth, I pointed at the paper with the stem. "What do you make of it?"

Abraham set the paper down on the counter between us, tapping it in a depressingly absent-minded fashion. I had hoped that he would have an immediate answer, even if it meant I had overlooked something incredibly obvious in my diagnosis. Not wanting to interrupt his thoughts, I contented myself with chewing on my pipe. A childish habit perhaps, but a forgivable one when compared to the habits of some of my peers.

But as the silence bore on, my mouth asked the question my mind was screaming. "Well, have you seen anything like it?"

The older man sighed, clearly annoyed at my insistence, but he hid his irritation admirably. Bent almost double over my notes, he stood up, crossing his arms across his chest protectively. "How did you know I was a Jew?" he asked with preamble, the blunt directness stunning me for a moment.

"Excuse me?"

"How did you know I was Jewish?" he repeated. "It is not a fact that I advertise about the community. The reasons for this should be painfully obvious, and yet you came in asking for me by name. I certainly do not believe that I look like a Jew, if such a thing were even possible, so tell me, how did you know that I was?"

"What does this have to do with anything?" I asked defensively.

"Just, just... play along," he requested. "Sarah said you pointed something out in particular."

I realized what he was getting at. "It was the *mezuzah* on the door frame." I saw him smile, taking that as an invitation to go on. "I've heard that it's used to 'write the word of God' on the hearth and home. Like I said to your wife, you would be hard pressed to find a Christian house with a similar decoration. Couple that with your name in the first place and..."

Abraham snapped his fingers. "Exactly! You see the signs and add up what they must mean, considering everything at one time. Very good." He began to pace, one hand at the small of his back, the other raised as if he were a priest blessing the masses. "As I'm sure you know, very often we cannot diagnose what is wrong with the body on the basis of a single symptom. Sometimes a fever means a cold, and sometimes it means rheumatism of the throat, and sometimes it means something altogether different."

I knew all of this; that kind of diagnosis was second nature to any doctor worth his name. Regardless, I motioned him to go on, though he continued without even looking at my direction. "It's the combination of factors that give away what we are dealing with. Taken on its own, the gangrene could be any number of things, but that is exactly where the sickness wants us to look! It seeks to steer us away from the giveaway symptom."

"The swelling yes," I interrupted, though, again, he carried on as if I had been invisible.

"It's the buboes that tell us that we are dealing with plague, and a particularly nasty one at that. I have heard of an illness that consumes a man from the inside out, that it ravages his soul and tears it from him, the body behind decaying without the breath of God to animate it. Yes, it is a very nasty one. In mere days, the diseased will die. Worse yet, it is highly contagious, and will pass from man to a woman or a child without any consideration for race or class."

He stopped his pacing, his body turning slowly towards me, his gaze boring fiercely into mine. "Where is the body?"

I feigned surprise, my expression one of carefully cultivated innocence. "What body?" I asked, though inwardly my mind was racing. Highly contagious? Had I infected myself, condemned myself to the same cruel ravages of this disease, this plague? I shook, unable to fully suppress the fears that shattered any lingering sense of comfort I had vainly held in my chest.

"Please," said Abraham. "You came to me for my help, and I cannot provide that from the shadows, much as I might like to." He extended a hand towards me, and I was struck by the eerie similarity to the promise I had extracted from Max and Wilderich several days before. His eyes softened, pleading now instead of accusing. "Please do not hide something like this from me."

I examined his face for deceit, looking for any reason that I could back away from him without cursing myself, but I saw none. I saw instead the look of a man who was haunted by what had appeared on his doorstep, no small feat when I remembered his nationality. I wasn't speaking to Abraham the *apotheker*, nor was he only a Jew out to save his skin. No, I was speaking to another son of Vienna, a brother who saw danger where I had seen a puzzle.

I cursed myself silently, angry that I had allowed myself to believe that I could solve this on my own. I should have come earlier; clearly Abraham had seen what I hadn't, or, at least, what I hadn't allowed myself to see. I stood up carefully, as if I wasn't quaking inside at what Abraham's revelation meant. We both knew that I had already come to my decision, but he allowed me the chance to say it aloud, to let me seal our partnership in blood instead of silence.

"There are others who know of the body," I said, ignoring the slight smugness that came to his face at my revelation. "Three, in fact, and though I have sworn them to silence, I don't know how long that kind of secret remains that way."

The *apotheker* nodded. "I have read in your Bible that 'Nothing is covered that will not be revealed in its time.' Who knows?"

"A watchman, Max. He'll say nothing; he and I have known one another almost our whole lives, and he knows more about me than anyone else, save my sister." Abraham nodded. "And a bishop, Wilderich of St. Stephansdom. I know less of what he'll do."

Abraham's lips stretched thin, his face grimacing fiercely. "A man of your God? I wish I could trust him more, but his kind called for mine to be ejected from the city in the first place!" He spat off to the side in derision, disgust etched in each hard line of his face. I found it strange to see that his face could be hard at all. Even when his eyes had pierced me before, his expression was more grave than gruesome. If anything, it nearly terrified me more than the sickness that this man, so kind and welcoming to a stranger like me, could hate so deeply.

The hate in his face faded slightly with time, though his face remained twisted in distaste. "*Hgh...*" he growled, "It can't matter. What is to come supersedes all other hatreds. If you will be with us whenever we are forced to be together, I will work with him."

I nodded, trying to project the image of calm authority. He noticed my effort, laughing at my attempt at gravity. "I'm sorry," he said, "I am putting so much on the shoulders of someone so young! Do not worry. I will control myself in his presence." He held up his hands. "Wait a moment, please. I need to speak with Sarah and then we will go."

"Go?" I asked, slightly confused. "Go where?"

He gave me a final grim smile before disappearing through the door with the *mezuzah* on it. "To the body, my *frayund*. To the body."

V

⚜

A Question of Theology

True to his word, Abraham wasted no time in coming, returning from the back of his shop having traded out his apron for a coat. In truth, I was surprised by his energy; given the way he had described the sickness, I hadn't expected him to be so... excited. Then again, given that I had expected wary reluctance at best, I supposed (keep it in the tense) anything more willing than that would have seemed excited.

Of course, his constant chatter didn't help, his hands pointing in every direction as he told me of where his cousin's sister used to live, or which of his neighbors had once made the best *lokshen kugel*, (whatever that was). It was during these times when he injected some strange term or a memory that I realized how unlikely a pair we were, even more so than Max and me. My friend and I were separated by class and class alone, but Abraham ate differently, lived differently, believed differently, even spoke differently.

·I had often looked down on those people who seemed incapable of seeing the Jews and the Muslims of the city as anything but unearthly, but even with an open mind, I could not help but understand how others might look at Abraham's people as a completely different species.

He seemed to sense my line of thinking. "You are wondering how it has come to this." he accused.

"How it has come to what?" I asked, looking off to my left towards the Prater. It looked so picturesque, peaceful to the point of being too quiet. When the Turks had come a hundred years ago, they had killed every animal in the forest there, or so the stories said. It was hard to believe anything that supposedly happened then; the history books were too full of religious imagery and personal heroics for my liking.

"A Jew and a Christian working together," he said. "Doesn't this bother you?"

I allowed a moment's consideration before I shook my head. "No," the simple answer even easier to say than I realized. "We are completely different, you and I, but with what's coming, do those differences matter?"

He stopped walking for a few steps, vanishing from sight as my directness stunned him. I drank in the quiet that came from his momentary disappearance. It didn't last long, his face re-appearing before I had gone far. "I like you, Dietrich. There are not many of your people that I like, but you? You I like."

His statement brought a smile to my face, and more than a little more warmth to my heart as we continued back to the estate. Unfortunately, Abraham decided that our new friendship should be sealed in a new round of one-sided conversation, proceeding to be my personal tour guide as we approached the center of the city. He broke off his monologue to ask, "Where was the body?"

I walked him to Stephansdom and pointed. We walked over to the place, taking great care to not disturb anything in the area. He bent over, scrutinizing the ground carefully. I half expected him to pull a ruler from his pocket, calipers to take in every last measurement but he did nothing as he just stared at the ground underneath.

"Dietrich! Dietrich!" I turned in the direction of my name, seeing Wilderich hurrying towards me, his cheeks puffing mightily. "*Gruß gott*, lord bishop!" I greeted. "What might I do for you?"

The shorter man almost skidded to a stop in front of me. "Dietrich,

I was hoping you might be able to tell me where-" he stopped as he realized Abraham kneeling at my feet. His lips worked frantically but he found the necessary words. "Where is it?" he asked, stressing each syllable carefully.

"Where is what?" I inquired calmly. "The body?" I added, enjoying the embarrassed flush that came to Wilderich's face. I saw him glance quickly at Abraham and then back at me. "He knows."

"Oh, does he?" If anything, the flush in the bishop's face deepened, matching his rose-red skullcap, until I reached out a hand to steady him. He brushed away my hand, instead asking me icily, "I thought we were looking to keep our conspiracy as quiet as possible? Who is he and why am I keeping still if you are telling half the city!"

Abraham took it upon himself to enter the conversation before I could make any response. "My name is Abraham, and I'm a Jew. I believe you are Wilderich, the bishop Dietrich spoke of?" He extended his hand in greeting, a calm smile on his face.

The bishop looked aghast, recoiling from the hand as if it were a snake and not a greeting. "He knows who I am? By God, what have you done? This is holy ground!" he asked me, falling back a step from us both.

"Can we take a step back for a moment?" I massaged the bridge of my nose. I tended to indulge in my pipe whenever I felt any kind of head pain, but I knew that there wasn't enough tobacco in the world to stem the oncoming headache. "Bishop, might we go inside a moment?" I inquired, indicating the cathedral with my hand. "It might be better if we discussed things in there."

But Wilderich was adamant. "Bring a Jew into my church? Not a chance!"

Abraham shrugged. "Not a problem for me." Glancing at the bishop, he quipped. "Bishop, what's the harm in it? Look at it this way. If Jehovah objects to me entering, I will burst into flame when I cross the threshold. If I do not, then he must not mind."

I stifled a chuckle, seeing the humor for what it was. Wilderich took it far more seriously, mulling it over before nodding slowly. "Very well but know that I'm doing this for the good of the city. Once this conversation is over, then I never want to see you again. Leopold evicted you from here for a reason."

"Well, I will do my best to accommodate you, *amoretz*," conceded Abraham. "But if this what I think it is, then I am afraid we will be together more often than you might like." Thankfully, he said nothing else, instead following behind me as I followed Wilderich inside the cathedral. Passing through the so-called Giant's Door, Wilderich glanced over his shoulder to glare at Abraham as the non-believer stepped inside.

Much to the bishop's dismay, Abraham failed to erupt into a living torch when he crossed the threshold, though he accepted this with a grim nod and said nothing more. Abraham, for his part, was more or less respectful, his earlier chattiness falling into a similar silence, both men turning to face me as soon as we passed the banks of prayer candles inside.

I waited for Wilderich to make the first move, which he did without any warning. "Where's the body?" he asked pointedly. "You promised me that the body would be here after three days so that I could pray over the dead and send him to Jesus' side."

Abraham shook his head definitively. "Don't pray over him, Wilderich," he said, his use of the bishop's given name earning him a glare. "You'll only infect yourself with the sickness."

"And how might I do that? Dietrich and I were near the body and yet neither one of us is ill." Wilderich threw his arms out to the side. "For that matter, I don't even know what this vile affliction is, only that it rots the body."

The *apotheker* nodded sagely. "And destroys the spirit - or so they say."

Wilderich clapped his hands, his face lighting up. "All the more reason for me to pray for the dead man's soul! He needs God's love now more than ever!" When the Jewish man said nothing, the bishop threw his hands in the air. "What would you have me do instead?"

"Burn it?" I guessed aloud.

I looked at Abraham for confirmation, seeing his head bob slowly.

"The sickness will continue to rot and fester unless we destroy its home." he said.

I wished I there were words to describe the expression on Wilderich's face. "You cannot be serious!" he exclaimed. "You know more than anyone that once the body is burned, destroyed, it cannot be resurrected. I can believe the heathen suggesting this, but not you!"

Abraham came to my defense. "God is all-powerful, yes?" he asked rhetorically. "Then he can manage to work against a little thing like a burned body, yes?" He waited for the grudgingly given nod from the bishop. "Then, I must insist that we destroy the body."

"Now?" I asked. "Before you've seen it?"

"No," he chuckled. "I would see it first, and then dispose of it."

I winced at the cavalier response, preempting Wilderich's outburst by only an instant. Despite Abraham's simply stated argument, the bishop took offense to his off-hand solution. "'Dispose of it'!" He thrust a finger at Abraham, who did nothing at all in response. "Listen to him, Dietrich! He'd destroy us all if he could! How do we know that his people didn't do it?"

I opened my mouth but needn't have bothered. "Because if my people were involved in this sickness, it wouldn't kill you. It'd make you better cooks and less filthy!" interjected Abraham. It was true: the city was undeniably beautiful, but that was in spite of the state of hygiene than because of it. "Honestly, I am here to help you and you instead want me to confess to unleashing some horrible disease?" He crossed his arms, leaning against a pew. "Let me ask you this... Would I stay in the city with this corruption running rampant and risk my wife?" When the bishop said nothing, he gave a grunt of superiority.

I interjected. "So the point remains, what are we going to do now?" But neither man said anything, instead looking expectantly at me, and I realized that my question was not meant for them at all, but for me, a fact that made me more than a little uncomfortable. I was only a young man, for God's sake! I had no business making decisions this important!

Then again, I had discovered the body, and I had involved both of these men, and others, in the growing secrecy. Though I hated to admit it, every step of the way I had been the one to move us further and further forward. It fell to me again now.

I cleared my throat, swallowing hard in an attempt to clear the lump that had materialized in it. I was only partially successful, though neither of the other men said anything, seemingly content to wait for my direction. Such calm acceptance of my authority only terrified me further. Turning first to Wilderich, I said, "Out of the three of us - four, if we include Max - Abraham knows the most about this disease. We need to defer to his judgement. If he says the body needs to be destroyed, then it needs to be destroyed."

The bishop scowled but nodded anyway; for some reason, his begrudging acceptance helped slow my racing heart. I favored Abraham next with a look. "We are going to do everything possible to preserve the body; if we can get by without completely destroying the body, we're going to do so."

The Jew shrugged as if it didn't matter. "I sometimes wonder why your God demands the body be in one piece to get into the afterlife. Isn't your god and my god the same one?" He turned to the bishop, his earlier impudent tone disappearing, in its place a soft sincerity to melt the hardest heart. "Wilderich, I know you and I will not see eye to eye on many things. I know you love this city as I do; like Dietrich here, I hear your name whispered by Jew, Muslim, and Christian as a lover of all men. I, too, love this city, regardless of what she might have done to my people. Perhaps you and I set aside our mutual disdain for a time? Perhaps we could find more common ground as we fight against this darkness?"

Wilderich looked thunderstruck. I watched him carefully as his eyes darted one way and then the other, as if Abraham's words had trapped him on the lower moral ground. It certainly seemed that way to me; while Abraham had needled him earlier on, his olive branch certainly would have come off as sincere to any bystander, regardless of their creed.

The seconds ticked on, the two of us waiting for the third to accept the hand stretched out before him. An expectant sniff escaped me, the sound reverberating from the cold stone of the cathedral. It was smothered an instant later as I heard multiple people thunder into the cathedral. At least two, but I could have been wrong.

The first face around the Giant's Door was instantly recognizable. "Max?" I asked, stupidly., "What are you doing here?"

My friend seemed as surprised to see me as I was him. "Dietrich? What are you doing here?" Looking over at the bishop and Abraham, I saw his head tilt in confusion. "Who's he?" he asked, pointing at the *apotheker*.

"That's really not important right now. Astrid, what are you doing here?" I asked, looking at the smaller woman at his side. Given my astonishment at seeing Max, I had failed to recognize my sister's house servant at his side, the already tiny woman diminished further by Max's considerable size.

She curtsied gently, always the proper maid. "My lord Dietrich, your Excellency and..." she faltered as she glanced Abraham's way, though she recovered quickly. "I've just come from the estate."

"The estate?" I interjected. "Is everything ok? Is my sister all right?"

"Yes sir, at least she was when I left. It's..." she shivered, though I didn't think it had anything to do with the cathedral itself. "It's one of the local grocers. His man came to the estate begging for him. He says there is something horrible over at his master's place!"

Max cut back in here. "I was coming by the estate to see if you needed help moving the- er, you know, and I saw the grocer's helped there..." he began, words flowing from him in a conflicted deluge.

What followed was a confusing mass of conflicting narratives, Astrid overriding Max at times, in others allowing herself to be overridden. By the time they each stopped for a breath, my head was swimming as I tried to puzzle out the series of events that had led them here. As near as I could tell, the grocer's man had arrived at the estate looking for my sister, begging for her help. My sister had listened to him graciously, as was her wont. Realizing that there might be a connection between our body and unfolding events, she had sent Astrid with Max to Abraham's shop to find me.

Somehow, they had missed us, but they had taken anything but the shortest path to the apothecary, meandering all over the city in the hopes of finding me. When Sarah had directed them back to the estate, Max had thought to come to Stephansdom, reasoning that the bishop might have figured out where I had gone, or, at the very least, might be able to get a message to me if they didn't run into me by then. I would have thought that it would have been better to wait for me at the estate, but then I suppose irrationality had overridden good sense.

"He's nearby, lord," finished Astrid. "The grocer, I mean." She looked at me earnestly, her unsettlingly large eyes pleading for deliverance. Despite having been born into nobility, I was always uncomfortable when other Austrians looked to me for leadership. My sister was the leader of the family; I preferred my books and the relative facelessness of nighttime. "His grocery is near to the walls, by the Burg Bastion." She turned away, clearly expecting me to follow.

I opened my mouth to call her back, but she was already racing from the cathedral. Shaking my head in resignation, I turned towards my unasked-for followers. "Can I leave you here alone without seeing another religious war?"

Wilderich smiled grimly, his lips pressed tightly together. Abraham nodded, but made to walk out with me. "My *frayand*, I am going with you. If this is also the sickness, then I will benefit more from seeing fresher victims than the putrefying body at your estate."

I shrugged away my own objections, knowing that Abraham would come whether I wanted him to or not. "What about the body?" Max asked. "Should I still bring it here?" He looked between the bishop and me for an order that never came. I stared at the bishop, daring him to oppose me again. He looked away in surrender, though I knew we hadn't fought over my decision for the last time.

"No, Max," I said. The next words were hard, my stomach twisting in knots as I fought the urge to relax my earlier position. But whether I wanted to lead or not, I couldn't afford to look unsure of my course forward: Wilderich would seize on any sign of weakness to replace me as the head of our little conspiracy. Despite this, I turned away from Wilderich and Max, ashamed of my course even as I committed to it.

"Burn the body. Burn it all."

VI

⚭

A Carnival of Rot

"*Gruß gott*, Wilhelm."

"I'm not sure God lives here anymore, Lord."

I looked quizzically back at the grocer's man, a sandy-haired young man with a soft chin and softer belly. He didn't have the look of most Viennese, his slightly darker skin marking him as some kind of farm-hand who had moved to the city. "What do you mean?"

His eyes fell, staring my feet fully in the face. "I can't say, Lord, but I know that if God lived here, I wouldn't have needed to run to your family's estate this morning."

Still confused, I shook away the question on my lips. "Has anyone been inside since you came across... whatever it was you saw this morning?"

"No, once I... "I watched his Adam's apple bob a moment as he tried to steady himself. "Once I saw him inside, I locked the door and ran to your family. Once I told the Lady von Rohan what happened, she sent Astrid to find you and told me to return here. She swore me to secrecy, telling me to turn anyone away with any story I could come up with." He looked about uneasily. "I've been here since."

I nodded, as much to reassure him as myself. "You did very well, Wilhelm. Would you like to go home now? You should not have to see this again."

But he rejected my suggestion with a brave smile. "No, my lord. I couldn't do that. Kalb took me in after my family's farm was burned outside the city. He is... was the closest thing I had to a father since then. I would like to stay and help, if I could."

Kalb. A Turkish name. As with Abraham, I was surprised that any Turks still lived in the city; With their brethren to the East ruthlessly invading Christian lands, I had assumed the remnants here had been forced from the city as brutally as the Jews had been. To know that a few remained was strange, but then the last days were very quickly re-defining the meaning of the word strange.

"Very well," I allowed. I took a deep breath; if Wilhelm's face was any indication, I was sure it would be the last clean air I would taste today.

"Let's go."

– – –

Upon seeing the grocery, I wished that I had not eaten breakfast.

Already unsettled, my stomach threatened to overwhelm any sem-blance of self-control I had left, bile building in the back of my throat. Struggling to remain composed, detached, I forced the gorge in my throat back down, swallowing hard as my own body warred with me. The sound of retching behind me told me that someone - either Abra-ham or the grocer's man - had failed to keep their own stomach as re-strained.

Yet, somehow it was more pleasant to smell the sick than to focus on the reeking stink emanating from the cornucopia of good things decayed. Everywhere I looked I saw more to turn my stomach, every corner of the shop a vision of decayed, festering rot. Artfully arranged pyramids of produce melted into disgusting piles of sludge, bread molded in carefully arranged display cases, meat was smothered in swarms of flies... No matter which direction I looked, the store was a vision of pestilent death.

The shop itself did not escape decay, the very walls sagging under the weight of the putrefaction, the ceiling above me bulging dangerously as wooden beams whined pitifully. Even as I looked about the scene, a shelf at the back collapsed, glass jars exploding as they tumbled to the molded stone underfoot.

Throwing my scented handkerchief over my face in a vain attempt to block out the smell, I turned to the grocer's man. "In God's name what happened here?"

His tear-streaked face stared blankly back at me. "I don't know!" he cried pathetically, his entire body shaking as if he were afflicted with palsy.

I tried to form a question, stopping to spit out the vile taste that found its way to my tongue. "Where is Kalb?" I finally managed. Casting my eyes about the store again, I didn't see anything remotely human, a fact leaving me further unsettled. "Is he alive? Wilhelm, where is your employer?" A part of me knew Kalb was dead: Wilhelm had already told me as much, but I had to pretend some measure of hope, the better to steady the young man behind me.

But Wilhelm said nothing, his mouth working open and shut as he gasped for deliverance. His hand thrust towards the near corner. "He was right there, lying in a pool of blood. His wife was there as well." His voice cracked in misery.

My face twisting, I turned to look at Abraham. Somehow the Jew remained completely composed, his gaze clinical as he looked about the store. I tried to learn from his example, by force of will twisting my face into some semblance of normality, waiting until he looked at me to ask an unspoken question. He shrugged back, as if to say that he was as overcome as I was. I jerked my head softly towards Wilhelm, silently looking for support that Abraham gave me.

The *apotheker* moved closer to the distraught employee, an arm extended carefully to drape about quaking shoulders. "It's alright, my boy. It's alright. Why don't we go outside for a moment, get a breath of fresh air?" He turned Wilhelm away, though the younger man attempted to glance back. "No, no," chided Abraham. "Tell me about the day Kalb took you in... Yes, there's a good lad."

I let the two leave before I turned to the corner, not even moving until the sagging front door wheezed shut. I tried again to remove the stench from my nose, tying the handkerchief loosely about the lower half of my face. For a few moments the putrid stink left me, the miasma dissipating as I ground the perfumed cloth against my face.

My eyes closed of their own accord, the pleasant smell of the perfume taking me back along memories half-forgotten. Mother had always loved this particular scent, ordering it from merchants in Milan at no small cost to Father. He had never complained once at the cost, in no small part because he loved doting on every one of us. Smelling it again now soothed my rebellious stomach, my guts unknotting in surrender, my mind quieting itself once more.

I let my eyes open, feeling the same detachment Abraham must have felt upon first experiencing this horror. The smell momentarily at bay, my mind began to catalog everything, internally calculating and cross-referencing every last detail, seeking some manner of order in the room. Nothing was immediately apparent, but I refused to let myself submit to despair. I moved tentatively towards the corner Wilhelm had indicated, my feet vainly seeking some uncorrupted portion of the floor.

I was somewhat successful, though my right shoe was enveloped by some slurry of matter that I refused to analyze more closely. Removing my coat, I tied its sleeves together about my waist, desperate to keep it from dipping into the same sludge half of my shoes now tasted. My eyes peered at the mold, my hands dipping into pockets to extract a set of gloves I had absent-mindedly grabbed this morning before leaving the estate. Given the comfortable weather, they had remained unused, but I found myself grateful now that I had grabbed them at all.

Crouching carefully, I probed the mass in front of me, the piles oozing one way and then the other, each tug coating my fingers in a sucking, elastic soup. Ignoring the gurgling burbles emanating from it as best I could, I jammed both hands into muck, prying the mountain apart with my hands, digging into the unnatural crust to get a look at the core beneath.

I was rewarded with a glimpse of fabric, my heart skipping a beat as I spied the small shred of color concealed in the morass. I had almost missed it, the mold's surprising vibrance hiding the grey tunic scraps in plain sight. I practically dove after it, hurling the muck to one side or the other as desperately as I could, fistfuls of the un-mountain splattering wetly against the walls as my hands dug in again and again. I felt my handkerchief twitch as shrapnel from these missiles spattered against the formerly clean cloth.

My mind focused on digging through, I almost jumped in shock as Abraham laid a hand on my shoulder. "Easy, *frayand*, Easy. Do not destroy something that might be important later."

I stopped for a moment to consider him. He didn't look back at me, his free hand reaching down to brush aside the slime gently. "Are you sure you want to touch that?" I asked. "Weren't you the one who said that it was not a good idea to handle something that could be so... contagious?"

He gave me a thin smile. "I have handled things far more deadly than sludge like this. This is disgusting, but this is not our plague." He stopped his digging, his hand looking like a frog's foot with the goo arcing from finger to finger. He pointed with his clean hand. "That on the other hand, you may touch."

I looked back around, my eyes widening as I followed his pointing finger. Revealed - at least, in part - was an arm, though who it belonged to, I couldn't say. At first, I didn't understand why Abraham had refused to touch it; most Turks I had met were darker, swarthy men, and I mistook the dark coloring of the arm as a consequence of a life spent out in the sun. But after I heaved it from the disgusting mess, the pile of decay stubbornly refusing my persistent tug, I realized two very uncomfortable facts.

One was about the nature of the arm itself. Like our first victim, every inch of the flesh was bare of hair or skin, necrosis boiling across every surface, though this one didn't look decayed.

The second was that only an arm came out from underneath the muck. Utterly revolted, I dropped the unattached limb to the floor, my fingers unwilling to hold onto to such a small piece of a man. Worse yet, it looked... gnawed upon, as if a great beast had been chewing on the diseased appendage, worrying it until a more choice morsel had come along.

My stomach reeled under this new assault, and I felt the room spin slowly, my feet refusing to remain beneath me. Abraham grabbed hold of me before I collapsed into the muck, steadying me as my mind struggled to make sense of the disgusting artifact. "Are you alright? Would you like to go outside with Wilhelm?"

I shook my head unsteadily. "No," I said weakly, the lack of strength in my voice earning me a look of concern from him. "No," I repeated more forcefully, trying to focus on the perfumed air that had begun to fade in the face of this new vicious assault. I gave a vague wave at the ownerless arm. "Is this what you expected to see?"

I watched him stare at me a few seconds longer, his eyes examining me for weakness. When he found none, Abraham knelt by the body, pulling a small knife from inside his own coat to prod the darkness. He drifted closer to take couple small sniffs, the action more canine than man. "No," he decided finally. "At least, not exactly."

I felt myself sag in exasperation. "Of course it isn't." Shaking off my self-pity, I asked, "What does 'not exactly' mean?"

Abraham chewed on his lip. "It means that the arm has all the hallmarks of the plague I thought of before, but there is more here than a simple sickness. Several things, actually. One is the timeline. If Kalb was ill, neither he nor his wife should have died for several days after contracting the plague, more than enough time for Wilhelm to find help. If the two were infected last night, they should be ill this morning, yes, but not dead.

"Then there's the rest of the shop," he continued, indicating the entire scene with his pointing knife. "I've never heard of any plague that would rot an entire grocery, especially not in the time it supposedly took Wilhelm to find us." The Jew stood carefully, his eyes cast back down at the ground and the arm still lying there. "And lest we forget, there is an arm here that is absent an owner. That's not even considering the fact that it's been... nibbled on." He looked over at me, for the first time looking a little green. "Might we go outside a moment?" he requested.

I wanted to chuckle, to laugh somehow and lighten the mood. I wanted to pretend that I was just fine inside, but I couldn't stand the crippling reek any longer either, so I nodded, and we left, heaving the creaking door open and stepping outside.

The air outside was sweeter than the best wine; I happily gulped in breath after breath, instantly pleased to be away from the rot inside. The street was full, with more than a few pedestrians looking at me in puzzlement, their expression enough to remind me that I needed to downplay where I had just been. Turning back towards the grocery door, I yanked the cloth from about my mouth, suddenly desperate to hide any sign of foul play.

Smoothing out my clothes as best I could, I put my coat back on, trying hard to seem as normal as possible. Well, as normal as I could under the circumstances. I turned around to see Abraham comforting Wilhelm once more. I waited for him to make eye contact before waving the two of them over to me.

"Wilhelm, can you remember exactly what you saw this morning? You said before that the shop wasn't... like it was now. Was there anything strange?" I tried to give him as little restriction as possible - if I had primed his memory with any words, he would latch onto them unconsciously, and I wanted his thoughts as natural as possible.

It seemed the time outside the shop had done the younger man some good, because he answered me almost immediately. "Kalb told me to come in later, what with it being my birthday, so I took a walk early this morning across the city because I could. There is a bakery over there that makes..." I nodded, not quite listening, as he continued his rambling story, struggling to grasp the idea of celebrating a birthday. I had heard of it happening in other parts of the Holy Roman Empire but hadn't come across it very often here in Vienna. The Church claimed that to be so focused on earthly matters only invited the Devil, and despite my continued absence from Mass, God and I were in agreement here. "Go on," I instructed.

He nodded, his hair fluttering softly. I hadn't realized how thin it was. "When I arrived the store was still closed, which was odd because Kalb always was open before the sun came up. He said that it was so we could cater to the drunks who were coming home from the alehouse, but I never saw any there."

I waved my hand in a circular motion, trying to usher him on politely. Abraham's glare told me that I failed in that respect, though Wilhelm seemed not to care. "I tried to open the door with the key his wife gave me a year or two ago, but the door wouldn't budge. At first, I thought it was the lock when I heard something going on inside. I tried looking in the window but could only make out vague shapes."

"Something going on?" Abraham repeated, his head tilting to one side. "Something going on like...?" he prompted.

"Like a fight. I heard crashing like someone was smashing the store apart," his voice began to accelerate, the memory unbalancing his humors. "I tried to break down the door, I kept hurling my shoulder at it again and again, but by the time I had gotten it open-"

His face fell, his composure beginning to break once more. "By the time I had gotten it open, Kalb and Samira were in the corner. They were..."

"It's ok," I said weakly, trying hard to be as consoling as Abraham and failing as my words rang false. Thankfully, it seemed that my words were all that was necessary; Wilhelm forced a brave smile across his face, though it never reached his eyes, his pale stare still mired in sorrow. "You said that the shop wasn't like we found it. Can you remember anything else? Did you see anyone else there?" I scanned the people passing by, the hair on the back of my neck standing on end as some sixth sense made itself known.

The sorrow left his eyes for a moment, the smile twisting into a look of reflection. "There was someone else there, someone who shoved past me to leave the store, but I didn't get a very good look at him. A little taller than me, maybe? Very thin, with a drawn long face. I'm sorry, I was just so focused on..."

"Sh," commanded Abraham softly. "It's alright. You've told us everything you could. It's more than enough. I think, though, that maybe you should not be by yourself tonight." He looked at me for support.

"Of course not," I said. "We have room for you on the estate if you like. You should come to stay with us for a few days, at least until this whole business is resolved."

"I couldn't, my lord," opined Wilhelm, confused. "I mean, I'm just a grocer and you're..."

"I'm Dietrich," I said, trying to sound as friendly as possible "and right now I am doing exactly what Kalb did when you first came here. You need some place to stay for now, and I would like to give you that. As it is, Abraham and his wife were coming over for dinner, weren't you?" I looked back at the Jew who nodded quickly. "I'm sure Astrid and Max will be there as well, and we have some space in our guest cottage where I stay."

"Are you sure?" he asked, looking overcome by emotion. "Is there anything I could do to-"

I cut him off. "No, not at all. Absolutely nothing." I pursed my lips in thought realizing that I had just misspoken. "Actually, there is something you could do for me."

"Yes, lord?"

"Please go to Stephansdom and ask Bishop Wilderich to dinner as well. Tell him that he and I need to discuss some matters of grave importance. Please use those exact words."

VII

A Pleasant Evening Spoiled

"Good night, Onkel Dietrich! Good night, Bishop Wi'drich!"

"Good night, little Knuddelbär," I smiled, gathering up my niece in my arms and planting a big kiss on her cheek, relishing the squeal of delight that sounded in my ear. Prying her loose, I picked up Freddie next, taking great pains to not give him the same treatment. Despite being younger than his sister, he fought like a fiend against any show of affection other than a warm embrace.

He accepted my more restrained goodnight with his usual quiet reserve, his tiny arms reaching about my neck to clasp at the back of my head, his tiny face level with my own. I gave a goofy grin, winking with one eye and then the other. He grinned back, to my joy tilting my head gently down and giving me a quick peck on my forehead.

Not wanting to ruin the moment, I set him back down on the ground where he and Katarina turned to the rest of the guests. One bowing, one curtsying, their nurse ushered them away to their rooms upstairs.

"Lady Sophie, your children are delightful," complimented Wilderich, a small tear appearing at the creases of the bishop's eye. "It makes me wonder what would have happened to me had I not taken my Holy Vows." He had enjoyed chatting with Katarina during dinner, showering her with attention that she eagerly consumed to the last. Unfortunately, this friendliness was not extended to either Abraham or Sarah, the clergyman continuing to extend his frostiness to the non-Christians seated at the table.

I let his careful distance slide, as neither of the Jews seemed to care much; while Sarah focused on stealing as much of Sophie's time as she could, Abraham chatted amiably with Max and me. I was pleased to see that the bishop's casual racism had not extended to Max, the night watchman leaning in as he drank in every syllable of the *apotheker's* stories and jokes.

Wilhelm had been with us for a time as well, but had begged to be excused a short time, the young commoner clearly feeling the odd man out among our dinner party. He had departed to the guest cottage to relax there. Once everyone had gone home, I would check in with him. With the plagued body now gone – destroyed by the bishop's own hand – I appreciated the thought of having another house guest, especially one with a pulse.

The conversation around the table continued for a few minutes more, each of us clearly unwilling to broach more serious subjects than how enjoyable the food had been or how wonderful my niece and nephew's innocence was . In the meantime the house maids and servants had come in, some to clear away dishes and to refill mugs and glasses, some to replace the candles that had burned lower during the course of the evening.

I watched one servant adjust a reflection disk that had fallen loose from its position against the wall. The offending reflector had spent a good deal of the dinner resting against a burning candle, a fact now evidenced as the first attempt to adjust it ended with a whispered curse and a seared finger.

At length the house staff retreated as well, taking with them any semblance of normality. My sister cleared her throat, her role as the hostess resumed as she called everyone to silence. "Well, I have had a lovely evening with you all, and I do so enjoy seeing old friends," she said, looking at Max, "and making new ones." She looked at the Jewish couple and the bishop in turn, giving a small smile to each. "However, I think it's time that we discussed the events that happened earlier today. So, where are we?"

Her frankness disarmed most of the others at the table, unused to such direct words from a noblewoman. I would have spoken then, but I waited as those on the outskirts of the conspiracy looked to those further inside. Eventually, all eyes found their way to me.

I opened my mouth to respond when the bishop cut in instead. "I don't see any need for us to talk about the whole affair. While tragic, there is nothing mysterious about either of the deaths. One was unfortunate, yes, but the other was a heathen." He reached out a hand as if calming a small child. "They are freak incidents, nothing more."

Sophie's eyes grew cold. I knew that look all too well, leaning back in my chair as she pinned the bishop to his seat with an icy stare. "Lord bishop, I have nothing but respect for the church, and because of that respect, I will overlook exactly how insulting your tone was just now. I am neither my daughter or my son, and I will not be spoken to like them, and certainly not in my own house!" She half stood from her seat, her arms placed carefully on the table.

I watched the bishop carefully lean back in his seat, trying to politely put as much distance between the two of them as possible. Seeing the effects of her words, my sister sat back down, her gaze and tone softening. "Now I know only a small portion of the events of the last several days, but I know enough that I know the body found the other day was not a 'freak incident', nor is the discovery of an arm absent any other body part something to be laughed away. So I ask again, where are we?" She looked over at me.

I shrugged, unsure of where to begin. She and I had spoken briefly about the day's events in the time between my return and the arrival of the others, but I had not had the time to more completely bring her up to speed. "Where should I begin?" I asked.

"Wherever you would like, brother dear. Perhaps start at the place that allowed Abraham and Sarah into our little group?" she responded, which I took as carte blanche to start at the very beginning. Recounting quickly but leaving out nothing, I took her through the day's events, beginning with Abraham's suspected diagnosis and continuing through the whole affair with Wilhelm and the grocery. Throughout my telling, I deferred when others around the table interjected to clarify or insert their own perspective.

I appreciated the chance to more fully explain everything; my brief chat with her had left out too much, at least in my own mind. If nothing else, my retelling allowed me a chance to more fully absorb what had already happened today.

"And that brings us here, around this table." I finished, taking a sip of wine to soothe my irritated throat. Given my own preference for parchment over people, I was not used to speaking as much as I had today. Between Abraham, the grocery, and this evening, I had had precious little time to myself.

Sophie nodded. "Seems fairly open and shut then. We are dealing with plague."

Abraham shrugged, "Well, we might have been dealing with plague."

Wilderich was, surprisingly, the one to ask the next question. "Why do you say 'might have been'? Weren't you the one saying before about how dangerous this was?" He leaned on the table as if intensely interested, though there was a smug smile on his face.

The Jew looked at his wife, the two of them having a quick discussion in some dialect I had never heard before. Some of the words sounded German, but I couldn't completely understand what was said. "Well," he said, "we have no bodies to study for one, short of the single arm which I admit to having only briefly looked at before we left the grocery. Given that the bishop has destroyed the only complete case study we would have had – I would like to think that we are ahead of the beast, but I do not want to give false hope."

Wilderich shifted in his seat, his superior look fading into a more neutral mask. Strange, considering the fact that Abraham had neither condemned nor complimented him, but I was more focused on the *apotheker*. "False hope?" I asked. "I'm not sure that I would call it that."

He shrugged, though it was Sarah who spoke next. "I think I would, *Herr* Dietrich. We may have reported cases of this plague, but in times past, this sickness hits a place in waves. I admit I haven't read all of the books Abraham has, but believe me when I say that Vienna would be very different were the plague truly here."

Wilderich's face shifted again, his interest as piqued as mine at Sarah's comment. "You read?" he asked curiously, his head tilted to the side in bemusement.

"Of course, Lord Bishop," answered Sophie from her place. "I do as well. I admit my family upbringing was different than Sarah's here, but I missed the place in the Bible where it said women shouldn't learn the same as men." She glanced at Sarah, her tone light but pointed. "Does the Torah overlook this, too?" she asked irreverently, drawing a chuckle from the more literate at the table.

The bishop adopted a conciliatory pose, holding his hands up in surrender. "Forgive me. I meant no disrespect to her, of course, Lady von Rohan." The apology was awkward, but it was one given more freely than before. He turned back to the Jews, a wary respect in his eyes. "So are you saying that we are past the threat of plague?"

"Not completely, perhaps, but our chances are good," said Sarah. More than one set of shoulders sagged in relief at her words, including mine.

Max, quiet so far, objected. "Are you sure about that? I mean, what about Kalb and his wife and their shop?"

"True," I admitted. "If we can believe Wilhelm, there was a struggle of some kind there. At the very least there is a murderer on the loose."

"Why do you say 'if we can believe Wilhelm'?" asked Sophie, her pose still relaxed and thoughtful. She had already followed my thoughts to her own conclusion, but she was trying to make sure everyone else present understood. Especially the bishop, given her glance his way.

"Well, Wilhelm told us that the shop was perfectly fine when he left last night, yet when we arrived there earlier, the entire place was overcome by rot."

"It's not uncommon for plague to be accompanied by rot," opined Sarah.

Abraham shook his head. "Not at the speed that this would have spread, *liebchen*. You know as well as I that with all the preservatives that are in food these days, it would take a week or more for most items to decay. The shop today was a glimpse into Sheol itself, hell made real." He reached out to pat her on the forearm gently as he ducked his head apologetically. "I am sorry I didn't tell you earlier, but you worry so when I am not in the shop."

I watched as Sarah looked irritated, then amused, at the admission. "It's only because I know you're helpless without me. It's a wonder you can get out of bed some days," she said, leaning into her husband's shoulder lovingly.

Sophie, Max, and I all smiled as husband and wife made peace with one another. Wilderich used the moment of quiet to ask again. "So the shop had been allowed to rot. How does this affect our belief in Wilhelm? I can't say I know the boy personally, but he seems to be an honest man, even if he did find employment with a heathen *Ausländer*."

I sighed at the destruction of innocence, massaging at my nose in irritation as I marshalled my response. However, it was Sarah who piped up again. "Bishop, I realize we are testing your limits with the inclusion of Abraham and I in this group, and while I am sorry for your discomfort, do you think you could keep your small-minded views to yourself for now?"

I hissed at the remark, the air gasping between my teeth as I imagined the older man's response. She wasn't wrong: the bishop had been nothing if not openly racist more than once, but he was still a bishop, and due at least a small amount of respect given his position. For his part, Wilderich flushed bright crimson, but he said nothing, instead inclining his head in silent deference, a tight grimace on his face.

I tried hurriedly to refocus us. "What I mean," I said, coughing until he looked back at me, "is that the spoiling in the shop is uncommon in the extreme, which makes me wonder if perhaps some of his story isn't quite true?" I let the word hang in the air, waiting for someone to challenge my mistrust.

I hadn't expected Abraham or Sarah to come to Wilhelm's defense, nor did I anticipate Sophie making any comment. But when neither Max nor Wilderich said anything I felt my eyebrows rise in astonishment. Perhaps the bishop wasn't keen on being scolded again, but Max had always had an almost dangerous level of naivety as far as humanity was concerned. It was something I appreciated constantly, but it was sometimes disconcerting, especially considering all of the evidence we had experienced to the contrary walking the streets at night.

With no resistance, I continued. "So if Wilhelm isn't telling us the truth, what do we do believe?"

Sophie held up her fingers one at a time. "Is there a murderer on the loose, or is there one now staying on my estate?"

"Our estate," I corrected.

"My estate," she repeated. "You live in the guest house, and while you are my brother, I have the final say on who remains here." I nodded meekly, knowing that any further discussion was pointless. Truth be told, it was all good fun when Sophie put others in their place but being on the receiving end of her dominance made me feel no small amount of pity for Wilderich. Her authority again established, she held up another finger. "If Wilhelm is telling the truth, who is the killer?"

Abraham cut in, his tone carefully subordinate. "I do not think he did it." When my sister gave him a nod to continue, he did so. "You did not see his face this afternoon. It was not the face of a killer."

"And you have experience in understanding what a face of a killer looks like, Abraham?" asked my sister skeptically.

The Jew didn't give an inch, his tone becoming more definitive rather than less. "You remember, of course, the nature of my business. I have customers who request all kinds of things from me," he said, stressing each word carefully. "If we are looking for the face of a killer, there are those around this table who fit that bill far more easily than Wilhelm."

All eyes turned to my sister, eager to see how she would respond to the challenge. She said nothing, merely nodding in agreement. "I'm sure that is true. People certainly have the ability to horrible to one another, don't they? We are fortunate that the five of us here are not so inclined to evil," she deflected, the response drawing a shiver from me. It was ironic, I realized, that I was so concerned about being in charge of this conspiracy. If anything, my authority paled against that of my sister; each decision would be ratified by her or not at all.

Wilderich bravely re-entered the conversation. "Well, might I suggest that we bring him back to tell us again what this intruder might look like? I realize that he may not have gotten a good look at the man, but perhaps he has remembered something since Dietrich and Abraham spoke to him before."

It was a reasonable suggestion, and there was a refreshing earnestness to the older man's face that made me warm to him again. "Makes sense," I agreed, my approval earning a gentle nod of appreciation from the bishop. I looked over at Max. "Should we go get him?"

"Both of us?" he asked quizzically, his eyebrows furrowing. "He's just one man."

"True," I shrugged, "but I would prefer that we are ready for absolutely anything in case Abraham is wrong about his innocence." Neither of the Jews seemed particularly pleased, but between Max's muscles and my words, I preferred to leave nothing to chance.

Nodding politely to the other four, Max and I stepped away from the table, retreating into the soft darkness of early evening, a retrieved lantern in my outstretched hand. Through the open door leading outside, I heard uneasy small talk began behind us, uncomfortable but bravely breaking the tension.

Max's voice intruded on my satisfaction. "Dietrich," he began, "I need to tell you something." His tone was uneasy, guilty in the most childlike of ways.

I grunted in acknowledgment of his words, though admittedly I was only half-listening. "Mm? What is it? Did you finally make a pass at Astrid today and she turned you down?" I meant my words at a joke, but I saw him wince as if I had struck him. "I'm sorry," I said, reaching out my free hand to pat him reassuringly on the shoulder.

"It's alright," he claimed, though I still saw his hurt look. "I'm serious, though. I need to tell you something, but I'm not sure if I can."

His grave expression gave me pause. "Max, what's going on? The last time you acted this way was when Linda told me that she had kissed you after she had sworn you to silence." Despite the twinge of half-remembered adolescent pain, I smiled reassuringly. "You told me anyway, but it wasn't until you had practically beaten yourself senseless over it."

My friend gave his own weak smile, but it was as fake as my own. "I want to tell you something about the bishop, but he made me promise not to tell anyone, even you. He even told me that God wanted me to keep this secret."

My earlier re-fired appreciation for the bishop was quenched in an instant, smothered by this new revelation. I struggled to not snap irritably at the big man. "Max, I know you're a good, devout Christian. It's one of the things I love about you, your trust in something greater than this world."

He stiffened, suddenly awkward because of my word choice; I had forgotten that Max was uneasy with any kind of affection between men, a stance that had seen him always keep a cautious distance from other men. I recalled trying to hug him the day I had become an uncle, an attempt that had ended with me tumbling head over heels when he unconsciously pushed me away.

"Oh, come off it," I snapped irritably. "You know what I meant." Letting my voice soften, I continued. "You always believe that there's something else out there, a higher power, a reason for us to come together and believe in one another. I never have, or at least I've kept it at arm's length. But while I admit I've not believed like you do, I do know one thing: There is no place in the Bible that says we should be dishonest. So whatever it is, you can tell me."

I watched his eyes flicker from one side to the other, practically analyzing his mind as he weighed and measured his next actions. I looked past him at the cottage: we had stopped just short of it, and it was curiously quiet for being so early in the evening. I had not anticipated Wilhelm to have every light lit, but there was enough of the deepening gloom that we had brought a lantern for our walk, and the cottage had a curious atmosphere emanating from it. I even felt a strange scent tickle my nose.

It smelled like... rot.

I pawed my hand in front of Max's eyes, my attention firmly fixed on the guest house. "Max... Max!" I managed to look at him as he jerked his own gaze at me. I pointed with my hand at the dark house. "Something's wrong."

His head tilted to the side in puzzlement. "How do you know?"

Then we both heard the screams.

VIII

⟨※⟩

A Death in the Dark

I threw myself at the front door of the guesthouse, rebounding when the wood failed to budge under my weight. "Max!" I bellowed, jerking a pointed finger at the door.

The screams had faded into silence long moments ago; yet, even in that blessed silence, they echoed over and over, a cacophony of freakish misery that made me clutch at my chest in agony.

I threw myself to the side as Max thundered in, barely making it out of the way before the huge man fell headlong against the stubborn wood. It shattered into kindling, every piece of it exploding as it fled his brute strength. Not even waiting for Max to get to his feet, I leapt over his prone form, throwing myself into a clumsy somersault deeper into the guest house.

It was a disaster area, not as corrupted as Kalb's grocery had been, but then I had never been one to keep food in the cottage. Despite this, everywhere I looked I saw signs of desolation. My writing desk against the window had been smashed in half, my papers having fallen like snow across the created peaks. To the other side, an overstuffed chair, once my father's dearest possession, now mine, had been gouged, its sawdust stuffing bleeding out in a puddle on the floor.

I heard Max rise behind me, favoring him with a quick nod as I tried to figure what had happened. He stared back, his head jerking twice towards the stairs in a calculated nod. "Dangerous?" I whispered, my sudden attempt at secrecy idiotic considering our entry just now.

"Probably," he hissed back. "Me first or you?"

"Me," I responded. "You have your club on you?" He shook his head, his response causing me to swear softly. We hadn't been expecting any kind of trouble, but the shriek had me suddenly fearing that Max's brawn wouldn't be enough to face whatever slunk about upstairs. I crossed quickly to the small fireplace, tossing him one of the bigger logs there, selecting the fire poker for myself.

Armed, we carefully made our way to the stairs, our eyes squinting in the deepening gloom, my lantern carelessly discarded outside. I felt my body straining to glean anything from the scene, trying desperately to understand anything. Part of me wished that I had never come across the diseased body days ago. Perhaps I would be blissfully ignorant of everything now, going about my business and my books without a care in the world.

I shook my head to clear it of distracting thoughts. I couldn't afford to lose focus now. Making the landing, we moved forward one slow step at a time, each of us unwilling to be the first to Wilhelm's room but equally unwilling to allow the other to go alone. We arrived all too quickly at his door, the flimsy portal slightly ajar, the room's contents out of sight.

Though the dark robbed me of my sight, my ears perked up at a strange new noise. It almost sounded like a nursing child, a soft insistent sucking that might have been almost soothing in any other situation. Holding out my hand gently, I eased the door open slowly, so slowly it almost was as if I barely moved it at all.

Inside was as ruined as the rest of the house seemed to be, though I couldn't make a sure assessment with light fleeing further minute by minute into night. As it was, I barely made out the hunched shape bent over a still body on the floor, but as my eyes adjusted I bit back on the curse that nearly slipped from my lips.

Though I had barely known him, the unmoving form was definitely Wilhelm, sandy hair carelessly falling across sightless eyes that now accused me quietly. Why had I allowed him to leave the dinner table? Hadn't he told me that there had been someone else at the grocery store earlier today?

Max nudged me, his meaty finger indicating the shadow atop Wilhelm's corpse. For the first time, I noticed that it was bent over the dead man, soft sipping sounds coming from where its head and Wilhelm's chest met. I looked back at my friend, nodding slowly at his unspoken plan. We might not have been able to save Wilhelm, but we could bring his killer – and Kalb and his wife's killer as well? – to justice.

My heart in my throat, I called out, my voice so weak the shadow on Wilhelm's body didn't even notice. With a confidence I didn't feel, I ordered the figure to stand, trying desperately to inject steel into my voice. The hunched shape paused, the suckling sound slipping to silence with a last slurp. Slowly it uncoiled, the outline rising to its feet before turning around to face us.

I heard Max gasp in horror, stumbling backward against the far wall of the hallway. I wish I could say that that I stayed where I was out of courage, but in truth I stayed only out of a fear so deep and sudden that my heart nearly froze in my chest because of it.

It was hideous, its face gaunt, one side cruelly singed by some manner of tattoo or brand seared into the caved-in cheek, the mark expanding and contracting as it respired, deliberately, each breath a menace. Eyes, absent anything humanity, bored into my soul, scrutinizing me the same way a man examines an insect under a magnifying glass. Teeth, red and wet, gleamed dully in the last vestige of illumination.

I tried hard to break its dead, predatory stare, instinctively knowing that to be lost in its eyes would be to be lost forever in hell. It was almost completely naked, but for a loincloth bare to the elements. Perilously thin, cadaverous grey skin stretched across barren arms and legs so finely I thought it would split with every muscle twitch. His hands were splayed like claws, a feral bestiality emanating from a soul sure to have discarded any mortality a long time ago. It swayed sinuously from side to side, the motion both alluring and repulsive, turning my stomach with its wretched seductiveness.

I gasped, having forgotten to breathe, only now forcing air back into my burning lungs with conscious thought. "Who are you? Why did you kill him?"

The questions were darkly humorous, for it cackled in apparent delight. "I have saved him, little morsel. Saved him from the divine damnation about to visit this city. You would fall to your knees and ask for my mercy as well, if you knew what was to come."

I shivered as it spoke, nearly doing as it asked and surrendering meekly. It spoke. It was human. Unaware as I was, I could feel the foulness of the revenant in front of me, I knew that any resistance would be futile at best. Yielding was the intelligent option, the wise course of action. I should submit and beg for deliverance.

But a tiny part of myself, something hidden and ignored, half-forgotten in the face of a life built on rationality and science, resisted. I reached blindly back for Max with one hand, the other raising the poker in front of me defensively. By some miracle I found my friend with my clutching hand, drawing strength from his closeness, from a lifetime of support and loyalty.

The man-thing tilted its head to the side. "Curious. I invoke His Will, reveal His Plan, and you resist. Do you not know God and tremble?" He paced, stalking from side to side, back and forth tracing the breadth of the room. I could feel an insatiable hunger coming from him, a ferocity that terrified me in its intensity.

A small voice came from my side, a soft innocent prayer for deliverance coming from Max to feebly clutch at the air. I had never seen my friend so cowed, and the thought of unsettled me further, but I refused to give in to the fear. I barely recognized it as such, prayer something I discarded for all but the most dire of times: my voice aped Max's, the half-forgotten given breath in the growing dark.

Our resistance seemed only to puzzle the man-thing further. "They know and they do not give in." He looked past us, his voice softening as he wondered, "Master, why do they deny you?" I whirled around, my

poker raised as I tried to find off another attacker. But I saw nothing
and cursed myself for being so easily duped. I was already diving to one
side as Max called out a warning, throwing myself to the end of the hallway as Wilhelm's killer threw himself after me.

The next few moments were a blur of frantic motion, my survival
happening more by instinct than any conscious thought. By the time
my whirling mind finally made sense of the scene, I had managed to
make it back to my feet, though not without cost; several long, ragged
scratches joined other souvenirs gained breaking up bar fights and stopping burglars, each one dripping blood to soak into my torn shirt.

Looking about, I managed to find Max, my friend no longer his
length of wood, gripping instead Wilhelm's killer in a chokehold so
fierce I thought he would explode under the attack. Seeing him subdued, I allowed myself to sag against the wall, barely standing but confident in the knowledge that the man-thing would soon collapse into
unconsciousness.

Which made it all the more shocking when the murdered bent
nearly double, snapping his body forward like a spring, hurling Max
into the wall opposite with a crash that sounded like a mountain collapsing. Getting his bearings, he turned towards me, a feral grin on
bloody lips.

I attacked my would-be killer, swinging for his head with my poker,
hitting him once, twice, three times full across the face. He accepted
each blow placidly, his head snapping from side to side as my blows
landed. Nonplussed, almost bored, he allowed me to thrash wildly, letting my anger slide out in every furious swipe, a devilish smile blossom-
ing on his face once my pumping arms began to slow.

I grunted in pained disappointment when he floated out of the way
of my latest blow, my breath exploding from me as he buried a balled
fist into my stomach. The poker nearly dropped from my hand as I collapsed again, though I managed to hold onto it, if only weakly.

I tried to rise from my back, but my limbs refused to listen to my
bellowing mind, lying akimbo as the man-thing leered down at me.
My eyes flew to Max, cold logic knowing that he couldn't help me. Be-

sides, even if he could, what good would it do? I had never seen anyone fling him around so bodily, certainly not by anyone who looked so frail. Even the poker in my hand had done nothing to him; his face remained whole, practically unmarred but for the small cut on his forehead. Even as I watched, he pressed one clawing finger to it, letting the dark liquid collect there before slurping it from his finger as if it were the finest wine in the world.

His eyes, moments ago barely glimpsed, now seemed to erupt in fiery zeal, gleaming as my vision began to gray at its edges. "'You, O king, are the most powerful king on earth. The God of heaven has given you the works: rule, power, strength, and glory. He has put you in charge of men and women, wild animals and birds, all over the world—you're the head ruler, you are the head of gold.'" The words tumbled from him in unholy fervor, as if he were praying in church and not preparing to tear into me.

I heard another roar of thunder, this time accompanied by a flash of lightning from behind Wilhelm's killer. My ears ringing, my sight fading, I let myself slip away into unconsciousness as he fell towards me, his mouth wide, his teeth flying for my naked flesh.

– – –

I woke to rough slaps on my face, the sting of it not enough to truly hurt but enough to snap me from my unconscious stupor. Groggy, I felt my eyes pry themselves apart, the action agonizingly slow as if my brain carried out my will only begrudgingly.

"Oh, get up already," snapped a voice irritably to one side. "It's been two days and you've been in bed for all of it."

A weak smile came to me as I looked at her. "I'm sorry I'm such a disappointment, Sophie. I did just almost die, though, you know." I indicated the gouges on my chest, the bandages no longer spotted with blood but still necessary. "I'm lucky they're not infected."

"You mean infected with stupidity?" she fired back, sitting on the edge of my bed. "What were you thinking, going after that thing with just Max?"

I tried to shrug, the motion delicately painful as it tugged on my healing wounds. "You saw him. He was so thin; how were we to know that he was so..." I felt my voice trail off, my mind struggling to successfully label the thing I felt two nights ago. As it was, my own recollection of the events was incomplete, everything I knew after my bout of unconsciousness, I had learned from everyone else.

Max had come earlier that day to help me relive the evening, his body shockingly unwounded but for some bruises and small cuts. Neither one of us understood how he had come through the entire affair so comparatively unwounded. Abraham had been the next to arrive, fiddling with the small pistol that he had used that evening to wound Wilhelm's killer. Between the three of us, we did our best to reconstruct the encounter, all of us completely befuddled by the ease with which our opponent had nearly killed us all.

Sophie's face relaxed, changing from older sibling to something more motherly. "I know," she said, nodding. "From what I've heard from Max, from what I've seen of the guest house..." She shook her head helplessly. "I've seen a lot and I'm still at a loss for words."

I grimaced, the expression appropriately ugly. "Did I make a mistake sticking my nose in this, Soph?"

"Probably, but you were always the gentler of us. More foolish as well, but we'll let that go for now." We shared a small chuckle. She thought a moment before speaking again. "No, I don't think you made a mistake involving yourself in this. If anything, I almost wonder if you were the perfect person for this to happen to?"

My brow furrowed unconsciously. "How do you figure?" I asked.

"Well, you're a student of medicine, a man of not-inconsiderable means – even if most of those come from me." Her lips curled slightly at the sides. "Can you imagine Max stumbling on that first body without you there?"

"Perhaps... but he would have found me, and we'd be right back here."

She laughed again. "Dietrich, Max is a wonderful young man and without a doubt one of the most loyal people I've ever met, but I would never think him guilty of having too much good sense. He would have touched the body, not realizing that it was plague and then we would be far more worse off than having to deal with a few dead bodies and a ruined grocery."

Something in her response gave me chills. "How do you do it?" I wondered.

"Do what?" she asked back.

"Remain so cool about the entire thing." I said. "Four people are dead, and you seem so at-ease with that having occurred."

Sophie got up from the bed, moving over to the casement window, pulling the opposing sides together and latching them shut. Despite this gesture, the temperature in the room remained cool. "I suppose I am at-ease with it." She turned to look at me, her arms spreading wide in resignation. "I have to be. Though I love this city as much as you – and sometimes more, I think, since my business depends on it – I also have to be prepared to lose parts of it."

"I don't understand."

"I know," she said. "Despite all the death and ugliness you have seen, you remain more or less pure, little brother. You are able to put the cynicism to the side so easily, see the world as a place of puzzles instead of pain. I can't, which means that I also have to realize that sometimes there will be a balancing of the books." Her hands went up and down in a pantomime of a scale. "Good fortune means ill fortune at times, and at times ill means good."

I felt myself get a little angry at the apathetic response. "So it's ok for people to die so you can benefit?"

Her eyes hardened, her tone sharpening just so. "Don't you dare mistake my long view as being uncaring. I'll have you know that I used to import food from Kalb, and that it's with my money that Wilhelm is being buried in something more than a common grave!"

My anger cooled quickly, remorse replacing reproach. "You're right," I agreed. "I should have thought about what I was saying before simply opening my mouth. 'Tis better to be thought a fool...'"

"'Than to open one's mouth and remove all doubt.'" Sophie finished.

"One of Father's favorite sayings, if I recall correctly." She walked to a nearby chair, tossing a shirt at me. "Get up, you've got work to do."

I grumbled, but I swung my legs out from underneath the covers. "I know. I need to examine the attacker's body as well as Wilhelm's before he is buried."

"Examine the attacker's body?" asked Sophie. "He's not dead. At least, he isn't yet." She waved away my confused look. "No, I meant that there are more deaths that reek of plague. At least four separate cases, near what used to be the Jewish quarter."

"Are Abraham and Sarah-"

"They're fine." She confirmed. "With their permission, I moved them and their possessions here. As the other night shows, I cannot prevent someone coming in, but at least here they might find some safety from the sickness." She looked back over at me. "What I need you to do is to go down and learn what you can from Wilhelm's attacker. Once I know more, I'll be able to make a decision about what to do next."

"Oh," I said as lightly as I could. "Have you taken over the lead of this little group now? I don't want to play any political card but-"

"Then don't," she interrupted. "To the rest, you can be in charge, but behind closed doors, it's going to be me calling the shots."

My eyes narrowed uncomfortably, my unease voiced a moment later. "I would be willing to share some level of control, sister dear, but I can't give up complete control."

"Why not?" she inquired. "You know your books, but you do not know the world or the way that it works. You could learn a lot from my direction."

"Perhaps not," I agreed, "but without me, you have no medical idea how to combat this sickness. Abraham has yet to see a complete victim, and if there are other outbreaks, then my know-how is as necessary as your common sense."

I expected Sophie to throw her weight around, to act the older sibling and demand to take charge regardless of my stance. But she surprised me when she nodded instead. "Fine."

While I certainly continued to feel the weight of world on my shoulders, I was honestly relieved to have Sophie's support. Though she was less medically inclined, I would need her strength – and definitely her money – if we were to survive this spreading sickness.

My face grimly set, I got up, tugging the offered shirt over my head and settling it into place. "From your answer before, can I assume correctly that he's still alive? The killer, I mean?" I waited for her nod, making it halfway to the door before acknowledging the chill that surrounded my lower body. Looking down, I glanced over at Sophie. "Sister?"

"Yes?" she asked innocently.

"Pants?"

She shrugged, the older sister mentality reasserting itself. "You want to share power, then you share in the responsibility. Find some yourself."

I sighed. Siblings.

IX

⟨≈⟩

An Enigmatic
Conversation

I pushed open the door to the pantry, a last breath all the preparation I allowed myself before meeting my attacker of the other evening.

The inside was well-lit, my sister's insistence on exploiting natural light welcome; after the events of the other night, I had no desire to be left in the dark with a killer again. Honestly, I had no desire to be in there at all, but I couldn't allow my own fears to rule me.

An upturned bowl lay off to one side, a prisoner's meal rejected out of pettiness or distaste, I didn't know. I let my eyes rove over the chained man next to it, my unease quieted somewhat as I was more easily able to see him without fear for my life.

He was as thin as I remembered, withered almost, his frame as devoid of any spare flesh; I would have thought him a dead man come to life had I seen him this way in the dark. His skin was sallow, its colorlessness only adding to his air of undeath. Turned away from me, I saw the bandage on his back, the white fabric drowning in dark, purple stains. Unconsciously, I put a hand to my side, wincing as questing fingers brushed against my healing side. My own wounds were already well on the mend; even shot, shouldn't his wound have stopped bleeding by now?

He sniffed, suddenly a predator smelling prey, his crouching form slowly coming about to face me. I shuddered at the sight of his own face. As demonic as it had seemed in the dark, his cheekbones sharp, almost jagged, I could finally see the brand on the left side of his face for the first time now, a stylized 'M' expanding and contracting with each breath racking his entire body. I did my best to ignore his eyes, but felt myself drawn to his depthless gaze, the dark wrath promised in them making me take an uncomfortable step backwards.

"He comes, he comes, the curious man, alive and well, or so it stands." I nearly jumped at the sound of his voice. Far from being monstrous as I remembered, it was almost childlike, playful. But there was no innocence to it, the absence of any youthfulness making it sound more mad than anything else. He tried to move closer to me, his sunbathed body jerking to a stop as he hit the end of his restraints, the metal chains clanking echoing from the stone walls of the pantry.

"I wanted to speak to you, my friend. Do you mind if we talk a little?" I kept my tone friendly, trying hard to suppress my disgust as I tugged a stool forward. Settling it just out of reach of his manacled arms, I sat, my hands clasped carefully in my lap. "Can you tell me who you are?"

His eyes quivered back and forth. "On Virgil's seat, the master stands, the hour of reckoning close at hand. Despair then, you doubting city, for God's kingdom comes, bereft of pity."

"What are you talking about? Where is Virgil's seat?" I asked. But he ignored me, turning away from me, away towards the darkness, tugging on his chains until he was half-hidden in the darker piece of the room. All the while, he repeated his rhyme again and again, his voice changing pitch slightly with each repetition. He babbled the words, sometimes singing them, sometimes barely whispering them, but all the while ignoring me completely. I needed to figure out a way to communicate with him, or this would be nothing but an exercise in futility.

I frowned, running through possibilities. Pain wouldn't motivate him; he had accepted my assault the other evening without batting an eye, completely untroubled by the assault that had left me exhausted and him unmarked. My attempt at geniality had come to nothing, either. What remained?

I sat in silence, a madman my only company. The light in the room shifted, shrinking as the sun rose higher and higher in the sky. Oddly, my companion grew less restless as it did so, no longer tugging on his chains as harshly as the intruding rays retreated. But despite this, he refused to speak to me, or at least, he refused to say anything intelligible more than his insane couplet.

A servant came by to drop off a plate of meat and cheese for me to eat, a small goblet of weakened wine to wash it down. The killer received a new bowl of broth, though he immediately threw that at the wall, shocking the servant into an undignified retreat.

All the while I thought. At length, a third option came to mind, but my stomach turned slightly at the thought of it. The other evening Max and I had found him hunched over Wilhelm, sucking, it seemed, at his chest. Was there more motive to that madness than just insanity?

I tugged my shirt back off over my head, reaching down to my side to delicately peel back the bandages covering my wounds. I hissed at the tugging of the cloth against the closing gashes in my side. Far less harrowing than they had initially appeared, I was far from completely healed, some strange infection in the gashes as yet unconquered. My nose wrinkled in disgust at the rancid smell, my stomach turning as the scent of ruined eggs weakly slunk from the half-sealed gashes.

It had a profoundly different effect on my captive audience, the killer going deathly still, his head slowly rotating around to peer at my side. I saw thirst in his empty stare, insatiable craving that was terrifying in its boundlessness. The same feral grin from the other night alighted on his mouth, each sharpened white tombstone appallingly bright in the pantry.

"The morsel bares itself to Belial, yes. Have you come to know His will?" my captive asked. "Have you come to be taken to Eternity and away from the Wrath that is to come?"

I did my best to ignore the feeling of dread that erupted in my chest, smothering it as best I could under an air of quiet confidence. "Belial?" I asked instead. "Is that your name?" It wasn't an Austrian name, that much was for sure, but neither could I label it as firmly Ottoman, or anywhere else for that matter.

The chained man nodded slowly. "It knows the name, but not the true nature of the Ascended before it. What a shame, that the morsel teases and taunts, seeking information without offering anything truly in return."

Though I felt as if I already knew the answer, I asked regardless. "What is it you would want in return?"

Filthy, jagged talons indicated my side genially. "A small taste of water is all I ask. For that, you may have the answers you think you seek in return."

My eyes narrowed without thought. "You want to drink my blood?"

He nodded, the feral grin fading to a more considered smile. "A simple taste of the humors, yes. Is that too much to ask?"

"After seeing your handiwork, I think it best that your lips and my side stay separate." I pointed at his back. "How about this - I will unbandage your wound and you can taste your own 'humors.'"

He waved my sarcasm away with a clank of chains. "The morsel teases. Very well, I'll relent if for no other reason than boredom. Please, ask your questions; I'll not be here for long. The Master comes after all."

I felt a surge of annoyed frustration. "'Boredom?'" I cried. "You've killed at least three people and you talk of boredom?" I got to my feet, moving to a nearby shelf, piled high with liquor and wine, selecting one of the thickest bottles there. Belial watched impassively, even insolently, offering me his unprotected face when I came back to stand before him.

I took him up on his offer, swinging with all my might, the bottle thudding dully into his face. A part of me prayed for the bottle to break, that somehow I would be given a perfect excuse to swing it again at the smirking face. But it didn't, remaining completely unblemished.

Belial's face didn't fare as well, his lips splitting, dark, discolored droplets of blood flying forth in a small spray of violence. He didn't yelp or cry out in pain, his only response to lift one manacled hand to his lip to feel the moisture collecting there. Looking down at his hands, his grin only grew wider, only vanishing when he put his dripping fingers in his mouth, sucking the dark fluid from them with the same sucking sound I had heard the other night.

Some of the madness fled from his eyes, a measured nobility infusing him now. "The morsel has teeth, but does it feel better committing violence against one of His chosen?" Belial moved away from me, kneeling down off to one side out of the softer light that continued to come through the pantry window. "Or should I offer my face again, to be struck a second time?"

I suppressed the urge to try and break the bottle again across his face, ashamed at the burst of violence. I was a healer, and even when I rose my hand, I only did it to defend the lives of others. I could hear my Father admonishing me from beyond the grave, his face loving but disappointed in me for my moment of weakness. Setting the bottle down carefully, I moved back to the stool. "I would like to ask you some questions, Belial."

"And I would like to answer them. I am an angel, after all. But I must ask the morsel: will he listen to my words or only hear them?"

"Stop calling me 'morsel,'" I demanded. "You will address me as 'my lord.'" I despised throwing around my title, but neither did I want to be referred to as a piece of meat.

"In the eyes of God and his messengers, there are no titles." His head tilted curiously. "I will call you Dietrich, for that's your name, isn't it?"

"How do you know who I am?" I asked.

He gave a small chuckle from the floor. "I am a messenger of God, his Ascended. I have watched you for longer than you know. Shouldn't I know who you are?"

The hairs on the back of my neck stood on end at his claim. He was a madman, a killer, and a malcontent; surely he wasn't anything divine, was he? Thinking carefully, I tried to remember if he had simply heard my name somewhere before instead. That would make far more sense.

He seemed to read my mind, bloody lips chuckling darkly. "Relax, little Dietrich. Your pitiful existence isn't worth the attention it would take to truly know you. I saw you the other day, when poor Wilhelm saw something he was not supposed to."

The hairs fell slightly, though a question in their place. "You were the figure from the grocery, then?" He nodded. "What did you do to Kalb and his wife? Why did you kill Wilhelm? Why did you try to kill me?"

Belial shrugged again, his pose relaxed. "Wilhelm died for seeing too much, Kalb for seeing too little, and you? You would have died for convenience, for prying into something beyond your comprehension." He turned towards the window, his face creasing as he looked towards the light.

Disinterest poured off of him, an apathy that told me I would find out little else from him. There was a chance I could press him a little more, find out something else, but I wondered if it even mattered. All of his answers so far had only bred more questions. For that matter, how much of what I heard could I even trust? His madness had swung into seeming sanity, but that could vanish as quickly.

He continued to look out the window, his face crumpled in distaste as if the brightness offended him. "Belial?" I asked, not eager to leave the pantry without some new piece of information. "You said you're a messenger. What kind of message are you bringing?"

His eyes were bright as they turned back towards me, the cold fire in them enough to make me shiver. "My Master comes, Dietrich. And with Him comes Judgement for this whole city"

X

A Lesson in Leadership

"You can't be serious," I said, my face falling in dismay. I scanned the faces of the others at the table, my words barely heard over the other conversations in the common room. Most of them looked nonplussed, even openly dismissive. The few that didn't had seen too many years, or too few.

"But I am, Dietrich," said Lukas, leaning forward on the tavern table. "I understand that you're concerned about a few deaths here and there, but there are other, bigger things to worry about."

Another at the table nodded, his face bleak. "He's right. Even if we wanted to go hunting around for some malcontents, the Turks continue to thump their chests to the east, and we need to make sure that we're ready for them to come back."

I threw my arms up into the air. "What's the point of being ready for the Turks if the city dies before they get here?" It was a mistake to show some emotion, but I had been fighting the same fight for over an hour, and after three mugs of strong beer, I was short on patience and restraint.

Lukas' head tilted to one side, somehow amused by my frustration. "Vienna has been here since the Romans! You think a little cough could

FIRST, DO NO HARM - 79

kill her?" I resisted the urge to remove the smug look on his face with my fist; without his family's money, the city watch would be weakened almost to the point of dissolution.

One of the youngest men there piped up bravely. I knew whatever he was about to say would be completely ignored - he was a second son of a family more minor than mine - but I gave him a reassuring nod of support. "Is the issue just one of money?" He looked around for confirmation, continuing after one of the gray-haired men there shrugged noncommittally. "If I increase my family's contribution, will anyone else match me?"

Lukas scoffed. "To what end? There are over two hundred thousand people in this city, and we should be nervous because a dozen or two die from some mystery illness? I think more of the royal family died last year of consumption than that!"

The old noble who had nodded before scowled back. "Mind your tongue. That's the Emperor you're speaking about!" His grimace only deepened as Lukas merely sneered in return. "Be civil or you'll be answering to my second."

"Gentlemen, please! This isn't just some illness," I cut in, desperate to head off the impending challenge. "This thing ravages more than the body!"

"So you keep saying," drawled Lukas, all pretense at civility gone as he yawned expressively. He looked at the others at the table. "I call for an end to the meeting. Anyone second?" When no-one objected, he gave me one final exasperated shake of his head before leaving.

One by one, the other benefactors and leaders of the city watch left. Some, like Lukas, quit the tavern completely, content to stagger back to supposedly safe homes while death prowled unseen in the streets. Others retreated to other corners of the tavern, unwilling to listen to my warning but willing, perhaps, to be convinced if I could provide them with a better case than I had previously. The handful that remained looked to me for some kind of plan, anything that could help us in my request for further investigation.

Would that I could have given them any kind of direction. Almost all the clues we had gained had been destroyed beyond all possible use: we had Wilhelm's body destroyed, burned to ash in the hopes of staving off the theorized infection risk. The other recent victims shared the same fate - I had burned almost all of them myself. (Wilderich had assisted me only on two occasions, unhappy moments when we discovered children among the victims.)

I had left Wilderich with instructions to keep an ear out as he circulated throughout the city, eager to have at least one friendly shoulder on which I could lean. He had accepted my given task, though his face looked guilty, the reason for which I was completely clueless.

As it was, I had not revealed the source of my information any more than to describe the sickness in the first place - Sophie had suggested silence and I agreed with her thoughts. In the wake of the disastrous conversation, however, I wondered if I had made another mistake keeping still.

"Dietrich, you have that look of a man deep in thought," commented the gray-haired noble, a wizened smile on his face. "I'd offer a penny for them, but I imagine it'd be better spent in the city's defense."

I tried to keep my tone light. "Herman, I'd offer them free of charge if I thought it would do anything." Seeing the effect of my pessimistic words, I tried to rally flagging spirits at the table. "I'm sure we can manage to find the source of this on our own."

Herman glanced around the table. "I've no doubt of that. Lukas might bankroll our funding, perhaps even our supplies, but he doesn't walk the streets like we do night after night. There are more than a few who feel like us, they'll not need money to help out."

I was touched by his encouragement, though I didn't know how exactly we were going to manage it on our own. Lukas was right in that the number of victims was still comparatively small. All of us on the watch had seen our share of disease, some of us even quarantining a building or two to prevent any kind of epidemic.

A thought looped in the back of my mind, repeated over and over that we were on the brink of something horrible, as if we had conquered a molehill and now falsely believed ourselves somehow invincible. Belial's claim to a master only increased this sense of unease, especially as none of the most recent cases had had the same puncture marks on their chest. This had only confirmed in my mind their source, their perpetrator chained up in the pantry.

That even increased my confusion; why didn't they have them? So far, Belial had been at each scene, sipping on each victim's blood. Forgetting his seeming ability to infect people at will, he came off to me as a killer eager to take credit for his work. He didn't comment on these people the other day when listing his victims.

Were there other madmen in the city as well? Other lunatics with their own predilection for death and with the same dark power to spread the disease?

I did my best to banish the dark thoughts, but the evidence was plain as day. Belial had been in our custody when the other cases had been reported to my sister. Seeing how quickly the disease progressed, they had been infected within a day or two of Kalb and his wife, which pointed to other culprits.

The others shifted uneasily in their seats, awkward small talk springing up when I failed to immediately respond to Herman's trusting words. I nursed my drink, bitter at the thought that Lukas' blindness would mean the doom of the rest of us. It was true that there were others who could help pick up the slack financially, supply the watch with the means to sniff other madmen like Belial, but the cost was too great against the immediate reward. Any who could give more had already done so; what remained were the few pennies painfully extracted from the more unwilling members of the watch and the poor.

A skirl of pipes intruded on my despondency, primitive screeches of sound shattering my self-pity, a small cheer coming moments later from the assembled patrons about the common room. I looked up from my mug to see a man blowing madly into a strange bag cradled under one pumping arm. His hands danced up and down a wooden flute that came from the bottom of it, his stomach partially obscured by several other giant wooden splinters that jabbed across his chest and beyond his right shoulder.

Dressed in the motley of a medieval fool, the man stopped for a moment to cheerfully call out to us, "*Gruß Gott* everyone!" His voice dropping, he bowed his head delicately in a short nod of greeting. "For those of you don't me, I am Marx Augustin, poet, minstrel, bagpiper, and artist extraordinaire!"

I had never heard of him before, but clearly someone else had, for a voice called out from one side. "Don't forget town drunk!"

A rough chorus of laughter tumbled on the heels of the heckler's comment, but Augustin took it in stride, making a grand show as he doffed the floppy hat on his head. "Ah, my reputation precedes me then!" More laughter came, and I realized the comment for what it was, a way for a showman to warm up his audience.

I leaned over to Herman, the old man perhaps the only one besides me who wasn't listening to the piper's rapid-fire showman's patter. "I may head home for the evening."

He nodded. "Are you sure you want to leave now? Augustin is something of a celebrity of the people. A bit of a drunk, like he says, but he is quite talented with those pipes of his."

"Talent?" I asked, raising an eyebrow. "I didn't know causing an instrument to howl like a cat was considered talent." I pressed a hand over my heart, making a great show of inflicted pain. "Why, oh why, did I waste my life obsessing over humors and muscles! I should have picked up... whatever he's holding there."

It was Herman's turn to raise an eyebrow. "You are quite in the mood, aren't you? Why don't we take a walk?" He rose from the table with an energy I found surprising, considering his age. The other survivors of our disastrous meeting jerked at the sudden movement, half-raising to their feet before the old man waved them back down. "We'll be right back, boys." He pointed at his empty mug. "Get me a refill in a few minutes?"

Not waiting for a response, he guided me in and around the tables of the tavern towards the door. Despite the close quarters, I was only dimly aware of Augustin's show, a few short bleats on his pipes interjected between the constant chatter coming from the rotund man.

It was cooler outside, the night sky overhead darkened by the clouds that swallowed the city from the beginning of winter until summer of the following year. I tugged my coat tighter around myself, the action more a reflex than a reaction to the season's chill. I considered heading towards home, but Herman gently pulled me towards the city's center, his stride slow and measured.

We ambled more than walked with any purpose, the two of us on a path that wandered with no destination in mind. I tried to focus on counting the windows that passed slowly on either side of us, some lit dimly by candles, others dark and cold as shopkeepers and families slumbered inside. Streetlamps, thoughtfully kept burning by the night watchman who had not been at the meeting tonight, lit our way, each lone beacon standing guard over us as we aimlessly went on the cobblestones.

"Lukas was in rare form tonight," observed Herman, his hands coming together awkwardly at the small of his back. His face tightened, and I wondered not for the first time what had happened to him to cause that stiffness. More than once I had almost asked that very question, each time letting my inquiry die on my lips unspoken. Herman had already been an old man when I was very young, a confidante of my fathers who had become a confidante of mine after his passing. We weren't close in the same way that Max and I were close - Max was loyal but less intellectually inclined than Herman - but Herman was, in many senses, the closest thing that I had to a role model these last years.

I nodded weakly. "He is just so... damn stubborn," I finished, biting back on much harsher words that I decided better kept to myself.

"I seem to recall another voice in that conversation who was as stubborn," Herman chortled. "Always so sure of himself and the righteousness of his plan, that voice would always go on and on about how much smarter he was than everyone else."

A sigh escaped me. "If you suggested we come on this walk because you wanted to scold me, I'm going home." The old man coughed in response, the unspoken rebuke angering me until I realized his coughing was becoming sharper and sharper. "Are you ok?" I asked, resting a hand on his back, petting it gently in a vain attempt to clear whatever obstruction plagued him.

It was several long seconds before he stopped convulsing, the end of his coughing coming more from exhaustion and self-suffocation than any recovered sense of well-being. "I'm ok," he lied, brushing off my concern, though he allowed me to lead him over to sit on a low wall outside a graveyard. I did my best to not focus on the dark promise of the scene. Seeing my gaze, Herman laughed. "Sooner or later, we all end up here, you know. Well, for a while anyway."

I felt my head cock to the side in confusion. Seeing my face, Herman shook his head. "Most of us end up here, anyway. You and me, Lukas, most of the table tonight, we end up in crypts, familial haunts squirreled away somewhere on our estates, but almost everyone else ends up here for a while."

"For a while?" I asked, still confused.

"Yes," he nodded. "Take a look at the stones. Tell me if you notice anything strange about the dates on each headstone." I did so, peering at one after another, not seeing anything amiss with the situation. "Does it seem like every one of them is recent? Died in the last fifteen years or so?" Not waiting for my confirmation, he went on. "Despite what priests might tell you about letting the body slumber for eternity until Jesus Christ comes 'round again, the truth is most bodies stay put about a generation before the monks dig them back up and clean them."

"Clean them? What for?"

Herman gave me a smile that, under the circumstances, could only be called ghoulish. "The only word I could successfully use to describe it is construction." He pointed off to the church adjacent to the cemetery. "Though there is more than a few that are just set aside for nobility and clergy, some churches are more to the dead than to God." His gaze bored into me. "Do you know what an ossuary is?"

I shook my head, though I hazarded a guess. "Something to do with bones I would think?"

His eyes flashed, his mouth curving in satisfaction. "From 'oss-', very good. Your father always said you were a smart one. A remarkable man he was, and nearly as willful as you. Thankfully he had your mother to balance him out, but... When are you going to find yourself a wife?" he asked suddenly.

"Herman, the ossuary?" I prompted, wondering why I was being reminded of my lack of a wife right this moment.

"Oh, of course. How silly of me," he apologized. "More than a few churches have houses underneath their foundation, whole rooms of stacked skulls and fingers laid carefully next to one another in designs so intricate it would shame the finest architect." His hands rose in front of him, tracing unseen images in the air. "You should see them... column after column, piles and piles of them. It's so macabre and, yet, so darkly beautiful."

I tried to imagine the scene in my mind. Strangely, in spite of the number of bodies I have seen - and some of them all too recently - my mind recoiled from the exercise, unwilling to envision so much death at one time for fear of willing it into existence. I settled for nodding sagely. "How do they know whose bones are whose? Or do they just not care?"

"Oh!' exclaimed Herman. "It's the most interesting thing. They paint the owner's name on each piece. That way, should any examination be necessary in the future, they are able to reconstruct the body as needed." He shrugged, his tone tending towards irreverence. "Now me, I prefer to think that God won't need help re-assembling the dead on the day of Resurrection, but I am an old man! What do I know?"

I felt my lips purse on their own. "Herman, this conversation is... enlightening, but why are we here? Now?"

His tone continued to be disingenuous. "Well that is a question for the philosophers and priests, my boy. Even with all my years I'm not sure-"

"Herman" I half-demanded, my eyes closed, my fingers massaging at my temple. "I have other matters to attend to. A funeral to plan, a watch to somehow supply in the face of something that I can't even pretend to understand. I really don't have time for this."

My eyes opened to see his face, the expression on it as grave as any of the tombstones around us. "You need to make time for it, Dietrich," he observed, one old hand extending to point back towards the tavern we had left some time before. "Those men - and a few women, I might add - are looking to you for guidance. They don't understand what's coming their way - I know I don't, and I've been unfortunate enough to see some gruesome things throughout my life. All we have going on right now is your word and your observations."

"And Max's, and Abraham's, and..." I listed.

He shook his head. "That doesn't matter. Until they see something for their own eyes, it will make no difference. Until then, they are like children, from the oldest to the youngest of them ignorant of what's coming. They need someone to tell them that everything is going to be alright, that their families will be safe, regardless of what comes to their door each night."

"Why can't that someone be you?" I asked despondently. "I have no more authority on this than any of you. I don't even know exactly what we're dealing with."

He reached an arm out to pull me closer to his still seated body, tugging me gently down to sit next to him. "Now I don't believe that. You told Lukas it's plague, and any idiot with half a brain and moderately balanced humors would - and should - be terrified of that. He might not be, and that's his cross to bear. Yours is that you've seen the plague's effects... well, that and the person you say is controlling it somehow."

The old man fell silent a moment, lost in his own mind or maybe just unsure of what to say next. I took the opportunity to protest. "But I don't have answers for them!"

"That's the burden of leadership," he noted. He pointed to his hip. "Do you know why I have my limp?" I knew the question was rhetorical, though I shook my head anyway. "Well, I was a younger man then. I couldn't tell you exactly when or how, but I found myself drafted into the Emperor's army and we were marching towards the Ottomans. An officer, I was given the task of clearing a village on the border between the Turks and us."

Herman leaned away from me, too close to me to accurately reminisce. "We came up on a town, just a few of us. Reconnaissance, you understand. The villagers there were supposed to have been friendly, but there was some tension, some... thing that had me on edge. But I had just come into my post, and didn't want to look the fool, so I said nothing while every part of my body screamed that something was wrong."

I saw tears form at the edges of his eyes, his hand falling to massage his side. "Twenty minutes after we arrived, they attacked, every one of the villagers, down to the last man, woman, and child, out for our blood." He looked over at me, pain bleeding from his gaze. "We broke free, fighting back with every last ounce of ferocity that we had. Dozens of them died; we tried to reason with them, but they just kept coming, wave after wave even as we fought back with harquebus and pikes. I lost six men, five others, including myself, alive but wounded in some way. I could have saved all that life, could have prevented that bloodshed if I had not been afraid to act, if I had been willing to take responsibility for all of them."

I opened my mouth to speak, but nothing seemed an appropriate response. Everything sounded cliché, trite, fake unto the point of being insulting. I settled for something between cliché and truth. "It was war. You had no choice in it. If you had not fought and suffered, someone else would have. Who's to say that someone else would have done anything differently?"

It dawned on me then, an unexpected lesson tentatively peeking out from its hiding place. A ghost of a smile stole over my friend's face, wistful yet prideful. "That was going to be my point. As little as you want to be responsible for this, for us, you are. Would that had come to someone else. A royal physician, a true plague doctor ahead of the infection. But it did not, which means that it has now fallen to you."

He rose slowly, the weight of his own history preventing any quicker movement. "Indecision and fear of making the wrong judgement will kill us quicker than any disease."

"But what about Lukas and-"

"Lukas be damned," interrupted Herman. "He will come around or he won't. Until then, we need to continue to move forward. Even if the decision turns out to be the wrong one, we must move forward."

I nodded slowly again, though this time there was purpose behind the motion and not simply an idle attempt to please an old friend. "We're going back to the tavern, aren't we?" I asked, getting back to my feet.

"Are we?" he asked me, though there was no ambiguity to his question. We both knew the answer to it.

I held out an arm to steady him, having just watched him age more than a few years in these last few minutes. He gratefully took it, and I realized that he would have willingly accepted my help had I but offered it when we had first left the tavern. "Even if I don't know what to say to them?" I asked him.

"Especially then, but then, success has always been built on more than just a plan." Herman frowned thoughtfully.

"It's built on faith."

XI

❧

A Dearth of Answers

I returned to the tavern and Augustin's show, a smile grafted to my face, an air of good humor about every initially faked gesture and joke. I was stunned to find that the facade faded into something more true, more honest, the longer I sat there listening to the balladeer Augustin. I had to admit that Herman was right about the fat man; despite being altogether too loud and crude in most of his humor, he was very talented, switching between bagpipes and ballads as easily as man might change his mind. His voice, strong but lyrical, was as intoxicating as any beer, and I found my spirits lifted by his seemingly unending stream of material.

Now and again he would set aside his instrument to recite poetry, often of his own writing, and it was in these moments that I most appreciated him. Though a couple were unmistakably focused on the sexual, he had more than a few that silenced the entire tavern with their serenity, long stanzas of home, heartbreak, and healing that moved me as surely as any of the great poets. At the end of each, he would look about the tavern slowly, and it felt like in that moment all division between us was removed. Nobility, peasant, Christian, agnostic, or otherwise, we were unmistakably linked in our humanity.

I imagine that was part of Herman's lesson in convincing me to return, encouraging me to remember that my leading was not a reflection of my nobility. No, it was a reflection of my humanity, a sense of human decency driving my duty to the others around our table and about the tavern.

At length, Augustin finished his performance, its finale leaving all of us laughing and crying at his antics. A final flourish played on his bagpipes, he bowed low, one sweeping hand reaching out to snatch an unattended mug of beer from a nearby table. Straightening, he downed it in moments, some of it escaping his mouth to splatter on his faded shirt.

I considered waving him over to talk, but he was immediately rushed by others in the tavern, Lukas among them. Given our recent conversation, I decided to leave instead, making a far more graceful exit than before, and vanishing outside.

The streetlamps had burned lower in the interim, a couple of them sputtering into darkness as the flame consumed every last inch of tallow. Thankfully, there was still enough light to make my way home, which I did with only a little difficulty, the beer and ale of the last hours only slightly dulling my sense of balance. Stephansdom sounded in the distance, her bells pealing mournfully. I counted the low sounds, each one coming time with my heart. Thanks to my drinking before, I lost count as my mind wandered to my surroundings. While I appreciated Herman's company before, I enjoyed his absence even more, content as I was to slowly make my way home.

There was something undeniably peaceful about the evenings in Vienna. Even in the wake of the horrible deaths, I couldn't help but drink in the cool silence of her streets, the nearly barren cobblestones quiet except for the sound of my footsteps. Sophie had accused me a long time ago of joining the city watch to get away from the rest of humanity, to pretend to be a part of humanity while standing carefully off to one side, apart from it. She was, more or less, right, though I don't think she ever quite grasped the reasoning behind it. She assumed that I had done it to honor Father in a way that allowed me more time to be with my books.

I guess there was a measure to that, the idea that I was walking the same streets as he had for a time, but there was more beyond it as well. Though I loved the city herself, I had less affection for its people, and it seemed very often that they had the same confused distaste for me. They were raucous and loud, dirty and small-minded, too busy hiding behind their preconceived notions of one another to fully appreciate their world. While I walked around the streets at night, my head held high as I took in every last roof, every last brick or shop's stall, they scurried about the daylight, completely ignorant of the luck they had in living in this paradise on the Donau.

There were a few I had come to appreciate who lived their lives in the daylight, Abraham, Sarah and, to a lesser extent, Wilderich, but these were few and far between. As to the rest... We inhabited the same space, but we weren't of the same people. We were a breed apart, my eyes open and looking about, theirs starring stubbornly at the ground.

I shook my head, approaching the gates to the estate. Whether or not I was correct in my judgement of mankind in this city, I couldn't allow myself to see only the differences. If I did that, I risked becoming something more akin to Belial than anything human.

The thought of the murderer cleared my mind in an unsettling way. When last we had spoken, - only a couple days before, though it seemed a lifetime - he had mentioned a master. At the time it had intrigued me, but I had half-forgotten in the wake of his other utterances all mention of it. It was a rather unwelcome realization: Belial had tossed around Max like a child, had nearly killed me without effort, and seemed able to inflict others with sickness at will.

If he could do this, then how much horror could someone more powerful inflict?

My mind resolved to learn more, I crept into the house, nodding a greeting to the doorman who sleepily rose from his post next to the threshold. Doing my best to make as little noise as possible, I moved quickly to the pantry, shaking awake a second man who sat outside the impromptu prison. Taking the key and an offered lantern from him, I unlocked the door with a dull thunk, sliding open the creaking wood and ducked inside.

There was no mad clanking of chains this time, no capering from side to side from the chained man. Instead, it was the back of his head that first smiled at me, its face twisted away from me towards the window. His hands were clasped together, his head bent in prayer if the mutterings from him were anything to go by.

Part of me wanted to intrude, to see my questions answered without delay. But I said nothing, my good manners extending to the killer who had nearly seen me dead, letting him sonorously drone on in his meditations. I lifted the lantern slightly higher in the interim, content to examine the wound on his back, more than a little surprised when I noticed that it still bled.

"Thank you for waiting for me to finish, Dietrich-morsel." I jumped, startled by his unexpected welcome. Turning about, he nodded a greeting to me. "Our paths have not crossed in a few days. Have you grown bored of me?" His face was more gaunt than I recalled, his already flesh-spare face somehow stretched even tighter. His eyes had begun to bulge slightly, the whites of his eyes ringed in the red of sleep deprivation. Despite the gloom of night, his teeth were easily visible, his lips peeled back in a genteel snarl.

Putting on a brave face, I dragged the stool from its place next to the door and sat before him. "Oh, not at all, my friend," I said, inserting as much sarcasm as I dared. While I had little desire to truly being anything but his enemy, Belial remained a useful resource, and antagonizing him might see him refuse to answer my questions. Under the circumstances, I needed to remain as polite as he, even if it made my skin crawl.

He smiled wanly. "I'm sure." He rotated his legs around in front of him, drawing his knees close to his chest. "Well?"

"Well, what?" I asked, curious.

"What is it you hope to find out? My master is not yet here, that much is for sure."

"How do you know that?"

"Were he here, you would have already released me and begged for me to give you the death I offered days ago." His tone was matter of fact, as if his promised doom was so inexorable that neither God nor science would be able to halt its coming.

I shrugged his answer away, as if I were completely unafraid. "We have you already, Belial, and your murderous rampage is over. This visit is, more or less, a formality of sorts. A polite offer between gentlemen."

He scoffed. "Spare me your lies, morsel-"

"I warned you before," I snarled, hating his smug apathy. "Do not call me that."

"I treat you with the same scorn you treat me," he said, rolling his eyes dismissively. "You may believe you hold all the cards, though you would be quite deluded to believe that. But if you have nothing further for me-?" He let the unfinished question hang, the glove dropped at my feet in challenge. Realizing I had sprung to my feet during my outburst, I sat slowly back down, smothering my disgust as best I could. Grimacing, I nodded an apology, one he accepted with an inclination of his own head. "Thank you, Dietrich. I suppose I owe you more than a little gratitude for allowing me to complete my prayers. I am told that such courtesy was not always extended to my kind."

"Your kind?" My head cocked to the side. "Hebrews? Hungarians? I admit I have absolutely no idea where you come from."

His eyes grew distant, the dark orbs growing until it seemed his entire face was one great shadow, underlined in a soft, wistful smile. "I was once one of those people, though I couldn't tell you how long that has been since I've been human. No, my friend, I am from somewhere more distant, though you would say that you know it well."

Lips pursing, I pressed him more information. "If you aren't human, what are you?"

"Divine." His arms spread wide, revealing barren legs that were veined by darkness. "I am a messenger and a soldier, a spy and a prophet."

It was my turn to scoff. "'Divine.'" I repeated, working to keep my tone on this side of civil. "Humanity has left divinity behind, or haven't you heard of things like the Renaissance?"

"Yet you still go to mass, pray to the saints, tithe..." he countered, ticking off the points on his fingers. "You have just suffered schisms in your own church, yes?"

"You're speaking of Martin Luther and the others?" I waved away his confirming nod. "A passing fancy. Luther died, buried after receiving Last Rites. Zwingli died in battle, his own followers scattering to the four winds." I held up my own fingers one by one, dropping them as I continued further. "This is Austria, the seat of the Holy Roman Empire. Yes, we hold to some scraps of the past, but it doesn't mean that we remain the same creature that once looked up at the Sun and prayed to it."

"No," he agreed. "You're more like the extinct creature who looked at primitive man and thought 'they'll never survive as a species.' And just like all of those now-dead beasts, it's that ignorance that will necessitate the arrival of my kind."

I frowned at the metaphor. "You keep prophesying death and destruction of everything that I know, but you are here, alone and in chains. Your particular brand of corruption is gone, died with your victims. Soon you will die, too."

Belial chewed on this thought for a time, conceding the point with a furrowing brow. "You call what I create corruption. Why?"

His question was, surprisingly, sincere, the purity of it throwing me off-balance for a second or two. "Could it be anything else?" I asked. "You kill and spread decay. I've seen the bodies - I've burned more than a dozen myself."

Part of me thought that my numbering of his victims would inspire some manner of sorrow, some kind of contrition. Instead, there was a light in the darkness of his face, a spark of infernal joy that my words had had the opposite effect. "More than a dozen? Then perhaps my master is already here, because I can only claim four. They were the beginning of my ascension to full divinity, you see. Earning my place in the final Kingdom."

"The final kingdom?" I asked, not understanding.

Belial looked at me, pity plain on his face. "I forget sometimes how ignorant mankind is."

"And how arrogant the divine must be." I retorted, my patience running out. "You do nothing but speak in half-truth."

"No," replied Belial. "I tell you everything you need to know, Dietrich. But to paraphrase Aristotle, wisdom is terrible, as it brings no profit to those like me."

"The wise?" I let an eyebrow arch. "Belial, will you be honest with me?"

"I have been," he claimed. "But you've only been hearing and not listening." My initial patience, long wearing thin, finally snapped. Springing up, I leapt over to him, my hands flying out again and again to smash against his face. I knew it would do nothing, but it would go a long way to helping release the frustration that had slowly built within me.

I had expected him to accept my punishment with a smile the same way he had a few days before. But he shrank from my first blow, an instant of fear on his face before my hand blasted into his nose. He didn't cry out at all, suffering that blow and the others that followed in complete silence.

His body was less unresponsive, thin watery blood erupting from his nose, his mouth to spatter at my feet. Stunned, my assault ceased almost as quickly as it had begun, my fists cocked but not falling as I struggled to make sense of the last moments.

He weakly pushed me away from him, arms that had once easily tossed me around not bereft of that otherworldly strength. Given space, he spat to one side, a thick goblet of fluid arcing to the stone floor underfoot. His hands probing his face, Belial desperately cupped the blood that fell from his wounds and lapped it as if he were a dog. "You've killed me," he accused.

Confused, I sat, hands still bloody though my mind was focused elsewhere. "How?" was all I managed. "How am I killing you?" Raising my hands before my face, I examined them for some kind of miracle, but they were as they always were: just flesh and blood.

His eyes bitter, Belial spat back. "You starve me, and you expect me to remain untouchable?"

"You've been given food," I responded, still confused.

"No," he disagreed, his civility faded into outright hostility. "I've been given filth. You deny me the Body and Blood of Christ, you degenerate animal. When my master comes-"

"When he comes, I'll starve him then, too!" I shot back, not caring that my words would echo throughout the house. "You could have avoided this," I hissed, my voice quieting. "Why do you do this? Why do you cause such... destruction?"

His eyes full of malice, Belial snarled back. "If you have looked outside, you know as well as I do that this city doesn't deserve to live. All of you exist by God's will alone, and he has decided that it is time you were reminded of that." He looked pitifully at his hands, the thin droplets of blood in them matched by tears that diluted them further. "Be gone and let me die in peace."

I tried hard to keep my heart hard, to keep steel in my voice, but a part of me did go out to him. As a man I despised Belial, but as a physician he was no different than any other and deserved my attention as surely as another sufferer did. "If I were to want you to not die," I asked, "how would I do that?"

"Feed me body and blood and I'll live," he whimpered, all pretense of power gone. I was stunned by the transformation. Minutes ago he had seemed so strong, a rock that no assault could shatter. What sat before me now was a shell of a man, wounded in mind and body, a weak, frail thought of a creature. "Please," he plead. "Save me, and I will save you and yours when the master comes."

"Dietrich?" I heard my sister's voice from behind me, turning to see her in a dressing gown, the guard next to her with a small candelabra. "May I speak with you?"

"Of course," I nodded, turning back to Belial. "I will come to you tomorrow with body and blood. I promise you won't die." If he heard me, he gave little indication, rocking slightly back and forth from his place on the floor. I reached out a hand to reassure him somehow but thought better of it at the last second. I had known enough nobles wounded as they tried to comfort wounded animals; while Belial wasn't an animal, per se, I had no desire to find out otherwise.

I dragged the stool back to its place by the door, leaving without another look back.

XII

❦

A Change in Dynamic

"Ok, you've made me wait. Now can we talk about last night?"

My sister's tone was irritated, entirely understandable from someone rudely interrupted from her sleep the night before. It had taken more than a little convincing for her to wait with any discussion until I had gotten some sleep myself. Tired as she had been, I considered it a massive success that she had waited until breakfast had been cleared away before pressing me on it.

Deciding to enjoy this rare moment of power a moment longer, I took a sip of coffee from the small cup in front of me, marveling over the invigorating effect gained from the bitter drink. Only recently imported from the New World, I imagined that soon it would become a staple of diets everywhere, once the issues of supply were solved. Though the process needed to enjoy it seemed a little silly - first beans were ground, then hot water allowed to stew through it - there was a robustness to it that was as enjoyable as it was unique.

Sophie put any further delusions of grandeur to rest before my cup was back on the table. "Little brother, remember that I can put you out on the street anytime." Her tone was light, but I heard the gentle growl behind her words, a she-bear slowly rising to anger.

Realizing that I had pushed matters as far as I could, I began to speak about my late-night conversation with Belial. As always, she listened passively, interrupting only for a minor bit of clarification now and again. Given her role as jailer, I had expected a more intense questioning from her, but she said little, musing more than actively involving herself in my monologue.

"Have we considered he might be telling us the truth?" she asked.

"About what?" I responded. "Some shadowy master, some secret cult hiding in the shadows waiting to bathe the city in prophecy and destruction? I doubt it."

It was false bravado, and she knew it, her eyes considering me with no small amount of bemusement. But she didn't immediately respond, instead acting as all older siblings did when feeling superior to their younger brethren. "Have you ever been to Venice, Dietrich?"

"You know I haven't," I answered, a little unsure of where she was going with this.

She went on. "There's a strange place there, opened some fifty years ago. The Venetians call it the Ridotto casino, whatever that means. Some part of a palazzo there or something." Her hand waved airily as if the facts were irrelevant. "In any case, when I was there, I played these games of bluff and lying. According to those who run it, I was quite the sensation there, able to win more than any one woman has won ever in that place."

"What's your point, exactly?"

A small smile creased delicate features. "Considering how poorly you lie, remind me to never let you go there. Our family would be ruined."

I winced in phantom pain, holding a hand to my chest. "Ouch."

She chuckled softly. "Oh, knock it off." She leaned forward on the table, her hands clasping one another in solidarity. "I think we need to entertain the idea that Belial is telling the truth. After all, dear Horatio-"

I cut the air with one of my hands. "Don't quote Shakespeare to me. You know I prefer Goethe."

Sophie grunted. "Hn, too dark for me, but the same thing applies. We don't have the luxury of assuming that he's telling us stories. You've said yourself that you find it hard to believe that he killed those other people beyond Wilhelm."

"True," I said, conceding the point with a shrug. "He was with us, for better or worse."

"It does," she agreed. Snapping her fingers, she exclaimed softly, 'Oh! I meant to tell you, Max dropped by last evening, looking for you. I guess he didn't know you had your meeting with the rest of the watch council."

"He didn't," I confirmed. "Max was on watch last night." My eyes narrowed. "Is everything alright? Did he need something?"

My sister shook her head. "He didn't say, exactly, though he was certainly agitated. He said something about the bishop, but little else. Anyway, back to our houseguest..."

"Ok..." I waited, filing away a note to stop over at Max's after breakfast. "What about him?"

"Well, it's clear to me that this house is paying host to a madman of some kind. That much is without doubt." I nodded agreement. "You said that he wanted the 'body and blood.' Is it possible that Belial is some sort of cultist?"

"Perhaps, but 1666 has come and gone. Anybody concerned about the end of the world now is a little late, right?" I leaned in myself. "We're also ignoring his claim to divinity, too."

"Considering the state you left him in last night, I should think so." Sophie gave another soft smile. "For all your bookishness, you can be quite fearsome yourself when you want to."

I shifted in my seat. "I don't like fighting, but I've been forced to defend myself more than once at night. Cutpurses don't care whose money they take. But, returning to Belial, I think you might be right about the cultist label. He went on both times about this master, and, again, on both occasions he went on and on about doom for the city."

"Right," said Sophie. "Do we have any idea what doom looks like?"

"I would think plague or sickness, if the last ten days have been any indication. But as much as I don't want to downplay their deaths, plague is usually a little more..." I struggled to find the right word.

Sophie supplied her own. "Wide-reaching? I would agree, but then if we assume that there are others out there, then we are on the brink of it, not in the midst of it. Divine or not, I would assume that anyone with whom Belial associates would have the same kind of dark power."

My face twisted in a grimace. "I am uncomfortable suggesting that he has any kind of 'dark power.' It flies in the face of all reason. There has to be a natural reason!" I proclaimed.

My sister seemed less convinced. "You know I'm not any kind of superstitious sort. But even I have to admit that there is... a possibility that such a thing is possible. Didn't Abraham say that this sickness progresses faster than even he thought possible?" She gained momentum from my nod. "And then there was the business with the grocery. Wilhelm noted that there was no rot in there when he had arrived that morning correct?"

"Sure," I relented, "but Wilhelm was a wreck. There's no telling if he misremembered, or he..." my voice trailed off as I tried to think of other reasons for an errant memory.

"Even so," Sophie allowed. "There is more at play here than some freakish illness, and I think it would be a bad idea to completely close ourselves off to any possibility."

I saw another question in her mind. No, not a question, an expectation of compliance. "Something else on your mind?" I probed.

"Yes," she said, her tone becoming more business-like, almost perfunctory. Her hands folded before her, she went on. "I would like my pantry back."

I played dumb. "Where do you intend to hold our newest member of the family?" Given the dark look I instantly received from her, I backpedaled for a moment. "You want to kill him."

Sophie rose from her seat, turning away from me as if she were ashamed of her next words. "I do," she admitted. "He's a murderer and a monster."

"He's also a starving prisoner and our only link to whatever vile cabal he claims is behind everything." I got up myself, walking around the table to stand next to her by the window. "He's no threat to us."

"'Us?'" she repeated. "Who is us, Dietrich?" Some of her reserve faded, a note of hysteria threatening to undermine her usually firm mind. "I go to bed each day praying that he dies somehow when no one is looking. Do you have any idea what it's like to imagine what that beast could do if he got free?"

Pointing to my side, I raised my eyebrows in mute answer. When her expression refused to soften, I tried to placate her. "Of course I do. Forgetting, just for a moment, the meeting that saw him chained here, do you really think that I don't worry after Katarina and Freddy? Are you trying to imply that I don't care what happens to them, or you, or Max?"

"Then you agree that he needs to die," she said.

"I do, but it won't happen now, today."

"Then when?" she asked, her arms flying out to the sides. "Tomorrow, a week? He hasn't eaten since his capture. Do I have to wait for him to starve to death to get what I want?"

"If you are, you will be waiting a long time." I promised. "Before I head to Max's I will be taking some of the more raw meat to him."

Her eyes hardened dangerously. "What?"

"He asked me last night for 'the body and blood.' I intend to give him some."

"You can't." she opined. "I won't allow it."

I shook my head. "I will, and I don't think I was asking for your permission." Even knowing what my resistance represented, I was unprepared for the pure look of shock in Sophie's eyes. I suppose it never occurred that I would stand between her and Belial; our entire lives I had eventually relented to all of her demands.

After I had completed schooling and enrolled myself in the watch, she was the one who had practically ordered me to stay on the estate, though since then she acted as if she let me stay out of magnanimity. Originally, she had painted her role in our group as the power behind the throne, and in any other circumstance I imagine I would have allowed her to continue to rule from the shadows.

Unfortunately for her, my conversation with Herman the night before had me come to the realization that to lead the conspiracy meant that I was responsible not just for Sarah and Abraham and the others but for Belial as well, an epiphany that had surprised me with its far-reaching implications.

Sophie's jaw hung open slightly, her mind apparently still whirling in the wake of my resistance. She didn't look like a gasping fish - a fact for which I was profoundly thankful, respecting my sister as much as I did - though her eyes did have a somewhat glazed expression. Shaking her head roughly, she smiled icily, frost gathering at the edges of her expression. "Well," she huffed. "If that is what you decide is best for our little consortium, I wouldn't dream of standing in your way, brother *dear.*"

Turning away from me, she sat back down, taking a hold of her own coffee cup and lifting it to lips. Even with a sip of coffee, her tone remained cold. "Don't you need to see Max now? I would not dream of keeping you from your appointments. Don't worry about your pet monster. I'll make sure he gets something to eat more suitable to his tastes."

I tried to mollify her with a brotherly kiss on the top of her head, though this was denied as she brushed me away. I settled for a mumbled goodbye and went out to see Max.

The city seemed a little colder, though it was hardly my sister's fault. Autumn had been here for quite some time, the dark clouds overhead failing to keep any warmth in Vienna once summer had fled the city. Her people were a little more brusque as well. What were once normal smiles of geniality gave way to thinner, tighter grimaces of false welcome, tenderness jealously guarded to be parsimoniously meted out over the winter months to come.

What chilled me more than the blithely displayed apathy was the cautious suspicion that creased more than one face. Perhaps the city knew about the deaths that had occurred within her; people talk, after all, and the absence of even a few would spread quickly. In lives filled with humdrum routine, the smallest change meant a new morsel of gossip. And the disappearance of some twenty people was anything but a small change.

Someone somewhere knew.

I did my best to ignore the whispers hissing from the back of my mind. There was no way that the secret was out. Illnesses happened, even sudden absences that took entire families. We were no longer in the Dark Ages, the seventeenth century a far cry from the serfdom and servitude of earlier times. People were able to come and go as they pleased, I repeated, over and over, to myself.

Thankfully I arrived at Max's home before logic shattered my conjured illusion. I knocked, adjusting my coat sleeves and smoothing out my shirt. It wasn't that Max would care about my appearance - we had looked far worse more than once - but there was a certain expectation, at least, in my own mind.

The door cracked slightly, my friend's face appearing from behind the portal. Upon seeing my smile, he gave a weak one of his own, the door heaved back to allow me inside. Ducking in, I reached out a hand in welcome, my head cocking slightly to the side in confusion when he took it only tentatively.

"What's going on?" I managed before he stepped back, holding up huge hands to silence me.

His mouth opened and closed several times before he said anything, his mind waging some internal war that I could only guess after. "Dietrich," he began, motioning me over to a small table, "I need to tell you something."

"I figured as much when you came to see Sophie the other day," I smiled, as much to cut the tension as to reassure him of my support. "What is it? You act like you've killed someone," I joked, though his face grew more pained rather than more amused at my comment. Max chewed his lip furiously, his teeth bared slightly as his hands wrung each other anxiously. It had all the hallmarks of a guilty man, my face falling as I came to the obvious conclusion. "Wait, you didn't kill someone, did you?"

His head ducking lower in shame, I barely heard him whisper. "More than one."

XIII

◎✖◎

An Admitted Crime

Had it been anyone else, I imagine I would have leapt to my feet, infuriated or appalled by that kind of admission. Instead, my backside remained rooted to my chair, my hands pressing themselves into the table in front of me as I struggled to comprehend what Max had just told me. He looked stunned at my response, understandable, I suppose, but after more than two decades of friendship, something about his claim didn't sit right with me.

"Now when you said you've killed, who did you kill, exactly?" I asked, each word tentatively leaving me as I fumbled about for information.

"All the people who just died of plague?" he asked, "I killed all of them." Max's face grew haunted, his eyes hollow and tired. "It's my fault. They're all dead because of me." His teeth continued to worry at his lip, small spots of blood marring the off-white as his jaw worked back and forth.

I felt a shiver slip down my spine unconsciously, logic trying hard to square Max's claim against the man who had been my best friend for forever. "That doesn't make any sense," I replied, my hands coming off the table. "You just said that sickness killed them, and you think some-how that it's your fault that they got sick?" I asked.

He nodded pitifully, the motion heartbreakingly small. It confused me how a man so large could engender such sympathy so easily, but he did it almost without effort. I could see in the way he continued to writhe under my gaze that he was seeking some kind of punishment for his imagined crime, a penance extracted from a man thinking himself sinner and not saint.

I reached out a hand to pat at his shoulder. Surprisingly, he didn't pull away, his phobias too drowned in self-pity to come out now. "I wanted to tell you," he said softly. "He made me promise to say noth-ing."

"Who did?" I asked, my brow furrowing in disquiet. "Belial?"

His sorrowful expression vanished for an instant as he looked con-fused. "No," he answered carefully. "I don't want to be anywhere near him."

"Then..." I prompted, extending a hand towards him as if I could draw the answer from him myself.

He obliged me a moment later. "Bishop Wilderich," he clarified, holding up his hands as my face flashed in anger. "No, no, it's not what you think."

"Not what I think?" I repeated. "And what is it that I think?" I in-quired with false deference.

Max went back to chewing on his lip. I watched his mind try to com-prehend mine even as I began to put the pieces together on my side. I had not seen Wilderich in several days, not since he had assisted me in disposing of the plague victims around the city. The bishop had been cagey those days, not engaging me in anything more than the absolute minimum of conversation. At the time I had chalked it up to having to destroy the bodies of unfortunate children who had died, but there now seemed a far darker reason behind his distance.

But Max cut in, interrupting my thoughts before they could fly from me too wildly. "I think you want to blame the bishop for them dying, and it's really not his fault. It's really mine."

Had I not earlier had my row with my sister, I imagine I would have been more conciliatory. As it was, I took a more aggressive tone with him. "How in God's name is it your fault, because I'm pretty sure that he completely ignored what he was supposed to do and had the first body buried instead of burning it as we discussed!"

Max's guilty expression confirmed everything, the action only stoking my anger hotter and hotter. "For that matter, Max, explain something to me." I waited as he furiously nodded his head, a dark part of me relishing my next words. "How can you call yourself my friend when you go and betray me like this? This must have happened over a week ago!"

My friend, so large and imposing in the light of day, shrank from my explosive outburst. "Well, I tried to tell you, but he went and told me not to, and then Wilhelm happened and Belial, and I wanted to tell you, I swear... The first body was just too heavy for me to handle alone so I asked the bishop for money so I could hire them to help and -"

I cut him off with a slice of my hand, my eyes as cold as Sophie's had been earlier. "But you didn't tell me."

"I'm trying to make amends now," he whined, but I was in no mood to hear excuses. "I didn't know it would happen. I mean, why did they get the plague but neither of us did?"

Something about his question caught me wrong-footed. Shocked by this shockingly canny observation, my anger abated. Mostly. "Wait, what did you say?" I asked, unsure that I had heard him correctly.

"I'm trying to make things right," he said, confused. His voice faded as I motioned for his other response. "Neither of us got plague?"

"Yes, that," I replied. "Why did neither of you get the plague? You tried lifting the body, right? The bishop had to handle the corpse, blessing it and... whatever people do when they bury the dead."

"Right, but I couldn't move it by myself. Or, at least, I couldn't bring myself to do it on my own." Max's face turned a putrid shade of green. "I mean, the body was slowly falling apart. It made me sick to my stomach."

I nodded furiously. "*Ja, ja*, not important. You touched it but you didn't get sick. Wilhelm saw the bodies of Kalb and his wife and didn't get sick. Both Abraham and I touched it, albeit with gloves on." I scratched my chin, thinking. "It isn't enough to just be around the bodies, there is some connection with touching them. But what? You touched it and didn't get sick."

My voice trailed off as I threw myself headlong into this new tidbit. Was there a measure of hygiene involved here, a way to mitigate any further spread of the disease? I needed more data to know. I looked back at Max, his broad face still meekly considering mine. His voice small, almost like a child's, asked, "Are you still angry with me?"

In truth, I should have been. He had hidden information from me that had ended with the deaths of others; I imagine he had only come to me now because the guilt had gotten the better of him, not out of any noble desire to help.

But I had to remember that his omission had been anything but willing, coerced by a man of the cloth who, no doubt, condemned false witness. More than that, Max tried harder than most to never cause any hassle. Even when his own hopes and dreams were at risk, he preferred the path of least resistance, an approach to life that, I admit, always confused me.

And more than all of this, he was my friend, a brother in everything but blood. Whether or not he believed differently, that bond would not so easily be sundered.

I shook my head, trying to reassure him once more. "No, I'm not angry with you. Though," I clarified, a slight tone returning. "I am annoyed beyond all measure that you thought it acceptable to allow the bishop to hide something like this from me. We have been friends a long time, you and I. I'd like to think that our bond is stronger than yours with him."

He managed a weak smile. "I shouldn't have but... He is nice to me and talks with me about books and we pray together."

I wasn't sure what religion had to do with it, but I waved off the apology either way. There was little benefit in staying angry, at least not with Max. "Is he at Stephansdom?" I asked.

"The bishop?" he asked, as if I could be referring to anyone else. Max looked above my head as if consulted some higher power for the answer. "He should be by now. Usually he is out to see the poor today, and then spends his day in Magdalenskapelle preparing."

"Preparing for what?"

The big man's face grew morose. "Requiem masses. With the cold weather coming, there are always a few people who will die because they have nowhere else to go." My forgiveness given, his voice regained some of its former strength. "Bishop Wilderich doesn't like to conduct mass for the newly dead with Advent right around the corner. He says that we should be focusing on new life and not death when Christ's birth comes around."

I felt my face twist into the grimace on its own. "So what happens to those who don't have the good grace to die before Advent?" I asked, sliding my chair back from the table and moving towards the door.

Max shrugged, my sarcasm lost on him. "They are placed in coffins under the chapel and after the Advent season the bishop does a special mass for them." He followed me to the door, trailing me not unlike a lost puppy. "Sometimes the coffins are stacked up to the ceiling! It's... sort of unsettling, seeing all those who died during Advent." He finished, his initial wonder fading into a more appropriate sobriety.

I reached for the door, though my exit was stopped by his meaty hand pressing delicately on the door. I looked up into his eyes, seeing a wealth of contrition and wounded affection in each dark orb. "Dietrich," he said, "I *am* sorry. You should have been told." He pulled his hand off the door, though he wasn't yet finished speaking. "I'm not sure I can be forgiven for what I did. Whether it's my fault or not, those families died, and I did not. How can I ever pretend to make up for it?"

In mid-step, I stopped, turning around to consider him. There was likely nothing he could do, not at least in any meaningful way. But seeing the hurt in his expression, I did my best and lied myself. "God has already forgiven you," I said. "Otherwise, he would not have spared you from becoming a victim. And me? I've already forgiven you, too."

He looked mollified, a measure of peace stealing its way across his face. His mouth twitched towards a smile, but he suppressed it, instead giving me a firm nod of farewell.

I opened my mouth, but there was nothing else to say. Giving him my own nod, I left, closing the door behind me. If there was a God at all, he would know Max for what he was - one of his most devout children. He had no need to ask for forgiveness.

Unfortunately, I could not say the same for me.

XIV

A Holy Man

Had it been placed anywhere else in the city, the Magdalenskapelle would have been lauded as a beautiful church. Indeed, I had walked past it many times during my night watch, marveling at the simple, regal lines of the chapel, the stark sharp stained-glass glimmering in the light of lamps and torches. Though it could never approach the royal atmosphere of St Michel's Church or the rude dignity of Rupert's Church by the Donau, there was something about the smaller building that endowed it with a measure of intrigue.

Unfortunately, it would never shine as the other buildings in the city. For while St Michel's bent the knee to the royal family, and St. Rupert's lived on by its solitude near the river, the Mary Magdalene chapel huddled in the shadow of Stephansdom, outdone by the sheer size and scale of the gleaming limestone cathedral.

As I walked up to it, I had the strangest premonition. It was as if an unseen power had peered deep into a looking glass, gazing ahead to the end of time and had whispered in my ear that Magdalenskapelle would never see its place in history recognized. No, whispered the power, the chapel would be ground into the dust like the mortals it served, reduced to nothing and reborn as something else entirely. Somehow, that whispered idea gave me comfort, my steps becoming less tentative and more sure as I heaved the church door open and went inside.

The inside of the chapel was less wondrous. An altar, as simple as any found in some poor, country church, considered me, distaste plain as its gaze bored into the quasi-unbeliever who had dared enter in. The stained glass I had marveled at from the outside looked broken, every translucent pane weeping muddied color as the weak sun outside struggled to warm the inside of the chapel. There were few pews present, and even those that existed were rude things, simple wood with the occasional attempt at ornamentation their only nod to decoration.

It was... a shock for me, to see the chapel so rude and unassuming. Had the builders of it given up when they had realized that their hard work would never be as admired as the cathedral next door? Or was this barren scene intentional, as if the mass for the dead required the world to be as lifeless as the next world might be?

Whatever the case, I tore my eyes from the simple sight and looked around, seeking some other sign that I was not here alone. I was given this when a small door off to the rear of the chapel opened, two men coming out clothed completely in black, their heads bowed in prayer. Though it took a moment, I recognized the trailing man as Bishop Wilderich, or at least I recognized the top of his head.

The other man I didn't know, though he moved with the vitality of a man more my age than the bishop's. Unlike Wilderich, he was more lean, though I couldn't say how much more he was, given that he was in vestments that easily hid his true size from me. We were about the same height, which put him a few inches taller than Wilderich, darker hair surrounding his dark skull cap short and simply cut.

The anger I had felt at Max's surfaced again, the unnecessary victims coming to mind easily as I now espied the reason for their death. Regardless, I coughed gently, looking to announce myself without tipping my hand prematurely. Neither man looked at me immediately, absorbed, I imagine, with speaking to God, though Wilderich did favor me with a sad smile when his head finally rose.

"Dietrich, my friend," he welcomed me. "I didn't know you were coming. I have been... distracted by other matters." He motioned the other man off to one side, towards the rude altar. Not even looking at me, the priest went over to kneel in front of the altar, his hands spreading wide in supplication. "The winter is coming, and there are matters to deal with before the beginning of the Advent season."

"I know," I responded. "Requiem masses, if I hear correctly."

His eyebrows rose in gentle surprise, as if he hadn't expected me to know what he was up to. Though I never pretended to have any committed relationship with God, I hadn't realized that I had portrayed myself as such an unbeliever. "That's right," he confirmed. "I like to ensure that our minds are on the Christ child's coming, and not on the departure of loved ones and friends." Wilderich moved closer, his voice dropping into a soft whisper. "Regrettably, it seems that there are more than a few that need to be prayed for these days."

My lips drew tightly across my face. "What do you mean?"

Wilderich looked up at me, confusion on his face. "You haven't heard?" he asked, then shook his head in understanding, looking away. "Of course you haven't. I've only just heard myself. There are more houses affected by our plague. At latest count, at least two score households. I was going to send someone to you later today to tell you, just as soon as I finished up here," he promised, though I couldn't help but hear the lie in his words.

"Oh?" I asked icily. "And where are these cases located?" My mind was already supplying an answer, but I wanted Wilderich to condemn himself first.

He did so with his next words. "It's the strangest thing... Most of the outbreak seems to be centered by the last round of victims. In many cases just next door to where neighbors used to live."

"How strange," I agreed, my tone barely on this side of mocking. He gave me an askance look, clearly unsure why my attitude was so frosty. "Wilderich, I need to ask you a question, and I am sorry to say that I need you to be honest with me." I waited for his unsure nod before continuing. "Did you destroy that first body like I asked you to?"

He bristled. "Of course I did!" he claimed, a little quickly for my liking. The other priest turned around at the outburst, his eyes suspiciously considering us both. Wilderich dismissively waved him back to his prayers before fixing me with an affronted glare. "Who said I didn't? Was it the Jew? I knew he was just waiting to stab me as soon as I reached my hand out in friendship to him."

I shook my head, laughing darkly at his claim. "Reached out your hand in friendship? Please, don't make me laugh! You work with him because I've forced you to, so let's dispense with any more lies?" He opened his mouth again, but I cut him off and a rough slash of my hand. "No," I demanded, staring the other priest back to his prayers when he turned again.

Grabbing Wilderich roughly by the arm, I pulled him near the entrance, all the while spitting him with my own furious stare. "No," I repeated, my voice a venomous hiss. "I heard that you decided to bury the body, *in spite* of everything Abraham and I told you!"

"Lies," claimed the bishop, clutching at his story with the grip of a man dangling over a precipice. He threw off my arm with a violent jerk of his arm. "And take your hands off me. I'll not have a doubting Thomas accuse me without any kind of proof!" His eyes softened as my intense stare lost none of its vehemence, so committed I was to my position. "He told you..." accused Wilderich. "Max opened his mouth and told you."

I nodded grimly, my mouth twisted in delicate derision. "And you stood there and swore that you knew nothing. 'Of course I did!'" I mocked, with each word feeling my soul slipping deeper and deeper into sin. My parents, more religious than I, had demanded that I always respect the Church, even if I did not attend it as often as they did.

After their death, I had striven to live by their commandment, determined to honor their memory even as they decayed in the family's mausoleum. Until recently it had been easy, though the events of the last ten-day had found it more and more difficult the more I learned about Wilderich. Beloved by the poor or not, if a man of God could lie and sin as easily as any layman, then why should I respect a man who did not respect his God's creation?

But my ridicule of Wilderich was not the sole reason why my soul felt dirty. I realized that all too quickly. No, that came as my mind chalked it up another transgression committed in defense of the common good. Through most of my life thus far, I had managed to remain safe, my soul clean as I upheld the common good and healed the harm that others created in the world.

And now last night I had beaten an unarmed man and today I had viciously grabbed at a bishop. That Belial had almost killed me should not have mattered - he was chained, and I was not. He was starved and I was not. Murderer of not, how could I pretend any part of the moral high ground if I abused him as he abused his victims?

Part of me prayed Wilderich to make a show of resistance, to justifiably snarl back as I scorned him. I deserved as much. But he did not, instead his face falling to the floor, his shoulders sagging in genuine sorrow. "Yes, I had him buried," he admitted, walking over to one of the pews and sitting down. No, he didn't sit, I realized. He sagged, his body bowing forward as his choices broke his shoulders under their weight.

I sat next to him, my anger and derision turning to a curious, cautious pity. "Why?" I asked gently.

Wilderich shook his head as if he barely knew himself. "I believed that a nameless soul deserved one last chance for salvation. He died alone, in the dark of a city that was not his home. He died alone, in a city of thousands, outside of Stephansdom! I could have helped him, or at least given him some peace of mind as he died."

It was a rather empty reason, at least to me, and I said as much. "You can't know that," I countered, though my ire faded as I wondered if I would have done the same in his position. Of course this supposed I had not been considered the corpse from a medical mind. Sighing, I sat next to him. "Why? Why didn't you tell me at the very least of what you were intending to do?"

"And listen to a lecture on the evils of not listening to a Jew and a nobleman's decree?" A mirthless smile crossed his face as he looked sadly at me.

"Aren't you nobly born, yourself?" I asked.

He straightened for the first time, his arms spreading wide for my inspection. "Do you see any trappings of nobility here?" he inquired. "I left those behind when I entered the priesthood. The oaths are not always the easiest to keep, but then Rome takes care of our worldly needs. Why should I keep anything around from my previous life?"

I pointed to a signet ring on his left pinkie. "What is that, then? Does the Church have houses these days that I've never heard about?" I wore my father's ring on my own hand, a constant reminder to honor our house as best I could.

He allowed himself a weak grin, though it was devoid of any true entertainment. "Yes, we call them bishoprics, and this is a reminder of that," he said, turning over his hand and extending the band for my inspection. "I have never enjoyed the touch of gold on my skin," he claimed. "Why should I wear gold when others go hungry, or cold, or sick? But the Holy Father demands it, so I relent to his will."

My mind struggled to even name the pope, constantly successive names completely befuddling me. If I remembered correctly, it was an Innocent, but then there were many innocents running around, and none of them were the heir to the Church. It was unimportant at present anyway, and I dismissed the thought with a half-shrug. "Do we come off so...?" I stumbled for the word, trying to avoid offending myself but also trying hard to not be dismissive.

"Harshly?" he supplied. "No," he decided after a moment's thought. "I can think of others who are far more likely to reject my suggestions out of hand." He leaned against the pew's back with a creak of strained wood. "But perhaps I've allowed myself to become complacent in recent years." He indicated his body, taking great care to indicate his waistline. "Look at me, I'm sixty-two years old and I have a congregation of thousands under my care. My word is law to so many people, so many good people who believe that somehow I am able to intercede on their behalf in Heaven. After a while, you begin to feel more divine than man, as if your thoughts carry more weight than a Jew and a nobleman a third your age, *nicht wahr?*"

I nodded solemnly, considering my next words carefully. Part of it was out of consideration, though part of it was out of shock. Although I knew myself to be more practiced in all matters of medicine, it was still surprising for me to hear someone else acknowledge it so plainly.

He removed any chance for me to speak, though, favoring me with a contrite expression before continuing. "I was wrong to not follow your direction. Any that die from here on out are on my soul. Perhaps it's God's way for keeping me humble, reminding me that, while I know His word, there are many other things about which I remain ignorant."

I tried to shrug off his apology, muttering some empty phrase of support, but he shook his head definitively. "No, I was wrong, and maybe I came here in the knowledge that I'll be spending more than a few long days here. What I can promise in the meantime, however, is that you will have no more resistance from me. I hope that God can look past my failings and see fit to bestow His grace when my time comes to leave this world." He rubbed at his leg, his face creasing slightly.

I stood up, resting a hand on his shoulder. "Lord Bishop, I hope that time is a long time coming. I don't believe that there are many on this earth who would have the strength to admit a wrongdoing, even fewer who would even have the strength to listen to a people who are seen as a blight rather than a boon."

Neither of us said anything further, but as I left, I realized there was nothing left to say. In a single morning, I had become the sole authority in facing the growing crisis. Though I'm sure it was only in my mind, the air felt somehow heavier as I left.

I could only hope that I was still breathing by the end of it all.

XV

❧

An Offering of Peace

I wandered throughout the city for the remainder of the day, unwilling to go home to my sister's cold shoulder or back to Max's home to be his shoulder for a crime he didn't commit. For a brief time I found myself in a tavern, staring deep into the eyes of a mug of ale, neither one of us blinking until I had had my fill of his reflective surface. But that time passed quickly, and I found myself back walking the city streets again in short order.

Eventually I found myself in the part of the city where the plague had begun to rear its head. It was an unsettling feeling, knowing that behind every door could be a picture of fetid death. I had smelled the stench more often than I cared to already, and one I was keen to forget though I know it would be impossible. Eager to create a more pleasant memory than the ones I currently possessed of the neighborhood, I ducked into a small cafe, ordering a small coffee and watching the passersby.

The coffee was smooth and fine, but I found the taste souring in my mouth as I studied the strain on most of the faces coming and going past my place by the window. Though I never pretended autumn to be a time of good cheer in the city, few expressions didn't betray some kind of worry or concern, nearly every set of eyes furtively looking around as if they were hunted by some devilish monster hiding in the shadows.

Somehow that made it more heart-wrenching for me; I barely understood what was happening and I possessed some much more a wealth of knowledge than they. How must it be for them to watch death stalk them without knowing what stole their health from them? They knew there was something out there, something that was taking their neighbors, their parents, their children, but they knew nothing of its true nature. All they knew, perhaps, was that there was little to be done to keep it from happening, that despite their most fervent wish otherwise they might die for a reason that surpassed all explanation.

My spirits fell as the dark mood took hold of me, though it did remind me of my undone responsibility back at the estate. I was unsure still of what to give Belial for his 'flesh and blood,' unclear as to what bread and water was for a creature of his stripe. I pondered this as I returned to the estate, my trek taking me far longer than it should have as my wanderings had taken me to the opposite of the city from home.

An idea formed by the time I arrived back home. It was not one I was particularly pleased with, but under the circumstances I would try, if for no other reason than to keep true to my word to Belial. It was a strange thought, to feel any kind of loyalty to the man, but I had made him a promise, and I would keep my word, my soul unclean enough in the last weeks.

I attempted to mend fences with my sister first. Her reception was cool, but at least lacked the frost I had experienced earlier in the day, the bond of siblings enough to see her consider my perspective more fairly throughout the day. We spoke briefly, enough for me to tell her of my plan to feed our prisoner. Sophie's face tightened, but she didn't make any attempt to stand in my way, instead sending a houseman to the yard to select one of the chickens that clucked and chattered outside.

He returned with the scrawniest specimen possible, a decision made, I believe, to mollify his clearly disapproving mistress. Sophie nodded acceptance of his tribute, one of her fingers flicking towards me, her eyebrow arching delicately. "Do you want to...?"

I looked back quizzically, unsure as to what she was referring to. When she brought her hands together and then sharply apart, I felt a little sick to my stomach. I imagine I turned a little green because she smiled somewhat smugly at me and sent the houseman away. "Little brother," she said, turning more completely towards me, "are you sure you want the responsibility?"

I know she meant to unseat me a little bit by her question, the innocent inquiry a gentle offer to take power back from me in the conspiracy. "That's quite alright, I'm ok," I replied, my voice infused with more confidence than I felt.

It was a deft play on her part, delicately trying to undermine my conviction, though I purposefully reinterpreted it instead as deference. There would be a time that I would need to do far more grisly things; my encounter with the dead notwithstanding, I had struggled with Belial physically and mentally, and would do so again in just a few minutes.

I heard a brief gurgle from the next room, the ignorant clucking stilled by a pair of strong hands. The houseman came back then, the newly-dead chicken's head flopping back and forth unsettlingly. "Not going to clean it at all?" I asked my sister.

"Dietrich, I am sacrificing a chicken only because you are my brother, not because I want to feed the creature in my pantry. If he wants to see it plucked and cleaned, then he can do it himself. It's my best offer under the circumstances."

Her face brooked no argument, and I made none, instead taking the corpse from the servant with a nod of thanks. Though I doubted she was particularly concerned, I assured Sophie that I would return for dinner after my conversation, if for no other reason than to spend time with Katerina and Freddie.

As before, there was a guard by the pantry door. Part of me wondered if that were necessary under the circumstances; last time I had spoken with Belial he was... diminished somehow, less the terrifying whirlwind of evil passion he had first seemed and more docile, whipped somehow into a measure of submission by his imprisonment.

Regardless, I waited as the door was unlocked and unbarred, the heavy portal swinging open ponderously this time to show a figure curled into a foetal position in the middle of the room. A small pool of thin fluid was by him, connected to him by a slow drip from his still bleeding forehead. It was strange to see his wounds still bleeding; I didn't think that I had abused him that much last night. Although I didn't expect them to be completely healed, they should have, at least, closed.

I wondered for a moment if his accusation last night was true, that I had managed to kill him during my rash beating delivered last night.

I pulled the stool from its place by the door, letting its scraping squeal announce my coming. Belial made no move to look at me at first, despite his eyes staring emptily at my feet. I set the chicken in front of him, my mind struck by the strange resemblance between the murdered fowl and the fouled murderer.

His hands finally moved once I sat down out of his reach, one shaking, palsied hand extending slowly to grasp the chicken and dragging it slowly over to his mouth. I half expected some measure of complaint as to its state, but he said nothing, his head finally coming off the stone floor to bite deeply into the side of the thin body, its white feathers dying themselves crimson as blood fled from the wound.

Belial didn't eat like any man I had met before, his face remaining grafted to the side of the chicken's body instead of tearing the flesh free from it. No, instead I heard the same curious sucking sound first encountered the night Wilhelm died, barely more than a gentle sip, as if Belial was a sick man drinking a cup of medicine.

His body certainly reacted to it as if it were medicine, over the next several minutes undergoing a most curious transformation. Color slowly returned to his greyed face, and while it didn't approach the glow associated with someone more healthy, it did at least approach the sallow yellowed brown I had seen in him several days before. His posture recovered slowly as well, his initial pathetic position on his side rising from it into a cautious cross-legged sit. The chicken he now gripped with both hands, his face grinding itself deeper and deeper into its side.

It may have been a trick of the early evening light, but it almost looked at if his wounds slowly closed, but I'm sure this illusion was a consequence of his changed posture. After being so obviously wounded, no one recovered so quickly, even if there was something inhumanly different about him. The blood from before must have made the cuts seem longer and deeper than they were.

At length he let the chicken drop from his mouth, his lips and teeth covered in a disgusting slurry of blood, feathers, and small bits of viscera. Apparently, he saw the look of disgust on my face, for he wiped the sight more or less clear with a backwards swipe of one hand. "Sorry," he mumbled, the humble apology changing my disgusted expression to something altogether more curious.

"It's... quite alright," I said, leaning forward, my arms resting on my legs as I peered at him. "How are you feeling?"

I surprised myself with the gentleness in my question, and while I admit to having a clinical interest in his health, I found myself equally concerned with his well-being. Though he had been crazed, almost insane, during our first meeting, he had steadily become more lucid since. Indeed, the transformation in personality had been so relatively quick that I could not help but feel that there was more to him than the murderer he had first shown himself to be.

He seemed equally unmanned, his hands slowly setting the chicken down as if unused to such a question. "I am less hungry, at least physically." My eyes narrowed in an unasked question, which he answered an instant after with a question of his own. "Why did you feed me? Why didn't you let me starve?"

"You're a human being. While you've done some horrible things, I took an oath to preserve life whenever I could."

"Yes," he said, "but I tried to kill you." His eyes flitted this way and that as if he sought to find the answer somewhere off to one side of me. "You are supposed to punish me for it."

I shrugged without lifting my arms from my legs. "There are others that certainly want to punish you, and I admit I still will see you face justice for what you've done but let that be their business. It isn't mine. For what it's worth, I am sorry I beat you last evening." It felt strange to apologize to him, but so far confrontation hadn't bred any success but perhaps kindness would. "You have to understand that you have done some horrible things these last days, but you are not to blame for all of them."

He looked back at me, a spark of fervor lighting his eyes. "I've only done what God has commanded me to do. When I stand before him again, I will do so in glory." I was struck by the change in tone from him; where before his answer would have been self-righteous and passionate, he was more subdued now, as if his days in chains had shackled him to the truth of his actions.

He reinforced this idea shortly afterwards as his eyes fell away from me, his arms wrapping around his legs, tugging them close to his chest as if the action alone were enough to comfort him. "Why doesn't the Dietrich-morsel punish us, Master?" he asked the empty space. "You said he would punish us if we failed in our Work." Belial looked back at me when the emptiness didn't answer. "You say I am not to blame for all the things. What do you mean?"

I smiled inwardly, working to keep any sense of premature victory from my face. Where before Belial had been vicious and aggressive, he seemed almost childlike now. Not childlike in the same way as my niece and nephew: they were truly innocent. No, he seemed childlike in his sense of astonishment, the way a child looks when seeing a bird fly for the first time or being out on the water with no land in sight.

It was quite a change, and I was eager to see what I might learn from this new side of him. "I mean that I know you are to blame for Kalb, Wilhelm, and others, but there have been more deaths since you have been here. I thought you caused them somehow, your ability undiminished despite being kept here, but I've discovered that there are others who have done your work for you."

That small spark brightened into a weak flame. "Others?" he said hopefully. "My brothers are here? They've come to welcome me in?" His jaw began to grimly set itself, his back straightening in what I could only imagine as being due to pride. His mouth twitched on either side, though he prevented more than a whisper of a smile from showing, surprising restraint considering his former conduct.

I smothered the spark of delight as quickly as I could. "No, I'm sorry. You're all alone. No, unfortunately these others died because of an oversight on my end. Nothing to worry yourself over."

His face fell somewhat at the news, though he regained a measure of certitude a moment later. "Dietrich-morsel, do you think you are more powerful than God?"

"I've never given it much thought," I supposed. "Assuming he exists, I'm sure there are those who would say that he's far more powerful than I." Shaking my head, I tried to push the conversation more towards where I wanted it. "But tell me, what do you mean when you mention your 'brothers?'"

Belial frowned as I parried his question into another of my own, but he answered me anyway. "God didn't send me among the heathen and the sinner without company. Not even Jesus would send out the Twelve without preparing them first for the journey."

"How many of you are there?" I asked, my stomach twisting in fear at the potential consequences of facing more than Belial's 'master.'

He seemed to draw strength from my unease, though he kept his tone barely respectful. "In total? I'm not sure," he shrugged. "I am only recently arisen."

"Arisen?" I asked, growing tired of the ever-deeper hole. Leaning back, my hands went to massage my temples. "Belial, I have asked you before, and you've dodged the question... What are you?"

He gave me a serpent's smile, thin lips almost vanishing as they drew tight across his face. "That is a very difficult question to answer, and one I am not inclined to answer still chained and clothed like this." He lifted his shackles out before him with a dull clank, his bare, emaciated chest silhouetting the iron in pale flesh.

"I don't have any way to set you free," I lied.

The murderer scoffed at my bluff. "Dietrich-morsel, the key is with the guard outside. Don't think I've not heard it when he gives you the key to unlock the door." I worked hard to give no reaction, though my pulse certainly quickened at his comment. How had he heard something like that? I know I had never heard such a thing and I wasn't sealed inside the pantry.

Maybe it was a simple guess. It had to be. The pantry door was heavy and thick, the walls adjacent equally so. I had fled to it when I was young to be alone with my books, shrouding myself in silence away from the clamor of a running house. There was no earthly way he could hear through either of those, right?

But then, I was constantly learning new limits of reality daily. I had thought plague a stately disease that allowed a certain amount of time before killing. I had thought man unable to commit the atrocities that Belial had committed on more than one occasion. I had thought men of God would be an example of faith and morality instead of ego and human error.

Perhaps this was another limit I had yet to understand.

XVI

⧉

A Spreading Contagion

I was in a haze much of the next hours, barely going through the motions of eating and conversing with Sophie and the others, so disturbed was I by the end of my recent talk with Belial. (Part of my mind wanted to call him Thomas, demystify the thing that had killed so casually, but I wasn't able to separate man from murderer.) I had hoped that somehow I might turn to him a more significant advantage, that an enemy might be changed to a friend. Or at least something less horrible than the monster he had initially appeared to be.

There was a certain part of me that saw myself in him during his more lucid comments. Not the would-be murderer - though in the last days, I had begun to wonder if there wasn't a darker side to me as well - but in the lonely air that so often was hidden by his more violent traits. Without Sophie or Max, I had no doubt that I would have found myself isolated much as I suspected he was, keeping as much as I did to my books and evening patrols.

It was equally pitiable that he refused to use his original, Christian name, though that he remembered it told me that he did still recognize the man he had left behind. That it was Hebrew was a little strange, as was the meaning behind it; I would have thought that any cabal would have preferred a more subtle way of naming its members, the better to hide in plain sight, but I suppose Belial's accented German and deathly look was more than enough to mark him as an *Auslander*, so why bother with the pretension?

But worse than both of these things were that Belial spoke of brothers, betters that would come and judge the city. My mind swirled this way and that, unable to relax under the implicit threat that there were others beside this amorphous master yet to descend on the city. Even if they were only half as deadly as Belial, they could cause death on a scale not seen since... the only time I could successfully think of was the Ottoman siege one hundred and forty years before. Even then, most of the dead had been soldiers and mercenaries and not citizens in the city itself - their leader, Nicholas, supposedly had been buried under his stature in near the Hapsburg Hofburg palace, though Father had told me that his sarcophagus was hidden somewhere in one of the various churches of the city.

Sleep eluded me for the most part that night. What little I ended up getting was plagued by horrible dreams of decay and desolation. I watched the city burn, powerless as its people shambled from shallow graves and slit trenches on the side of its streets to smother the living in misery and disease. My nose shriveled on my face at the wicked stench assaulting it, the wretched stink so thick I feared it would be captured in every pore, becoming a part of me for as long as I lived.

It was a scene of Hell, of madcap, gibbering terror and horror that I almost lost my mind at its expression. My dream-self, overcome, curled upon itself in surrender, begging for the end to come. Even knowing it to be an image of things possible and not reality, I almost gave in, praying for the release of eternal sleep, if only to get away from the sights, sounds, and stench.

But I managed to wake to the light of day instead, though the rotten scene remained fresh in my mind. Drenched in sweat, I did my best to drown my skin in the water from the basin near the armoire in my room, scrubbing ferociously to rid it of the smell that I was sure had followed me from the fever dream.

I had nearly managed my task when a knock sounded from my bedroom door. Setting my wash basin aside, I quickly pulled on a shirt and a pair of breeches to find Astrid outside the door. "Miss Sophie wanted to know if you were coming down to breakfast at all or if she should begin without you," she said. Murmuring some kind of half-answer and a promise to come along as quickly as I could, I shut her out of my room despite her offer to help me get ready, unwilling to deal with her particular brand of ignorance more than absolutely necessary.

That wasn't fair, I scolded myself. She had managed to break me out of my self-imposed isolation of the last evening, even if she hadn't done out of her own agency.

I did my best to ignore the dark thoughts that reared from the back of my mind. There would be time to consider all that hideousness later today. I desperately needed a moment or two of respite from the horror and breakfast with my sister would be exactly what any physician would call prescribe.

I was somewhat gratified to see the half-hidden smile on Sophie's face when I came downstairs; hopefully it signaled a return of relations to almost normal, the ordinary infinitely preferable to other matters.

Nodding a hello, I sat down, my hands extending to snag some sausage, a couple boiled eggs, cheese, and bread all to my plate, my stomach growling in ravenous hunger. "Well, I'm happy to see your appetite is returning," observed Sophie, her eyebrow arched knowingly.

I waited to answer until the grumbling about my middle was quieted by the sausage. Washing away the smoky taste from the meat, I asked quizzically. "Was I not myself last night?"

"A bit of an understatement," she replied. "The children were wondering about you, and I'm sure Abraham and Sarah were equally concerned. You managed to slide some food about your plate, but that was about the extent of it. If I was anyone but your sister, I imagine I would have wondered after you as well, but I'd like to think I know you better than that."

"Oh," I managed to utter around a mouthful of bread and cheese, the single syllable failing to convey anything more than a vague acceptance of the night before. I swallowed hard as my sister's face hardened at the unacceptably minimal response. "I'm sorry. I guess I was a little bit uneasy last night."

"Belial?" I nodded. She scoffed knowingly. "I might have guessed. What did he say now?"

I began to relate his thoughts, beginning with his apparent identity crisis and meandering towards his claim of doom and death. "I'm sorry," I repeated, "I was already afraid of facing down Belial's mysterious master, whoever and wherever he is. And now, it looks like there's an entire cabal of them-"

"An entire group of men with delusions of grandeur?" cut in my sister, laughing softly. "I would pretend to be surprised, but that's always been the course of history, men believing themselves movers and shakers while the true power lies in the fairer sex."

I allowed myself a small chuckle as well, grateful that Sophie was willing to play the role of jester for the time being. "Is that why I barely see your husband around the estate?"

She waved his hand airily. "One of them. It was quite the rude awakening for him when I announced my control over the business affairs of our marriage. He was cool to the idea at first, but then I sicced Astrid on him and he became far more agreeable." I felt my head tilt in confusion. "She's very convincing when she wants to be," clarified Sophie.

"But she seems so... empty-headed. What could she possibly have done to convince him otherwise?" I asked tentatively, though I admit that I knew where my sister was heading.

She confirmed this a moment after. "An act. She uses the only thing most women have right now: her body." Her eyes rolled as my mouth dropped open. "Oh, stop it. You know as well as I do that a woman has only a few roles open to her, and I refused to be a nun or a housewife. Astrid is another less willing to accept her lot in life."

I let the matter drop, my respect growing for the seemingly empty-headed housemaid. It was irritating, to put it mildly, to learn that I had been so eager to dismiss Astrid as unimportant when she was clearly more sophisticated than I gave her credit for being.

I opened my mouth to probe further what Astrid might have done to convince Baron von Rohan to give up his concerns regarding the family business, but my words were overridden as the doorman burst in, flustered and out of breath. It took multiple attempts before we understood what he was saying, the words flooding from him in a torrent of frightened emotion. Though he had managed to keep them at bay, there were several men and women at the entrance to the estate, each begging for an audience with Sophie.

Ever magnanimous to those who might later help her, Sophie agreed to let them in one by one, dismissing the doorman with some additional assistance. She turned to me after he had left, saying, "I asked Abraham to return to one of the regions originally affected by plague. I'm beginning to wish I hadn't done that. I would prefer that he was here for this, if for no other reason than to help in understanding just how widespread this might become."

I tried to pout and failed, breakfast puffing out my cheeks like some rodent. "Do you think I am really that incapable of keeping any kind of notes myself and consulting with him later? It was me who brought him in, after all."

"True,' she allowed. "But that was after I suggested it?"

She was right but I was unwilling to concede the point, so I shrugged instead, continuing to consume the food on my plate, going back for seconds once my plate was cleaned down to the last crumb. I stopped only once Sophie's visitors arrived one by one, ducking out to the study to return with pen and paper on which to scribble my notes.

I almost wished that Abraham had been there to take my place as stenographer. Each new story brought with it images of horror and death on a scale that was beyond sobering. I felt the illness creep into each new sheet of virgin paper, soiling it in corrupted misery, the pulp wilting under its enfeebling touch.

Eventually Sophie had each first eat their fill of the food on the table, ostensibly to give them a moment's respite in the face of personal tragedy, but I saw the way her face slowly turned a putrid green I had thought only reserved for bile. Nothing on that table was appealing anymore, not after hearing each tale of disease and rot. In the same fashion that I had lost my appetite last evening, I imagined my sister would be eating little herself for the rest of the day.

Our morning and afternoon were spent at that table, the initial few visitors replaced by new tales of death. I had to leave twice for more paper and was grateful for the moments away from the table. By the end of it all a small mountain of grief had pushed itself out of the tablecloth, the mound of molder drawing my eye time and again despite my best attempts to look anywhere else in the room.

At length we were left alone with our thoughts and each other, the last inconsolable sufferer having eaten their fill and departed back to the woe of the world outside. I saw something then I had never seen before in my life: my sister sagged. She slumped, all of her careful poise and elegant control completely abandoned in an instant of pure, abject fatigue.

My entire life, Sophie had been the bedrock of my existence, the indomitable foundation against all of life's trials and tribulations. When our parents had died, she had borne up under the strain of raising me on her own, had funded my education when I had fled the city to further study medicine. She had courted a man without any assistance, founded a house that dominated Viennese society (even if this was only done quietly), built in the name of two children who were, even put mildly, the epitome of childish innocence and ability. She was all-knowing, all-powerful, and here she was completely overwhelmed by the stories recently heard.

It was terrifying.

She said nothing for long minutes, her gaze empty of any true consideration. It was as if her humors had rebelled in her body, fleeing and leaving behind nothing but a barely animate corpse. I tried to pretend to be engrossed in the notes, but I was sickened by the lightest perusal of them, disgusted by the way each sufferer had expired in cruel, unmitigated misery.

A more logical part of my mind attempted to restore some semblance of logic and order, forcing away the nausea to focus on the facts of the spreading sickness and not the vile images that continued to fester in my imagination. If nothing else, it would fixate me on something other than my suddenly comatose sister.

Most of the victims were concentrated in two areas: near the river and down by the warehouses near the most industrial part of the city. I felt my brow furrow in thought. Up until now, the sick had been dotted around, though this could have been written off as a function of Wilderich's mistake. Even more oddly, though there were a couple new reported cases in those areas, it seemed almost as if the plague had burned itself out.

Or maybe we had burned it out. We had, after all, destroyed all the corpses we could. Was there some manner of correlation between sickness and killer?

There was another piece of the puzzle that I found uncomfortable. Belial had claimed that he was able to kill others at will, that he decided who would live and die through his use of the sickness. Given that others had died outside of his direct influence, I wondered if he truly had the power he pretended. Though the knowledge had come at the cost of so many new victims, perhaps this sickness was something natural than it had first appeared. Unnatural in its ability to spread and kill, of course, but not unholy in its origin.

If it was natural, we could fight it. If it was natural, we could kill it.

Unless, of course, Belial had been right in his predictions. Though I was loathe to admit it, he had claimed that others would come far more powerful than he, other 'brothers,' other so-called 'angels' who were the face of God's wrath here on Earth. At minimum, there remained his hidden master. Could these new outbreaks be because of them?

My thoughts were interrupted as Abraham burst in, the older man panting as if he had just run a great distance. Sophie finally reacted, her gaze languidly focusing on the Jew looking oddly pleased with himself. "I have some news!" he exalted, his tone completely out of place given the events of the last couple hours.

Flummoxed at the sudden shift in atmosphere in the room, I couldn't even form the obvious question. Thankfully, my sister seemed recovered enough to ask it for me, though her inquiry lacked anything close to true energy. "I fail to understand how visiting the houses of plague victims would lead you to be so pleased?"

Abe's face sobered somewhat, the bright moment of happiness in the room falling back to its shade of grey. "That's true," he allowed, sitting carefully in the seat where all the previous guests had been, his posture sagging as the ghosts of their stories weighed down on him.

I found my voice. "Well, what did you learn?"

He looked towards me, though his eyes drifted upward while he carefully called his experiences of the morning to mind. "There is nothing remarkable about the victims I was able to see. I would have liked to bring a sample of the tissue back with me, but given that we still don't know what we're dealing with-"

I cut him off. "Good idea. We know for sure that we are all healthy - if we were otherwise, we'd be dead by now or at least would show more than a few symptoms." My eyes narrowed as Belial again came to mind. "Did any have the marks?"

The Jew shrugged. "Not sure. I didn't find any, though I might have missed something. I was more concerned with the neighborhood. A bit of a mess: lots of garbage everywhere, sewage is practically all over the place, and the entire community is infested with rats."

"Is that why you rushed in?" I asked acidly as he took a plate of food for himself. "To tell us part of the city is disgusting?"

"No, but I suppose I'll get to that in a minute." He looked carefully at both Sophie and me. "I admit, I had expected a warmer reception. What happened?"

I relayed the events of the morning, taking a perverse pleasure in the way Abraham's face fell. It wasn't that I enjoyed making him upset per se, but there is an old saying of misery loving company. It soothed me to know that the pain and horror was being suffered together.

"Well, I'm sorry to hear all that, *mein frayund*," he offered soberly. I nodded away his indirect apology, content to have brought him down to our level emotionally, though my head tilted as his eyes brightened against all expectation. "Well, perhaps what I have to say will put a spring in your step then. I met someone while I was out on my little fact-finding mission."

"Oh?" I asked, trying to emulate the light tone he had infused his words with, desperate to buoy my spirits. "Does Sarah know of this new love?"

Clearly appreciating my attempt to make light of the situation, Abraham chuckled lightly. "Oh, I don't imagine she'll care. Knowing my stubbornness, she'd probably be happy to be rid of me. But no, she has nothing to worry about. No, I think this 'new love' would be far more your type than mine."

Sophie might have laughed, but I was less amused, my eyes rolling on cue. "Abe, I'm not sure now is really the best time to find me a woman."

"Who said anything about it being a woman?" he grinned. "Actually, I invited him to come by because I figured that you two would hit it off famously. I imagine he'll be here any moment."

I glared at him. "I understand that I'm a bachelor in his late twenties, but I didn't think that meant I would prefer crossing swords with another man instead of a woman."

A house man came into the dining room, crossing over to my sister and whispering in her ear something about another visitor. I was puzzled by the change from the usual; I was good enough to know the identity of every other guest, and my sudden exclusion made little sense. Flicking a glance in my direction, my sister shot me a look that I found myself unable to identify, her sudden scrutiny more than a little unwelcome. When I shrugged, helplessly lost, she looked back at her man, nodding entry for this latest caller.

He disappeared, vanished back towards the front door, I imagine, to get the visitor. I spread my hands wide in mute protest. "I realize you own the estate, but is there any reason I'm suddenly kept out of the loop?"

A touch of color had returned to my sister since our experiences earlier, a similar tidbit of her personality in the soft, superior smile she sent my way. "I'm sorry, little brother," her cheeky tone earning her a similar, crumb-filled grin from Abraham across the table. "I just wanted your first experience with your new lover to be a surprise."

I realize that I should not have been as annoyed as I became in that moment, but before I knew it, my feet had found their way under me, my chair shoved roughly back as I stood, sharp words on my lips.

I never got the chance to use them, however, a muffled greeting rumbling in from the doorway. My eyes hard, I looked over, ready to lash out at the unfortunate guest who had chosen the wrong moment to intrude.

And found myself face to face with the dark revenant.

XVII

❦

A Clarion Call

Wary, I stood and went to the guard, taking both the shackle key as well as the pistol at the man's belt. Moving back inside the pantry I tossed the key at Belial's feet, sliding the stool closer to the door and sitting down. I nodded toward the key. "Make a move other than at my express direction and this," I lifted the pistol slightly and cocked it, "will put an end to you. Are we clear?"

"I understand, but wouldn't that be a waste, to shoot me after giving me food?" he asked smugly. His hand slowly moved towards the key, snatching it to himself when I made no protest.

I surprised myself with the steel in my voice. "I gave you food because I took an oath to do no harm, but I *will* shoot you to prevent you from doing it to others."

From the bemused look on his face, I doubt Belial had expected to hear such conviction in my words either, his somewhat resurgent snideness vanishing in the blink of an eye. Rubbing at his wrists, he inquired politely, "May I stand?" I nodded. He stood slowly, his hands exploring all over his body as if he were seeking the extent of the damage suffered in his days of captivity.

I let him a moment or two of self-consideration before pressing him for an answer. He turned away from me, holding up a hand to shield his eyes from the soft light of the evening. "You will laugh," he accused. "They have always laughed, my master has said."

"Maybe," I agreed, "but you made your answer contingent on being released from your chains. I've delivered, and a deal is a deal. Remember, I could have let you starve."

"But then you would be breaking your oath," he replied easily, but he continued before I could make any response myself. "I am a messenger from God, come to do his work."

My eyebrows fell suspiciously. "A messenger," I repeated. "Are you asking me to believe that you are a prophet of some kind?"

He went off to one side, out of the weakening light, leaning against a set of shelves and slowly sagging to the floor to sit, his back pressed tightly against the wood. "No," he snorted, "I am not any so high in God's eyes. I bring His will about, I do not reveal it. My master calls us Monarchists, for we serve the King in heaven." His eyes sparkled with half-felt fervor. "But one day, when the swords are beaten to plowshares and man lives morally, I will be free to take my place at God's feet with Peter, Michel and the rest of my kind."

"The rest of your kind..." I fought to keep disbelief from my response. "You think you're an angel."

"Not yet, but one day, perhaps," he said wistfully. He fell silent then, heartbeats passing as we sat in mutual solitude. I studied him carefully, seeing in his posture something that I had noticed before, a stiffness to his back, a proud aspect to the way he held his head high, even under the weight of his monstrous deeds so far.

I took a shot in the building gloom of the room. "You weren't always this way. You were someone human once." I avoided acknowledging him as an angel; though I was sure he was just a man, there was no need to antagonize him, and denying his delusion would be the easiest way to see this new rapport destroyed.

He half smiled, his eyes drooping as his lips rose on either side. "I was, yes. Thomas Venner, though that name hardly means anything now. No, Dietrich-morsel, I am Belial, 'the worthless one,' a contemptible speck of nothing who deserves only derision and mockery."

"Why?"

"Because I was to spread the judgement of God here, and in so doing show my brothers that I was worth more than my name suggested." He began to bang his head against the shelf behind him, each thud causing the items on the shelves above to clatter back and forth.

I opened my mouth to order him to stop but needn't have bothered: his face suddenly lit up, his gaze flying to me. "How many others have died, would you say?"

"Excuse me?"

"How many others have died?" repeated Belial. "You said others had died that were not my fault. How many?"

Seeing the infernal glimmer return to his eyes, part of me regretted telling him of the other deaths, but it was too late now to turn back now. "Perhaps thirty, forty?" I supposed, though I knew for sure that the death toll was already higher than that.

He flew to his feet, his eyes so wide that they seemed fit to burst. Surprised, I barely managed to get my pistol in line with his body, although this turned out to be unnecessary as he just laughed, the hideous sound knifing into me as surely as any blade. "I didn't fail," he murmured.

"Yes, you did," I argued, but he laughed away my denial.

"No, you may have minimized the death for now, but my master has heard the beginnings of it. He knows that I have begun holy work here and he will call my brothers here to pass sentence on the city." I saw madness build in his gaze again. "On Virgil's seat, the master stands, the hour of reckoning close at hand. Despair then, you doubting city, for God's kingdom comes..."

He had muttered that before, the same words whispered in our first 'conversation.' "You've said that before, what does that mean?" I asked, though from the way he began to twitch I would get no answer. "Put the chains back on, toss the key over here." I ordered, half expecting him to make a rash decision in the wake of his supposed success.

He stared at me, his eyes losing their insanity as his expression became calculating, inquisitive. I felt like a bug under a lens, impotent as something far more powerful than I studied me with the callous concern of an unworried naturalist. If he made a move towards me, I would have less than a heartbeat to defend myself.

Fearing the worst, I let one hand curl around the hammer of the flintlock, hauling the spring back as my finger curled around the trigger. He was only a few feet away, and I would not be able to aim if he attacked me now.

But he didn't attack, instead sitting back down and slowly reattaching the chains to his wrists. When the last one clanked home I jerked the pistol barrel at the key, my eyes not leaving him as he tossed it back at my feet. My hand moving with the same slowness his had only minutes earlier, my questing hand fumbled about blindly on the stone floor for the cool metal, grasping fingers eventually finding the shard of metal and stowing it in my pocket.

Somehow knowing he was safely again locked away didn't make me feel any better, a sentiment he managed to read in my face. "I'm not going anywhere," he said, lifting his hands up as if I needed more proof that the chains were securely manacled. "You can put the pistol away."

"I don't know about that. You make it sound like now is the best time for me to be armed, if these brothers of yours come."

He grinned. "*When* my brothers come, this city will need more than a single pistol to save it from God's judgement." Unlike the other smiles of the last minutes, the smirk on Belial's face was genuine and without madness, utterly without any artifice or ploy hiding another agenda.

No, it was a look of pure happiness, and somehow that made it worse than all the others.

XVIII

⟨❧⟩

A New Ally?

My mind recoiled as quickly as my body did, my mouth letting slip an undignified yelp as I retreated from the masked monster who stood, uncomfortably still, in the doorway. Thankfully, it didn't chase me, instead its head cocking curiously to the side as it stared glassily up at me, the crow's face worn more than just an affectation for the figure. Of the rest of its body, I saw very little: a wide black hat hiding the top of its head, long black robes shrouding the rest of its form but for two hands. These seemed human at first glance, one tapping a long piece of wood intermittently against its leg, though given the motionlessness of the figure, I was unwilling to believe that anything less than a monster had sprung up from the earth to make my life somehow even more miserable.

I heard a titter of laughter from Sophie, Abraham's elderly chuckle gently underneath, the two of them somehow unaffected by the bleak avian face, the cold dead eyes. My gaze whirled to them, wounded betrayal on my face as the figure removed first the hat and then the bone-white mask across its face, settled the crow's beak down on the table.

Revealed for the first time, I saw an old face, a wizened, whiskered jaw settled easily under eyes that had seen too much yet somehow remained energized by a glimmer of un-diminished hope. "I'm sorry," he said, his voice richly infused with true regret and apology. "I didn't mean to startle you. Abraham told me that you would be expecting me?"

My heart still raced, hysteria still fueling my breathlessness, though I tried to affect some measure of calm. "No, forgive me for being surprised. I was told to expect someone far different than you," I glared my accusation at the amused faces of the *apotheker* and my sister. "Unfortunately, though Abraham mentioned that you would be by, he *did* fail to tell me what your name is, Mr...?"

He glossed over my question initially, instead asking, "May I sit?" I nodded him down, the unmasked man sitting slowly, his flexibility clearly tarnished by the touch of old age. "No title. I am simply Michel." Grasping hands clawed at a pocket, extracting a set of rivet spectacles and gently pressing them over his nose. I worried that they would fall almost immediately, seeing as how they weren't held in place by anything but his obviously frail flesh, but he seemed to not mind, instead reaching for an empty glass on the table and retrieving a small flask from his waist.

He extended it towards us half-heartedly. "May I interest you...?" he wondered aloud. None of us partook, instead letting him pour an oddly viscous liquid into the empty glass before secreting the flask back about his person. Taking a fortifying sip, he sagged back into the chair in contentment, his eyes artificially grown by the magnifying spectacles.

I broke the silence that followed. "I take it this is my new lover?" I accused the others at the table. My cheeks reddened as the other three at the table laughed, embarrassed by their easily achieved attempt at humiliation.

Michel recovered first, reaching up with one hand to paw at his pasty white flesh. "That's what you told him?" he chortled. Turning more towards me, he nodded apologetically. "I'm sorry about that. I admit that I wanted to enter a little more... normally, but Abraham asked for me to enter with my tools of trade more close at hand."

Though I had little doubt as to what that profession was, I asked

anyway. "Your trade? I'm assuming it isn't haunting the houses of unsus-
pecting nobles?"

My comment was meant to inject a little levity, to show that somehow I could take a joke gracefully. Michel inclined his head again, giving
me a pitiful spot of laughter in reward. "Would that I was employed
that way," he said. Crossing his legs, he smoothed out the fabric as it
huddled, bunched, on his knees. "No, regrettably. I am a plague doctor,
come to do my part to ease the suffering in the city."

"A noble sentiment," I said, though my brows rose in surprise anyway. "I didn't realize that the Emperor had asked for outside physicians
to come to the city?"

"He hasn't," agree Michel. "I was on my way through when I came
across one of the infected locations in the city." He reached up to point
delicately at Abraham. "It was there that I met Abraham here, who in
turn explained the situation in the city." Old eyes smiled at me. "I hope
you don't mind that I did?"

I knew that I should have responded graciously, accepting him into
the conspiracy with all possible speed. Given Abraham's clear approval,
I imagined we would be lucky to have him as one of us, but there was
something off about him, his aged frame out of place here in the middle
of the rising tide of death and discord. I wanted to chalk it up to his
entrance, my embarrassment still quite fresh in my mind, but there was
something beyond pettiness in my desire to reject him.

It was positively insane, after a fashion; the old man had done nothing to earn disrespect from me, at least not in the way that my stomach so violently reacted, acidic bile churning in my guts. Despite that, I
found myself glaring at him, peering deeply at his artificially large eyes
to discern the secret beyond his pale exterior.

Sophie's gentle cough snapped me back into the present, and I realized just how much time passed since his question. Eager to cover
up my ungraciousness, I mumbled some manner of welcome and apology, which he took with an inclination of his head, his spectacles still
perched precariously on the edge of his nose.

The next minutes was a perverse cocktail of polite deception as I tried to share what we knew as I studied Michel further. Between Sophie, Abraham, and I, we went over every interaction with the sickness infecting the city. When one of us took a breath to sip at a drink or to collect our thoughts, one of the others taking up the skein of the tale, words flooding from us in a torrent that would have drowned anyone else in information.

But even more than Sophie, Michel seemed to take all this in stride, nodding thoughtfully, noting some apparently important details down on a pad secreted from somewhere in his robes. I tried to sneak a look at his notes to better help me understand what we missed on our end, but I was at a loss at the strange collection of squiggled lines that didn't read as any language I had ever seen before. My distaste from before turned into an actual jealousy at the way we suddenly deferred to the plague doctor - not even a repeated reminder to myself to be cordial could completely erase the groundless animosity that swelled inside me.

He was here to help us against this spreading disease. Why couldn't I accept that he was only here to help?

No answers immediately rose to my question. Stymied, I felt myself withdraw as the other two continued to speak, only reentering the one-sided conversation when they, too, fell into complete silence. "What do you think?" I asked, a little too much vinegar infusing my words.

Michel ignored my tone, examining his notes, paging back and forth, a queer smile on his face that I found repugnantly innocent. He almost looked like he was enjoying the stories we had just relayed! He carefully lifted his spectacles from his nose, laying them flat on the table before he responded. "I have excellent news for you. You have the black death here."

Abraham looked aghast, his mouth plunging open in shock. "How can that be an excellent thing?"

"Well," began Michel. "If you had a more... virulent strain of disease, there might be nothing I could do for you. But we have here a strange moment where fate, faith, and fortune all coincide." The old man rubbed his hands together in what seemed excitement. "I have seen this before! Don't worry, we've gotten to it early, and it should be more than an easy problem to remedy."

Sophie's head tilted to the side, her posture echoing mine as our arms crossed in skepticism. "I'm a little unclear how this is an easy problem. Dozens dead, this is popping up in different areas all over the city. Isn't that a little uncommon?" she turned to ask me, her tone expecting support.

Equally doubtful, I gave it to her gladly. "I would say so. If you look at Avicenna-"

Michel cut me off. "Don't mention that Muslim here. He was a hack, and there's not a shred of proof for his wild conjectures."

"But every doctor-" I began, a hot rejection on my lips.

It went unfinished as the old doctor cut in again, his hands flicking my response aside disdainfully. "As near as I know, Avicenna never faced a sickness like ours. What's more, he lived when, 700 years ago? More? His thoughts belong in the dust with savages, not in a more enlightened time."

"Ok," I agreed slowly, my tongue firmed clenched between my teeth to prevent any sort of outburst. "If you know this disease so well, then what might our best option to fight it?"

"Collect the people in places where the diseased have been," he answered authoritatively. "Expose them and their bodies will become accustomed to the disease. We will starve it of any fresh victims."

"But what about the plague's miasma?" asked Abraham. "Won't the healthy be infected by the plague's bad air?"

"Nonsense," said Michel, his kindly exterior fading into something more dictatorial. "The plague isn't caused by some atmosphere."

"It isn't?" asked Sophie. "Then how are they getting sick?"

Michel shrugged. "A lack of faith?" he hazarded aloud, his surety ebbing just for a moment. "Does it matter if I know how to make them well again?"

She snorted. "Yes, I should say so."

Pasty white flesh flushed crimson. "Madame, I will do my best to keep my humors in balance, but I will not be spoken to by someone who has not battled plagues their entire life!" Heaving himself to his feet, he reached for his glasses on the table. "If I will not be respected for my centuries of learning, I will take my knowledge elsewhere! Good day."

He turned to leave, an action I was shockingly fine with enduring. I read it for what it was: a bluff. Michel wanted to stay, he wanted to match his wits against this plague again. Unfortunately, the other two were less inclined to try their luck, both calling out for him to stop, to wait, to sit once more and speak more candidly.

The black robes came back, though he didn't sit, his gamble successful. "I'm pleased you could overlook not knowing the more unnecessary details of this plague," he noted piously. "Sometimes it is better to put your faith in God as opposed to the ideas of man."

"You are remarkably religious for a physician," I observed, trying to reassert some manner of control over the conversation. "I don't think I have ever heard so many calls to faith in such a short time."

If he heard the sarcastic tone in my words, he didn't take offense to it. "When you've seen the things I have, you learn that the support of God is a necessary requirement in our line of work."

"Oh?"

I admit I was hoping for some kind of story, anything to justify the smugness that, it seemed, only I could observe coming off him. He denied me that, though, instead gathering his materials from the table. "I would tell you stories that would age you well before your time. But if you'll indulge me, I need to rest, and I wouldn't dream of imposing on your hospitality more than necessary. I will return in a few days, after I've had a chance to more completely see the state of the plague in the city."

"A few days?" repeated Sophie. "That would allow for the plague to spread further. Shouldn't we begin to gather support, rally the people together? We could even go to the emperor and request his physicians move about the city to help the infected."

But Michel shook his head, his wide-brimmed hat settling back into place overhead. "That's premature, but I would ask that Dietrich might escort me out. It would be nice to have a moment alone, between doctors, to speak a little further."

I would have preferred to stay behind, but manners were manners and Sophie's face told me that I had pressed my luck too much as it was in the last minutes. So, despite being drained by a morning of horrific stories and then suffering the inclusion of someone else into our growing circle, I got to my feet and fell into slow step next to Michel.

There was a peculiar aroma around him as we crossed the threshold to the outside, a scent that was equal parts sweet and sickening. Somehow, I had not noticed it before at the table with the others, but now that we were alone, it reeked almost of death and life, as if somehow Michel walked somehow between devil and divine.

"You don't like me very much," he told me as we slowly descended the front steps. "Is it because I represent something that you aren't? At least, something you aren't yet?"

I pretended ignorance. "What do you mean?"

"Well, it's clear to anyone with eyes that you are uncomfortable around me. Your attitude was hostile at best. I would have understood that from Sophie or Abraham - she's a woman and he's a Jew after all - but you are another man of science. Shouldn't we find common ground in our learning?"

My eyes narrowed at his casually disparaging comments. "We could, but that would also require you to respect those who are close to me."

He smiled thinly, acknowledging my implied criticism. "Point taken, forgive me. But I think at some point, you and I should speak in a day or two, after I've had a chance to see Vindabona. It's been ages since I've been here."

"Vindabona?" I said, confused. "Do you mean Vienna?"

He looked surprised, though he recovered quickly. "Of course, forgive me. Like I said, it's been quite a while since I've been here." Reaching the gate, he extended a hand, withdrawing it when I didn't put out my own. "Dietrich, I would very much like to be friends. I think that, if you and I were to spend a little more time together as we fight the disease in the city, we could be far closer than you think.

"But until then," he said, tilting the brim of his hat with a gentle tug of his hand. "I am your humble servant." Without waiting for any response from me, he left, a tiny whistle escaping from pursed lips.

I returned inside to find the atmosphere largely unchanged from before, Abraham and Sophie in soft conversation that guttered out as I sat back down. "What did he want?" asked Sophie.

"He wanted to set up some social call on my part in the next couple of days. He said that he noticed my unease and wanted to ensure there was no bad blood between the two of us," I said, omitting his commentary on my sister and Abraham.

"That might not be a bad idea," opined my sister. "It was certainly tense in there for me." I glanced over to see Abraham's nod of agreement.

My lips pursed. "Maybe, but I can't shake the feeling that he is hiding something from us. Something about him that strikes me as... "I shook my head as the word escaped me. "Wrong." I finished lamely, hating the imprecision of my answer. "As it is, I'm not particularly happy that we know so little about him and yet we're willing to give him de-facto control of our group."

Sophie shrugged. "I admit I don't really enjoy his attitude either, but he could be a God-send. A man who's seen and struggled against the plague before? After all of our work, I feel like we haven't accomplished anything. Michel could be the one to turn that around."

Abraham murmured from his place at the table. "Do you think that maybe you could look past his coarseness and instead at the good he might do for us?"

I nodded, though my mind continued to swirl darkly. When I had begun the conspiracy, there had been three. By necessity we had grown to seven to combat the growing threat.

How many more would need to join us before we would see the sickness defeated?

XIX

❦

An Unremembered Name

I spent the rest of the day - and most of the next - in my head, unable to completely shake the increasing depression that hounded each of my steps. A more intelligent man might have been able to diagnose the reason for the wave melancholy; I managed to understand it only in the most basic sense, which, in turn, depressed me all the more.

In that time, more died, new stories of horror surfacing to haunt me at nighttime. I had begged off from patrolling for the time being, unable to rest for long before being dragged through a fresh nightmare that left me smothered in sweat and unease. Max had - thankfully - taken up my duties, though this had, in turn, left me without a shoulder upon which I could lean.

I had seen little of Sophie, Sarah, and Abraham since Michel's visit, in part driven by my need for isolation though they also spent a large amount of time correlating data from the reports the sufferers and their neighbors had delivered days before.

In one of the few windows of time that we had had together, a minor argument had broken out as I pushed to advise the emperor so as to secure his help in this growing time of need. Sophie had come around to my logic, though the Jewish *apotheker* and his wife had staunchly defended Michel's advice. "There is no need to warn the crown yet," he had claimed. "Besides, do you think that he would listen to any of us? We're a group of Jews, minor nobles, and watchmen! I imagine I would be lucky to leave with my head attached to my body."

Frustrated, I had dropped the subject, fleeing from the estate to walk the streets as I tried to rid myself of my anger.

Though I walked with no destination in mind, I was nevertheless surprised when my feet stopped outside the Magdalenskapelle. Facing it, for the first time in more than a decade I felt the pull of something greater than myself, a tugging of something beyond the tangible world.

Not really knowing why, I went inside. It was quiet, as last time, something about the stillness shredding the smothering blanket of ennui that I had had wrapped around my shoulders. My mind quieting for the first time the last days, I found a seat, my hands clasping of their own accord, my head bowing in submission to something I had rejected a long time ago.

I prayed, or at least I think I did. It was an odd sensation, to speak to no one. My words vanished into the emptiness of the chapel, vain whisperings seeping into the empty air to fall to the ground or to rise somewhere else. I didn't know which occurred then, though some part of me hoped that somehow someone could hear what I had to say.

The alternative was that I was losing my mind and was only talking to myself, the only separation from Belial that I muttered madness to a socially accepted delusion. No, there was more that divided that two of us, but for now I would settle for the simple distinction between murderer and myself.

A soft voice interrupted my thoughts. "Dietrich?" I looked up to see Wilderich cautiously shift towards me. Not knowing how to finish my attempted prayer, I glanced mutely towards the altar and shrugged, hoping that, if there was a god, he would understand my inappropriate ending.

I tried to encourage him over to me with a smile, though by the way he crept towards me I was only barely successful. I felt ashamed as he slunk towards me, seeing in him the whipped shuffle of a beaten dog, the memory of my rough treatment of him fresh in my mind.

I tried to make amends. "I realize that I have no right to be here after the way I treated you when we last saw each other."

"No, this is a place for all children of God. Even the wayward ones," he added bravely, a tentative smile on his lips. "I am surprised to see you here, I admit."

A small smirk creased my own face. "I am as surprised to be here, at least for anything... otherworldly."

"What brought you here?" he asked.

"A new face is in our conspiracy. A plague doctor, from somewhere to the east," I remarked carefully, trying to marshal my thoughts. "He is... unsettling in his ways."

"He is an older man?" the bishop guessed. "Completely covered in black, with a long beaked nose?" When I peered at him, he nodded slowly. "He was here this morning, said something about being drawn to the place. Asked to see the bodies of the newly dead. I wasn't keen on letting him disturb the final rest of so many, but he was quite insistent and promised that he would take nothing from them that they hadn't already given. It seemed reasonable at the time, so I left him for a time while I held a mass in Stephansdom. It *is* Sunday, after all," he admonished.

I shrugged away the rebuke. I lived my life without consideration of the day of the week, each melding into the next without any real concern. "If you say so," I said, if for no other reason than to acknowledge that he spoke at all.

His eyes narrowed in caring suspicion, his former fearfulness falling into a more paternal tenderness. "What's wrong, Dietrich? You were less... unsure, the other day."

I forced my gaze to match his, looking as deeply as I dared into a face that had lied to me so easily less than a week before. I wanted to snap back at him in anger, to tell him to mind his place and to keep to God, but the words died, unuttered. I had no right to shout at him, now or as

I had days before. In the face of the spreading plague, we were exactly the same, two men bound together by growing misfortune.

The realization melted away some of my iciness, though I still felt hesitant. Up to now in life, I only had revealed myself to Sophie and, to a lesser extent, Max: to unburden myself to someone who wasn't blood - or close to it - seemed a dangerous moment. But if not now, to whom and in where could I do it? He was a man of God, a man of faith.

Wilderich revealed himself as more perceptive than I gave him credit for previously. "Would it help if we did this more properly? The confessional isn't especially spacious, but then, it was made after God blessed Vindabona with Stephansdom."

Nodding, I almost made it to my feet when I finally comprehended what he had said. "Vindabona?" I asked, my head canted to one side. "Where's Vindabona?"

The bishop's face twisted in confusion. "Why, here, of course."

I pointed dumbly at my feet. "Here?"

"No," he said, opening his arms wide and rotating slowly. "We live in Vindabona. Or some of us do, anyway." My mind ransacked my memory unsuccessfully, Wilderich chuckling while I stayed silent. "Max told me you were a man of learning! How is it that you haven't studied the history of Vienna?"

"Bricks and mortar aren't exactly living things," I retorted.

"What is architecture, but a childless labor of men?" I opened my mouth to ask what he meant, but I could see the gates of a hidden passion opening, words coming out of him before I could speak. "This city sits on what used to be an old Roman fortification." He looked around, orienting himself before he pointed one way. "Depending on the source you read, some claim that there are still ruins underneath Josefplatz by the Hofburg." He turned around, the back of his head to me as he went on. "By the Donau there are supposed to have been officer's quarters. Some even say that there are remnants of the Roman defenses underneath our own city walls."

Something clicked in my mind. "Like underneath the Graben?" I felt a small smile whisper into being as he gave me an encouraging nod. "I always thought 'ditch' was a strange name for a road."

"Exactly!" he said, snapping his fingers knowingly. His tone remained light, though his eyes asked the question he repeated aloud a few seconds later. "There aren't many who know that name. Where did you hear it?"

"Michel," I replied. "The plague doctor? The man in black?" He nodded at last in understanding. "He made a comment to me that he had not been about Vindabona in quite a while."

Wilderich's eyebrows met as he frowned in thought. "Well, it could be anything really. He's studied as much as you, of course. And by his age I imagine he is more well-read than either of us give him credit for being."

"Perhaps," I said, giving ground grudgingly, "but when was the last time anyone used that name?"

"The thirteenth century?" hazarded the bishop. "That's the most recent citation I can remember." He massaged his chin with one hand as he paced for a few moments. "Yes, that sounds about right."

"Exactly!" It was my turn to snap, as much in emphasis as it was to indirectly tease the bishop for his action only minutes before. "I've spent most of my life in books, and I've never heard of it. And I've lived here nearly all my life! When did you hear of it? How long did it take you to even be aware of it?"

"Years ago," he allowed. "Though I suppose that was a bit of a chance encounter. But honestly, Dietrich," he asked, "why this... inquisition? He isn't a Protestant, and certainly isn't a heretic if his actions before are anything to go by?"

"I'm not sure what I'm getting at," I admitted, shaking my head slightly as if I needed to confirm my lack of defined purpose. "It is... strange, is all. Two days ago, Sophie and I spent the morning listening to the stories of plague survivors, or at least those who were plague adjacent. I haven't heard yet of anyone who has had the plague and lived."

Wilderich blushed. Though it was very likely his fault that the plague was spreading, I tried to reassure him otherwise before continuing. "We are overwhelmed, outmatched by a disease that spreads faster than we can understand it. I realize that only a few have died so far, but that is more by luck than by anything we have done, and I see no reason that more won't die."

I ignored his stunned expression, trying to get to my point before he could recover and unhorse my thought process. "And now, now of all times, a plague doctor arrives? A man who should understand the nature of the disease magically appears and tells us that he knows the best way forward?"

Wilderich drew himself up, claiming piously, "God works in mysterious ways."

Despite an admittedly complex relationship with religion, I found it impossible to not scoff. "Would you mind explaining to me why God would kill his faithful with such a horrible plague?"

"If you could tell me why he would waste his power on creating the Muslim and the Jew, I would be more than happy to," Wilderich retorted before softening his tone. "I'm sorry, I told you I would work to be more agreeable to Abraham and his people, but my point is that you are asking things of God and not pushing further on your own. It is not for us to determine what His plan is for the world, but to find our place within it."

"Then why do we pray?" I asked before realizing how hypocritical it sounded coming from my lips.

The bishop made no comment on my phrasing. "We pray because we hope that his plan coincides with our desires. If anything, it is the purest form of faith we have, to hope that we are important enough in God's eyes to be worthy of inclusion in his plan."

It was, oddly, both a reassuring thought and an unsettling one in equal measure to think that a single man could move mountains only so long as a higher power allowed him to do so. It managed to lift some of the burden off my shoulders, though questions remained about Michel and his strange knowledge of my home. "Did Michel tell you where he would be when he left?"

"He did, actually," said the holy man. "Actually, he told me if I should run into you to tell you that he was staying at the tavern two streets over."

"How did he-?"

"Know to leave that knowledge with me? I'm not sure, now that I think about it. I never spoke of you, nor did he know that we were acquainted." Wilderich mused. "It's possible that I did mention you and simply forgot, but I couldn't tell you for certain either way, I'm sorry."

I smiled wanly, pretending that the revelation didn't unseat me overly much. The truth was that I found myself more uncomfortable than before when it came to Michel. I thanked Wilderich for his company, doing my best to reassure him of my respect before I turned to go. I stopped, though, asking the bishop one final question before I left. "I realize this will be outside your area of expertise, but I need to ask you something."

Wilderich seemed surprised that I was looking for his input. "What is that?"

"If you were looking to stop this plague from spreading, how would you do it? Would you bring everyone together, sick and well, or would you keep one from the other?" I knew that his response was absent any real experience in the area, but I felt myself seeking some measure of reassurance; something continued to rankle about Michel's suggestion the other day.

The older man clasped his hands over his stomach, his thumbs slowly twirling in orbit around each other before he answered me. "I don't know. In faith, to combat sin we seek one another out, the better to resist the devil and his lies. In health?" he shrugged, "I know as little about that as I do of money-lending." His head tilted to the side. "Michel suggested to bring everyone together didn't he?"

I nodded confirmation. "How did you know that?"

Another small shrug, though a small smile traipsed along behind it. "You want me to burn the bodies of the dead. When I didn't, the plague spread. I am a fool in many ways, but I still possess the occasional moment of good sense when the good Lord allows. Dietrich," he said, a whisper of hope appearing on his face. "I know that your relationship with God is troubled, to put it delicately, but should you find yourself needing a... confidante. I know I haven't given much reason for it, but I am here, should you need me."

I was touched by the gesture, both in the recognition of past failings and yet the hope of something in the future despite it. Saying nothing, I offered him a simple nod instead as I left the chapel.

XX

A Doctor's Discussion

I would be lying if I said I left the chapel with my enthusiasm restored, though I did find a glimmer of hope in me that I had thought extinguished forever by my ambivalent cynicism towards God. A single prayer didn't faith make, but I had to confess that the silent whispered monologue had left me feeling somehow renewed if not entirely excited to wage war against the sickness once more.

Yet there remained too many unanswered details, the least of which circled Michel like a vulture eager to feast on carrion. It was queer that he seemed almost omniscient about my circle of conspirators: already he had appeared when Abraham was in one of the many plague sites, and now had informed Wilderich as to his lodgings despite not knowing of our previous association.

It shouldn't be surprising, then, that my feet sped towards the inn the bishop had mentioned. It was a five-minute walk at best, the lodge a staple for the foreigners and transients in and out of the city. It was probably the first normal thing the man had done, which was impressive, considering that his strange writing and silent musing was unsettling, to say nothing of his profession, garb, and harshly direct attitude.

Walking past it in the night often, I had long seen the inn as being something of an eyesore, especially considering its location in the center of Vienna. Seeing it in the light of day, my view became that much more hardened. There was an alien feeling that shone dully from the dirty windows, warped wooden beams twisting madly as if the inn swelled painfully in an attempt to contain all the exotic blood residing within.

The interior of the building did little to combat my perspective. It was dark and gloomy, the soiled windows allowing precious little light to seep in. The air stank, a putrid concoction of sweat and musk that almost made me wish I had stumbled upon another plague site instead of a room full of the living. I was stunned at the incredible amount of noise inside, my ears ringing in time with slamming mugs and chopping knives.

My eyes tearing in pain, I shouldered my way past several thick beards - not all of them on masculine faces - to shout a question at the bartender. Spitting off to one side, she looked me up and down, a vague sense of disgust on her face. She said something back that I couldn't hear, though based on her cruel smile, it likely had something to do with the strangeness of my presence there in that place.

I slid a couple coins to her, trying hard to keep my face composed despite my touching wood that had played host to thousands of hands before me. My fingers had barely retreated from the metal before she snatched them up, her face softening marginally as she pointed over to one dank corner.

I forced a smile to my face, nodding a silent thanks to her, though she already had turned away to ply more alcohol to a drunk customer who was clearly in his cups. Pushing past more sweating bodies, I managed to glimpse Michel sitting calmly in the corner, his paleness surprisingly bright considering the conditions inside.

He noticed me quickly, old lips twisting up in a rictus that might have been welcoming on a younger face. As it was, I felt my stomach twist uncomfortably, as much due to my surroundings as to his attempted smile.

Pushing through the last few bodies between us, I stood over his table, shouting a greeting that immediately lost itself in the maelstrom of noise. His smile became more genuine, though I couldn't understand what he said in return, my eyebrows rising as my head tilted forward in an ageless expression of deafness.

He extended one hand towards the stairs, a clear invitation to speak elsewhere. While I didn't wish to be alone with him, neither could I speak with him at all under the present circumstances, so I nodded dumbly, waiting for him to lead the way upstairs to the dubious silence of the rooms there. He moved unhurriedly, the crowds inside the common room parting before him like the Red Sea, all of it done without a single word. Then the moment passed, and the other customers flooded back into the vacated space, even collapsing into the newly opened booth.

I felt my jaw fall open in shock, an unconscious reaction I immediately regretted as my tongue suffered the same fate as my nose had before. Nevertheless, the repulsive taste snapped me back into action, and while my passage was more strenuous than his, I followed Michel upstairs and into one of the rooms off the landing.

The private rooms were little better than the common room downstairs, as disgusting and dingy, though they did have the benefit of having far fewer people contained within. There was a small bed in the corner, covered by a blanket that was, I assumed, infested by lice and other insects. The only other furniture in the room was a small table with two moldering chairs, one at either end. Michel, already seated in one, motioned to the other silently, the twisted welcoming grimace still on his face.

I sat carefully, mindful that the smallest shift in weight encouraged the stressed wood to whine and complain piteously. I was aware that the noise downstairs had thankfully fallen away to a dull roar that was only occasionally punctuated by a round of raucous laughter, though it remained at the edge of my awareness.

"I'm happy you came to visit," said Michel. "I wasn't sure that you and the bishop were close, but I suppose that sometimes dumb luck is necessary in bringing two extraordinary people together."

I let his flattery slide overhead, putting instead a smile on my face. "Well, I realized the other day that I was a little unwelcoming and wanted to apologize."

He waved a hand. "No need." He pulled out a flask, the contained somewhat bigger than the one he had used at the estate, pouring a generous measure of crimson liquid into one of the glasses he had taken from downstairs. "Would you care for some?" he offered. His tone was, at first, pleasant until I declined, at which point it took on a slight edge. Where I come from, we move past old insults and celebrate new friendships in a drink."

I opened my mouth to reject him again, but remembered Sophie's desire for me to be more polite, so I awkwardly agreed, sliding forward the other glass on the table, grimacing as he put as much or more of the liquid into my glass. Sliding it back over to me, he raised the one in front of him, waiting until I matched his gesture. "Salvatus est," he toasted, tilting the glass to his lips and drinking deeply.

I was more restrained, letting the liquid moisten my lips before setting the glass back down. It wasn't wine, that much was sure. It was far too sweet, even more so than any port that I was familiar with. I had heard stories of some Scandinavian drink that was thick like honey. Perhaps that's what sat before me now, but my non-taste wasn't enjoyable enough to inspire me to drink further.

Besides, I preferred to have my wits about me.

Michel wasn't as restrained, refilling the missing portion in his glass until our glasses were fraternal twins, though I imagine his was slightly larger than mine. While he took another drink, I dug slightly. "I get the feeling that you know a great deal about me, about this city, but I know very little about you. Where exactly is it that you are from?"

"Oh, a long way off," he told me enigmatically. "Across a sea or two," he said airily. "Suffice to say, I am much happier to take up residence here again than there." Eyes grew distant. "It's been... thirty years since I was there, though I'm not keen to go home."

"I'm surprised a man of your profession calls any one place as 'home'. Aren't you always traveling where your skills are needed?"

He nodded. "These days, yes. It seems every year a plague surfaces here or there. Often I find myself heading from east to west across Europe as some new contagion flows in from the Orient." A ghost of a smile. "I suppose it's true - I am in a place just long enough to watch it live or die, and then I'm off, on to another Godless place, a pilgrim in another unholy land, working as hard as I can to bring new, everlasting life to sufferers there."

"I know I said this the other day, but you act sometimes like you are more a missionary than a man of medicine." I accused softly. "You spoke Latin before, correct? Outside of the occasional lifelong scholar, I don't know many who know a dead language, or dead names of bygone times."

I was angling for a question on his strange of Vienna's past, but he answered a different unasked inquiry instead. "I admit I've been around for a long time, Dietrich." He leaned in, though his chair didn't make the faintest whisper. "Do you mind that I use your Christian name? I realize I should probably call you 'lord,' or 'baron,' or some title, but I sometimes think that that conveys too much pretension. Man is a simple creature, wouldn't you agree?"

I didn't enjoy hearing my name said so cavalierly, but he had already preempted any other name I might have requested he used. "I think simple is a little dismissive." I said carefully, as it seemed he was judging every word I said. Fair perhaps, considering how I was judging his.

"If you say so. I guess when you've been across the face of the land as much as I have, you begin to see people as predictable, basic after a fashion. Sure," he continued disdainfully, "there is the occasional outlier that can - and has - surprised me in the past. But by and large man is... like a dog. More to drink?" he asked me before I could question his metaphor.

Looking at my glass, still very nearly full, I politely declined. "Is the vintage not to your liking?" Michel's eyebrows furrowed in concern.

I picked up my offered beverage, carefully swirling it around in my hands as if I intended to take a drink. "Not at all, though I don't know exactly what it is that I'm drinking. I have read of some thicker liquors from further north, outside the Empire?"

"You're talking about mead?" The plague doctor shook his head. "It's not that, though I admit it is rather close to it, in terms of consistency and body I imagine. I *am* surprised that you've never had it before. Everywhere I go, there is a different vintage served, it seems, in every house. The one I keep here," he said, tapping the flask bottle, "is Mediterranean. Greek, if I remember correctly. Only about eight years old, excellent body." He laughed at my confusion. "Each city, each country calls it something different. I wish I could tell you its actual name, but they all run together. I call it the 'elixir of life.' A little dramatic, but in the broader scope of my life and work, it's woefully unimportant." An almost childish look came to him then. "But you didn't come here to speak to me about liquors and previous lives. Tell me why you really came here."

I had no desire to tell him, but some strange part of myself felt compelled to share my thoughts anyway. "I met with Bishop Wilderich -"

"Of St. Stephan's cathedral?"

I nodded. "- and he said that you had come to see him about the same idea you raised at my family's estate."

"Exposing the people of Vienna *en masse*?" I nodded again, drawing a small frown from him. "Dietrich, I thought we had discussed this."

"We had considered the possibility," I began carefully, setting down my glass to pick at some imagined piece of filth on my pant leg, the small motion drawing a squeal from my worn chair. "But I don't think that we were committed to the idea."

"And why not?" he asked me, the frown fading into a more considered mask as he leaned back soundlessly in his own seat.

"We don't know how the plague spreads. How are we to know that exposing people isn't how it passes from one to another?"

"Faith."

I jolted at the one-word response, my chair whining in similar protest. "How is that even an answer?" I fought to keep my voice level, even taking a sip of the liquid to cover for my rising irritation. Passing over my lips, it was even more sweet than I had first thought, a strange metallic aftertaste causing my mouth to twist in disgust.

He looked insulted, though that faded quickly into something more amused. "Well, faith in me of course!" he half-claimed, his statement punctuated by an oddly appropriate roar of laughter from downstairs. "You don't think that believing in God will save someone, naturally but, again, I have faced this evil before. This is a tried and tested method that has worked every time for me. If it eases your mind, I have other colleagues who have used this successfully to mitigate the effects of the plague on multiple occasions as well."

Searching his face for any kind of duplicity, I asked, "If you've been so successful in combating this disease, how is it that it still exists? Surely between you and your... colleagues," I said, infusing as much suspicion as I dared into the word, "most of Europe should be immune by now to it?"

Michel looked away for the first time in our conversation, abashed. "There are those who refuse to follow into the established traditions in dealing with the plague." Again his hand waved airily, a gesture that I was beginning to hate. "They pretended that by keeping affected areas dry it somehow prevents the plague from spreading about the body further. Some even prescribe emetics or bleed the afflicted!" His eyes took on an unsettlingly amused aspect. "Can you imagine, bleeding people already weak? Suffice to say, they cause more illness than improvement. But others like me work tirelessly to reverse the damage they've done."

The argument weighed heavily on me - I was loathe to admit it, but his reasoning did seem to make a kind of sense, if only loosely. "Besides," he said. "Though I will certainly ask others of my kind to come here, I wonder how much our skills will be needed."

I felt my brow furrow unconsciously. "What do you mean? Dozens are dead and more will die already. I would say that you are needed more than ever."

He smiled benignly, though it did little to put me at ease. "Yes, some continue to die, but the plague is consuming itself now, or at least that is what I have discovered as I've re-acquainted myself with the city over the last days. My suggestion to expose the people is more a preventative measure for the future than one to combat a sweeping contagion."

Having seen the bodies and witnessing the vile spread of the plague in the last weeks, I wasn't as inclined to agree. If anything, I had thought the disease was growing in strength, not withering as Michel suggested, but I kept my denial in my mind unsaid.

Another thought occurred to me, another idea that I had kept sacredly un-spoken until now. Though it was not my intent to see it slip past my lips, a single look in his eyes and I felt myself powerless to stop it from stealing past teeth and tongue. "There is something else, something that I don't believe we've shared with you when we first met," I said after a time, surprising myself that I continued to share what were previously guarded secrets. "Shortly after we encountered the first victim, there was... an incident."

For the first time, Michel's expression softened. "Go on," he encouraged.

My mind screamed at me to not go on, but the words came out regardless. "He is deranged, to say the least. Somehow, he is monstrously strong, in a way that I have not experienced in anyone of his size. I..." My voice fell to silence as I finally got a hold of myself. "He is no one, just a madman who raves of some reckoning coming for Vienna," I finished quickly.

Michel shifted, uncomfortably it seemed, though I wouldn't have known this had I merely listened for his chair; amazingly, it continued to bear his weight without any kind of comment or complaint while mine squeaked and squealed under the slightest movement. "A madman you say? I've found that occasionally that some kind of doomsday cult surfaces in the face of what might otherwise be certain death. You can do nothing but pity those poor souls, of course. Did he ever give a name?"

"Belial," I said, determined that that should be the last tidbit of information I would give up.

"The name of the devil, or one of his names at least," said Michel, stroking a pale-toned chin carefully. Though I might have blamed it on the light, his eyes lit almost infernally. After a few moments reflection, he shook his head, laughing lightly while his hands dropped to massage his legs. "I wouldn't think anything of it. I can promise you one thing, Dietrich: while I'm here, there's nothing I won't do to save your city. By the time we're done here, there will be nowhere for any madman to hide.

"I'll make sure of that."

XXI

❦

A Godly Question

I left shortly after Michel made his promise, leaving him to my remaining 'water of life.' He slurped my offering down in a heartbeat, his face flushing slightly as inebriation finally came to him. Though we were still strangers, I felt less acrimony towards the man who seemed to stylize himself our savior.

The reasoning behind his faith-filled rhetoric still eluded me, though.

Despite the inn receding into the distance behind me, the smell and the filth of the place clung to me like a horrible memory. I raised the collar on my jacket against the breeze that heralded a cooler night to come, shivering as my clothes did little to fight off the chill that cascaded down my spine.

I arrived home sometime in the late afternoon, finding Abraham and Sophie as I had left them, at the table debating possible responses and collating new reports of illness and contagion. It was almost as if the world had frozen when I had left after breakfast that morning, the only change that Sarah had joined them. There was an energy to their talks that I found surprising; two days ago Sophie had nearly collapsed against her seat after hearing all the heart-wrenching stories of loss and death.

Her posture now betrayed none of that recent angst. No, instead in its place was the very portrait of calm under pressure, an attitude that I had not seen since our parents died. She had cried only once then, the tears quickly dried as she aged overnight to care for me as well as for the family's finances and needs.

She would not be able to sustain the facade of control forever - I had seen that before as well. In the same way that I withdrew into my books for comfort, she would turn to me in the next ten days if the circumstances in the city had not gotten any better.

And yet, I felt for the first time that a light might have gleamed at the end of that tunnel. In truth, it was a weak light, one lit by the faintest hope and faith, but perhaps we would stumble all the less for it. But then, perhaps that was just another prayer I whispered unconsciously within myself.

I coughed, not wanting to interrupt their deliberation but neither willing to stand there without a definable purpose. I had been removed enough and wanted to contribute, should they want my input. Abraham and Sarah greeted me with a warm smile. Sophie was a little more succinct in her welcome, her mask of command firmly in place.

"What are we discussing?" I asked, my fingers pointing to the map spread out over the table. My stomach growling, I inquired, "For that matter, have any of you eaten since this morning?"

"Ah, always thinking with your stomach, little brother," replied Sophie lightly, her expression cracking slightly as a glimmer of good humor slipped through. "Food will be coming along shortly, but before you join us, I need you to speak with your pet."

"Belial," I gently chided. "Monster or not, he was once a human being, in body still if not in mind."

She shrugged. "Whatever he is, I caught him talking to Katarina earlier today."

My heart raced for long seconds before remembering that, were things more dire, Sophie would not be as calm as she sat now. Especially in the case of Katarina and Freddie. "Did he get loose?"

"No, thankfully, but he managed to lure her towards the door when his jailer went out to relieve himself."

"Odd," I said, "He's never shown any interest in the children before." Seeing her face harden, I backed away, my hands raised in submission. "Ok, ok. I'll see what he wants."

"Please do," she said, "she has been somewhat weak over the last day or so." For a moment her reserve cracked, a glimpse of the concerned mother seeping through from beneath.

I promised that I would, spinning on my heel towards the improvised jail, making it only a short way before my path was blocked by two short figures, one mischievously grinning, the other with a far more genuine, if weary, smile of happiness. "You're going to get me in trouble, Knuddelbär." I accused, turning around theatrically as if my sister could appear out of the dining room left behind.

At her side, Freddie continued to grin, silent as was his way. Katarina was less quiet, coughing for a few moments before answering me, the tiredness on her face painfully plain. "I didn't mean to, Onkel Dietrich. I just wanted to see you."

"And now you have," I agreed. "Are you alright?" I asked. Like most children, Katarina fell ill occasionally, but her face was flushed yet drained at the same time in a way that I had seen more than once before in recent weeks.

She cleared her throat before answering me. "I think Mama will send me to bed earlier tonight. I think I am... just a little tired..."

From the way she swayed unsteadily from foot to foot, she was more than a little tired, and I moved forward to pick her up. Freddie's smile faded as he watched me pick up his sister, though not, I think, out of any kind of jealousy. I called for a nursemaid, a quick hushed conversation ensuring my niece would see the inside of her eyelids before our next mealtime. With a small kiss to the top of her head, and another given to Freddie - grudgingly accepted, a sign of his growing age, I suppose - I continued on my way to the jail.

There were two guards outside this time; after hearing of the events of earlier in the day, I imagine Sophie was not keen for a repeat performance, even if it meant another body was largely wasted guarding a man in chains. Motioning for the door, I waited for the portal to creak open before ducking inside.

Belial turned to face me, his head rising from where it had been on the floor to consider me. I asked for and received his keys from the guard, tossing them to him with a mute nod of my head. Carefully smiling, he welcomed me sarcastically. "And the lord of the house returns, the self-styled savior of the city here to bellow at me for a conversation I didn't seek."

His read of me was hardly surprising - I could only imagine how furious Sophie had been - though I tried to hide my reason for visiting, at least for now. "No," I disagreed, ignoring his bitterly bestowed titles. "Or at least, not completely. We haven't spoken in a few days. What do you mean by your comment about a conversation...?"

I waited for him to unchain himself, carefully taking the keys from a tentatively reaching hand. "The little one visited me and asked me my name," he began, backing away from me towards the window, though he retreated further into a corner as the last weak rays of daylight caressed his feet. "I said nothing at first, but she sounded so sweet, so sick... I took pity on her in her last days and shared my name."

"So sick?" I repeated quickly, the edge coming, unasked for, to my voice. "What are you talking about? She has a cough is all. It's nothing."

I suppose I wanted him to explain himself further, but he ignored me, asking instead. "Do you think God hates children?" When I didn't answer, he looked at me in curiosity, a plaintive gentleness in his eyes that unsettled me not for its duplicity but for its authenticity.

As his greatest ally in the house (and, only then, in the loosest sense of the word), I kept my heart carefully closed off from feeling anything for Belial. He was a monster, that much was sure. Given the cruelty that simmered underneath the surface, it would be impossible to feel the same kind of wary pity that I could summon even on my darkest days.

But, part of me argued, hadn't he been different in the last several conversations? Though I was more concerned with the machinery of the body, I couldn't pretend that I had the same understanding of the mind. It had seemed to me that Belial had been more innocent since I had fed him, that he had become confused when I was seen for what I was and not what he had previously assumed me to be.

I ventured a careful answer to his question. "No, I'm sure God loves all his creation. Isn't that what the Bible says?"

The innocence on his face didn't leave, his entire body shrinking down until it seemed I was speaking to a small child and not a murderous fanatic. "What of Sodom? Gomorrah? The flood? The plagues? What of the power he's given my master and me? In all those times, children died with their parents, didn't they? Wouldn't this mean that God hates children as much as he hates the sinner who makes them?"

Many of his references I only barely understood; my recent attempt at prayer notwithstanding, I confess one book I rarely perused was the Bible. Dredging up every half-forgotten fact and half-heard homily, I responded. "Maybe, but all of that is Old Testament, isn't it? There is still the New Testament and all the forgiveness there for sins, right?"

Belial gnawed on my answer for a time, pacing to and fro, injecting the occasional glance my way as if to reassure himself that I remained there with him in the room. Unlike before, though, this was not the tread of a trapped beast. No, this was a wanderer's walk, a man slowly striving to understand the mysteries of the world, failing and trying again and again.

Eventually he stopped, his expression distant as he continued to find an answer to his question. "My master sends us out to punish the wicked. But children are wicked only because they are born, and even this is not of their own choice. I know that I do His work, like my master and my brethren, but I am no longer sure why must my work involve the killing of children?"

I felt my mouth open to respond, but he continued to speak. "There have been times recently that I wish that I had not come here, to this place. I feel my mind ripped in every direction except the one that I would choose for it." His hands began to furiously knead the skin on the sides of his head, as if he could push the distressing thoughts from his head by sheer will and the repetitive, never-ending motion.

His outward calm began to melt in the face of distress, the careful poise of humanity fading once more into the barren bestiality of the anguished. "I gave him everything to quiet these thoughts, gave him everything so he could set me on the path to righteousness through the purging of immorality. I have done everything I need to ascend, why is my mind so tormented?"

I nearly fled the room then and there, but he stopped suddenly, his frame going stock-still, his hands dropping to hang at his sides as he sniffed the air in question. "I smell more sickness in the city," he said, flickers of decayed vitality infusing him with quiet energy. "My master is here. I sense him." His voice came out in a hushed whisper, albeit absent the ardent fervor that he had expressed whenever we had spoken of his master before.

His voice was so certain, I found it hard to deny convincingly, though I tried regardless. "No, Belial. If anything, the plague has burned itself out. Yes, there are some who have died, but the plague is consuming itself and soon there will be nothing left to infect anyone." I felt a bitter taste on my tongue as I paraphrased Michel's words from before, but the words seemed to take the wind out of Belial's sails as his head turned one way and then another.

"No, no," he mumbled, his hands flying to the side of his head, his probing fingers massaging at rubbed-raw temples. "I can smell the disease. I can smell *him*." Eyes, shockingly bright in the darkening pantry glared at me, a careful, if still petulant, fury simmering behind a thin veneer of control. "You're lying to me."

A bitingly sarcastic comment almost came from me before I remembered that I was unarmed, my pistol back in my room. Even if he had not eaten in a couple days, Belial would be on me in moments, and I found myself doubting that even my help outside the door would be anything but a liability, should push come to shove.

I settled for shrugging, commenting gravely, "If I do, I'm doing it out of ignorance. However, I'm definitely not lying about the plague. Plague doctors have descended on the city in droves, and all of them tell me that the sickness of the city is passing."

The violence left his eyes, though the dark mirth that replaced was little better. "Doctors and physicians are curious things... They are made to heal, but between an immortal virus or an immoral victim, who's to say what they'll heal?"

XXII

❧

A Momentary Review

"Of course I spoke to him," I promised. The afternoon glow dining room - or perhaps the 'council chamber' as I had quipped a short time before - had faded into gloom, the sun more weary than the six of us sitting around the table. "There's no need to ask a fourth time, big sister."

Sophie opened her mouth to speak, the abrupt hardening of her eyes warning of a harsh response. At her side, Wilderich forestalled any response by gently patting her arm, though his gaze was as hard as hers. "I'm sure she simply wants to make sure that everything is done to make sure that our... guest remains secure." The bishop had been momentarily furious upon discovering that the man responsible for the recent death was held captive in our pantry; he had recovered quickly, though his face was still grimly set whenever Belial was brought up.

"He is locked up and there he'll stay," I claimed, glossing over the fact that I did not force Belial's chains back on him when I left. Though I still wasn't entirely sure that it was a good idea, there had been such a change in his behavior since his capture days before that I couldn't help but wonder if the kindness would further humanize him or encourage a relapse to his old ways.

If anything, he had become almost human in the last few conversations. I realized 'almost' might be the closest he ever came to being a true human being, but still the idea intrigued me. A dozen callous murders could be traced back to him, all the subsequent plague-death and misery already in the city lying at his feet, yet his claims and his passion sounded more like the ranting of a deluded cultist, as if he were a starving man vainly clutching at fruit kept by a talented torturer just out of his reach. He was a victim and not villain, and though he would never, could never, be saved from mortal justice, perhaps the humanity hidden behind indoctrination and inculcation might yet see the light of day again.

I shook my head from my reverie as I realized the others were staring at me, their faces filling the entire spectrum from curiosity to suspicion. My sister was far closer to the latter emotion, her eyes peering carefully at me for long seconds before shrugging, as if she were unconcerned about the matter, though the tension in her shoulders told me differently. I clapped my hands together, rubbing them together as much to warm my hands as to deflect any more questions. "Well, with Belial safely," I stressed the last word, "confined, where does that leave us?"

Abraham coughed politely. "It leaves us with a growing problem. Whether or not one believes Michel - and while I wish to believe, I am seeing more and more evidence otherwise - the plague is spreading." He pointed to the city map spread out in the center of the table, his pointer finger and thumb curled into the palm of his hand as his other fingers indicated sites all over the inner city. "At my latest estimation, maybe two hundred dead. Higher than usual at this point in the year, but the chill in next few months will lead to more dead than that without a sweat being broken. It is a wonder that there is not a larger outcry, but, then, it seems confined to single buildings, never growing beyond neighboring houses."

Max spoke up from his place, his face red with embarrassment as he cut in. "I've not been inside any of the houses, mostly because you told me it wasn't safe." He took a breath, looking fearfully around at the table, his mouth opening and closing as if he were reconsidering his potential contribution.

Wilderich gave him a supportive smile. "Go on, boy. Tell us."

My friend, so strong yet so meek, nodded in thanks. "Most of the sick people run shops. Groceries, apothecaries... this one here is a butcher," he continued, pointing at each in turn. "I don't know anything about the sickness, but could it have something to do with bad food?"

I wanted to laugh at the stupidity of the idea, but Max didn't often give his opinion, so I bit my lip instead as I looked at the map, a peculiar pattern arising the longer I looked at the plague sites. If Max was right, most of those areas were without easy access to food, medicine. My own gaze drifted to Abraham. "You've been inside these places, what did you see?"

"Mush," he said, "much like the first time at Mohammad's. The food was decayed and rotten. I wouldn't eat anything that remained there, that's for sure."

"Do you think that's an effect of the plague? The rot, I mean," asked Sophie, looking at the Jewish man first and then me.

I shrugged. "I am unsure what to think anymore. I have been examining every book on the subject, but I don't think I've ever seen a disease that affects both plant and man, certainly not like this." I looked at Abraham for support, my mouth mirroring his tight-lipped grimace. "I mean, the disease turns portions of the body black and rotten, corrupting the flesh underneath as it seems to spread using the body's own veins."

"Don't forget how light the body becomes," offered Max helpfully. "Remember how easily you lifted the body we found outside Stephansdom?"

"You're right," I agreed.

"Well, the soul has left the body. Of course it's lighter than it would otherwise be," cut in Wilderich, his face slightly indignant.

I ignored him, not willing to debate the point. "True, and then there are the bloody marks on the chest. Is that how the disease infects other people, maybe?"

Abraham's face tilted to the side. "What marks?"

"The two marks," I repeated, on the chest, right here." I indicated an area just around my pectoral. "Right by the nipple?"

His face darkened, his hands pulling out a small bound notebook and paging furiously through the notes therein. "I don't think I've ever seen anything like that." Eventually reaching blank pages, he closed and reopened the text, restarting his search from the beginning. I watched his eyebrows rise in soft surprise. "Here's something about those marks. The victim was that poor grocer's boy. 'Two puncture wounds on left breast... estimated distance between three and three and a half centimeters.' Hm," he mused, "I guess there was a great deal of activity around that time. After all, that was shortly after Sarah and I moved to the estate. Right around the time Belial took up residence here as well."

I didn't comment on his delicately sarcastic sentiment, instead asking, "You said that you haven't seen them on any other bodies?" My mouth drooped into a frown as he shook his head. "They were also on the body Max and I found outside Stephansdom. You saw them, didn't you, Bishop?"

But Wilderich shook his head. "I can't say that I had, Dietrich. His body was covered, more or less, when you brought him inside. We didn't even remove his clothes for the burial." His face flushed red at the memory of his failure two weeks before. It had since been discovered that he remained the only survivor of the burial party: the gravediggers had all fallen sick and died since then or disappeared, though where this latter group had gone was anyone's guess.

Sophie sighed, leaning back in her chair and crossing her arms petulantly. "Wonderful, another mystery. Will this list of amusements never cease to grow?" she asked dramatically.

Wilderich again tried to play the role of conciliator, his hands rising in a gentle plea for calm. "Baroness, please," he began. Strange, I thought, he never used my title with me. "I'm sure this is just a freak occurrence. In all the bodies the *apotheker* here has come across, he hasn't seen them, has he?" He turned to Abraham for confirmation. The Jewish man's eyebrows shot up in shock at the request for support, but he gave it anyway, turning to whisper secretively with Sarah next to him.

But though he tried to gloss over the subject, I was altogether less willing to look past the mystery. "I'm sorry to disagree, but I would prefer an answer to those marks myself."

"The mark of the Alpen," interjected Max from his place at the table, the expression on his face faraway and distant. We all peered at him, waiting for him to continue, but he didn't meet any of our gazes, his pallor growing grey as if his soul had died days ago, leaving behind a barely breathing husk of flesh.

When he didn't continue, Sophie looked at me to translate. "The Alpen?" she asked frostily, as if I had any clue what my friend was speaking about. I shrugged in reply, confused.

Thankfully, I was given no further chance to explain something I knew nothing about. "The Alpen," said Max suddenly, his eyes still gazing deep into emptiness. "The children of the devil. They come at night to suck the purity from men and women, leaving behind only evilness and corruption." His voice was emotionless, its tone absent anything like life as if he was merely the mouthpiece of stories almost forgotten and barely understood. "My *grossmutti* told me that when she was a child, they would come from the forests around cities and steal away the souls of the children who didn't pray before nighttime." His eyes finally rose from their empty contemplation to look at us each in turn. "They would make marks like that, she said," he finished definitively, pointing at his chest. "Two marks: one to let life out, the other to let evil in."

I don't think any of us, save Max, believed in such a fairytale. This was the 17th century; childish fantasies belonged in the benighted Dark ages, not in today's more enlightened times. Regardless, I saw fear in more than one set of eyes as I looked about the table, though its specific color was different from person to person. Max was on one end of the spectrum, his gaze tortured and unsteady. My sister was on the other, her eyes defiantly cold, though I could read in them concern of a nature I was unable to easily qualify. The others were somewhere between these two extremes, with the Jews closer to my sister and Wilderich to Max.

Other than that uneasy exchange of looks, none of us spoke for a short while, unwilling to comment on Max's addition to our conversation. I broke the uneasy silence, asking Wilderich. "Are you alright, Bishop? You look like you could use some air." He looked back at me, confused. I flicked a gaze over at my friend, emphasizing my next words gently while still removing all doubt as to why I was asking the question. "Maybe you could take Max with you?"

He realized my intent, rising to his feet with a great show of his middle age, one hand pressed to his back. "Oh, of course, a walk outside sounds wonderful. Max, if you don't mind, I wanted to ask you about your devotions the other night when you were by on your evening watch." Extending his other hand, he guided my huge friend to his feet, the kindliness of his gesture comforting and gentle in its softness. He gave me a glance as he left, one that demanded a full recounting of what happened in his absence. I nodded almost imperceptibly in response, careful to hide our wordless conversation from Max.

I waited until they had left before saying more. One hand pointing back along the path of the recently departed, I commented, "I've never seen Max like that before."

"Neither have I," affirmed Sophie. Though I was always closer with him, Max had been around my sister often enough for her to get the full measure of my large friend. To see him so haunted was uncomfortable, though I managed to pull a small measure of strength from the fact that I was not the only one unsettled by his abrupt personality shift.

Abraham carefully interlaced his hands, his fingers creating a ladder that led back to his half-covered mouth. "Are we buying into the idea of a demon coming in the night that killed these men?" His tone was deferential, neither dismissing nor buying into the recently related hypothesis. It was the tone I would have expected more from a lawyer or a noble, and my respect for him, already not inconsiderable, rose further.

"I wouldn't want to assume anything at this point," I said, "though I am very uneasy with the idea of some fantastic creature causing all of this death." I waved my hands in the air, as if I was erasing all my previous thoughts. "But forget that for a moment. Let's assume that there is such a creature attacking the population. Wouldn't someone have seen something, anything at all? Besides, we already have the man who claims to have caused all of it. Maybe he caused those wounds."

I could see from Abraham's expression that he didn't entirely accept my proposed explanation, but he shrugged, turning to Sophie instead. "Do you mind repeating what you've taken down so far as to symptoms, milady?" he asked formally, though a hint of mischief was visible in the one eye I could see easily.

"Corrupted flesh, blackened limbs as well as a theorized transportation system that uses the victim's own body for transmission." She continued on with the highlights of our conversation, her meticulous nature evident in each collated and controlled line of data. "Anything else?" she asked after finishing, her hand flashing across paper as she furiously edited already perfect notes on the plague's symptoms and our observations otherwise about it.

I nodded. "We've - or at least I've - seen victims be dizzy, fatigued, staggering one way and then the other, as if they were living their life on a boat and not on solid ground." I stopped as Belial's half-heard claim slammed into me like a bolt of lightning, feeling my body go instantly cold as if I had been drained of all my blood. "Oh, no... Oh, please, no..."

"What is it?" asked Sophie, dread creeping across her face.

"I think Katarina has it."

XXIII

❦

A Murderer's Confession

The sound barely made it out from between her gritted teeth. "Has. It?"

I tried to explain. "Belial said something before about her being sick, but I thought it was just a madman's wild claim. How could she be sick? She hasn't been exposed to anything!"

But Sophie's fierce gaze brooked no argument, the dread disappearing in the face of a wild flair of anger that swirled and sparked behind suddenly hard eyes. "Except for that monster, no." She rose to her feet slowly, her chair scraping harshly against the wood, only going quiet once it no longer felt her touch.

She shouldered her way past me, so brusquely shoving me with a thrust arm that I staggered from the force of her movement. My hand thrust out for balance against the doorframe towards the kitchen and the pantry beyond, I swung myself after my sister, seeing murder in her determined stride. Behind me, Abraham and Sarah belatedly rose to their feet, not as able as I in understanding Sophie's intentions but apparently not willing to be left out of the next moments.

I hurried to the pantry, arriving as Sophie demanded the keys from the guard, her free hand reaching out to clutch the flintlock pistol at the man's waist. Though his gaze flew to her hand at his waist, he made no move to stop her, and why should he? She was his mistress, and to stand in her way now would be to risk his employment (as well as his life, judging from her glare).

She had the door half open before I could manage to even lay a hand on the hard wood, shutting it again as I leaned against the portal with my full weight. "Sophie, don't-"

Whatever else I was about to say was completely forgotten as two eyes and an iron barrel stared me cold in the face. "Brother, I love you, but I love my children even more. I let you keep that beast around on the off-chance that he could be useful, but he is now more trouble than he is worth. Hundreds are already dead because of him. I will not have one of them be my daughter."

I swallowed hard, unwilling to be on the business end of a pistol but also unable to meekly stand aside while my sister killed Belial in cold blood. "Sophie, if it was him, she would have been infected weeks ago when he first arrived." Her face hardened further, until she looked more like a carving in harsh stone than a noblewoman of flesh and blood. "Please, Sophie! He's not an animal to be put down-"

A hammer clicked back into firing position in reply. "Don't pretend you can tell me he's human either, Dietrich. He lost his right to be called that the day he killed his first victim."

"But he's a victim, too! He wasn't always this way," I pleaded, but I doubted even that tack would breed any kind of positive result. My throat locked, waiting to exhale, as I tried to stare down Sophie.

I don't know how long we remained locked in that stand-off, seconds or hours passing, her with the barrel nearly against my face, me with one hand on the door, carefully remaining between Sophie and her target. A part of myself, clinically detached, carefully cataloged the damage that would occur once her finger caressed the trigger of the pistol. A smoothbore pistol, inaccurate at anything over twenty or twenty-five paces, would have no trouble hurling its leaden round into my exposed face at this range. The best I could hope for would be a straight shot to the brain, an instant death as opposed to anything more painful and lingering, but the possibility always remained that the ball could deflect and just maim me. Shutting my eyes, I found myself hoping that it would be quick.

And opened them a moment later as the barrel dropped out of my face, Sophie slowly releasing the hammer back into a safe position. My shoulders sagged as the single supporting breath held captive within me writhed free, fleeing into nothingness as I leaned against the door in relief...

Which is why I was blindsided by the pistol whip that hammered into the side of my head, hurling me to the side away from the door. Stars spun across my vision, my sight first greying and then going white as I fell to the floor.

Until my vision returned, I could only guess at the events of the next moments, though my ears told a tale all of their own. The pantry door slammed open, wood flung into stone as Sophie stormed the room. Shouts of alarm echoed, first from her and then from the guard outside - I imagine, once they saw how I left Belial. Steps and sounds of struggling. A pistol fired, but I heard no yowl of pain nor any body hitting the floor. I heard glass shatter and wood splinter all the while, but this was in the background of it all, the bass to the melody of the scuffle.

I felt soft slaps on my cheeks, my sight flashing in and out in time with the strikes. "*Freyund*," whispered Abraham urgently, "you need to get up quick!" Still groggy, I vainly dragged myself to my feet, my fingers clawing at the walls to drag myself to my feet. I felt Abraham's hands under my armpits, trying to lift me to my feet, though in the end I know I only made it because of my own efforts.

Standing straight, I thrust an arm to the side against the wall as my balance remained elusive, the world still spinning slightly despite my efforts to the contrary. All the while, the sounds of struggle continued to emanate from the pantry, though they fell silent as I shuffled through the open portal.

The room was in a state of disrupted disarray, with several shelves shattered and broken. I had heard glass breaking before, but I was unprepared for the sheer number of shattered fragments that littered the ground. Sophie stood off to one side, her clothes slightly torn though apart from a bruised dignity she seemed fine. Her man was in rougher state, lying prostrate across the floor while Belial stood overtop him, his chest heaving with effort as he held the pistol like a club over his head.

Upon seeing me, Belial dropped to his knees, the arm holding the pistol out in surrender. Unsure, I nevertheless took the pistol from him, though I keep it pointed at the floor. "What... is going on here?" I asked, as if I couldn't already guess.

"Is this what you call safely stored away?" Sophie spat from her side of the pantry. "Allowing this thing to escape his chains and attack me with a broken bottle?"

Belial's face shot up, his expression earnestly innocent. "I was not trying to escape, Dietrich-morsel. I was out of my chains, but I was here at prayer." He continued even as Sophie tried to demand the pistol from me. "I heard you fighting outside and did nothing besides defend myself. Please, don't punish me." His voice was small, in a way that unarmed me, even with the pistol in my hand.

It must have struck Sophie strangely as well, for she stopped dead in her tracks, her arms freezing in mid-grasp, her head glacially rotating about to consider the recoiling Belial.

To say that silence reigned in the pantry then would be an understatement; the room became a tomb for sound, still as death and as lively as a corpse, the barest mutter of noise emanating only from the prostrate houseman still on the floor next to Belial. I drank in every instant of it, my recently wounded head already throbbing painfully whenever someone spoke in. In the wake of so much noise, it was a glorious moment when the world stood - largely - still

But this blessed silence, too, did pass, with Sophie breaking the stillness, a harsh scowl on her face. "Don't punish you?" she asked, half in disbelieving anger, half in maternal confusion. "You've killed dozens, hundreds! You are the reason that I have a *trottl* living in my pantry and the reason that my daughter is sick upstairs!" A single finger jabbed first at the kneeling man and then at the ceiling. "How dare you ask *anyone* for mercy here after what you've done."

I opened my mouth to defend him, but Belial shook his head in my direction, standing his ground from his place on the floor. He bowed his head slightly, but his eyes remained locked with Sophie's. "I didn't ask for mercy, Dietrich-sister. I asked to not be punished." His voice lost some of its childlike quality, though an earnestness flooded in in its wake. "I have destroyed God's creation, and even if I do that to save mankind from himself, I deserve no mercy. I expect none. But what I did not do was infect the little girl. She, like the Dietrich-morsel, was kind to me. She is what I am here to protect. Innocence."

"Innocence?" Sophie laughed, her lips speaking my thoughts. "Yes, she is innocent. She and Freddie are perhaps the only innocent things left in this city. But what would a monster know of innocence?"

I looked away for a moment while Belial composed his own response, flicking my hands first at Abraham and Sarah and then at the guard on the floor. The *apotheker* and his wife nodded, doing their best to unobtrusively remove the wounded man from between Sophie and Belial out into the hall. I heard hushed conversation from the two of them, but decided I needed to remain where I was; even if Sophie hadn't gone for the pistol in my hand, there remained bottles and pieces of wood all over.

Belial finally seemed ready to speak though, his gaze finally breaking from my sister's to consider a life poorly lived. "I was innocent, once, before the Master came to me and made me a messenger of God. My days were empty of anything truly important, but though I murdered time as surely as any man, I did nothing that harmed another soul.

"I gave to charity, I ministered to the sick. Despite what my father told me to do - he always believed that the poor remained that way due to indolence and sloth - I tried hard to become that which any Christian might aspire to become - a good man." His eyes became even more faraway. "I remember coming across a farmer whose cart-horse had thrown a shoe. I couldn't tell you why, but I found myself moved to give him my own horse, a gift that my father had given me on my tenth name-day. Imagine the farmer's face! when some random rider gave him an animal worth more than what he would have made in years of toiling in the sun."

He chuckled, as if the memory were some joke and not the sad recollection it became then. "Mother was furious," he said, his voice dropping almost away to nothing. "When I returned home that day, she beat me, ordering me to take her to the pitiful *baumer* to whom I had given one of her prized horses. I told her no, and in return she gave me the first of these." He turned slightly, showing my sister what I had already known he possessed, the sight of the dozens of crisscrossed scars received and healed drawing a wince of sympathy from Sophie.

She tried to smother the momentary weakness with another spit of venom. "So you were beaten. That is your defense?"

Tears welled at the side of Belial's misting eyes. "No, but neither did I tell her about the farmer, and not just out of some sense of pride. We were rich! What did we need of one more horse, not when an entire stable sat outside! But mother refused to listen to any defense. She was angry, and though she beat me, I still believed my mother to be a good woman, a Christian woman, so I forgave her and, as the scars healed, so did, I thought, her love for me." He turned back around so Sophie could see the moisture that fell to collect on his unshaven chin. I was struck, momentarily, by how short the growth. I would have possessed a far more significant growth after a similar incarceration. "But she merely waited for my back to heal before she had me whipped again, striping my back time and again until I pled for her to stop.

"Can you imagine?" he asked Sophie and then me, "a woman beating her son for acting charitably. A woman who pretended to the name of Christianity, who prayed loudly whenever the bishop watched, but then beat her son as God watched her in private?"

I was the only one to answer in any fashion at all, my head shaking in sympathetic sadness, my heart moved to pity for the broken man. No longer could I only consider him as a murderer first and victim second. He was a shattered reflection of humanity, a husk of what Christian charity had become in recent decades. Brutality and dishonesty wedded together, I think I might have understood what drove him into the grips of the vile master who drove him to the spread of death and further violence.

But it seemed his tale wasn't yet done, because he went on. "Love for my mother died slowly, a piece at a time, scar by scar scourged from my body whenever I tried to be Christian, tried to be anything approaching human. Sometimes I stayed silent, not naming the beneficiaries who ended up possessing everything I had and freely gave. Sometimes I failed, and when I failed, my love for my mother died that much quicker as I was forced to watch her take my gifts back, often repaying the gifted with as much cruelty as I had given them in charity."

I risked a look over at Sophie, saw in her tightened jaw an expression that told me of the complicated cocktail of emotions swirling within her. I could see her softer side war with the heart of stone she cultivated whenever something threatened her children. She was moved to the same perspective I held; I could see that easily. The question was when she would allow herself to see it.

Her teeth unclenched long enough to hiss another question, though this one was absent some of the toxicity of before. "We all have demons, yet you turned from Christian to killer?" She tried to play off the barbarism, but, like I said, I could see her stony face eroding under the meanness of Belial's former life.

I heard a half-angry shout from behind me, the voice unmistakably that of Wilderich. For a moment I worried that the outburst would disturb the uneasy peace of the room, but neither party moved, Belial composing his next response, my sister carefully distant from him, her arms crossed in front of her chest.

Cursing myself for an idiot, I stepped outside. I had completely forgotten about Wilderich's walk with Max, and I raised my hands in a plea for forgiveness as the shorter man stormed towards me, Max trailing behind him almost like a puppy. Though I only managed a brief glance before the angry clergyman was upon me, I was relieved to see him more relaxed than he had been before.

Then I was forced to look down at the angry bishop. "What in God's name is going on here? I leave for a few minutes and-"

I raised my finger to my lips in an effort to get him to speak a little more softly. "Please, everything is under control. Just a small disturbance," I said, realizing the idiocy of my comment, given that there was a still wounded man lying on the ground behind me.

"Why are we here? I thought that the guest was safely kept quiet!" Infuriated hysteria threatened to drive his voice louder and louder, but I managed to hush him back to a more serene sputtering. "What have I missed, exactly?" he asked, affronted.

I tried to summarize everything for him as quickly and quietly as I could, anxious to return to the inside of the pantry and the uneasy conversation I was sure was going on there. At least there had been no new outburst of sound, so I thought it safe to assume that the awkward truce remained in force.

The harsh glare on the bishop's face melted slightly at my suspicions of Katerina being ill. "Poor child," he said, crossing himself. "If it's plague after all... How is the Baroness taking the news?"

I blithely tossed a thumb first toward the wounded man and then the pantry. "I believe you might be able to assume her thoughts on the matter." I waited for several heartbeats until pity bled across the other man's face. "Please believe me when I say I didn't think we would find ourselves here. I am trying to keep the peace, though, so could I manage to...?"

I left the question to hang in the air and was gratified when the bishop nodded agreeably. "But of course." He mused a moment before snapping his fingers. "Perhaps I will visit with Katarina then. If she isn't asleep, perhaps I could keep her company with a story or two."

It was a charming idea, imagining the bishop telling my niece stories from the bible or history, but a feeling in my gut caused my eyebrows to furrow of their own volition. "Bishop, I'm not sure that's a good idea. We don't know how the disease is transmitted. It might be polluted air, it could be a bite."

But the bishop wouldn't be dissuaded. "I have caused enough harm thus far. I would like, I think, to be the cause of some small bit of comfort for the suffering. It is one of the reasons I took Holy Orders. Besides," he said, smiling, "I have been near several of the diseased already. If I was to get sick by foul air, I would have done so. So would you, I think!" he continued, lightly patting my shoulder. "If you need either of us, you can find us visiting the children."

Turning away from me, he approached Max once more, extending an elbow as if my friend were a fashionable young lady as opposed to a low-born man. "Maximilian, would you care to accompany me to visit young Katarina and Fredrick. Max looked at me for something - permission, I supposed - which I gave him in my soft nod. Drawing himself up in an image that drew a chuckle from me, the two men, arm in arm, strode off to visit my niece and nephew.

I could only hope that Katarina's spirits would be similarly buoyed.

Turning back to the pantry, I risked a glance inside to see Sophie's arms no longer crossed. Instead, her hands clutched at each other, softly wringing her fingers in distress while Belial continued to speak, the man still on his knees before her. I turned away to kneel beside Abraham and Sarah. "How is he?" I asked, pointing to the man on the ground.

"Contusion, maybe a few bruised ribs," answered Abraham. "I can only guess at his full injuries."

Sarah confirmed his diagnosis with a jibe. "Well, that's why I handle the afflicted and you stay behind and work with your chemicals, my dear." When I favored her with a glance, she nodded briskly. "He is right in this case, however, absent some small cuts and splinters. Nothing bed rest won't fix." She reached a speculative hand out towards me. "How is *your* head?"

My vision was still imperfect, my sense of balance similarly impaired, but I tried to shrug away her concern. "I'll survive. If it's one thing I have confirmed in recent weeks, it is how durable a man can be when he must be."

Abraham laughed lightly at this, and my spirits were further buoyed by the fact that my fellow conspirators could laugh even as the world decayed around them. "I am aware of this, *freyund*. You don't seem slowed by your injuries, and you managed to find yourself introduced rather forcefully into a wall recently."

I realized he was right, surprised at how little consideration I had given to the injury I had sustained when I had first encountered Belial. Shrugging again, I tried to steer the conversation. "I want to check in with my sister and Belial. Can I trust you to handle him?" I asked, pointing at the supine man.

"Of course," Sarah said, dismissing me with an airy wave of her hand. "Go."

I flew as quickly as I could back inside, though I did my best to appear as calm and collected as if I were taking a stroll outside and not returning to the disarray of the pantry. Sophie was slumped against the wood shelves along one wall, her shoulders arched under the weight of Belial's words even as she half-sat against a surviving shelf. Belial sat before her, his legs crossed in front of him as if he were some Far East monk preparing to meditate, his arms relaxed on his knees. His drooped head watched as one hand idly traced the lines of the floor, one pale finger sliding gracefully in and around the detritus there. As if I needed any assistance to know, I could tell from tear-streaked faces that the mood of the room remained far from delightful.

Sophie was asking, the harsh tone gone from her voice, "Why join him, though? It seems this Master of yours cares as little for you as he does for life?"

Belial shrugged, his head still cast down at the floor. "He is God's right hand? When he speaks, so does the Lord. Obeying him obeys God." I was afraid that I would hear zealotry color his voice, so used I was to the abrupt shifts in his personality, but it never came. Instead, he seemed... tired, like the last whispers of butter spread over a crust of bread. There was no fervor, none of the passion that would and had frightened me in previous conversations. Instead of some deranged cultist murderer, I saw a weary, exhausted young man, old far before his time.

I think, perhaps, that Sophie saw this, too, though I could only guess this tangentially from the momentary glance she flickered my direction.

I still saw the concern for my niece, thoughts for her sick child enough to deserve the lioness' share of her worry. But there was something else now, the concern too complex to be just that for a daughter who may or may not be slowly dying. Yes, there was a pity there, empathetic yet not pathetic, caring yet not vulnerability in its feeling.

"I hope I'm not intruding," I said carefully. "Are we ok in here?"

"No," said Sophie, "no, we are not ok. I have a sick daughter upstairs and I wish that I could take out my anger and frustration and concern on... on... Belial," she finally finished, giving a name at last to the man who had lived these past weeks in her home. His head flashed up at the sound of his name, cocking itself to the side as if he were unused to hearing it said. "But I cannot and I will not, if for no other reason than to begin to make up for my own failings as a Christian recently."

I was unsure of exactly what she meant, as my sister only barely acknowledged the existence of the heavenly more than I. But I nodded slowly, seeing it as a way for her to explain away her inclination to mercy and refuse to recognize it as a reaction to Belial's story.

But then I knew my sister. Belial did not, showing this as fresh tears fell from his eyes. His hands rose from his knees to clasp in front of him in thanksgiving. "Thank you, Dietrich-sister-"

"Baroness," she interrupted, a hint of soft anger there.

"Dietrich-Baroness," replied Belial.

Sophie looked at me as if Belial were mad, which I imagine was still true, even if this new flood of information put that insanity into a still mildly-confusing perspective. I shook my head softly, so she went along with his new name. "I must leave now, Belial, but I will make you this promise: you have killed and destroyed part of my home, you have harmed my child and my servants, and you have attacked my brother. For that I can never forgive you, but what I will do is turn the other cheek. I will see you clothed and fed, even if such an action sees your demonic talents return. Master or not, let it never be said that all women are such vile creatures as the monster who was your mother."

I wondered what had been revealed while I had retreated to deal with Wilderich and the others, but my sister's lips sealed and didn't re-open. Instead, she rose to leave, stopping only when Belial crept over on his hands and knees to grasp at the hem of her dress. Despite my belief in the scraps of humanity that lay within him, my hand went for the pistol that I had almost forgotten at my waist, unconsciously worried for what he could have done. He ignored me, large pleading eyes fixed only on my sister. "Please, I asked only to not be punished. I don't deserve anything that you would give to me."

But Sophie would not hear it, either out of a sense of spite or out of true Christian charity I failed to know, cutting off his objections with a knifed hand. "Then repay your debt to me.

"Heal my child."

XXIV

A Surprising
Transformation

My sister's mask of control settled back into place, her back straightening back into her pose of careful poise once more. Looking at me, I could see her delegation to see her will done, the command communicated in the gaze of the older sibling. Without another word, she left, going, I knew, to her daughter's side.

I looked back at Belial, no longer seeing a detested enemy. His tale of woe had been too pitiful to hold any real rancor against the man. That was not to say that I saw him as an ally: Despite my newfound flow of pity for him, there was the lingering sense of suspicion hanging in the recesses of my mind. He was, for now, an ally, though I couldn't help but see him more like the deck in a game of faro or basset - depending on the whim of the dealer, we could come out ahead in spades... or we could find our very souls mortgaged to pay our debts.

I reached a hand down to him, dragging him carefully to his feet, straining against the strong grip that could have pulled me from my feet without a second thought. Even in his diminished state, Belial could still have torn me limb from limb, the reminder enough to return my hand to the pistol at my waist. Even then, I wondered how much good that had done me so far, what with him having taken a round from point blank range and still coming through more or less unharmed.

I tried to push the dark thoughts from me, failing as I became infuriated by my own powerlessness in the broad picture of the last weeks. Despite my having located the disease and, in a sense, having brought together the motley band who met at the estate, I had done very little to fight the disease itself. Sure, I had gleaned some small fragments of knowledge, some infinitesimal measure of success more by accident than design, but I was more a cabin boy than the captain of my own destiny. I was, at best, a bug in the cosmic scheme of the world, a loathsome insect waiting to be squashed by fate or by God.

That supposed that there was a God, and though I had attempted so recently, I was still uncommitted to the notion. If there was no higher power, then I had the worst damnable luck in the history of man.

If there was a God sitting in judgement, then he was enjoying his torment of me.

Belial, the architect of all the darkness in my mind, intruded. "Thank you, Dietrich-morsel, for intervening." His tone was earnest and kind, or as close as he could manage through a terrifyingly sharp-toothed smile. I found my eyes drawn to his canines; somehow, I had failed to notice how feral they seemed from up close. My mind idly imagined him having made the marks on the bodies I had found so far, but I dismissed the idea immediately. What kind of man would want to drink the blood of diseased corpses?

A man who had given up all notions of humanity a long time ago, another piece of me answered.

I tried to smile myself, a pale and wasted grimace coming through in reflection. "You're welcome. She is acting only out of concern for her daughter, of course."

He noticed my wariness, his head cocking to the side. "I didn't do anything to her, Dietrich-morsel. She is of the Innocent. I do not harm the pure of heart. That would go against the word of God and the Master."

"Then how is she sick?" I asked, watching his face curl in thought as we slipped outside towards proper clothes and a sick niece. Motioning him to one side of the hall, I angled my body to allow a small troupe of servants to pass through towards the pantry and the mess therein, brooms, dustpans, and small buckets in their hands. I needn't have bothered, given the way they shrank from Belial until we had nearly the entire passageway for ourselves.

Leaving them behind us, I slowed as the hallway widened and we returned to the house proper so Belial could walk abreast of me, allowing that vaguest sense of egalitarianism between us. He was, in some ways, my opposite - where I tried, in my own way, to bring life, he brought death. Where I tried to heal, he tried to destroy. My eyebrows rose in astonishment that we were two sides of the same coin, for the first time recognizing him for what he was.

Despite the chasms that lay between us in so many ways, he was my equal.

"That is the curious thing, morsel," Belial answered finally, his own brow furrowing in consternation. "I am not sure. Save the touch of God coming here on its own, I didn't call it here. She was not around any of the Sinful who have died already, was she?" I shook my head. "Then I don't know."

"What about your claim to kill everyone in the walls with your powers?" I asked, curious. I was cautiously skeptical of the claim from the start, and his own confusion of the source behind Katarina's infection confirmed for me that he was the omnipotent being he had first seemed.

He looked chagrined, his pale face flushing a shockingly crimson color. "I may have tried to call down God's judgement on you when you first brought me here-" His hands rose as he anticipated my response. "since I came here to send the boy for judgement," he amended.

I didn't comment on his euphemism for murder, content that he acknowledged it at all for now.

"Either way, my prayers were unanswered, in a way that I cannot help but wonder if God has special plans for you." His eyes narrowed as he considered me suspiciously, though I was astonished to realize that the predatory flavor that had been so rampant in it recently was gone, curiosity instead infusing the expression. "But I swear," he continued, crossing himself feverishly. "I had nothing to do with making the small one sick."

I stopped to look at him, weighing and measuring the earnestness in his eyes. His earliest rantings aside, he had always spoken of the wicked being punished by his hand, and though I was unclear why or how it was that he made the delineation between evil and not, his claim of innocence would make a peculiar sense.

Regardless, I let him writhe under my consideration for long seconds. I should not have enjoyed the way he quailed under my gaze, to all the world a whipped dog in a man's body, but the darkness in me enjoyed his fear. The fear lasted all too short a time, but the flame of happiness that flared into life on Belial's face was worth it as I nodded in acceptance of his profession.

We said little else to each other as I let him into my room so I could see him dressed properly. He seemed confused by the idea of true clothes, used to, I imagine, the shapeless robe he had worn for who knows how long. At length I managed to convince him of the necessity of dressing more appropriately, but I handed him clothes that hung more loosely on his spare frame.

By the end of the entire session, he might have passed for any other citizen of Vienna, if only one didn't consider his eyes. They remained as they always had, expressive beyond all measure yet plummeting into deep pools of nothing at the drop of a hat, a cold reminder of the absence where a human soul would otherwise reside.

But soulless or not, he was bound to our cause now, or at least he was bound to my sister, so I did my best to set the matter aside and motioned him towards the door and towards Katarina.

There was a small crowd outside the door to my niece's bedroom, a gaggle of gossiping servants there, it seemed, to pay homage to Katarina. Although I swiftly ordered them to return to their duties, several persisted in remaining behind, disobeying me as they looked fearfully towards the bed and its lone occupant.

I understood their devotion. When Belial had claimed before that Sophie's daughter was innocent and pure, he had missed the mark entirely, though this was due to exposure more than anything else I imagine. She was like the fairies one reads of in children's tales, flitting from one place to another with an inexhaustible energy, vibrant and untainted by the cares of the adult world. Any who spent longer than a few minutes with my niece were instantly captivated by her mischievous giggle, the gentle laugh enough to soften even the heart of the old stable-hand who still snarled at every request I ever made of him.

All who knew her were hopelessly devoted to her, myself included. Truth be told, of my sister's children, she was my favorite; I loved my nephew as well, but Fredrick's withdrawn nature had long since driven a quiet space between the two of us, content as he was to keep his thoughts to himself. Sophie had told me once that he is as I was at his age, though I admit I have tried hard to repress my memories of that time, given its proximity to my parents' deaths.

I saw my sister tense from her place next to Katarina, her very skin going taut as she fought down the gorge that I was so sure was in her throat. She gave us both a small smile of welcome instead, as if we came unannounced to visit with her daughter.

Max and Wilderich were less welcoming, each man's face twisted differently at the sight of Belial. Wilderich was the more politic of the two, his eyes frigidly cold while praying hands became more like talons clutching at one another. Max was less diplomatic, allowing a hiss to escape from him even as his face became so ugly and ferocious I was thankful that Katarina couldn't see it from her place in her bed.

I cut off any chance of a voiced objection as I fairly flew to Katarina's side. "Someone tells me that you are a little sick," I said, as if she and I hadn't spoken earlier. "I wanted to bring a friend of mine who wanted to help you get better. Would you like to talk to him?"

She favored me with a brave smile, "I wish you hadn't bothered him, Uncle Dietrich. It's just a little cold, Momma says. I'll be better in a little while." I couldn't help but return her courageous expression, amazed that a child of her few years could be so fearless. She had to know that her illness was more than a simple cough, but she took it in stride instead of falling to pieces as others her age would have.

She was her mother's daughter, after all.

Belial knelt next to the bed, his face soft and yielding. "Hello little one," he said. "Do you know who I am?"

"Yes," she said, nodding weakly. "You're the angel Uncle Dietrich was keeping in the pantry!"

I thought I saw Belial's face flush a little in embarrassment, but he nodded sagely. "I am!" he agreed gently, though he moved his hands away from her when she reached towards him. I saw Sophie nod, mollified by his decision to be more distant. "I have a secret to tell you, little one. Would you like to know what it is?"

She naturally nodded as energetically as she could, sagging against her pillows afterwards after the exertion.

He leaned in slightly, close enough that I imagine she could smell his breath without trying. "God has great things in store for you, little one. And right now he wants to test you through me to make sure you are worth receiving his gifts. This means that you might not feel well sometimes, and I want to make sure that you understand that, despite anything I do to you, I am doing it out of God's love for you."

I was afraid I would hear the old zealotry appear in his words, but Belial's face was completely calm; that was not to say that he was dispassionate, for I could see he fervently believed everything he had just said. I wondered if he did not see his actions of the past weeks in a similar light against the entire city, but discarded that as secondary to seeing my niece well and healthy again.

She, for her part, seemed to relax at his words, not even flinching when he leaned over to kiss her forehead in some strange form of benediction.

Would that everyone else around that bed reacted so agreeably, though it fell to Max to be the most active in his response. Max fairly leapt to his feet, his hands half-raised until he realized where he was:

even then, he only barely managed to force his hands into quiescence. His face a taut expression of disapproval, he glared at me. I could only wonder what Wilderich had said to him in the interim but given the fiery glare I saw in the bishop's eyes, it was far from complimentary.

I tugged on Belial's shoulder. He accepted my unspoken order without complaint. "Little one, I will be back soon. I need to retrieve a few things to test you, if that's ok?" I was, for lack of a better word, stunned by the transformation. Katarina, unknowing of the animal inside him, smiled and nodded in response slowly. She was still in the early stages of the disease, or so I guessed, without the lumps and rot that marked so many of the other victims we had seen or heard about in the recent past.

I hoped that those same symptoms would never blemish her skin, but it was out of my hands as to whether or not they would. No, her salvation was in the hands of Belial. I suppressed a shudder as he nodded a goodbye to Sophie. "Dietrich-Baroness, I will need several things to heal her. Have you any antimony on hand?"

Wilderich hissed, his teeth baring themselves in a snarl that he tried - unsuccessfully - to turn into a bitter smile for Katarina's benefit. "Baroness, it's a poison!" he whispered.

She ignored him for the moment, her concern for her child overriding all else. "Unless my brother has any in the cottage, I don't believe that I keep any of that here. If you had needed arsenic, I imagine I could have been more accommodating, but that seems unimportant right now..." Her voice trailed off, but I saw that she took strength from Belial's question, seeing in it as I did a committed direction as opposed to the flailing about that had so far marked our own response to the plague.

"Perhaps Abraham has some in his apothecary," I offered helpfully. "Maybe we will take a quick walk there and see what we can find."

"Good," offered Wilderich venomously. "I imagine Belial will enjoy seeing the fruits of his handiwork."

"Outside," I ordered, pointing to Wilderich. "Belial," I continued. "Go to the bottom of the stairs and stay there. I will be along shortly."

He nodded gamely and padded out with a final - surprisingly respectful - shallow bow to both my sister and Katarina, his feet making almost no noise despite being wearing the noisiest, most uncomfortable pair of shoes I had ever owned.

I waited for him to leave before I bid my sister and niece goodbye. This time, Sophie accepted the supportive kiss I gave to the top of her head, Katarina looking on as I promised her a kiss of her own and more once she was all better. Jerking my head to one side, I ordered Wilderich into the hall, waiting until we were halfway to the staircase before I caught him by the shoulder and spun him about.

"How can you trust him?" he asked me, his entire upper body tensing and relaxing in repressed outrage. "You would put the life of your niece in his hands?"

"Do you have any better of an idea?" I asked. "We have nothing without his help."

"We have a plague doctor!" he half-shouted back before dropping his voice back down. "How in God's name have we gone from imprisoning him to trusting him in a day?!"

I opened my mouth, but I had no good answer for him. He was right; Michel would have at least as much understanding of the disease and, though I doubted his methods, would surely know as much as Belial in how to heal Katarina. "I don't know," I said. "But do you see how he is around Katarina as opposed to the rest of us? Did you even hear his story?"

"No," he said icily. "I was nurse-maiding Max while you decided to speak with him!" I recounted it then, leaving out only the pieces that I had yet to hear myself. His face fell when I told him of the beatings, of Belial's abusive mother and crippled commitment to Christ. I thought I had broken his frosty resolve, but he instead reminded me. "How do we know that any of what he says is true?"

"We don't," I admitted, taking the wind out of his sails. "But I have spent more time than anyone else in this house with him. I can tell you that he came to us a madman, raving and insane. Explain to me how I can square that with the man who just told my niece that he will make her well." I waited for an answer from him, receiving none. "I will not forgive or forget what he's done - he is the architect of every cruel death in the city and will cause more yet, but isn't my duty as a Christian to believe that he can become something more than he was?"

I don't believe that Wilderich expected me to use religion in Belial's defense, for his own mouth gaped open and shut foolishly. "I'm going to see if Michel will come by," he eventually said petulantly, his arms folding across his chest. "Regardless of your good intentions, I would prefer the lamb lying in that bed to be entrusted to a man who has seen and beaten this devilish thing before."

I shrugged in response, knowing that any response at this point would be futile. "As you will, bishop, but if his own prescription gets in the way of my niece and her health, I will throw him from the house myself."

We both nodded, keeping our own counsel for a short time.

"What if Belial's method doesn't work?" he asked me as I turned away to meet Belial at the bottom of the stairs. "What if all your faith in that... thing comes to nothing?"

I felt my heart grow heavy with grief that I hoped never to feel.

"Then she will die."

XXV

◦⊰⊱◦

A Supply Run

The day outside was fading as I strode from the estate with Belial next to me. I had a thicker coat on, the cold of October settling in too uncomfortably for my liking. Belial, however, was invigorated by the chill, his back straightening as he drank in the growing gloom. His face twitched, canting to one side and then the other, his nose sniffing at smell that was beyond my ability to detect.

"Do you smell that?" he asked me, the question cautiously asked and answered by a slow nod of a white lie on my part. "Do you know what it is?" he pressed, his eyebrows rising expectantly.

I pretended to, nodding dumbly as my mind focused on more immediate matter, namely the shortest route to and from Abraham's *apotheke*. Planning what I hoped would be the shortest path, I simply began walking, all social graces going by the wayside. Thankfully, Belial was ignorant of such considerations and fell in step behind me.

I focused more on our path than our surroundings, only the barest glimpse of reality enough to compel me to turn one way or the other, though a piece of me struggled to identify the odor in those first silent minutes of walking. Despite the earlier hour of the evening, there were few people out, a phenomenon I had not noticed until we had passed several taverns that all seemed to be shuttered and closed. Stranger still, there seemed to be only a few watchmen out for the evening, the street-lamps unlit along several avenues.

"What's going on?" I finally wondered aloud, the inquiry escaping unintentionally from my lips. My nose, finally given a moment of recognition, flooded my awareness with a sulfurous reek, the stench like an entire coop of chickens' eggs left spoiled in the summer heat. I felt the gorge in my throat rise, my stomach tying itself in knots of sympathy.

I heard Belial's response an instant after. "It's God's judgement," he said simply, as if those three words were enough to explain the entire current state of reality to me. When I stopped to spit him with a confused look, he went on, if a bit begrudgingly. "The plague, Dietrich-morsel?"

I realized with a sinking feeling where I had smelled the fetid miasma before: back in the grocer's shop, and then a second time only hours later at my family's estate. "It spreads so quickly?" I asked, aghast.

"Not naturally," he said, his hands rubbing at each other in an almost soothing manner.

"Not naturally," I repeated. "What do you mean? Speak plainly."

"The Bible claims God works in mysterious ways, but have you read His word?" He sighed as I stared at him blankly. "The truth is he works with the tools at hand. Imagine... God sent fire and locusts to punish the Egyptians for the bondage of Israel, the Philistines to punish Israel... Wormwood will poison the wells of the Earth at the End of Days. Why should his judgement of this sinful city be any different?" He shrugged, his hands rising to indicate the streets around him.

I hammered one hand against my leg. "I *knew* that there was no mystical, magical reason behind this! But then... "I faltered, "how is it spreading so fast?"

Belial carefully rose to his full, skeletally-thin, height. "'The soul who sins shall die, though the iniquity of the father shall not pass to the son, nor from the son to the father.'"

I itched at my cheek, regretting the decision immediately as the skin on my hand puckered in the chill. "Belial, I am a man of science. If this is a natural thing, then it spreads because of something we do here and now, not because our souls are unclean." I held up a hand to forestall his answer, summoning my weak knowledge of Christianity. "Let me ask you this... man was born with original sin, yes?" He nodded. "Then we are, all of us, unclean, correct?" Another nod. "Then shouldn't every sickness, every cough, flood through us like this plague does now?"

He pondered my logic. "But there was no sickness until I came," he opined.

"So are you sick?" I asked.

"No, I'm saved, soon to be one of his messengers," he claimed falteringly, his voice unsteady for the first time in memory. "But... I spread the sickness, didn't I? I spread the plague and infected those who were weak in spirit, to prepare the way for the rest of them and my Master."

I answered, but motioned him along, unwilling to lose more time while Katarina lay ill. "But if the plague infects only the weak in spirit, then why is someone innocent like Katarina infected?"

He no answer for this either, or at least nothing intelligible, resorting to snorts of frustration as my logic stood against all of his responses. "Belial," I interjected, as much to ask more questions as to calm him down. "Why does your Master ask you to spread the plague?"

"It brings the sinful before him for judgement," he said matter-of-factly, as if it was so appallingly obvious that even I should have managed to understand. "It is our divinely-inspired mission to take on the sin of others so that they can be sent to God free of their flaws."

"Divinely-inspired..." I responded, uncomprehending. "Wouldn't that mean-"

"My Master sits at the right hand of God," he interrupted quickly, amending his words before I could assault previously held dogma with more mortal logic. "Thus, he acts as His messenger, and we as his," he finished, one hand falling step by step, lower and lower in the air before him. "Maybe divinely inspired is the wrong term... maybe God-given is better?"

I felt my lips tighten, cautious derision held in check behind the taut, fake smile. "Perhaps we should focus on the task at hand."

I felt hurt pour from my walking companion. "You don't believe me."

"No, no," I said quickly, looking to salve his wounded ego. "I am just... Confused, I suppose. You have to understand-"

He cut me off, prideful pain in every syllable. "No, *you* must understand, Dietrich-morsel. When it comes to God, not everything need make sense by the laws of man. We are his creation after all; it was not until the sixth day when we first breathed. We are an afterthought, an image of God as a caretaker."

Belial opened his arms, taking in the entire scene. "And what have we wrought by our hands? War, lies, sin of every kind forbidden to us by a merciful God. Can you tell me that living in filth is better than dying to join God instead? Even if it is in judgement?" I wanted to deny his logic, but in my heart I couldn't help but agree with the condemnation. Even only considering this city on its own, there was crime, rampant poverty, small minds bickering over the last dregs of decayed, perverted morality... I was beginning to understand the twisted rationale driving Belial, the realization raising the hairs on the back of my neck.

I almost managed a question when Belial continued, likely believing my silence to be acceptance of his reasoning. "After all, God struck the world more than once by fire and flood, didn't he? From Noah to Gomorrah, the Philistines and the Babylonians, the Romans, the Christian world was devastated whenever they allowed licentiousness and the devil enter in their body and mind. Even in the end times, may they be a long time coming," he said, crossing himself, "the world will be destroyed by fire and flood, wormwood and the sword. As I look around, I cannot help but wonder... From now, where is the difference?"

Pessimism sought to wheedle its way into my thoughts, only held back as I thought of the righteous few I could name personally. "But what about those like my sister, the bishop, my niece?"

"Your sister poisons her rivals as it suits her, the bishop preaches hate against the less evolved of God's people. I only help you now because of the niece's innocence." He scratched his chin thoughtfully. "Strange... you name others but not yourself to be righteous."

I wanted to ignore the question, leading him on a quick left and then a right, passing quickly by Stephansdom. Abraham's *apotheke* was close, but Belial pulled me to a halt now, his grip gentle but firm. "Why do you believe others to be more clean than you? Others you know to be less virtuous than yourself and yet you hold them up as examples of Christianity?"

I shrugged, as much to remove his hand as to deflect the uncomfortable feeling of his scrutiny. "I'm not a saint. I live as best I can, but I drink and swear. I was given so much, and I do so little with it."

Again Belial's eyes softened, and I wondered not for the first time if the way they looked now was as they had when he was younger. "Dietrich, the essence of Christianity is not that we are perfect or that we claim to be perfect. Many can and have done that." He pointed to the sky. "Only God is perfect. All that remains for us is to become him, as best as we are able, and to serve his Creation as it deserves." He raised one thin hand, pointing at my chest. "And the first step of all is to forgive ourselves of this flaw, for we are all short of deserving God's grace."

A curious peace settled over me, a warmth from somewhere else infusing my chilled limbs with a soothing strength. In an instant, the chills that threatened to overtake me vanished, chased away into oblivion.

I allowed him to see a genuine smile on my face, feeling closer to him than I thought possible. "I wonder sometimes why you did not enter the priesthood. You could convert a rock to the church." I made the comment lightly but realized how much truth was contained in my jest the moment my mind had a chance to process my remark. Though he had come to me a raving madman, whenever Belial spoke lucidly of religion I felt a part of myself drawn towards believing in something beyond my books and learning.

For the second time in perhaps an hour, Belial flushed, my compliment enough to embarrass him into silence. We walked further, each of us together yet alone with our thoughts, passing by Stephansdom with little more than a nod of recognition of its grandeur.

We were nearly to Abraham's *apotheke* when the stench of death grew obnoxiously, its fetor enough to drag unwilling tears from me. Belial stopped in his tracks, his entire body leaned delicately forward in the stance of wary predation, his nose twitching as it had before. "The touch of God has been here," he said.

I choked on my words, coughing violently before managing a semblance of carefree composure. "Hardly surprising. You said that this plague spreads naturally."

His eyes were bright. "Yes, but this goes beyond natural order. I've not smelled this since... Master?" he asked warily, turning to favor me with his gaze. "My Master is here. I can smell his touch."

Unsure of how to respond - and barely able to, besides - I tugged a perfumed handkerchief from my pocket, wrapping it around my face like a highwayman in a pathetic attempt to banish the rot from my nose. The sweet reek of chemicals was nearly as bad as the smell of death, but my breath returned to me, though my eyes continued to weep anyway. Nodding for us to continue, I pulled the pistol from its place at my waist, checking to make sure that the hammer had not been accidentally pulled into a firing position. If trouble loomed, it would not do to go off half-cocked. I had become attached to what I had below my belt and had no wish to see it truncated by a momentary lapse of judgement. "Which way?" I asked, pointing one way and then the other with my pistol.

His hand flicked out, its aim unerringly indicating a building a short way up the road. Unable to fully comprehend where my human blood-hound pointed, I made my way carefully into the night, whispering for Belial to keep close and silent. He had no trouble with my command, even spitting me with a questioning look as my every step obnoxiously rapped against the cobblestones of the street.

I wished I had thought to bring a lantern along with me, but then I had been surprised by the swift onslaught of darkness, the world conspiring with the stench to smother my senses. But the idea was a day late and more than a few *pfennings* short.

Belial, somehow less affected, made it more than a few steps from me before noticing I was no longer behind him. Glancing back and seeing my apparent discomfort, he ducked to one side of the street, grasping an unused torch that someone had carelessly discarded and handing it off to me. I nodded appreciatively, uncocking and returning the pistol to my waist while I fidgeted with the torch and my tinderbox, retrieved from another pocket.

Coaxing the dark wood into incandescent flame, I loathed and loved the light that suddenly surrounded me. As grateful as I was to be able to see more clearly, I had sacrificed all pretense of stealth, hurrying to the building Belial had indicated, a shop with smashed mirrors and an askance *mezuzah* on the doorframe. Belial was a step behind me, his entire body tense and alert, almost like a hunting dog in the way his face peered for a quarry.

Crossing the threshold, I realized with a sinking feeling that I had managed to find both Abraham's *apotheke* and the source of the stench at the same time. The shelves that had been packed with chemicals and concoctions were broken, their contents strewn about the floor in shattered pieces of offal and glass. I looked over to where I recalled seeing a jar of pickled eyeballs: the containing jar was cracked, a jagged fissure in one side allowing more than a few to pour onto the floor. The fallen eyeballs stared at me emptily, and I fought to suppress the shiver that slunk down my spine.

I despaired at the sight of the shattered shop, knowing that I would have to convey the sad news to Abraham of his livelihood, though I found solace in the fact that the jar was still bleeding liquid. Whoever had trashed the apothecary was still nearby, perhaps hiding in the room at the rear of the building.

Leaving Belial to find whatever he thought important among the detritus of the shop, I crept through the shop, pushing open the half-ajar door between business and the bedrooms beyond. I needn't have bothered, my slow hunt coming up empty but for two bodies messily disassembled in a pile of clothes and blood. I ignored them at first, stepping cautiously over them to examine each dark corner for a murderer hidden in the dark. After finding nothing, I returned to their side, strangely eager to learn more about the two newly deceased.

My skin went cold as I rolled the first body over, seeing the face

of my fellow night watchman Lukas. I had not seen him since our impromptu council meeting, and to come face to face with him now in
such a state stole away any attempt at rational thought. His face, so often arrogant and smug, had none of its usual contempt, his mouth a
frozen rictus of pain and fear, his unseeing eyes wide and bereft of any
kind of conceit. There was a jagged wound on his shoulder, deep and
pulsing yet, crimson oozing from it to fall to the floor in an ever-grow-
ing pool.

His chest fell then, the sigh that escaped from him causing me to fall
away from the corpse in fear. Was he still alive, somehow clinging to
life even after such a terrible gash? Unwilling to approach too quickly, I
ghosted delicately towards Lukas' face once more, tensing as I strained
to hear any other sound from him.

But nothing came. I swallowed hard, forcing the gorge in my throat
down painfully as I tried to explain away this last gasp of life. My mind
spun wildly, beleaguered logic trying and failing to find any good reason behind it all. At length, I realized that no one cared to know besides
my own peace of mind, so I did my best to shift him and my concerns
aside so I could look at the other body beneath him.

I struggled with both until Belial appeared beside the bodies, his
hands full of jars containing all kinds of herbs and minerals. Setting
them aside, he heaved along with me, hauling Lukas aside so I could see
the state of the other victim beneath.

I didn't know the second man, a fact for which I was profoundly
grateful. Whether or not Lukas and I had gotten along, seeing him dead
before me was jarring; it was far easier to pretend to immortality when
the dead were those with whom I had no connection. Muttering some
kind of thanks to Belial, I examined the other man. He had all the signs
of the plague, the edges of his limbs rotted and foul, flesh collapsing in
the disgusting way I had come to associate with the disease. I reached
out to push aside one of his arms when Belial's arm shot out, gripping
my wrist in a steely grip.

"Problem?" I asked cautiously, unwilling to antagonize him with my
hand in his grasp.

"It is not right for you to touch the sinful," he said.

"Belial," I said, attempting - and failing - to extract my arm from him. "Hundreds are dying in the city. I have a duty to heal them, or at the very least learn from them so I can heal Katarina."

But he didn't release me, firmly but gently pushing my extended arm down until it was near my side once more. "Ask me, and I will tell you. I will not allow the tainted to infect the righteous."

I wanted to ask what he meant, but I focused on the more pressing question. "You said that you know how to cure this," I said instead. "How?"

He indicated one of the jars at his side. "Antimony. It allows the soul to hurl the corruption of the plague from the body."

"Poison," I confirmed skeptically. "You want me to believe that the way to save my niece is to sour her further?"

He nodded slowly, sadness plain upon pale skin. "As I told her, I don't do it out of malice but out of God's love for her."

I wanted to say something back at him, anything that could perfectly capture my doubt. Perhaps it was the earnestness in his eyes, or perhaps it was the complete lack of anything productive to say.

Whatever it was, words escaped me, so I said nothing, standing up instead and looking about Abraham and Sarah's now-desecrated home. I wanted to find something to cover up the bodies, to find some pathetic shawl or scrap of cloth that I could use to attempt a measure of a clean-up, but there was nothing that I was comfortable seizing. What if I made a mistake and grabbed something priceless, an heirloom or the like that had been passed from one generation to the next? The blood would ruin anything that touched it, to say nothing of the potential for corruption via illness that ran rampant throughout the home. I'm sure Abraham would accept any attempt at decency for the well-intentioned act it was, but I could already imagine how his face would fall at hearing the state of his house, his way of life.

I had no desire to heap more desecration on his life than already existed.

Resolved to come back with a proper burial for Lukas and the other victim, I nodded to Belial and turned to leave, hearing the soft ringing of jars behind me as he gathered his newly found possessions, slipping them, I'm sure, into the pockets of the clothes I had given him earlier.

Without another word, we left.

XXVI

᠙᠙᠙

A Scuffle in the Dark

The night was as quiet as before, all sound smothered by clouds that now obscured any view of the night sky above. In light of the absent moon, it was somehow colder than before, the night's wind slinking along the city walls, leaping from the shadows to claw at the back of my neck with frigid talons.

I held the torch closer in response, surprising myself with how jealously I clung to the weak heat which stuttered from the burning wood. Belial, noticing my discomfort, asked, "Why do you clutch that so tightly to yourself?"

"What do you mean?" I responded, trying to buy a measure of time to more eloquently answer his question. For some reason, admitting to being cold seemed an infantile, inadequate answer, even if it was true.

But he pressed me in a different fashion. "Why do you feel that you need a light to show you where your feet go?"

"Would you prefer I stagger through the night like a drunk?" I said irritably.

"No," he said, ignoring my tone. "I would have you trust in God to have made the path straight before you."

"I'm not sure that he and I are such good friends," I quipped, shivering as we turned a corner to run face-first into a gust of wind. "Haven't you noticed that I'm not quite as... devout as you?" I finished, unwilling to be more biting in my label. I should have been more genial about the conversation, should have supported Belial's attempts to humanity. But I was cold, and good manners had flown along with my comfort when we had left Abraham's shop. Too much was on my mind: Katarina, Lukas... I had little patience to discuss the divine again.

Despite this, I fought to have at least some kind of civility in my voice. Whether or not I wanted to speak about God, Belial deserved better treatment than what I was giving him. Cold, I led us down a street more covered from the wind than the one we had taken before, a measure of composure returning to me once I no longer felt goosebumps along every bit of exposed skin.

Thoughts of Lukas and the other victim crossed my mind once more. "Belial," I ventured. "You said you smelled your master. It was what sent us to the shop in the first place. I need to know. What we saw back in the *apotheke*... Was that his work?" He nodded, which only prompted me to ask further. "How do you know it is him and not another - I've forgotten what you call yourselves." I admitted.

He smiled gently, the soft expression oddly reverent. "Monarchists," he supplied.

"Of course... How do you know it was him and not another of your group? I'm not sure if you recall, but when you first... came to us, you claimed there would be hordes descending on the city."

He shrugged. "I know the same way that I knew it was him in the first place, Dietrich. Faith." He laughed at my disbelieving expression. "And by scent. The Master's touch smells differently than the rest of ours. It is purer, more divine."

My eyes narrowed, squinting to see in the dark as well as show my skepticism. "Belial, do you really believe what you're doing here is divine? That by killing hundreds, thousands even, you are doing God's work?"

He didn't notice my look, his head twitching again the same way it had before we had come to the *apotheke*. "Dietrich-morsel, we are not alone."

"No?" I asked, peering into the darkness, the torch held before in a vain attempt to see deeper into the night.

"No," he confirmed, a thin arm stretching out to point further along the street. Straining, I could make out dark shapes, barely shadows at all flying in and out of a house, thin and quick as they disappeared inside, bulky and slow as they exited.

"Thieves," I said, feeling my voice wither in distaste. "They're breaking into that house there."

I could feel Belial straining next to me, eager to involve himself but unwilling to go without my express consent. "Morsel, will we do nothing?"

Given the importance of what we currently carried with ourselves, I was tempted to say no. There was an entire city's worth of watchmen to step in, wasn't there? Even if poor Lukas had been responsible for the closest area around Abraham's home, by now we surely must have wandered into another watchman's patrol area. We had more important matters to attend to, the least of which was saving my niece's life

Yet, as callous as it seemed – and was – to think, there was little point in saving Katarina if the city around her fell to pieces while she healed. And the city *was* decayed – there was no doubt about that. I knew that even before Belial had cackled the idea in the pantry weeks ago. It was a wretched, husk of what it could be, a mess of diseased poverty. Its moral character was no better than its physical form, entire sections of the population carved brutally from its own corpse for no other reason than malicious racism.

I shook my head to clear it, desperate to loosen the dark mood. The night was heavy enough without my bitterness. I turned to Belial, in that moment feeling a strange kinship to the cultist. "What would God have of us?" I asked, half in jest, half in seriousness.

He seemed to understand my comment for what it was, a carefully predatory grin whispering into existence. "The Commandments come to mind," he quipped. Even knowing him as I did, my stomach twisted in terror as the torchlight flickered across his face, inhuman shadows dancing and writhing along sharp cheekbones and sunken eyes to create something monstrous.

I forced myself to speak. "Stop them but do not kill them," I ordered. "We show mercy." Belial muttered something, clearly unhappy with allowing 'the Sinful to run rampant without punishment,' but he nodded, which I suppose was good enough.

His – begrudging – acceptance gained, I started forward, drawing the pistol from my waist even as I drew air in to give the thieves a single warning before we charged. But I needn't have bothered, one of the robbers seeing the light of my torch and bellowing out a challenge. Objects rained from his compatriots' hands to clatter to the street, replaced by lengths of metal and wood. I raised my pistol on the off chance that the sight of it would convince them to abandon their break-in. But they took no notice, one even laughing at my implied threat of violence.

Belial raced past me, his hands hooked like claws, his face a feral leer which shocked one of our would-be opponents into flight. Realizing that he would be dreadfully outnumbered by the thieves, I quickened my own pace, drawing a bead as best I could on one of the men on the end of the rough line forming ahead. Drawing the hammer to full cock, I tightened my finger so slowly that the shot even surprised me, my arm jerking as the ball sped down the street to hammer into my target's leg.

He went down with a shriek, one of his fellows dropping to help even as another fled, courage flown in the face of diminishing numbers. I wanted to be pleased at the new odds – one down with three more fled or taken out of the fight, but for every one incapacitated, more remained. My heart in my throat, I realized we had had the misfortune to run into a small army of thugs tonight, and my desire to act morally had overreached against my good judgement.

But Belial did his best to shorten those odds further, throwing himself headlong into the fray, his outstretched arms pulling two over even as he shoulder barged a third to the ground where the reformed cultist pummeled the burglar senseless with great, sweeping blows. Belial barely regained his feet when another struck him full across the face with a powerful blow, the club in the man's hand cracking with the effort. The cultist seemed not to care, another wild strike bowling the man over to whimper on the stoned streets.

Then my world shrank as two men came to attack me, both barrel-chested men who moved with a swiftness that belied their muscled bulk. I half-threw the pistol at one, as much to free my hand as to distract him, bending quickly to snag a discarded pipe while I kept my torch high above my head to ward off the second attacker.

Embers cascaded down, fiery comets flooding my vision as my improvised defense stopped a furious, overhead smash from the other man, a hiss passing from me as skin singed under the heat. I vainly kicked out, off balance and half-blind, earning a high-pitched squeal as I connected with somewhere very delicate on my opponent.

But I was given no time to revel in my success, my opponent's friend rejoining the fray with an oath, swinging and jabbing his club in a riot of feints and assaults. I picked off most of them, doing my best to break up his momentum whenever I could with my own attacks, but more than a few snuck past my guard to thud painfully into my chest and arms. Despite the pain, I knew he would tire soon, so I bided my time, letting his anger and fury exhaust itself before counterattacking.

My window came soon after, a wild, frustrated swing exposing his head and shoulders for a counteroffensive. My arms sore, I whipped my torch arm out wide. Like a moth, his eyes followed instinctively; I had all the time in the world to whip my other arm around in a blow that blasted him to the ground.

Unwilling to beat a man so obviously defeated, I spun back to the melee that continued, unabated, in the middle of the street. Belial had acquitted himself well, a small ring of would-be thieves moaning and writhing on the ground around him. But his success was costing him, two of the remaining footpads on either side of him, gripping him tightly while another pounded him again and again with a length of wood.

Scooping up my pistol from the street, I made a show of shoving a new ball down the barrel, cocking it ostentatiously and shouting, "That's enough!"

The struggle didn't stop immediately, Belial's abuser getting in one final, thunderous strike with his club. I winced as I heard the wood splinter under the force of the blow, though Belial did nothing but grin ferally through it, though his eyes were glazed and unfocused. I ordered them again to stop, my thrusting pistol enough to force into a sullen quietude. "Release him."

I heard footsteps stomp against the stones behind me. Risking a quick glance, I saw more torches, the faces underneath partially in flickering shadow but still recognizable as other members of the city watch sprinted at long last towards the disturbance. "About time," I scowled.

"Sorry," said Herman, the old noble one of the dozen or so watchmen arriving. "We were just at an apothecary near the city walls northeast of here. Lukas..."

"-is dead," I finished for him.

Herman's face scrunched in confusion. "Yes," he said, his head tilting. "How did you know?"

"I was just there. If we hadn't come across this here, I would have informed you," I lied, omitting why and how I had happened upon him. "Looked like he had been attacked."

Herman nodded slowly. "Yes, by some kind of wild beast, it looked like." He scratched at his chin as the other watchmen moved about the scene, collecting the robbers and thieves even as another knelt by Belial's slumped form. I knew the attention was largely unwarranted, having seen Belial's constitution in action more than once before, though for some reason I found the flickering of fear in my guts, genuine concern for his welfare pulsing through me. I wanted to believe that my concern was only as a byproduct for Katarina's well-being, but I knew it for the lie it was.

Murderer or not, cultist or not, I was worried for Belial. Over the past weeks I had come to understand the reason for his rabid fanaticism; even if I could not forgive his actions, he remained as much a victim of the disease as any body discovered in his wake.

I was startled by Herman's jostling of my arm. "What?" I asked, at a loss.

"I said that he should have listened to you. Lukas, that is. He might be alive if he had listened to what you had to say in the tavern." Herman favored me with a sad smile. "There is a bright side to this, at least."

"How do you figure?"

"Lukas was rich, and by all reports he was, more or less, happily married. You were concerned about financing the watch. After this, I doubt his widow will object to using his money to find the culprit behind his murder." I watched him, looking for the punchline in his words, but there was no mirth in his eyes, nothing save a dark, weariness that sunk deeper by the second.

"What was he doing here, anyway?" I asked. "His contributions were always just financial. It doesn't seem like him to have come down from his estate to a random *apotheke* inside the walls." I omitted any foreknowledge of whose shop it was, unwilling to entertain more questions than absolutely necessary. As it was, I could see the way Herman was beginning to peer at Belial, the wheels of his mind turning as he tried to work out the cultist's relationship to me.

"Hm, what?" he asked. "Oh, you haven't heard... The plague isn't just affecting those in the city. There have been reports around the upper echelons of society as well. Rumor has it that the Emperor was infected," he continued, pursing his lips, "but I wouldn't believe that."

"Why not?"

"Because I was with him yesterday. He had some grand war council in preparation for fighting the Turk, not that we needed it." Herman, a loyal Austrian if there ever was one, snorted. "I think he knows that there is something rotten in the city and he's petrified."

"Why?" I asked, confused. "He's one of the most powerful men in the world."

The old man didn't answer at first, interrupted by another of the watch who asked about dispersing the prisoners until someone could set in judgement over them. Addressing the issue quickly, he said, "The Emperor's confessor is convinced that we are in the End Times and is

218 - K. AVARD

filling his head with thoughts of hellfire and brimstone. I want to believe that the emperor isn't listening to his pontificating, but you can see his nervousness. The Emperor I mean. The war council is just a way for him to focus on something concrete, something tangible for him to measure himself against."

I nodded, understanding. Though our paths hadn't crossed in quite some time – what with my self-imposed exile from the imperial court – I still remembered the Emperor's personal priest as a man who saw even the smallest iniquity as cause for eternal damnation. He and I had nearly come to blows back when I had opposed his characterization of the non-Christians in the city as little better than animals. Given how much trouble Christians were causing in the city at this point, I found myself unable to feel anything but cynical bitterness at him.

Trying to distract myself, I nudged Herman again, watching the last of the robbers finally escorted away at dagger point. "I'm sorry I've been away," waving away his assurance that everything was understandable and, he claimed, all right. "You seem to act like this is not uncommon."

His eyebrows rose. "You mean robberies?" He wanted for my nod before giving one of his own. "*Ja*, you know we've always had them, but it has been worse in recent weeks." He shrugged. "You ask them, and they say they're taking only what others have left behind, as if the world has died and been left in trust to them, but their actions have only escalated in the last week or so. We used to have to deal with a cutpurse attacking a drunk... now it's roving armies of them. I won't pretend the city has always been a safe place to live, but with the plague, everything is beginning to come apart at the seams."

He answered the question I gave with my eyes. "It's all coming apart," he repeated, extending one finger after the next. "Some hide. Some flee. Many pray. But some of them let their baser instincts out, and they prey on their fellow man and pretend that it's merely a crime of opportune coincidence. Truth be told, some days I wonder why I bother getting out of bed."

It was a bleak viewpoint, and not one I wanted to consider.

So I said nothing, unwilling to respond to Herman's dark words.

Standing alone together for a time, we watched the last signs of the struggle were cleared away, though its effects on Belial and me would be longer in fading. The old man pointed to Belial. "Mind if I ask who he is?" My ally was, at long last, on his feet, though from the way he swayed back and forth I wondered if he was injured more than I had already thought. Though he had kept his more animalistic nature in check around the other watchmen, I could see his unease being around so many others, many of them as sinful in his eyes as the men we just fought. Despite this, he was admirably restrained, though he shrugged away any attempts at assistance, even when each motion threatened him with an undignified stumble.

"He's a... friend," I said cautiously, unable to completely explain away my thin comrade. "He's from outside the city and has more than a little experience with the plague."

Herman's eyes met mine for a short time, aged wisdom examining me for falsehood, though he quickly broke that off with a shrug. "There's more than a few these days who have come to Wien with that kind of knowledge, it seems."

My expression darkened. "Oh?"

"Yes, I've seen more than a few of those bird-beaked doctors in the last few days. Sometimes by day, sometimes by night when I'm out walking." He smiled wanly at my raised eyebrows. "Yes, with some on the watch getting sick or disappearing altogether, some of us old timers have picked up where the others left off. Anyway, I see them when I'm walking about, always poking at the plague dead. God help me, but I cannot help but think of them like crows."

"Crows?" I asked, my eyebrows meeting in the center of my furrowed forehead. "Why's that?"

"Their appearance for one, their worrying of the dead for another," he said matter-of-factly. "How else could you think of a man who dresses completely in black and is obsessed with a dead man?"

"Well, in that case, I would call him a priest," I said sarcastically. Herman scowled, not appreciating my irreverent humor. Coughing, I tried to gloss over the remark, remembering that Herman had been supportive of me when Lukas had still been alive. I was not blessed with enough friends to go about mocking their beliefs. "Where are they when they are not dealing with the dead?" I asked.

He gave me a shrug, shifting uncomfortably from foot to foot in a way that told me I had pushed too far with my comment. "I don't know. The von Bock's out to the east of the city hosted a few of them for a few days, welcoming them with a rather nice dinner, if rumors are true. I didn't go, of course, busy as I was with a patrol that evening." His shoulders rose and fell again. "Just as well. I heard that the house was stricken with plague soon after the crows left."

I winced. "I hadn't heard anything about that." The von Bocks were a more progressive family in the city, and their support had been invaluable in keeping my sister as head of our family after my parents' passing. "How bad?" I inquired, already knowing the answer.

"Their house is more a memorial for the dead than a manor for the living. Someone said there was a child or two that might have escaped, but I don't know if anyone has gone up there since the stories started. Not even the crows have returned there." We were both quiet a moment.

When Herman finally spoke, his words were weighed down by every one of his years. "I have walked these streets for too many years, Dietrich. I've seen the worst of man at night, and sometimes even during the day. When I see something like this," he said, pointing at the cleaned up scene before us, "I can't help but wonder if it would not be better if we all just picked up and left. Go our separate ways and start over." Shining eyes, slowly feeling with pained tears, turned towards me. "Is that wrong?" he asked, his voice soft and childlike.

I struggled to comfort him, platitudes and cliché falling from my lips in equal amounts. I suppose he was comforted by what I said, which was more than I could say for me. Lukas, the von Bocks... the list of the dead continued to grow while I was powerless to do anything about it.

The last of the attempted robbery was cleared away, one by one the watch returning to their routes until only Belial, Herman, and I stood in the street. Belial, keeping his distance from me so long as I stood near

Herman, gave me a questioning look, clearly eager to be back to the estate and away from other prying eyes.

I nodded wearily, turning towards Herman with my hand extended, a goodnight on my lips. He looked more exhausted than I, looking like little more than an old man dragged down by circumstance, a barely animate corpse going about the pretense of life. Our eyes meeting each other, I looked for any spark of hope, any tiny flame that I could steal for myself.

But there was nothing, so I said goodnight and left him, alone, in the darkness.

XXVII

A Second Lesson

Belial left me to my own thoughts for the rest of our return to the estate, waiting until we crossed over the threshold before he intruded on my deepening depression again. Though part of me thirsted for any kind of companionship to offset the darkness, I didn't wish to endure any further existential questioning.

Not that my new ally had any knowledge of this. "Why didn't we kill those men?" he asked, true confusion coloring his voice.

I tried to sigh, the action causing me to wince in pain as my newly acquired bruises tugged painfully at my mind. "Because killing is easy. And killing is hard." I didn't need to look at him to know I hadn't fully answered his question; I could practically feel his eyes boring into my face, seeking an answer.

Despite my desire to avoid deeper thought, I indulged him. "When you kill a man, he is gone. His opposition to you is gone, yes, but so is everything he stood for. His dreams and goals, his passions, his flaws... all of it dies with him. In killing, you create a world in your image, but who is to say that your world deserves to be the one that exists?"

Though my question was rhetorical, Belial leapt at the chance to interject. "God, of course. His will surpasses all of men's wishes. His plan is everything!" he exclaimed, crossing himself furiously.

"You're far more knowledgeable in terms of Scripture and the Bible, I'm sure," I remarked, meeting his questioning gaze. "But doesn't God tell you to love your neighbor as yourself? Doesn't he say something like 'whatever you do for the least, you do unto me'?"

"Matthew 25:40," he confirmed for me. The torch in my hand, burning low after striving so long against the night, still gave off enough light that I could see him writhe uncomfortably in the grip of my logic. "But God says -"

I flicked a hand to one side, cutting him off. "If God says the most important thing is to love another, then you would believe that you must love, yes?" I waited for the tentative nod. "Like I said, you are likely more learned in the Bible, but I'm sure the bishop would remind you – and me – that the most important commandment is to do unto others as you would have them do unto you."

Our feet tromped up the front steps into the manor house, each hard stride sounding like the final tolling of a judge's gavel. Belial, condemned to deeper thought, only asked one more question of me. "So how does God's will come to pass if the sinful are left unpunished?"

I was at a loss of how to answer at first, or, at least, I was at a loss of how to explain to a man so deep in his faith that what he was doing was wrong. It wasn't that the question was unimportant: as a physician I had struggled with it all through my school, but since then I hadn't given the matter much thought outside of the faithless moral code that I sought to practice. Nodding a greeting to the yawning doorman, I waved Belial upstairs back towards Katarina's room.

"Condemn them to life," I decided. "Let the sinful be punished by God at his leisure and not at yours."

I don't think he expected my answer, for he stopped short on the stairs as my words hit him harder than any of the would-be thieves had earlier. Waiting until I reached the top of the staircase before I turned around, relishing the thunderstruck expression on his face. I saw in the surprise the shattered reflection of a man whose entire worldview had come crashing down in front of him. There was pain there, true, but pain healed in time.

But I was more concerned with the tiny spark I saw in his face. It was barely a whisper: even calling it a whisper would see it fly into nothingness, so insubstantially did it lay on his face. It defied any label I could have laid at its feet, but that it existed at all breathed fresh life into my own ailing flame of hope.

Trying to reassure him, I waved him forward. "Come. We have a child to save."

XXVIII

A Second Crow

Though we had only been gone only a few hours at most, I found myself surprised by how similar the room looked to just before we had left. My sister, still the doting mother, was perched on the edge of the bed, whispering something soft and obviously soothing to my niece. Max still knelt by the bed next to Wilderich, his head bowed and hiding behind his praying hands.

And my niece... She still lay in her bed. A part of myself had prayed – there was that strange idea again, praying – that somehow I would come back and I would find her up and about, scampering around with Freddie trailing gamely behind, that innocent, wicked giggle brightening a house so recently depressed by the death outside its doors. I had hoped that somehow the sickness would leave her alone, knowing that she was too pure, too young to take so soon.

But that was a hope as frail as she was now, and there was little point in wishing for that which wouldn't come true. Very little came to those who laid in simple expectation. Or, at least, nothing worth having came in such effortless dreaming. Scars healed, but not before drawing their own price in blood and pain.

So lost in thought, I almost missed the dark shadow perched at my sister's shoulder, half-hidden despite the light scattered by the lit fire-place and the bright candles burning merrily from their place along the walls.

At first I thought it was Michel, that somehow Wilderich had scoured the city and found the plague doctor in the time it had taken us to go to Abraham's and come back, but there was a leanness to the shape, though the same wide brimmed hat hid his face, the same corvus -beaked masque considered me dispassionately from the bureau next to Katarina's bed.

The face underneath the hat was that of a foreigner, though the skin tone was unlike that which I had ever seen before. Though he possessed the same high cheeks of someone from the Kemet deserts in Africa, his skin was pasty white, closer to alabaster than the obsidian I would have expected. "Who're you?" I asked.

"Kalb," he said, inclining his head deferentially.

"Kalb... no last name?" I peered at his face carefully. There was something recognizably hidden from me, an unknown commonality to something I had seen before, but I was unable to place my finger on it. Other than being a shockingly pale African, there was little remarkable about him as far as I could tell.

His answer was syrupy but falsely eloquent, the words coming with the steady rhythm of long practice. "None, my lord. I am a humble doc-tor, here to heal the sick and to tend to the ill. I need no last name to commit myself to my life's work." He seemed bored with my considera-tion, his eyes flicking away from me.

They flitted around the room, settling first on Belial where they nar-rowed slightly as he considered the thin man next to me. It might have been a trick of the light, but something in his face seemed to be ignited by the sight of my companion. It vanished an instant afterwards, Kalb smothering his interest in Belial as his eyes were torn forcefully away back to my niece where she lay in her bed. "She has not been ill long," he said with the calm knowledge of extensive experience, "but she must be bled soon before the disease spreads further."

I felt my own eyes narrow, but Sophie made the comment before I could. "My daughter is *not* going to be bled." She raised a hand towards Kalb even as the pale African opened his mouth, forestalling his reply. "I realize that I am no doctor, but I find it hard to believe that there is wisdom in letting all of her humors if just one is out of balance."

The candles reflected dully from Kalb's eyes. "With respect, Baroness, but like you say, you have not the experience with this malady. If you want your child to remain here in suffering, then by all means, let some charlatan whisper magical prayers over her." His eyes, previously so bored, flared again as they turned towards Wilderich and Max from their place by the bed. "I'm sure God will know the pure from the sick when she goes to his side."

"Then thank you for your time, but for now I would like you to leave." I admit my mind had conceived the words, but it was Sophie who voiced them, her own voice hard and cold. "I would like my daughter to rest in peace and be without the excitement of so many outsiders in the room."

I watched Kalb consider and reject several responses, his lips carefully parting and then pressing themselves together once more. He settled on saying nothing, merely gathering his beaked mask from the dresser where he had left it and heading for the door, all the while muttering unintelligible somethings under his breath. He paused only once, a miniscule, momentary pause as he strode past Belial, each pale man staring the other deep in the face for an infinite second, and then he was gone, disappearing into the night.

I felt myself relax once the sound of his footsteps had faded, my shoulders sagging in relief as the breath I had held in my chest escaped me at last. Given his claimed title of doctor, I was unsettled by how little he acted like one, the vehemence in his voice uncomfortably bitter given the stakes at hand. "What was that?"

My question, meant for the entire room, was fielded by Wilderich from his place by the bed. "I am sorry," he winced, getting slowly to his feet. "After you left, I went to look for Michel. Like I said to you, I thought that his wisdom would be helpful in healing Katarina." That had been putting it mildly, but I didn't interrupt him. "I didn't go too

far from the estate when I crossed paths with Kalb. He had been examining another plague site and I asked for him to come and examine
Katarina."

"I didn't see much examining just now," I replied, flicking a look
back at Belial for his nod of confirmation. The thin man's eyes were distant, dark eyes glassy and unfocused as he acknowledged me from wherever his mind wandered.

"No," said Sophie from her place by the bed. "He spent most of his
time here telling me that we needed to drain the evil humors from her."

"Like he said, bloodletting," I confirmed. "I agree with you, Soph. I
don't know how draining her will make her better."

"He lies," said Belial from behind me, his words soft, as if his voice
was as far from the room as his mind was. "Letting her life-water drain
will kill her faster and not slower." He shook his head, his gaze refo-
cusing on us as he pulled the antimony from his pocket. "She must be
purged with antimony."

I was amazed that the jar had not broken after our engagement with
the robbers in the streets earlier. He gave me a soft smile. "I removed it
before we stopped the wicked." When my head tilted in confusion, he
let his smile grow. "Do you really think I would risk damaging her cure
to stop the smallest piece of evil elsewhere?"

I felt my lips twist upwards without conscious thought, touched by
his foresight as well as his concern for Katarina. "No, I suppose not," I
answered, the response lame and inadequate, but there was nothing else
to say.

"Pardon me," interjected Sophie icily. "The wicked? Antimony?
What happened tonight?" she asked, rising at last from the bed to cross
over to us.

I waved her away gently. "I'll tell you later," I promised. "Suffice it to
say, Belial saved my life earlier, and we can trust him to save Katarina's
as well." In and of itself, it wasn't a true lie, more a modification of circumstance which might still any further questions from my sister.

I could see her want to question me further, but she said nothing,
holding her own council as she crossed over to the thin man who cast

his eyes down towards the ground. Reaching out her hand, palm to the floor, she bid him drop to his knees. He nearly fell in his haste to obey. Laying her hand on his head, she drew herself up to her full height. "Belial, I take you into my house and into my family. When you came to us, it was as a captive and murderer. Though you still wear this second label, by risking your life for my brother – idiot though he is – you have earned a place here. Will you work for this family and this house until the end of your days?"

I was unsure exactly where her words came from; household servants were contracted employees in the service of my family long before my parents had died. If anything, Sophie's words sounded more like some archaic ceremony of binding, more an enslavement than an employment. But if Belial minded, he gave no sign, his eyes streaming as he lifted his head to nod upwards at her.

Mollified by the simple answer, Sophie nodded back. "Then stay here tonight and fulfill your promise to Katarina." Not waiting for a response, she turned away to look at me. Her face, for so much of recent memory unsure and stricken by sympathetic pain, had hardened, a measure of logical calm returning to her cool eyes. There remained the anguish of a terrified mother, but I took heart in the fact that she at least pretended to her former level-headedness. "Dietrich, can I see you and Wilderich outside, please? Max, would you remain here to assist Belial if he needs help?"

I saw Max's face twist into a grimace, my friend not immediately comprehending that he was an assurance of Belial's good behavior while we spoke outside. But he obeyed regardless, standing and taking a protective stance on one side of the bed even as Belial shifted around to the other. I took heart from the utter lack of bestiality in the cultist's movements, one hand moving with a surgeon's care to comfort the coughing child while the other opened the jar of antimony. "Dietrich-morsel? Would you have someone heat water and bring a medical mortar and pestle up for me?"

He turned away before I responded, but, then, he already knew that I would agree to do as he asked. Retreating to the hallway, I called his instructions down to a servant lingering by the foot of the staircase, confident that someone would be up shortly with the requested water and equipment.

Turning back to my sister and Wilderich, I found them already deep in conversation. "...I have to say, Baroness, I was... surprised as your actions just now. Wasn't this the same monster who killed dozens and, indeed, almost killed your brother!"

"And who, tonight, saved him." Sophie's mouth drew tightly across her face in response to the bishop's implied criticism. "If you had heard the story I had heard earlier, I would think you could find a bit of mercy and pity in your heart, Wilderich." It was a small thing, omitting his title, but I heard Sophie's voice taking the moral high ground. "Belial is a monster, but one that was created in part by circumstance."

"And that is enough to rescue him from punishment?" asked the bishop. "Surely he deserves to be thrown back into the pantry where we left him, not given the keys to the proverbial castle."

I cut in, trying to defuse the situation. "I think my sister is trying to note that we would be little different, had we been exposed to the trials and tribulations he had been." In truth, I was sure she was indirectly taking a swipe at the Church for tacitly allowing Belial's abuse to happen, but I admit I still didn't know the whole story, having had to step out to speak to Wilderich before.

"All the same..." sulked Wilderich, folding his hands before him.

"Anyway," said Sophie. "I asked the two of you out here because I am a little confused about something." She stared at us both briefly, chewing at her lip in a moment of nervous insecurity as she composed her thoughts. "Realizing, of course, that we are operating completely in the dark in how we are attempting to treat this plague, why is it that those who *do* have experience in the matter are not agreeing?"

The discussion of treatment caused me to realize that two rather important figures in the discussion were absent. "Where are Abraham and Sarah?"

"While you and Belial were away, an order of monks arrived. I believe they were called the 'Brotherhood of the Holy Trinity'...?" Her voice trailed off as she looked over to the bishop for support.

He nodded slowly. "They are a smaller order of the Church's somewhat more misguided Orthodox brethren." I considered remarked on his gentle criticism but discarded the thought almost instantly. Wilderich had come a long way since my meeting him weeks ago, and while his assumed position of moral superiority irked me, it was a far cry from the intolerance he had shown earlier.

Sophie's eyebrow curled in confusion. "I was under the impression that they were Catholic by nature? You're saying they are Orthodox? Don't members of the Eastern Church dress very differently from you?" she indicated his cassock and cope, the long cape almost dragging along the floor.

Her confusion passed to Wilderich, the short man's head tilting as he mulled over her thoughts. "Didn't they wear all black and have longer beards?" I tried to call an image of any Orthodox holy man to mind and failed.

Sophie had no answer either. "I don't remember. I've been a little focused with Katarina." She shrugged, shaking her head. "In any case, they have arrived in the city, come to ease the pain and suffering of the diseased. They asked if I would support them in establishing clinics and hospice-houses."

"Support them how?" I asked.

"Money, mostly, but they welcomed anything I would be able to spare. Cloth for bandages, grocers who might be equally sympathetic..."

Wilderich snapped his fingers from his place next to us, an answer finally realized as Sophie and I had had our side conversation. "Ah, Trinitarians! Yes, there is a small group of them, recently arrived from Roma. I admit I expected them early next year. They were to have journeyed here after celebrating the Advent season with the Holy Father." He rubbed his hands together, the action almost gleeful in its innocence, his eyes flickering to Sophie. "Baroness, if you'll allow me to go and meet with my brothers..."

"In a moment," she said. "As it is, how could we be sure that they are not your misguided cousins the Orthodox? I wouldn't want you to be forced into an uncomfortable situation." She gave a small smile as he scowled, a hand extending to pat him on the shoulder comfortingly. "Let Abraham be a liaison for now. He seemed overjoyed at the prospect of working with them and they seemed willing to work with a Jewish man. I'm sure you'll have a chance to speak with them more soon. For now, can we return to my question?"

"On why two plague doctors differ so widely in their pattern for treatment, and why they differ from Belial's intended decision?" I asked, shrugging myself. "It isn't entirely unreasonable that more than one way exists to fight something like this plague. But I'm a little uneasy myself. There is something that doesn't follow in my mind."

"Only one thing?" quipped Sophie, drawing another smile from me. I could see her old self returning in spite of all that was happening with Katarina. I knew she was concerned, but she had managed to divorce her fear for now, sinking her teeth into the question here in front of her.

"If we're talking only about their medical approaches, yes, one thing. If we're talking about them in terms of their character and actions, then my list grows somewhat."

"Why?" asked Wilderich.

"They are a little... morbid, aren't they?"

"Of course," said the bishop. "Can you expect them to be any other way, being around death so often?"

"Are you more right because you have a man's moral authority?" asked Sophie pointedly, daring the bishop to deny her reasoning. Wisely, Wilderich said nothing, instead folding his hands again and shifting uneasily from foot to foot.

"My point being," I cut in, as much to save Wilderich as to return our conversation to something resembling a clear direction. "is that we've met only two of them, so this may be premature, but isn't is strange that they are as pale as death itself? And they seem equally dismissive of any action other than what they suggest, despite claiming to have come across this plague dozens of times? Add in their claimed knowledge of every subject and it paints a somewhat awkward picture."

Sophie nodded immediately, though Wilderich conceded the point only after scratching at his chin. "I suppose that is a little strange. You *did* mention that Michel seems to have extensive knowledge of the history of the city, though I'm remembering now that he had an awful lot of questions about the city itself when he first arrived."

"What's more..." I continued. "Has the situation in the city gotten any better since they've arrived? I mean, I know it's been only a few days, but as far as I know more people are dying than ever. Entire streets sit in the dark because the city watch has been ravaged. I saw Herman before," I told Sophie. "I was told that one of these doctors visited the von Bocks and that barely a few days later the entire dynasty was devastated by the plague. He says that robbery and disorder is becoming more rampant." I pointed at my side. "Belial and I ran into some before; I have the bruises to prove it. The entire city reeks of death and disease."

Wilderich grimaced. "It's true," he allowed. "I've had little time to minister to the poor, or at least to the living poor. Far too many are lying cold in the Magadalenskapelle."

"Are these doctors inept then?" I wondered aloud.

A dark shadow fell across Sophie's face, her next words drawing a shiver from me. "I don't know that I was ever considering this, but is it possible that the doctors have a more sinister purpose for being here other than healing?"

Her unwelcome realization shattered all rational thought as each our minds fled in terror from the idea. Why an entire group of doctors would descend on a city and then do nothing to stop a disease? "Belial told me something a short while ago... He said that 'Doctors and physicians are curious things... They are made to heal, who's to say what they'll heal.'" I looked at the others.

"I think it's long past time we went to see the Emperor."

XXIX

A Royal Welcome

The Hofburg had not always sprawled like it did now. Once – centuries ago – it had served a more serious purpose, the tall peaked towers at the corners defending the personage of the emperor and his dependents from peasant and prince alike. The towers were still there, though the narrow slits that had once existed to defend the palace had widened to become something more welcoming and yet somehow cautiously opaque.

I had loved that version of the palace as a child, had marveled at the way the building stood, structured and proud, among the ocean of low buildings that lapped gently at the edge of the palace complex. It was an island of order in the city that had seemed so overwhelming and huge, a sole place of constancy, a haven of something permanent.

That version of the palace was gone now. No, gone was the wrong word, but it was concealed behind a brand new wing constructed, it had been said, to house the Emperor's wine cellar. Even if that particular rumor was untrue, there was a hideousness to the entire extension. It had nothing to do with the building itself, I suppose: the exterior of it was beautiful enough, clear and crisp lines of architecture giving way to an ordered symmetry.

My dislike of it had come from what it did to the old building that had stood so tall and proud. While it was ordered, complete unto itself, it had ripped all symmetry from the stately Hofburg, the now-Emperor's vanity reflected in the breadth of the entire expansion.

"I've always hated this place," I complained. "It's too pompous."

Sophie laughed at one elbow, while Wilderich fidgeting with a handful of cloth at the other. "Too pompous?" laughed my sister. "Don't you pay attention to where your own life is lived?"

I shrugged, conceding the point silently even as I stood my ground vocally. "Yes, but I didn't have an entire wing of a palace constructed to suit my own sense of grandeur."

"He's the Emperor!" interjected the bishop nervously, looking around to see if anyone else had noticed my irreverence. In truth, I had never seen him so deferential, any pretense or air of superiority gone. His voice dropped to a hushed whisper. "You need to show him some respect, Dietrich."

"Since when?" I asked. "He's the pampered son of a pampered son who's never had to do a hard day's work in his life."

"Again, little brother," cut in Sophie impishly. "How does that make him different than you exactly?"

"I'm not sure how you enjoy this so much," I complained, inwardly pleased that she was in so fine a mood. To tell the truth, I was as well. Though Katarina remained ill, Belial had given her something. 'A draught to draw the curse of God from her' had been his words, the words themselves doing little for me but somehow inspiring my niece to cease coughing for long enough to fall asleep.

"I enjoy it because it is the only battlefield where I am believed to be an equal to a man," replied Sophie easily.

Wilderich, still uncomfortable, tried to put on a brave face, injecting, "My dear Baroness, if any man doesn't believe you his equal, then he is a fool."

"Very kind of you to say," thanked my sister, looking past me to smile at the bishop, who blushed in return. "But there are so many arenas in which I am seen as somehow weaker than my more masculine counterparts. So I play the fool where I have to when I have to. This is one of those arenas where I do not have to do so."

"Soph, you know that I wish you could have had all the opportunities I have had as a man, but sometimes I feel lucky that you are only as powerful as you are. Could you imagine you with an acknowledged university education and not just the personal education gained through your devouring of father's library? You'd be ruling this empire!"

She made a big show of considering the idea. "Empress Sophie... I like it."

We all shared a laugh, the good humor defusing the tension enough that Wilderich managed to finally let go of the fabric he had been kneading between his fingers for the last while. I took a moment to rehearse my case; everything would need to be perfect if we were to gain some imperial assistance in combating the plague.

With luck, our visit would only be one of the many calling for the Emperor Leopold to involve himself in the affairs of the city and would ultimately not be necessary. After all, was there any possible way he could stand by and do nothing? The city was dying around him. It was, part of me said, a formality that we even needed to go before him and ask for help.

But then, the last weeks had hardly been marked by anything approaching good luck. Though I wanted to be hopeful, a more cynical piece of me recalled that the welfare of the city lay in the hands of a man who was more concerned with the ejection of the Jewish population than establishing any means by which he could help the poor who thronged to the city on a weekly basis.

"Whatever you're thinking, stop it," chided Sophie, reading the dark expression covering my face.

"Am I that transparent?" I asked, already knowing what she would say.

"To anyone else? No, I've seen more expression in some particularly dense rocks, but I'm your sister and have had to deal with your moods more than anyone else has had to suffer through them. You are practically an open book to me."

"Meanwhile there are times that I don't have a single clue of what goes through your mind," I answered honestly. "And I think you take no small amount of joy in that."

My sister's face became almost unreadable, save the roguish hint of playfulness in her eyes. "I have no idea what you're talking about," she claimed.

I nodded, letting the matter drop as we approached the entrance to the palace proper. A footman at the door stopped us. "Can I help, my lord? If you are here unannounced, you may be disappointed to find that the Emperor isn't receiving petitions today. I'm very sorry." The man ducked his head as if he expected me to scream at him.

I admit that the urge did come to mind, but I knew that the footman was hardly the reason for the disappointment. Nevertheless, I let me voice chill by several degrees. "He isn't? Not even for a personal adviser for his Majesty."

The servant peered at me cautiously. "And who might you be, my lord? I'm afraid I don't recognize you."

I opened my mouth to speak, but Wilderich stepped forward, sliding carefully in front of me. "You may not recognize him, my son, but I'm sure you recognize me?" Extending one hand laden with heavy rings, the short man tried to draw himself up to his inconsiderable height. If one squinted at him without taking his liturgical vestments into account, he might have been confused for an extremely civilized gopher pretending at humanity.

Indeed, I would have laughed had the servant not looked so stricken as he plunged swiftly to one knee and made the sign of the cross. "Of course, your Excellency. I apologize." His voice became small as he meekly took Wilderich's hand and brushed his lips across one of the rings there. "Will you bless me, Lord Bishop?"

Wilderich smiled benevolently. "But of course, Antal. Just remember that we missed you at Mass this past weekend." He raised both hands over the kneeling man's head, whispered Latin phrases escaping from his lips. Finishing, he made the sign of the cross, and called the man back to his feet. "Now, I understand the that Emperor may not be receiving petitions about earthly matters, but surely the Holy Church needs no introduction, having bestowed on his line the right to rule?"

Now I smiled, though I worked to keep it as tiny as I could, coughing when the muscles of my face threatened to force me to grin more broadly. Though he pretended to be nothing but a humble man of heaven, I couldn't help but see the manipulative streak in Wilderich. Though he lacked the ability to deftly maneuver in the more noble social circles, with the lower classes he wielded his influence as I might use a scalpel. Honestly, when all was said and done, I was the least socially skilled of our party, yet for some reason both the others deferred to me.

And now was not the time to dwell on the subject, I realized, our steps very quickly eating up the distance and a chamber ahead guarded by two perfectly poised soldiers in crisp clean uniforms. Armed ceremonially with pikes, each wore a grim expression that allowed for no deviation from their duties. As we approached, each tilted their weapon towards the other, barring our way in a dully gleaming barrier of steel.

I stepped forward, nodding a congenial welcome; less adept or not, if I was the head of our conspiracy, then the Emperor needed to hear my voice seeking an audience, not my sister nor the bishop. "Gentlemen, I need to see his Majesty."

My tone was clearly different than the officious attitude so many others gave them, as evidenced by the way the men looking at one another in mute confusion. "Do you have an appointment?" asked the one on the right eventually.

"No, I do not, but then I wouldn't have been let in by the doorman if I had not come on the most vital of missions, would I?" Our passing the doorman had nothing to do with anything, but I saw a chance to inflate our importance and took it. When neither one looked mollified, I asked, "Is there something the matter?"

"Well," began the one on the right.

"Keep quiet," said the left. "Excuse me, my lord. Your Excellency, my lady," he nodded to each Wilderich and Sophie in turn before sliding the door into the chamber beyond a crack and slipping through. I managed only a quick glimpse of figures rushing one way and then the other before the door closed, but I was surprised by the lack of sound that came from the room beyond.

But if I had hoped to wonder more completely as to the lack of sound, I was interrupted as the other guard intrude politely on my thoughts. "I'm sorry, my lord," said the remaining guard ruefully, flushing slightly as the guard tried to apologize for his less polite comrade. "There has been more than a little activity here in the last few days..." His face reddened further as he realized who he was speaking to with altogether too much familiarity. "Sorry, my lord," he muttered again.

"It's alright," I nodded agreeably. "Please, I've been away from the court for a while. Feel free to tell me more about what has been going on in my absence." Far truer than my last comment, I was relieved to see his shoulders sag gratefully: I would get more information out of him if he felt at ease.

The guard shifted his posture slightly, but it was enough that his pike stopped being a weapon and now became a walking staff for the tired, middle-aged man standing guard in front of me. Leaning heavily against the wooden shaft, he grimaced. "The sergeants, they won't let us out of the barracks except to patrol on their orders, so when we do..." His face twisted further, his skin practically sweating his fear through every pore. "The city is changing, lord. The streets are falling apart. Bodies everywhere. It smells, lord, like..."

The guard fell silent as the door opened back up, his companion returning with a deep scowl on his face. "I have been instructed to let you in to see the royal personage." The returning guard didn't look happy with this result, his anger only seeming to deepen as he saw his opposite number leaning on his pike rather than at painful attention.

"Thank you very much," I said equitably, as much to one guard for 'his' permission as to the other his information, little as it was. I received nods from each, one cold, the other as warm as my thanks. Retreating slightly to either side of the nod, my conversation companion reached out to tug the door open for our small group. Tugging at the hem of my coat, I straightened my appearance as best I could, looking to Sophie for her confirmation that all was in order before I entered the chamber before me.

Though I had not been at court in quite some time, I was surprised by the scene which greeted me on the other side of the doors. I was struck by the utter lack of dramatic vitality, the usual gaggle of nobles courted and scheming with one another utterly absent as I watched servants, each laden down with a chest or an artifact of some unknown importance, rush this way and that. It had all the appearance of a disturbed anthill, every chain of servants another train of mad insects scrambling around as their home was assaulted by some strange, unknowable invader.

More surprising was the lack of regal authority in the room, the vacuum of power almost tangible as I could not see the dark, haughty shape of the Emperor anywhere in the chamber. There was, in fact, no one at all in either of the chairs at the far end of the room, the thrones of both Emperor and Empress lifelessly standing sentry over the processions waving in and around each other.

My heart fell as I wondered why we had been admitted at all when a voice called off from one side of the room. "Sophie!" I turned to see my sister peel away from my shoulder to approach a beautiful young woman who detached herself from the servant caravans to embrace her warmly. Blonde curls, collected into two soft mounds on the side of a face that was severe yet affectionate, shook gently as my sister made some small comment that drew a laugh from the woman. The laughter died away as the woman turned to consider both Wilderich and me, dark eyes analyzing me from head to foot, a carefully contained intellect weighing and measuring every move that I made.

I would have been smitten immediately with her had my sister not spoken then. "Dietrich, this is Empress Elenore Magdalene Therese." Struggling to keep my mouth from falling open, I managed to awkwardly drop into a low bow, taking the offered hand in mine and brushing the back of it with my lips respectfully.

"Oh stop," said the blonde woman. "I'm not Empress yet, you know."

"Are you married to the Emperor?" asked my sister, waiting only for a brief, regal nod before continuing. "Then you're the Empress."

"Well, until I am officially given my title by the Emperor's sycophantic advisors, please call me by the name my parents bestowed on me," said the Empress – Elenore, I supposed – gently. I felt myself warm to her complete lack of pretension; where other upper-crust figures condescended to the lower tiers, she had descended delicately, brushing aside social convention and established protocol.

Given Wilderich's sharp intake of breath, I half-expected him to protest vehemently at this equality between the royal family and lower nobility. But he covered well, moving another step closer and bowing with a grace that belied his expansive middle. "My lady, I am sure you do not remember me but we met when you first graced our humble city –"

Elenore cut him off, but the interjection was as gracefully as she had been up until now. "Bishop Wilderich! Of course I remember you. My husband speaks fondly of your work with the poor and the sick. I think he is secretly jealous of your commitment as a hallmark of what it means to be a good Christian. I've discovered that far too often God's word is corrupted by those who would seek to elevate themselves instead of debasing themselves in service."

It was likely a lie, but it drew a deep blush from the bishop nevertheless. "My lady," he stammered, caught wrong-footed. "I seek only to match your good example."

She laughed, a merry sound that shattered the solemnity of the largely lifeless room. "Oh... you're too kind. Though I do wonder sometimes what would have happened had my parents not allowed me to become the nun I always aspired to be."

I was confused, my puzzlement apparently plain on my face as my sister leaned on to whisper *sotto voce*, "Even as a child, Elenore asked the less fortunate to treat her as one of them and not as one of noble birth." She turned slightly towards her friend. "I have even heard that your translation is about done?"

"Translation?" asked Wilderich.

"Yes, but I wouldn't make too much of it. It's a minor thing really," admitted Elenore humbly. "I just believe that the people deserve to read God's word as his holy men preach it to them."

"You translated the Bible?!" I asked, incredulous. It was a task that I had thought beyond any layperson. Even Gutenberg had not tried such a thing, contenting himself with revolutionizing the replication of the written word.

The Empress merely shrugged, the huge accomplishment humbly shifted aside with the motion. "Please, it's nothing." She looked away, truly embarrassed for a moment before returning her gaze to each of us in turn. "But what can I do for you? The guard was somewhat vague when he announced you."

I coughed, as much to clear my throat as to cover my own shame. "We had hoped to speak with the Emperor actually. As I'm sure you are aware, the plague has been making a mockery of the city's health."

She nodded. "Yes, hundreds are dead. I believe that one of the visiting doctors told my husband that the situation would get worse before it got better unless their methods for healing were used."

My heart sank. "They have been here already?"

"Who, the masked doctors?" asked Elenore. "Yes, they were here only a few days ago. Put quite the fear of God into my husband: he's already retreated from the city, although I cannot help but wonder if fled wouldn't be a better word to use." She and Sophie shared a grim chuckle. "He was quite insistent that his physicians and healers in the city take the advice of the traveling doctors." Her eyes narrowed then. "You make it sound like their visit was less boon and more blasphemy."

My sister leapt to my defense. "We are beginning to ask questions about these doctors and their methods for healing. The first to arrive, Michel, told us that the best way to heal the sick was to expose the healthy to them before the affliction spread. Another, Kalb, told me that the ideal treatment would be to bleed the sick of the evil in their souls."

"Kalb? An Arab in Wien? These are certainly strange times when a Muslim is not beaten from the city as soon as he arrived."

"It helps, Ele, that he is as pale as you or I. Honestly, I would not have known myself if he had not come to my estate when my oldest, Katarina, fell sick."

"Oh, no... How is she?" inquired the other woman, concern plain in her darkening face.

"She is... stable," I said, nodding in apology to Sophie for cutting in. "We are trying another treatment that may breed some results, but we are suspicious of this wave of masked men. They have been here how long? A week? Given how swiftly the sickness kills, surely they would have known some manner of success by now. And, yet, for all their planned treatments, matters are worse than they had been before they arrived!"

The Empress' mouth drew tightly across her face, lips pencil thin. "I admit I have been lucky enough to not have had this to cross my path personally, but I have heard stories. Flesh rotting in what feels like the blink of an eye, a cough that kills quicker than the cold, the arteries of the body engorging themselves on corrupted fluid. I have heard about the marks about each of the dead's chests: two angry welts, like the bite of a viper."

"Angry welts?" I interrupted, muttering an apology when Elenore's face momentarily hardened at the harsh intrusion. "I'm sorry, but we have not seen those manner of marks in quite some time."

"'Quite some time,'" she repeated. "Maybe you might tell me exactly what it is you know?"

How long I spent relaying the story up until then, I do not know. I do know that we retired to an adjacent chamber, one that would usually otherwise host the royal family between court visits by dignitaries or otherwise. Servants came in and went after delivering small goblets, each one filled with a delicate wine cut with a measure of water. I know that I spoke for most of the tale, my only breaks taken when hoarseness drove me to the drink in my hands.

I was struck by the way Elenore considered our tale, sitting back in her chair and absorbing everything said with barely a nod. Though it was not immediate, I could see more than a few parallels between my sister and her, the thought of which sent an odd chill coursing through me. Even as a son of a more progressive family, I admit to feeling superior to most women in many things. In between the short pauses I took, I absently wondered if perhaps man's primacy in the world was a sham, predicated on the notion that women, supposedly our inferior in all things not dealing with the reproductive, were too busy to seize power from us. What could a ruler like Elenore or my sister, unencumbered by the weight of masculine posturing, achieve?

Elenore appeared to read my mind, for she smiled surreptitiously at me, her face falling back to a more serious expression a moment before she asked me, "Why do you trust this Belial individual more than these doctors? He sounds more like a beast than a brother-in-arms."

Wilderich nodded smugly from his side of the table, while Sophie and I gave more noncommittal shrugs. "It's hard to say, Ele," said my sister. "I imagine if you had heard his story, you would feel altogether less animosity towards him. And I should know, considering how close I came to blowing his head apart with a pistol."

One regal eyebrow arched carefully. "A pistol? I know you and I are willing to go far to accomplish our goals, but that seems a little extreme, Soph."

I was surprised to hear someone refer so familiarly to my sister, but, then again, the two seemed on a vastly different level of intimacy. "You stay more in the light, Elenore: you are favored by God and the Emperor's wife needs to keep her hands clean. I am less constrained and, in the face of a perpetually absent husband, I am forced sometimes to resort to more definite means of achievement."

"But murder?" accused the Empress, crossing herself.

"You wanted to be the nun, not me," coolly replied the Baroness. "But morality aside... Elenore, there is something wrong about these doctors. You must be able to see it yourself. Their color, their extreme methods of healing."

"More than poisoning with things such as antimony?" Elenore held up her hands to forestall an objection. "Forgive me, I am just trying to poke holes in your argument to better understand myself. Playing the devil's advocate, if you'll forgive the phrase, your Excellency."

Wilderich made a sign of the cross playfully. "See that you are off to confession after this meeting and you have earned my grace, my child."

"Maybe we might be a little more serious?" I asked somewhat harshly. "Not to be too abrupt, but there are people dying every day and we are doing precious little about it."

XXX

A New Convert

Sophie and Wilderich spitted me with glares, but Elenore contritely nodded. "You're right to be angry, Dietrich. At last report, I have heard over two thousand have died, and more have and will have died by the time we are done speaking here. Knowing that, is your visit here still a waste? Is the occasional pun to give hope not worth a life or two while we determine what might be done?"

It was a deft retort and I bowed my own head in embarrassment. "Of course, Empress," I replied formally, acknowledging my lack of social grace. "But returning to the matter at hand? Antimony is a rare case of treatment, but there are mentions of its use as far back as the Romans in treating poisons and afflictions of the body."

"Yes, as a purgative, occasionally used to purge the soul of imperfection," she said, impressing me once more with her knowledge. It truly was uncommon to be speaking with someone with so wide an awareness and I understood why and how my sister connected with her so easily. Different sides of the same coin, light and dark mixed in them perfectly, one balancing the other.

"A purgative?" quizzed the bishop. I mimed the bodily response antimony encouraged, wincing as Wilderich turned a delicately putrid color of green. "And that's what Katarina is undergoing right now?" I nodded, and he made the sign of the cross again, this time without his previous good humor. "Poor child."

I nodded, returning my gaze to the Empress. "Belial is a murderer and a cultist of the worst kind but-"

"You mentioned the name of the group was the Monarchists?" interjected Elenore. I managed a short nod before she went on. "I want to return to that as well, but please, you were saying?"

"Belial is a murderer, but his identity is intensely tied to being a part of something. While I can't claim to be an expert, I wouldn't be surprised if he joined the Monarchists because they promised him a family of sorts. Given his history, he wouldn't know any different from his destructive past."

"So why would he be more inclined to cooperate if they have already given him a purpose, a set of miraculous abilities...?"

I shrugged, but Sophie picked up where I could not answer. "Belial seems to identify my brother as his advocate, a protector in a way – especially after my admittedly hasty attempt on his life. He rushed to save Dietrich last evening while they were away securing the antimony when they were set upon by would-be robbers. What's more, he seems to have formed a strange connection to Katarina. He sees her as pure, even where some of our other visitors have not."

Elenore mused on this for a time. "It is strange to me that he seems to be repeating a lot of the same rhetoric as a number of the doctors," she said eventually. "Though I can't begin to imagine why or how they are in league, maybe you're right and there is something more sinister at hand here." One delicate finger rose to tap at her chin, unexpectedly pulled away after a few quick touches. "Actually," she continued, sliding herself back in her seat and away from the admittedly un-ladylike lounge she had fallen into these last minutes. "Let me share something with you that might connect a dot or three.

"You may not know, but Leopold wasn't the first man to seek my hand in marriage." I didn't, though both Sophie and Wilderich nodded knowingly. "One of my earlier suitors was James, the Duke of York."

"He'll be the King of England one day," commented Wilderich.

Elenore shrugged, carrying on with her story. "But despite the prestige of marrying one of the few monarchs with holdings in the New World, I rejected the proposal."

"Why?" asked the bishop.

"There has been a great deal of upheaval lately in England, a consequence of the apocalyptic fever that swept across the continent recently." Now this was something of which I was far more aware. Numerology had predicted the end of the world in 1666, reasoning that it was, at minimum, the number of the Beast and therefore heralded the second coming of Christ. "If I recall correctly," continued Elenore, "there was a group active there who had briefly tried to remove the monarchy and install their own theocracy. I believe they were called the Monarchists."

"Were they doctors?" I asked.

The Empress shook her head, her hair waving in the negative. "*Das weiss Ich nicht.* As far as I know, they were largely commissioners and the like, local politicians blessed with conviction yet cursed with bad judgement. Ironic really. But I could still see some doctors numbering among them. In the wake of Westphalia, the Church is diminished right when it shouldn't be. There's bound to be a power vacuum."

"You think England is a power vacuum?" asked Sophie a little too lustily. "I was looking to expand business in a new market. London might be prime territory."

I laid a hand on her arm. "Let's focus on saving Katarina and the city before we try to make more money?" She grinned, though my mention of her daughter tempered the expression into something more complexly colored.

Elenore's mouth twitched slightly at the sibling camaraderie. "I'm beginning to wonder if our visiting physicians sold us a bad bill of goods. I won't say that I am completely convinced, but there are enough questions that I cannot help but feel some doubt about their commitment to the survival of this city." She leaned forward onto the table, once again abandoning femininity for a more businesslike posture. "What can I do?"

Sophie, again, answered. "Lend us your support. Simple as that."

"I can't." Elenore's face twisted in sincere apology. "I must meet my husband soon. As it is, I barely extracted his permission to remain behind as long as I have."

The mood at the table collapsed. "What can you do, then?" asked Wilderich sadly, his plunging mood infusing his words with a careful insolence.

The Empress ignored the understandable reaction. "I can distribute some of funds from my own accounts to assist in supplying anything you might need." Her face brightened. "Though I'm not officially their ruler yet, maybe a letter or two granting you authority in my name?"

Sophie's lips pursed thoughtfully. "That would be helpful, actually. I was just approached by an order of monks, come to lessen the suffering of the sick. Having your sanction would allow me to establish them more legitimately in the more afflicted areas. As for money, even a small amount would be helpful."

Elenore wondered aloud, "Would ten thousand be too little?"

I felt my jaw drop, my reaction mirrored in Wilderich's wide eyes. Even Sophie coughed in surprise. "That... that's extremely generous, your Grace," I stammered out eventually. "Are you sure?"

The Empress favored me with a soft smile in return, her eyes bright with delight at the reaction she pulled from us. "I'm afraid I cannot give more, but the Emperor only grants me a small stipend for my works about the city. Keeps me busy and out of his way, and frankly while I have little desire to even deal with politics, this is one area where I am more invested. So let me now invest in you.

"I'll also urge my husband to make a larger effort to return to the city; as it is, it seems that the rest of the empire is suffering as much as we are, if not more so. At least, I'll reach out to a few physicians who have remained. It may change nothing, but perhaps we might manage to survive the tide of disease yet."

She stood, the rest of us rising swiftly to match her. Hugging each of us in turn, she gave us a final brave smile, making the sign of the cross on her forehead, her lips, and finally her heart.

"Keep your faith. If you hide under a basket in times like this, who else will light the night?"

XXXI

A Patient Visited

There was a small break in the clouds as we left the palace, and for a moment the building almost managed to look regal again, even with the Leopoldine expansion perverting its old, stark strength. Or perhaps it was just my mind tricking me into believing in that the world bowed to my whim, that somehow the weather reflected my own heart and not some other, otherworldly master.

Whichever was true didn't matter in the slightest, though. Despite our failure to meet with the Emperor, we had gained even more than I had possibly dreamed: Elenore's "small" contribution would mean that money was almost no longer a concern, the mountain of money able to sustain us and our beneficiaries for weeks – hopefully longer than the remainder of these plague.

And it had to end sometime, didn't it? It was a cruel joke that the plague existed at all, but it couldn't be equally perverse to imagine that it was nearly over, was it? After all, it was better to hope for an impossibility than to consider the alternative: that all the death and misery was merely the appetizer to a far greater feast of doom to come.

No, it would end. Even the longest night gave way to day eventually. After living most of a life in a city perpetually grey for months at a time,

I knew this more than most. Vienna, Wien, Vindabona... Whatever its name, the city had been here long before me and would be longer after me. Our visit with Elenore helped me see that now.

However, any pleasure I had gained from knowledge of Vienna's immortality was lessened by the knowledge that Belial's brethren were an apparently international concern. It had been hard enough for me to believe that even a handful like Belial might descend upon the city, but to learn that there were dozens, maybe even hundreds sprinkled liberally across Europa was almost enough to cut hope from me once more. I continued to doubt in the existence of the powers Belial had claimed ownership over, though I did find it increasingly convincing that there was something otherworldly about him

Regardless, that we knew more about them meant something, even if we couldn't tie them to the plague doctors now entrenched in the streets here. An image of the masked men as blood-sucking ticks rose, unbidden, in my mind: bent over all the plagued dead, grafted painfully against each ravaged chest, my imagination saw them slurp at the putrid essence, good and bad humors vanishing into swollen, corpulent bodies that ballooned until they lost all humanity, becoming something otherworldly and terrible.

"Something the matter?" asked Sophie, intruding.

"Why do you ask?"

"You just shivered," commented Wilderich, "and it's cold, but I don't think I've seen you shake so violently."

"Did I really?" I asked, flushing. "I hadn't realized I was so cold," I lied. Neither believed my story for a moment, but both bishop and baroness said nothing, allowing me to hide behind my lie for the remainder of our journey.

We discovered a queer energy once we arrived back at the estate, the atmosphere thick and cloying like a prostitute's perfume – not that I had ever engaged any in my time, but I had heard stories. As it was, Max was there at the foot of the stairs to the manor house, almost hopping from foot to foot in irritation. Abraham lingered at the top near the entrance, straddling the darkness as if unsure where he needed to be.

He kept furtively casting a glance over his shoulder, each quick flicker of his eyes doing nothing but deepening the dread that seemed to come from his every twitch.

Sophie was infected immediately. "What's wrong?" she asked quickly, her earlier humor fading. "Is Katarina-?"

"She's ok," called Abraham from the doorway. "Sarah is with her upstairs."

"Sarah?" I asked curiously. "Where is Belial?"

Max answered this time. "He's... he's... stepped out."

"Stepped... out, you say?" said my sister, slowly, the four syllables hissed between clenched teeth. "Where, pray tell?"

"I'm not sure," replied Max, his head ducking in that same subservient way he had since our earliest days as friends. "He gave Katarina something that made her..." he mimed the action, "and then he said that he needed to go glorify God so he could save Katarina. I wanted to stop him, but I figured that, if it helped Katarina, he should go."

Sophie's expression softened somewhat as she turned towards me. "Did he say anything to you?"

My arms flew out to the side in a helpless shrug. "I have absolutely no idea. I've been with you!"

Max cleared his throat uncomfortably, waiting for us to look back at him before he spoke again. "Also, Michel is here. He said that the other doctor that was here came and found him. He said he wanted to check on Katarina."

"You didn't let him do that, did you?" I asked, my tone drawing a quizzical look from Max. "He's not with her now, is he?"

"He tried," said Abraham. "Even asked to be alone with her so he could more attentively concern himself with making her better, he said. Max didn't let him do that, though."

"Did I do that right, at least?" asked my friend. "You told me to stay with her, Sophie. Did I do that right?"

She smiled, pleased with the response but also to reassure him. "Yes, you did very well, Max. Where is Michel now?"

"The dining room, ma'am," he replied, the smallest bit of color returning to his expression. "I asked one of the housemen to watch over him. I asked him to pretend to be attending to his needs, but to be aware of where he was at all times." I grinned. All the time Max claimed to be unintelligent, always hiding behind the idea that every man was either given brains or brawn. But here he was, directing the house staff with the cunning of a spymaster, his actions deliberately forward yet full of misdirection.

"You did a good job, Max," I affirmed, lavishing my friend with well-deserved praise.

"Dietrich, could you see what our guest needs while I check in with Abraham about his efforts?" asked Sophie. "Bishop, perhaps you could visit Katarina, see if Sarah needs anything?" With her daughter's health assured – even in its current state – my sister's back straightened, the role of family matriarch again assumed.

"I would prefer to visit my niece first," I said.

My sister pursed her lips, thoughtful. "Maybe it's only me thinking this, but perhaps you could focus on the man who seems to be behind a lot of our troubles?"

"We don't know that for sure," said Wilderich. I wondered why he was defending the outsider now, asking him so a moment after. "Well, what if he is the source of the entire plague? It would mean that I caused more pain again by speaking with him about the state of the city when he first arrived. I left him alone with the dead; who knows what he was doing with them?" The bishop looked stricken, a far cry from the more jovial clergyman who had come and gone from the Hofburg earlier today.

I tried to reassure him, earning a weak smile of confidence in response, though I think that was more to reassure me than a reflection of his own thoughts. Either way, I looked over at Sophie. "Michel will keep, or he won't. He's here to accomplish something."

"What is that?" she asked.

"I don't know," I admitted. "But I would prefer to see my niece well with my own eyes before I find out what that is." She gave me a perfunctory nod, dismissing us with a gentle wave that remained somehow encouraging despite its seeming condescension.

Taking Wilderich gently by the shoulder, I led him towards the stairs, leaving him to his silence for now as we made our way towards Katarina in her room. I heard conversation begin behind us – Abraham's report detailing the establishment of the hospitals in the city – but I tried to focus on my visit with my niece. 'Business' could wait. Now was a time to heal minds as well as bodies.

I knocked gently on Katarina's door, greeting Sarah with a nod and a soft hug. She seemed surprised by the affection though she returned it gratefully with an embrace of her own, pulling in an unresisting Wilderich a moment later. Strange, I thought. Such a thing would not have happened even a few months ago: Jew, Gentile, a doubting Thomas... An unholy trinity of faiths made pure in the disgusting crucible the plague had created of the city. By ourselves, we were weak, flawed, corruptible. Here, in this time and place, in the support we gave one another we had become something more, not strong but not as frail as we might have been alone.

A small cough behind our joined embrace broke us apart, though the warmth of the gesture remained in all our hearts. I looked over to see my niece sitting up slowly in her bed, pale as death but determination set in every small crease of her face. Patting Sarah and Wilderich on the shoulders, I moved around to sit by her side on the bed. "Hello *knuddelbär.*"

"Hello, Onkel," she said gravely. I despaired slightly at the utter lack of mischief, but that could return later, I realized. For now, she needed to bend every last fiber of her will to conquering the disease. "How is Freddie?"

"He's fine," I assured her. "He told me that he wanted you to focus on getting better so you two could play."

"I'm trying," she replied. She grimaced, one small hand coming across to rub her belly painfully. "Herr Belial gave me something to drink before he went away. It makes me..."

"I know," I shushed, as eager to not speak about it as she. I could smell the sick in the room as it was, my mind fighting my nose's urge to wrinkle in the face of the smell. "He wants you to be better, too. He says he can't wait for a day that the two of you can play together, too."

"Herr Belial?" she asked. "I know. He told me that when we first talked. He said..." Her face screwed up in concentration as she struggled to remember. "that I would inherit the kingdom one day." Katarina looked up at me, disbelief in her face. "Is that true, Onkel? Will I be a princess one day?"

I imagined that Belial was talking about a very different kingdom, but I kissed her on the forehead in response. "There's no reason to say 'one day.' You're already a princess, *knuddelbär*." I kissed her on the forehead again and leaned her back slowly to lie against her pillow. "And princesses rest to make sure they get better so they can spend time with their subjects. Can you do that for me?"

"Of course, Onkel." Tiny hands reached out for the small cup on the bedside table. "Can I have a drink before you go?"

I looked over at Sarah from where she and Wilderich hovered, my eyes asking the question that she answered with a soft nod. Taking the cup in my hand, I took a quick sniff to ensure that the mixture of wine and water was not stale or soured. I waited while she took several small sips, returning the cup to the stand when she was finished. "I need to go for now," I confessed, rising only after she nodded in acceptance.

Wilderich took my place on the bed while I gently tugged Sarah into the hall. "How is she?" I asked her after the door to the room had closed.

She didn't answer me immediately, composing her thoughts with long moments of caution. "The antimony potion that Belial made seems to have helped. Given what we know about the plague already, I imagine she would have shown far more symptoms by now. She's weak yet – that's fairly obvious – but that she hasn't shown any of the blackness that others have under similar circumstances must be a good sign. The fever has yet to fully break, but she doesn't seem contagious."

"Contagious?" I asked.

"You're a physician," she accused, disbelief plain on her face. "The sickness hasn't spread because of her. I certainly haven't gotten it, which I imagine should have happened given all the time I spent with her."

"Of course," I blushed. "Sorry, I admit there are moments that my mind doesn't fully think things through."

"You're a man," she said. "I assume that's fairly often." She smiled to soften the blow, spreading her arms for another small embrace that I gave before leaving.

XXXII

An Indecent Proposal

Turning away, I tried to mentally prepare myself for meeting with Michel. I still had no idea what he could possibly gain by visiting: visiting with my niece, as dear as she is to me, doesn't seem an important enough occasion for a plague doctor to come by the estate. No, it seemed to me that he was visiting for a far more nefarious purpose.

I was still unsure of what that was when I sat down across from him. It was strange to think that I was so against the man, especially considering I couldn't provide anything more than some intangible feelings as the reason behind my mistrust of him.

He didn't give me any reason either as he nodded amiably back at me. "Baron Dietrich, thank you for taking the time to see me."

I tried to maintain my smile, but I could almost feel it twist into a parody of it, a sick grimace where a more congenial expression should have laid. "But of course!" I replied. "I only apologize that I was unable to meet with you sooner. I'm sure you have heard that my niece is quite ill."

Concern swept across his face. "Yes, I had," he said, scratching at his chin. "Kalb was kind enough to tell me of her illness. I regret that one so young and pure has been affected by this horrible sickness. I always imagine the wicked and the sinful becoming ill – after all, if they were not corrupted within, why would God allow them to be corrupted without? – so hearing of her... affliction certainly concerns me." His head tilted carefully, the motion thoughtful and unthreatening. "I actually had hoped to see her, but your large companion would not allow it. I felt almost as if he thought I couldn't help her." He adjusted his belt over his stomach – was it larger? I wondered.

"I'm sure that wasn't true," I lied. "I think that perhaps Max was just a little too zealous in following my sister's orders." Something flickered across his face, the polite mask slipping just for a moment, a dark energy infusing every crease on his face. Then the moment was gone, and his face was once again old and kindly. I rubbed at my eyes, making a show of fatigue as I tried to find the darkness on his face and failed. "I'm sorry. With her ill, few of us have known a good night's sleep."

"She has been sick for a while then?" asked Michel.

"No, just a day or two at the most."

"That is peculiar," said the doctor slowly. "I was given to understand that most who have this illness succumb in barely a day. To have a child so resilient... She must be quite special. Are you sure I cannot see her?"

I shook my head. "Sophie was quite insistent. I only barely managed to obtain her permission to interrupt the healing process myself." I allowed myself to chuckle lightly, the better to keep Michel at ease. "Her healer was furious with my interruption."

I regretted the lie almost immediately, for something lit in Michel's eyes. I had never noticed how dark they were, his eyes: without glasses I imagine his face would seem far less friendly than it now appeared. "'Her healer?" he asked. "I would love to compare notes with him – or her – if Katarina recovers under their care."

"I'll be sure to pass along your request," I promised, though I am sure he read for the empty promise it was, because he said nothing else. I waited for him to say something else, but he didn't break the silence that grew between us for maybe half a minute.

Eventually the look in his eyes became one of expectation. "Not to be

indelicate, but do you think that we might have something to drink?"
he asked.

"Oh, you weren't offered anything?" I asked, surprised. "I'll have to
have a conversation with our houseman."

Michel smiled wanly back. "No, no. He did offer, but I wasn't fond
of the options he had given me." He held up a hand to prevent me from
replying. "Let me try again. Can I have a glass please? I have brought
some of my own vintage to enjoy. I would offer to you, but I can't help
but wonder if it did not agree with you last time. You seemed... to not
enjoy it, to put it delicately."

A mask of civility on my face, I stood and moved to the nearby bureau to extract two small glasses from there. I called for the recently
departed houseman to bring some water and wine, giving a word of encouragement as the man fearfully entered to deposit two small pewter
vessels on the table.

Michel merely looked at the man, the servant turning an even paler
shade of grey before he politely fled the room. I offered both urns to
Michel before pouring a measure of each into my glass, favoring a little
less wine and more water. "Do you ever wonder why we mix water and
wine?" the doctor inquired as he extracted a flask from his belt.

"Something to do with the alcohol content of the wine, *nicht wahr*?"
I ventured. "Ancient vintners made strong wine if I recall correctly."

Eyebrows rose in admiration. "Very good," he said, opening the stop-
per on his flask and pouring a generous measure of syrupy liquid into
his glass. A second heady bouquet filled the room, mingling with the
strange scent that seemed to seep from Michel, the smell enough to encourage my thoughts to retreat to the memory of my last conversation
with the older man. Shaking my head roughly, I struggled to remain focused on his next words, but still managed to miss nearly everything
than his closing statement. "...It was said that only barbarians drank
undiluted wine," he concluded, looking at me curiously as he raised his
glass to me. "*Salvatus est.*"

I mirrored the gesture, taking only a sip of my beverage while my
guest poured every last drop of his drink down his throat in one rough

toss. Setting the glass down, he was halfway through his second pour before he blushed, though I chalked up the response to the effect of the alcohol as opposed to any sense of shame: he had done the same the last time we had spoken after all. "Do you see yourself as a barbarian then?" I asked lightly, indicating his glass. "If I'm not too rude in saying it, you are somewhat... cavalier with your intake?"

His eyes flashed, though he did his best to change the expression to one of merriment. "Oh, of course not!" he chortled. "Like I have said before, this is my private vintage. You don't think I could manage to minister to the sick if I got drunk every day, do you?" He fought to keep the tone light, but I heard the implicit threat in his words.

"Of course not," I said, repeating his words. "But I wonder if the rest of your particular doctrine feels the same way. I mean, of course, given the state of the city and all." No doubt my thoughts would anger him more than a little, but I wanted to understand the reason for his visit. "You must understand that – to the more skeptical, of course - the city's health seems to be decaying more quickly since the arrival of your... group. There are those who wonder what you might be doing to save the city."

A carefully considered grimace stole across the old man's face, as if he was calculating something time and again, each time coming up with a result he found distasteful. "I see. I would probably invite those skeptics to take a closer look at the plagued and see how difficult the work we do is. I imagine those concerned citizens would be more understanding then."

I raised my hands as if surrendering to his logic. "I understand the struggle you face completely, though I am curious of one thing on my end."

"What's that?"

"I understand that each of your doctrine comes from a different school of medicine, and that the plague probably has variations that even I – as another physician – could not appreciate, but I am confused by the multiple approaches that you seem to take in healing the disease."

He looked at me quizzically, encouraging me to expand my own answer even as he stayed silent. "Well, like you said, you were aware that Katarina was sick after Kalb came in response to the bishop's call. While you advocated exposing the healthy to the sick as a way of healing, Kalb told us that we should immediately bleed my niece."

"Ah," he said, nodding slowly as if the reason was as plain as could be. "My way is best used before the body becomes sick, Kalb's after the body has become sick." He spread his hands wide, as if the answer was as obvious as could be.

"Don't you think that that approach seems a little bit drastic?" I asked. "She is a child. Maybe if she were older...?" I had hoped that he would respond, but he merely shrugged with his face, as if the result, regardless of age, would be the same. "What about something like antimony? Would that help her past the sickness?"

I had caught him mid-drink with my last question, his face twisting as if his drink had soured during his last sip. The glass fell from his lips slowly as he seemed to ponder for a time. "I wonder," he said, "where some methods of healing begin. For some, there is a level of superstition that is never quite tamped out by logic. For others, environmental effects that see a single patient cured who should not have been saved. For others, still, there is a level of divine intervention, an allowance by God that surpasses all human understanding to make someone whole who, by human reckoning, should not have been saved." Michel seemed unconcerned with any potential response I might have made, instead peering deeply into the glass before him. "Are you familiar with the idea of 'trial by ordeal'?" he asked suddenly.

"Isn't that where innocence or guilt is created by a task?" He nodded sagely in response. "Depends what kind we're talking about," I said, shifting in my seat as I wondered what this had to do with anything.

"Oh, any of them," he said blithely. "Combat, the bitters, bisha'a-"

"Bisha'a? I asked, my brow furrowing. "What is that?"

"Oh, it's a trial that the Bedouin people use to establish guilt or innocence." His eyes found mine, and I felt the same irresistible tug I had felt the last time we had shared a glance in the tavern. I tore my own eyes away only after a concerted effort of will, though Michel continued largely as if our eyes were locked. "The people there heat a spoon in a fire, almost to the point of melting it."

I shivered as a curious relish filled his voice, his syllables congealing in almost ecstatic expectation as he went on. "The idea is that the accused licks the spoon three times, and that injury or nothing will name the innocent in a dispute between two men."

"Sounds barbaric," I said uneasily, my mouth tingling in imagined heat. "Are there ever false positives? An innocent condemned for some other outlier of behavior?"

"Perhaps, but doesn't that mean that the accused is as guilty anyway?" He shook his head, taking another drink from his glass." Perhaps not of that specific crime, but of another, one that he has managed to keep hidden from the sight of God and mankind? I would say that it is far worse for a man to escape God's justice than it is for an innocent man or two to be punished."

I felt my eyes narrow suspiciously, my mind trying to work through his bloodthirsty logic. "I am not sure what this has to do with our discussion..."

He looked at me quizzically. "Don't you? I would have thought an avowedly upright man such as yourself would understand what I meant immediately."

"I wouldn't say that I'm an upright man."

Chancing a glance at Michel, I saw him smother the spark of dark delight lighting the gentle smile on his lips. He reached a hand out to tap one of mine, the sensation enough to set my teeth on edge and my skin to crawling. "Yet you walk the night in defense of your fellow citizens. You fight off thieves and concern yourself with the public good for no other reason than the cause's inevitable righteousness. Isn't this the sign of an upright man?"

"I hadn't realized that word of last evening had traveled so widely about the city," I commented slowly.

He smiled easily, the expression reminding me of a black cat I had seen once as I had walked about the city, just before the first man had died, actually. "I wasn't suggesting that they had," he said. "But you could practically hear the city herself sing your praises. If you don't mind me saying so, you're a pampered noble, and yet you devote your energies to serving your fellow man. Isn't this noteworthy?"

My eyes remained as they were, narrow slits trying to hide the questions whistling through my mind. "No, I would think that this is the duty of every man." A glib remark crossed my mind. "I would say that every man should do one thing and one thing alone: 'First, do no harm.'"

A genuine chuckle came from Michel at my turn of phrase, even earning me a soft salute from the man who continued to build nothing but suspicion in me. "Well done," he congratulated, raising his glass slightly before taking a sip from it. "But why save the people who do not deserve to be saved? Why save the people who would do you harm, or do harm to those who you prize?"

"Because to cause pain with no honest purpose is evil," I said, surprising myself with the simplicity of the thought. "I became someone who healed because there is enough violence in the world without someone there to close the wound."

"Evil?" he repeated. "Even when that kind of pain advances the greater good?"

"Do you see that happening now?" I asked cautiously. Was he really that callous to suggest that all this death and decay should serve a purpose? He shrugged as if unwilling to take a stance, but I could see the truth in his face. "But if that's true, then why do you devote your life to healing the damage it causes?"

Michel peered at my face, leaning on the table to scrutinize me more closely. "I am not a heartless monster, Dietrich, no matter what you might think of my last response." He frowned in thought. "We forget sometimes that what we try to do on this earth has lasting consequences in heaven and the world beyond this one."

My head cocked to the side unbidden. "Then wouldn't my desire to heal - good and evil alike - a good thing?"

"If you could be sure that only the righteous would be saved, then I would be inclined to agree with you," he countered. "But how do you know who is pure of heart and who is not?"

"How do *you* know who is pure and who is not?" I returned, unease continuing to tease the back of my mind.

He retreated from the table now, leaning back in the chair but creating no sound as he did so. "I have been at this a long time, Dietrich. Long before you were born, and long after you die, I imagine. It's not a task that I relish, carrying out the will of heaven but I do it without complaint if it carries His plan to fruition."

"God?" I asked skeptically. "You would have me believe that God is the one telling you who is pure and who isn't?"

He smiled at my question, as if I had hit on the truth of it, but he shook his head a second later in denial. "I wouldn't presume to say that. The last who pretended to act in God's name was cast down and away."

"Are you referring to the Protestant Luther?" I asked. "I know you are German by birth."

"Oh, you do?" he asked, his accent vanishing in a heartbeat. "Luther is a sideshow to a much greater matter, but no, I wasn't referring to Luther. There is a much larger game to be played than the actions of a not entirely mistaken priest." His accent returned as swiftly as it had begun, but it had sounded as if each word spoken was infused by the touch of a different land, a different people.

Old hands reached down to smooth at his robes, pressing them enough that I could see the swell of newly gained flesh underneath the simple cloth. How was he gaining weight? While the estate itself managed to feed and water its inhabitants without struggle, I had heard of food shortages beginning to hit the city, starvation claiming its fair share of the dead. "Dietrich, I want to ask you... What do you think would happen if the plague is defeated in this city?"

"What do you mean?" I asked. "You act as if the sickness was sentient, alive as you or I are."

His head came up to consider me, his eyes meeting mine; thankfully I did not feel the same dark tug as I had the last time our eyes met. "I mean, what happens if the people are saved? Will they give thanks to God for their salvation? Will they understand how hard people like you worked to save them? Will their actions change from any past wickedness to thoughts of purity instead? Do they even know why the plague came here in the first place?"

"I feel as if the answers to these questions are beyond my ability to answer," I said carefully. "But if I was to say, I would say that what the people do – those who do survive, that is – is their own choice. Would I give thanks to God for surviving the ordeal? Probably not." His face glowered at my answer, but I pressed on. "Wilderich likely would praise God enough for us both, should he be as fortunate as I might be. Does faith in the beyond guarantee survival? If faith is enough to save us alone, then I might wonder what God would need of good works."

"That's entirely my point!" claimed Michel. "Would the people try and change in the wake of any salvation granted them by God?"

I shrugged, taking a sip of my drink instead, savoring the sweet sourness of the wine and water combined. "I don't know. But consider this – if this is somehow God's will, that the plague visit this city as some kind of divine punishment for wickedness, then he should be prepared to offer Vienna the same deal as Sodom or Gomorrah."

"A single good man in exchange for salvation for all?" I nodded. "Would you see yourself as that good man?" Michel asked me.

"No, I've told you already that I am far from a good man. I have beaten men, shot others, raged against them in public and in private... No, I am not a good man, but then you aren't looking for a good man, are you? You are looking for an evil man turned good."

"You would have one?" he asked me, expectant.

"I do, though I don't think he knows yet that he is a good man," I said, careful to hide any revelation from my face. "Tell me, if you were the cause of all the sickness, would you trade the health of the city for the sake of one fallen man working to turn away from his past?"

Michel didn't answer me at first, his eyes narrowing as he seemed to measure every last hair of my face. I, in turn, measured his. The last time he was here he had moved painfully slow, as if the weight of the world had borne so heavily on him that one falsely placed step would see him broken under it. He was kindly then, not deferential necessarily, but not as arrogant as he was now. No, there was a subtle arrogance now to him, a darkness measured not in any way one man might know another.

"No," he said eventually. "One flawed man come to God is not enough to save an entire people from their own moral filth."

"Then why are you here?" I asked, my hands thrown out to the side in loss. "If this black death is horrible enough only for God to send it as a punishment of the wicked – a wickedness you believe can only be expunged by death – then why are you here?"

He smiled then, the expression enough to chill me to the bone as I realized I had seen one like it before on Belial's face when he had first come to the estate. It was a smile equal parts considered insanity and feral calm, a smile which promised bloody retribution to any who stood between it and its goals. "Why, I am here to save the sick," he said, standing slowly, his own arms settling behind his back. His back was straight now, his bearing powerful but controlled, each action accompanied with a smooth indifference I had never seen in him before.

"What are you?" The question was implicitly stupid, something only a lost child might have asked, but I felt that way now. "You are not an old man," I accused.

"But I am," he said, his accent disappearing again to be replaced by a voice that dripped from him like quiet thunder. "I am older than you will ever be, and younger than you will ever understand." He brought one of his hands around, his gaze examining the fingernails for any imagined flaw. "Dietrich, I came here today with a very specific purpose in mind."

"What is that?" I asked, taking a deep drink from my cup as I sought stability from the wine and water therein.

"I came to make you a proposal, one that would see those whom you love and the truly pure rescued from this terrible disease. Would you care to listen to what I have to say?" His cheeks seemed to grow younger, a trick of the light I was sure, but the creases of his face filled, the years seeming to melt from him as he turned to consider me more fully.

I fought for a moment to collect my thoughts. "How can you promise me that? You are only a man."

The hand before him pointed at me. "But you just said I wasn't. Which is it?" His question came lightly, as if he was holding back laughter. "I can and I will save your niece, as well as... let's say forty others who you and you alone say are pure. After that, it will be up to me to say who in this city is worth saving and who is not. In fact, as a sign of good faith, I will save your niece right now." He closed his eyes, his brow furrowing for a few scant seconds before he returned his gaze to me. "It's done. She will be well."

"You're very generous," I said carefully, not wanting to antagonize him. "And what do I have to give in exchange?"

"You agree to serve me. My work is more than I can do alone, and I would have need of a man who is as committed as you are to your cause, misguided as it is." He reached a hand out towards me, beckoning as a man calls his dog. "Come, come and see your life elevated to something that will change the face of the entire world. Come and serve God."

"Serve God?" I asked slowly. "So you would claim to be divine yourself, then?"

His arms spread as if he were making ready to embrace me. "Can you not recognize an angel of God?"

I couldn't, but then I wouldn't know what one looked like even if he acted as Michel did now. "If you are an angel, then you are only a messenger, a herald. How do I know that you are something beyond man? I have dealt with men who have claimed to be more than mortal before; more often than not it was ale talking, though I would safely say there is no alcohol at play here."

There was a brief flash of fury in his eyes, though he quenched it quickly in an icy stare. "You require proof? Fine." His bearing stooped slightly, a sign of the old man returning, but his eyes gazed heavenward. "You lost your parents to a similar sickness twenty years ago, your mother and then your father wasting away in days before expiring. They were not easy deaths."

"Again, I do not wish to offend you, but you could have heard that from anyone, here or otherwise. My history is no secret here."

Michel scowled, but nodded, understanding. "You believe your skepticism about God to be justified. To you, the absence of the beyond in a tangible way is enough to warrant your lack of faith. Yet, these past weeks you have found something of God, even if you refuse to believe it yourself. You approach it now timidly, like a small child who has been singed by fire once before and yet approaches a flame again anyway. Is this proof more to your liking?" he asked me, irritation in every syllable.

Another shiver found me as his words penetrated the shield of my doubt. Though brief, every word of his comment was true, and I knew that I had done little to give away any hint of myself. Either he was beyond talented or he could see through me to my core: neither idea filled me with any kind of relish.

"May I have some time to think about your offer?" I asked, my pulse hammering in my ears as I struggled to comprehend the implications of the last minutes.

The old man smiled thinly. "A day, a week, a month, how long you take to come to your senses is of no consequence to me. This city's doom comes, whether or not you wish it. I make my own offer to you in recognition of my growing respect for your work, though, again, I note how idiotic you are in your commitment to folly. Regardless," he finished, sweeping his things from the table, "you may save the lives of you and yours, and I ask little in return for my favor."

A small rebellious piece of me, stubborn to the end, asked, "What if I were to refuse your offer? Generous as it is, what if I were to turn you down and place myself between you and everyone in this city? Good or evil, the people here deserve to make their own fate. If you are an angel, then you are a creature of mercy and not death. Show it now, and see the city grow strong in that mercy."

He sighed, placing the mask at his waist, his hands tracing the brim of his hat. He seemed to stoop again, bending forward as the lines of his face returning with time's unstoppable caress. "You are an obstinate people, man. We give you your free will, and you use it to kill and torture one another. We step in to give you Jesus, and you nail him to a cross. We give you the catholic church and you use it to kill and rape your way through the Holy Land. We give you the Renaissance and you use it to find new and inventive ways of oppression."

His eyes turned to me sadly. "We give you every opportunity to save yourselves. *I* give you every opportunity to save your loved ones; if there is a greater chance to see Christian charity, I don't know what it would be." He lifted the hat to his head, his face cloaking itself in soft shadow. "If you turn my offer down, then perhaps you are no different than the sick of the city.

"If you turn my offer down, then your fate will be the same as theirs."

XXXIII

A Changed Man?

I might have answered him, but in the blink of an eye he was gone, and I was alone. I could not even bring myself to my feet in surprise, so weak did I feel at the knees. Indeed, it felt like Michel had passed his weight to my shoulders. My life for my loved ones and forty others? Did I deserve such a responsibility? Did I deserve such an offer of mercy when so many others expired without it?

My mind would have endlessly rolled through its debate, waffling back and forth, had Belial not appeared in the doorway then. "Dietrichmor... Dietrich, may I speak with you?"

I dumbly waved him in, unable to make anything close to words. I let the silence fester between us, rotting in the same air that continued to reek despite Michel's recent departure. It was as if the world refused to allow me the chance to forget the last minutes, as if I could. I was more convinced than ever that Michel was somehow the cause of the sickness in the city, though I was still damned if I could explain to myself or anyone else.

Was he, in fact, an angel? Or was my first thought correct, that he was somehow just a crazy old man with delusions? There had been far too many questions that had gone unanswered, and I hated that Michel had left before answering even a fraction of them.

"You've met the Master," said Belial simply.

"That depends... Is Michel the Master?" I managed to croak out.

"I don't know his name. I only know him by the face that others wear once after they know him for the first time. You wear it now, just as I wore it when he first revealed his majesty to me."

A flash of flash flew from me. "His majesty? How could you serve a creature like that? How could I not have recognized him as anything but an enemy until now?"

Belial winced as my anger slapped him across the face. "Forgive me... I don't know how else to speak about him. He has been my lord for years. It is... hard to not hold him in awe."

Understanding quenched my frustration, extinguishing it as swiftly as it had come. "I'm sorry, Belial. I forget that sometimes, as well. You've come a long way in a very short time."

I tried to assure him with my last comment, and perhaps I did, for he smiled at me, a toothless thing that almost managed to still the whirl of thought that continued to rush about my head. "Thank you, Dietrich." His face grew dour again, though infected slightly by a curious thoughtfulness. "You asked how you didn't recognize him as the architect of all this. The Master is a lord of disguises. The face he wears now is just the one he has selected for the current age. He's worn different ones throughout mankind's life." He peered carefully at me. "Which does he wear now?"

"A plague doctor."

"He always had a sense of humor, the others said," nodded Belial. "It is said that when he first appeared to man, he came as his true self, striking down the eldest of Egypt with a flaming sword. But God called him to more subtle methods, to do his work among the people without giving them notice of his presence."

"He is a divine creature after all?" I asked, dreading the answer that could come back. "He is not some insane man pretending with his cries of doom?"

The other man shrugged. "I can only tell you what I have seen, Dietrich. I have only served him for a short time. Barely two years, in fact. Vienna was to be my chance to ascend to join him and my brethren."

I nodded. "So it was you who brought the sickness here?" I asked, knowing the answer, but wanting something, anything to be confirmed for sure.

"I am," he said, his face flushing with more color than I thought possible from his wan complexion. I saw his mouth gape slightly as if he thought to apologize; he didn't, a choice that I found as admirable as his choice to come clean about his past. "I would try and explain myself, but any words I could say would sound trite," he eventually commented. He looked down, away from me in shame. "Thank you for asking me."

His appreciation confused me. "I'm not sure I understand why you're 'thanking me."

"By asking me, you force me to confront who I have become." He stood up, beginning to pace as Michel had back and forth, though his step was without the same malice. No, it was open, innocent, the walk of a child teetering this way and that, each unsteady stride bringing him closer to a truer understanding of himself and his mind.

I said nothing, knowing that my own words right now could destroy any thoughts swirling in his head. "I know that you and the Baroness look at me as a murderer, a cultist bent somehow on bringing about an apocalyptic vision of the future." He held up a hand to prevent a response that I never tried to give. "And you are right to look at me that way. Until recently, I have done little to paint a different portrait in your mind."

I couldn't help but interject now. "But you have in these last days. Does your work with Katarina not count? Your confirmation of Michel as the Master? Defending my life last night?"

"Drops in the bucket," he said dismissively. "Do you know why I am here now, to speak with you? Do you know where I just came from?"

"I figured you would tell me when you were ready," I replied. "I know Sophie has been anxious to find that out.

He nodded. "I know. I have just come from speaking with her. She was... rather cross with me."

"My sister has always fiercely protected the health of her family. With Katarina ill -"

"Katarina will live," he said assuredly. "I would sooner allow myself to fall ill than to allow her to die. I would not have left otherwise." He stopped his pacing a moment, winning me over with the earnestness in his eyes. "I left only after knowing that she would recover. She will be weak for a few days, but she will be well, I promise."

I nodded in acceptance as he resumed his pacing. "I went to visit the house of one of the men we stopped last night."

"How could you possibly have found him?"

Belial never stopped walking, merely tapping his nose. "After you have tasted a man's life, you know that every body has its own scent. Finding him was as simple as trusting my own body. Anyway, I went to his home, to learn about the kind of man who would prey on others, living or dead." His tread stopped now, the gaunt face wistful. "I watched him play with his children. By God's grace, his family has not been touched by the Master or the plague, and I saw a man caper back and forth as if he were a child himself. In a rude house in a dank corner of the city, I saw a sinful man give joy and peace to others who will know no other existence than a short, brutal one achieving the dreams of another man while their own die."

He saw the guilty look on my face. "I don't mean to accuse you of anything. I only mean that I watched a man who, last night, pushed himself to pillage and rob another man. I watched him bring joy to those who called him family, watched him ignore the misery around him in the hopes that tomorrow would be a brighter moment, a brighter day." He looked down at hands that slowly clenched into fists. "And I still almost ensured that he would never see another dawn."

"What did you do?" I asked, a pit opening in my stomach, my mind calling to mind the feral man who had saved me last night.

"Nothing, I swear," he said, his hands raised. "Almost nothing," he amended. "I waited for his children to disappear around a corner before

I grabbed him and hurled him into a wall. I felt my hands close on his throat. I felt his flesh under my fingers retreat until breath almost left him completely. I watched his eyes flash in fear, regret, anger... all of mankind's ugliest emotions were on display in barely the blink of an eye. But I saw something else in there that caused me to stop."

"What was that?" I asked, on the edge of my seat now.

"Forgiveness," he whispered, so softly I strained to hear him say it. "He pitied my actions but didn't struggle. In that moment I let him go, threw him away to gasp on the cobblestones, and fled."

"Why?" I asked.

"Because I saw the same emotions in your sister's face in the pantry. I saw the same in yours. And perhaps, I think, I could see the same in God's... if he sees it good enough to forgive me for my sins. Given how many they are, I worry sometimes that he may not see me as worthy of his grace."

"But you are," came another voice, Wilderich's voice, the old man coming in tentatively from his place at the entrance into the foyer. "Forgive me, Dietrich. I wanted to give Katarina some time to sleep and came down here to hear voices." His lips twitched upward tentatively. "I can leave the two of you alone, if you like," he allowed, turning to leave.

A day or two before I might have sent him away, having seen the obvious animosity he felt towards Belial, but a new glimmer lay in his eyes now, earnestness mixed with polite piety. "No, please," I contradicted. "You are more qualified than I am to comment on this anyway." Calling for another glass for the bishop, I encouraged him, "You were saying."

"Belial, my son, I confess that I am at a loss towards you," he said. "You come to strike at my flock. As you said, you are the reason for the death here, and that cannot be forgiven by the laws of men." How long had he been standing there? I wondered silently. "But God," he continued, making the sign of the cross in the air, "God is all-knowing and all-merciful. Where I cannot see past the blood you have shed, he sees you for who you wish to be. Where I can only see frail flesh and a weak will bent to evil, God sees your soul, knowing you for who and what you are. You say you hope that God can forgive you. The truth is he already has.

He did that the day you were born, even as original sin stained you, he loved you beyond all possible measure. If he did not, then why did he send his son for you?"

At best an agnostic, I still felt my heart pull at the sound of Wilderich's words, my skin prickling as gooseflesh formed at the touch of the beyond. All my concern about Michel falling away for a brief, crystalizing moment of perfect peace. Was this the same kind of faith that seemed to infect everyone outside of my family? Was this why Michel was so quick to kill, why Belial was so eager to obey, Wilderich so eager to preach?

I watched tears form on Belial's face, watched them plummet down cheeks to collect at his cadaverous chin. Had his face not broken into a truly genuine smile, I'm sure my heart would have broken further. "May I pray with you, father?" he asked, the question eliciting its own kindly smile from the aging bishop, who nodded in return. Helping the older man to his feet, Belial and Wilderich left together, not arm in arm, but together nonetheless.

The servant came back from the kitchen to find its intended recipient gone. Apologizing, I motioned for him to leave the goblet on the table; if no one else ended up drinking it, I would.

I would have liked to have had more time with Belial, the better to learn about our newly revealed foe. To know anything about him more than rumors and my own limited experience might give us an advantage. But then to fully believe him to be our greatest enemy would be to completely ignore the plague. I could face one or the other, but not both. That much was obvious.

Which to give my attention to, though? My life's work would suggest that the plague was more important: I was a physician, and to turn away from the sick to combat some unknowable, seemingly-omnipotent angel of death would be to deny my entire existence.

But to completely neglect Michel would be to allow him to spread his influence further, permitting him to flit about the city doing whatever he wanted to encourage the spread of the sickness, to say nothing of the actions of his acolytes. If Belial was the barometer by which each of them would fight to further Michel's ends, then focusing on healing the effects of the plague would be like plugging my fingers into a leaking dike: for now it might be enough, but eventually the rising waters might break through elsewhere and drown all of us.

"A *pfennig* for your thoughts, little brother," interrupted Sophie, my sister sitting down across from me and removing the responsibility of drinking the other cup on the table.

"Michel is our enemy," I said simply, "And we cannot beat him."

An eyebrow cocked at my fatalism; I confess I was surprised that I could still be so negative in the face of the interaction between Wilderich and Belial, but the dark thoughts remained hunkered within my mind. "What makes you say that? If anything, I would have said visiting with Elenore helped us turn a corner."

"Two things," I said, holding up a finger. "First, you're not surprised about Michel?" She shrugged. "What did I miss? And why didn't you say anything?"

"You would not have believed me," she promised, though her aura of infallibility broke as she admitted, "I only put the idea together as I crossed the threshold here. As for what you missed? The coloration of Belial, Kalb, Michel... three men from disparate places, all of the same complexion? Two perhaps, but an albino African?"

"They do exist," I countered lamely, though I could see where she was headed with it.

"Add in the fact that an entire coven descends on the city, and the sickness gets worse after they arrive in their droves?" she continued. "Add in their differing healing methods, and I think I only Katarina falling ill prevented me from seeing it sooner." I nodded acceptance, pleased to know, at least, that my own misgivings had been echoed in someone else, even if that echo had remained private until now. "What was the second question?"

"How can you be so sanguine about where things are? The city continues to decay, both physically and morally. The Emperor has already fled. How long do you think the city can last with all of those important dead or gone?"

"Are we dead?" she asked me.

"No, but –"

"Are good people like Abraham and Sarah dead?"

"No, but – "

Sophie would not be deterred. "What about the brothers of the Holy Trinity, putting themselves in harm's way everywhere we cannot be? What about Belial? If a cultist can see the value in laying himself down for the city, then the spirit of Vienna remains."

I signaled surrender. "I get it."

"Of course, you do," she said. "You just needed to hear what you already knew from someone older and wiser."

"Definitely true with your claim of age," I said, as much to puncture her ego as to show that my spirits had been lifted. My hands clasped before me, I shared my recent thoughts with her. "Which way do you think I should focus my efforts?"

"I think you need to mobilize the city watch and go after Michel directly," she said without a moment of thought.

"But what about the plague? We have no definitive way of dealing with it. We could lose thousands in the time it takes to even find the plague doctors."

"Belial came to see me before he spoke to you, as much to appraise me of his... activities as to tell me about what we might do more realistically for the rest of the city." She pursed her lips, her gaze rising from me as she called to mind whatever message Belial had transmitted to her. "Antimony is not going to be a long-term solution: there simply isn't enough of it to go around. The lack of that means that we need to be proactive after using it on the newest cases we come across."

"Shouldn't be hard to find usage for that," I quipped bitterly, but I nodded for her to go on.

"For those who are more severe, I think we need to resort to one or two other ideas. You – or Abraham, since you're going to be hunting Michel and his ilk - would have to help identify the correct purgatives we could safely give someone."

"Belial seems to advocate increasing fluids to wash out all the symptoms," I noted.

"The monks also called for bandaging parts of the body that show clear signs of plague," she said.

"What will that do?" I asked.

"I'm not sure. They mumbled something about keeping the soul confined to the body and not allowing it to be corrupted by the rest of the world."

I tried to work my thread through the muddled logic, trying as hard as I could to separate the religiosity from any victim's health. "I guess that would keep most of the wounds closed and minimize the chance of an infection." I spared a glance towards my sister. "The city is dirty enough."

"True."

"There's one more thing we will have to do..." I said, feeling my face grow bleak as Sophie looked back at me in confusion. "Wilderich isn't going to like the idea, but it needs to happen."

Comprehension dawned on her, my thought coming from her lips a moment later.

"We'll have to burn the dead."

XXXIV

A Painful Confrontation

Surprisingly, Wilderich was largely ambivalent to the issue, raising little more than a vague protest to my call for the immolation of the dead. The last weeks had changed us all, in more ways than one, but the change I saw in him over the next days seemed the most pronounced. The man I had met a month ago had been an affable, friendly man to all he met, so long as they were Catholic; those less civilized in his eyes – the unbeliever, the 'heathen' - he had treated with a vicious contempt, his responses as zealous as a priest could safely be if his faith was attacked.

The affability remained, though the walls he had erected towards Abraham and Sarah, towards Belial, and even, somewhat, towards me had long since fallen. Though there were still moments that he remained guarded, especially towards Belial, more often than not I found him about the estate joking with the Jewish couple or locked in feverish discussion with Belial and my sister. His faith remained, too, but a new pragmatism had tempered it. "God will understand whatever sins we do now against His Creation," he said when I first suggested to burn the dead. "If he does not understand, then He is not God."

I imagine it was the closest he would ever allow himself to come to speaking against the Church or his own faith.

Whatever the case, there was a new industriousness about the estate over those days, every room in the house a riot of feverish activity. Mountains of food were created, the stores in every pantry and the barns emptied in an effort to offset to the famine rearing its head in the city. The Empress' contribution disappeared piece by piece as my sister negotiated emergency contracts that would see wagons full of cloth bandages, food, and medical supplies delivered to the estate.

Despite the whispers of doom that continued to infect the housing staff, morale was high, spirits helped by the joyous news that Katarina was well on the road to recovery. Even Freddie, not one given to any outburst of affection, almost bowled her over when she first came downstairs, though he kept resolutely silent otherwise.

My sister's network continued to bring stories of death and decay from the city, some of her spies about the city falling under the plague's touch even as other fled the morass to hide at the estate or other parts of the empire. Those who came to the estate were examined for signs of plague before being employed to the best of their ability.

Healers were dispatched to the hospitals the brave brothers of the Trinitarians established in the most afflicted areas; grocers and money-lenders were asked to contribute what they could; laborers were dragooned into augmenting the city watch as my own dwindling brotherhood strove to hold back the tide of barbarism that swelled in some parts of the city.

Those who refused to walk the street to protect its living were assigned to collect and burn its dead in pits outside the city; often those assigned this task grumbled bitterly, but swiftly fell to silence once Max spoke to them privately. I never knew what he said, but there were few who complained more than once.

And yet, regardless of our efforts, Vienna's still hemorrhaged each day, some headed for other cities, others for the pits that began to hide the eastern sky in thick, black towers of smoke. Worse yet, not all those who remained in the city were of our mindset: though their numbers were thinned by the plague daily, we had heard more than once of our corpse-collection carts being attacked as the more zealous refused to let their loved ones be burnt on the city's outskirts.

I heard about most of this second or third-hand, far too busy with my own matters to fully be aware of events outside my direct concern. With some of the more nobly born of the city watch dead or having fled, the remaining members of our impromptu council had named me *de facto* commander of the watch, a responsibility that weighed so heavily on me that I thought I would shatter in those first few days.

It was only after I delegated the day-to-day matters to older, wiser heads like Herman that I was finally able to concentrate on my own task of locating Michel and his cabal. But the task was easier said than done; for all their distinctiveness, it was as if they vanished the instant Michel had delivered his offer of deliverance to me. Now and again I would get a fragmented report from someone in the watch – all of them had been alerted to the true nature of the so-called doctors – but just as quickly our quarry fell from sight before I could react.

I started moving about the city myself, the better to react in real time instead of after the fact. Sometimes I was alone, sometimes either or both Max and Belial came with me. As strange as it would seem, a curious camaraderie had formed between the two men. They were almost a study in opposites, Max's large frame contrasting starkly with Belial's leanness, but both men moved as shadows to the other. Though I doubt there was anything close to true brotherhood between them, both were equally committed to helping me in my own search and, at least, suffered the other to be along.

Today saw us creeping about the center of the city, by no means the lodestone of the plague (that seemed to be opposite the estate in the city), but we were moving about St. Stephensdom in an effort to learn anything about Michel's whereabouts. Though Wilderich had not set foot in the cathedral in some time, his assistant Johann had reportedly striven to keep life as normal as possible, holding weekly mass for the few huddled scraps of the living still brave enough to sprint through the streets to holy ground.

That attempt at normalcy had fallen apart in the last week as the stench of death had permeated the stones so thickly that the small congregation had been driven outside the cathedral, unable to bear the stench of so many plague victims being dumped in the catacombs below the church. While we were not there to retrieve the bodies – others were being dispatched for that distasteful task – a lone watchman had seen lanternlight inside late last evening.

Remembering my last nighttime engagement with a member of the group – my opponent walked now behind me, guarding my back – I had opted to wait for the next day, taking the time between then and now to ensure that we were not walking into any kind of trap. Honestly, I would have wanted to bring more than Max and Belial with me, but manpower was thin enough with all other hands otherwise employed. And while I would have wanted to bring at least the watchman who had noticed the phenomenon, I decided it would be better that he be given some time away: his young wife was stricken with the plague, and after Katarina's struggle with plague, I knew it would be difficult for him to remain focused.

So it fell to the three of us, slinking from building to building as if we were hiding from a sun already absent from overhead. I readied the pistol in my hand, the wheellock somewhat less reliable than the one I had last used, but I had left that with Sophie for her own protection. Quickly looking over at Max and Belial, I saw Max grip his club tightly, his hands wringing the life from the dead wood, his eyes closed in silent prayer. The reformed cultist was only marginally less reflective, twisting his neck from side to side, audible cracks accompanying each movement, loosening his limbs, his inhibitions, for whatever lay inside.

Hissing at them to get their attention, I counted down on my fingers, waiting for the last one to fall before I sprinted towards the lifeless cathedral, vaulting the low graveyard wall and slamming into the heavy door. Max was a step behind, Belial several steps quicker despite having waited for my signal. Motioning to them both, I waited as they heaved the heavy doors ponderously open, slipping through the growing crack as quickly as I could, my eyes adjusting to the gloom inside quickly.

Far from the majesty of my last visit, the cathedral was bereft of any regal air this time. The prayer candelabras were dark, a few lonely blackened wicks the sole guardians over the silence. A quick look towards the chapels dotted on its perimeter confirmed what I already knew: God was as dead here as the stones of the church were, all touch of the divine flown in the face of the moldering dead underneath my feet.

My eyes were drawn to a shadow moving in the far corner, a kneeling figure barely seen in the gloom slowly crossing itself before turning to reveal the alabaster face of Kalb. Or something that had once been Kalb. Like Michel, his face seemed to grow younger before my eyes, a dark vitality infusing the cruel smile underneath his infernal gaze.

I heard a whispered oath from Max, heard him furiously cross himself to avert evil, but it was Belial who spoke for us. "Brother, it's time to leave this city."

The smile grew mocking, derision infusing Kalb's response. "Oh, you poor deluded fool. I didn't want to believe it when I came to visit the child – you *have* gone soft." He shrugged, crossing to look at us as we advanced towards him down between the pews. "You are as worthless as your name implies. I told him that you were beneath saving."

I held my tongue. This was a conversation between two men, one struggling towards the light, the other bathing in darkness. "This is wrong, Kalb," said Belial, his hands outward, almost pleading. "The Master has to know this. We came here to save the sick, but how many have we made by our own hands?"

"How many have you made, you mean," countered the African, his pale whiteness almost painful in its lack of color. "You made the first one by your own touch, by your touch and your faith." A skeletal finger jabbed accusingly. "You, who implored the Master to take in a whipped dog, who begged to be given a purpose in life. Why do you turn your back on that which made you truly matter?"

"I haven't," responded my former prisoner, quiet passion in every word. "I turned my back on the Master."

"Then you turn your back on God himself!" roared Kalb, his outburst causing each of us to jerk into a sudden guard. But the fury passed as quickly as it had come, and the albino laughed. "You are like an ant, Belial, in his sight."

"In whose, God's or the Master's?" he asked.

"Does it matter whose? You are nothing to either, not even a thread in the loom of the tapestry of his great plan. When we return to God, we are the ones who will be glorified for our efforts and not you. You, who came so close and yet threw it away to help... who?" asked Kalb, flinging his hand carelessly at Max and me. "An atheist and his pets? You fled your old life to become faithful, truly faithful, and you go right back to it?" I saw a glimmer of pain in Kalb's eyes, the African's harsh mien breaking for a moment as he considered a face that he had perhaps called a brother once.

"Would you have us drown the city in blood in an attempt to wash it clean?" asked Belial. "The Master has called us so many things. Monarchists because we celebrate God in his primacy." He crossed himself here. "Doctors because we save the healthy from the sick. Saints because we do God's work. But aren't we also murderers, to have consigned so many to His side? If my name is true in my worthlessness, then let yours be true now. Let your faith see you turn your back on the Master and the evil he would have us do." So close now, Belial reached out a hand in friendship.

It was swatted away by the other cultist, a mask of deranged zeal falling over Kalb's face. "No, it's you, isn't it? The Master knew when he brought you into our number that he was inviting the devil himself into our midst. That's how we know you... your name, your temptation would have us turn our backs on the Master and God!" Kalb became agitated now, backing away, his head whirling one way and then the other, his hands curling into fearsome claws. His eyes cored into Belial. "You are no brother of mine, and their city's tomb will be yours as well."

Belial didn't even look at Max or me, leaping forward even as Kalb turned to flee.

Seeing what he was intending, I called out, "Stop him!" Taking my own words to heart, I took aim with my pistol quickly, but when I clutched at the trigger nothing happened. Cursing fiercely, I shook the pistol, one hand flying to my pockets for a small crank that would prepare it to fire. I felt Max shoulder past me, heard a wild yell and a grunt of effort that quickly turned into one of pain. Attaching the crank to the pistol as swiftly as I could, I spun it as quickly as I carefully could, one last loud snap telling me all was in readiness.

I raised it again to see Max and Belial circling Kalb like hunting dogs bringing a fox to bay. Darting in and out as quickly as they could, I watched the three men parry and strike at one another with the speed of master swordsmen. That two of them used nothing but their bare hands did little to dull the savagery, every chop and jab delivered with lethal intent. I watched, helpless, as Kalb managed to sneak a blow past Max's guard, a kick landing hard on one leg to slow his frantic darting to an awkward limp. Max dropped a hand to his massage his injury, but his other hand still gripped his club and I could see determination in every painful step.

I could see Belial was already wounded, several parallel lines on his face already bleeding. They weren't enough to take him out of the fight – Max's injury was far more severe – but it was an abrupt enough reminder that the longer this fight went, the worse off we would be. Trying to stem the bleeding – literally and figuratively – I raised the pistol again, sighting carefully on Kalb's stomach. I didn't think a single shot would stop him, but if he closed the distance, I knew I would get the worst of it.

My finger pulled the trigger tightly, the wheellock mechanism spinning wildly with a loud *chikt*. But nothing else. Surprised, I half lowered the pistol, tilting it slightly to see that everything was as it should be.

Off-target, it was then the weapon fired, the ball flying from the muzzle to whine against the flagstone of the floor before ricocheting up and burying itself in Kalb's thigh. The melee ground to a halt, the three men half stunned by the sudden noise in so confined a space. Even prepared, I was half-deafened, my ears ringing as the cathedral reverberated with reflected noise.

Kalb recovered first, shaking his head to clear it of the ringing, his gaze falling murderously on me. He flowed like quicksilver in between my staggering companions, his body moving in ways that I couldn't help but call unnatural. Like Michel days before, his face seemed to change before my eyes, as if my bullet had shattered some vestige of control, but in the dim light I didn't know, couldn't know if I could trust my eyes.

I know I should have raised my hands to defend myself, that I should have gone for the knife at my belt or tried to reload my pistol, but I was frozen as I saw death hurtle towards me. But Kalb stopped short, his face so close to mine that I could smell old, stale blood on his breath, rancid and sickly sweet. It was as if I had bitten into a fresh corpse, yet even that thought was somehow more appetizing than having the albino so close at hand.

I heard a groggy shout from Max behind Kalb, but I knew that he was too far from me to even pretend assistance. "You are lucky that your life has been promised to you by my Master," snarled the cultist, making me gag as the stench filled every crevice of my nose and mouth. "But," he continued, the cruel smile returning, "he said nothing about you feeling a measure of the torment that we must endure in God's service."

I felt a fist thunder into my side, phantom daggers plunging into my ribs. I heard bones break and my breath shot from me. I tried to stay clinical, tried to catalog my injuries as dispassionately as possible, but the pain kept intruding. I had been through worse, but here and now I could think of nothing but the pain.

My mind, overwhelmed, retreated, my vision whiting out as I felt my legs collapse under me.

I didn't pass out, I know that. The pain in my side wouldn't let me. But I heard more than saw my companions rush to my side, though even then their voices were muffled and distant. More than one hand went to my side, drawing a shout of pain from me that sent the probing finger in retreat.

The whiteness across my eyes faded to grey and then faded further, resolving slowly into the inside of the darkened cathedral, Belial and Max's faces, the pews at the edges of my view silent and judging me for my irreverent sprawl in a place so formerly holy. I heard my name first, my senses returning enough to hear the repeated call over and over, as if the reminder of my identity would rid me of the pain.

I tried to wave them off, my voice coming weakly from me. "I'm ok. Help me up," I ordered, regretting it immediately. Falling heavily to one side, my vision swam, my breath leaving me in rough, ragged coughing.

At length, I stopped hacking, blessed relief coming as Belial and Max half-lifted, half-coaxed me into one of the pews. "Where –" I began, struggling to pull more than the shallowest breath, "is Kalb?"

"Gone," said Belial, his face abashed. "He left through one of the side doors after you fell."

"Doesn't matter," cut in Max. "Are you alright?" he asked me, one hand clutching at his leg painfully.

I tried to favor him with a brave smile, but I have a feeling that it did little to reassure him, his face growing more concerned rather than less. "I'm fine. A few bruised ribs maybe," I mused, though the pain in my chest told the truth of the matter: far beyond bruised, I had broken more a couple of my ribs, the shortness of breath probably due to a deflated lung. If Kalb's intent had been to torment me, he had been successful.

Max seemed to accept my response, but Belial's face was more skeptical. "You sure you're alright, Dietrich?"

I nodded, but the look in his eyes only faded once Max turned to look at him. "He's been through worse," said my friend. "He might be a noble, but he can take a beating," he finished proudly.

I looked around the cathedral. I remembered the first time I had come inside. There had been a choir softly singing to one side, light shining through the stained glass in such a way that the colors shimmered against the stones on the floor. It had been enough to bring a tear to my eye.

My eyes misted again now, though I could not pretend it was because of any imagined beauty. The music was gone, replaced by a chorus of voices inside my head that endlessly listed my failures, Kalb's escape adding itself to the long list. The glass still dully shone, even in the lightlessness, though the holy scenes gleamed with an infernal cast that caused me to shiver painfully.

I waved both of my companions to me, heaving myself to my feet, doing my best to breath as shallowly as I could to avoid another coughing fit. I had deserved today, deserved the injury for being foolish enough to believe that I could soldier around the city like some hero from a fairytale. Fairytales weren't real, and imagining myself as some storybook savior would get me killed, and to what end?

"We have gone as far as we can by being gentle," I muttered. "It is time for the gloves to come off."

"What?" asked Max.

I coughed, as much because of my injury as in surprise. While I saw Belial glance knowingly at me – of course he was listening, I thought petulantly – I didn't think that my words were loud enough that Max could hear me. Drawing in breath as best I could, I said, "We have been responsive this entire time to the plague, to Michel, to all of it. We set up hospitals in the areas where the plague rears its head, we burn the dead after they die... We only came here because we were chasing a rumor! That ends now," I promised.

"How?" asked Max, confusion plain on his face. "We can't keep people from getting the plague."

"That's not exactly true," I countered, dark inspiration striking me. "There are ways that we can, at least, minimize the spread."

My eyes met Belial's, the former cultist nodding slowly as he guessed the direction of my thoughts. "It can be done, Dietrich, but you will be killing as many as Michel. You will break every oath you have ever made to your craft. Is it worth it?"

"For those of us who might survive?" I asked, hating that my newly-minted idea was so devilishly attractive.

"It is."

XXXV

A Healing Wound

Going on the offensive was easier said than done, the pain of following days enough to sideline my ambitions.

The first of these pains was physical. My self-diagnosis, a knee-jerk reaction at best, turned out to be correct. Four ribs broken, one of them splintering enough to puncture my left lung. Abraham told me he could hear my chest hiss every single time I took anything more than the shallowest of breaths. Sarah divided her time between a recovering Katarina and me, admonishing me every time I attempted to go outside to see the state of the city for myself. It would be weeks before my chest healed, weeks that none of us had, so I did my best to evade her watch, sneaking out with Max or Belial whenever I could convince them to go.

They rarely gave in to my desire to escape the estate, Sarah's recommendations for my welfare prized above my own wishes. More often than not, one would pretend to go along with me while the other ghosted off to find my erstwhile jailer. I didn't hold it against them, my attempts to escape Sarah's assisted imprisonment enough to distract me from the other pains I in which I wallowed.

The city, so long decaying, had begun to change for the better, or at least that was the tale I heard from Max and the others of the watch.

Their reports streamed back to collect in the parlor that had become my war room, scraps of information barely managing to slake my thirst for knowing the current state of matters.

The established hospitals, though they were unable to find any true remedy for the plague, had slowed the rate of infection. Instead of hundreds dying a day, the number had dropped to mere dozens, though even that tally was too high, the towering pyres outside the city continuing to burn unabated. Thugs and thieves continued to enrich themselves from the plagued dead and dying, though the watch had managed to crack down on the more egregious looting. More than a few houses were seized and turned into impromptu prisons, slowly filling as these unrepentant opportunists were arrested.

But for all the good news, my morale sagged, if for no other reason than that I knew the cost of this recent success. For every neighborhood we saved, another was abandoned. While the lanterns were kept lit on one street, others were allowed to gutter out. Wherever I deemed the situation hopeless, I cut off all investment, closing the *apothekes* and clinics, withdrawing supplies from the groceries and shops, barricading the streets, and stationing guards to prevent any in the district from leaving.

I only saw the effects of my ruthlessness once, but that single visit was enough to give me insomnia the following night. I smelled the fetid reek of corruption, the stench enough to cause a painful coughing fit on its own, as if my wounds were not enough to cause suffering. I heard the wail of newly minted widows, the sound enough to set my teeth on edge. But the worst was the way that the starving stumbled into the street to join the other corpses. I was reminded of my nightmares months before, the shambling of the soon-dead sending shivers down my spine as they glared at me in unrepentant hate.

Before then, I had kept the guards at their posts for days on end. After that, I changed them daily, sometimes more often than that.

"Do you ever regret your decisions?" I asked Belial one day after another failed escape attempt. I took a fortifying sip of tea, the touch of honey in it soothing a sore throat that had developed in the last days since my injury.

"Which ones?" he asked, pretending confusion though his answer told me that he already read my question for what it was. "If you refer to my coming here, then I do, and I do not."

"No?" My eyebrows rose in surprise. "Given your activity these last weeks, I did not expect an answer that straddled the fence."

He smiled, the wistfully sad expression full of recovered humanity and uncovered misery. "Consider this from my point of view... I came here to kill and destroy, to turn my back on God and his creation even as I thought I was saving it. I came here, to this place," he continued, one hand pointing at the floor, "to kill you and everyone who might have seen me at the Muslim's grocery."

The reformed man shrugged. "You stopped me, and while yes, you chained me in the pantry, you showed me kindness, the first of it I have seen in years. You prevented others from taking their rightful revenge on me. You freed me, gave me a truer purpose. I am where I am now thanks to you."

"I also beat you, starved you, shot you," I countered, ticking off one finger after another, melancholy threatening to overtake me again. "I hardly think that I deserve thanks for my actions."

"True," he allowed, nodding slowly. "But you did it with the best of intentions!" he joked. We shared a laugh, one that turned into another coughing fit for me. He reached a hand out to steady me. "Are you ok, Dietrich?"

Covering my mouth quickly with a handkerchief on the table beside me, I waited for the fit to pass, delicately dabbing a cloth at the sides of my mouth as I felt moisture collect there. I folded the white cloth over quickly so as to hide the new spots of red now soaking into the fabric. "I'm fine," I lied.

Belial's head tilted curiously. "Why do you hide the depth of your injuries from the others?"

I deflected. "The others know, I'm sure. Sarah will have told Abraham, and Abraham my sister."

"What of Max? Wilderich? Your niece and nephew? Why save the city if you kill yourself in the process?" he pressed.

"I'm not dead yet," I commented, though I felt the ache in my side that could easily herald that. My ribs were slowly healing, my breath returning more with each passing day. But even if I managed to heal completely, these were the kind of injuries that would last a lifetime. My mind would be willing, but my flesh would be weak until the end of my life, however long that was.

He allowed me my lie, his questioning taking a different tack. "Why do you doubt yourself and the decisions you have made?"

I waved a hand out vaguely towards the city. "Have you seen the kind of misery my actions have caused? I have consigned whole portions of Vienna for death!"

"No," responded Belial, his head shaking softly. "If anything, you have given whole portions of Vienna a chance at life. Without your decisions, the efforts to save the city would already have failed. It would be as if..." he struggled to find the right metaphor. "...as if you were spreading butter over too much bread. I have noticed the way you eat. You scrape and spread, pushing the smallest pat of butter to all corners of your *brot*. You try to minimize the resources you use as best you can for tomorrow, hoping for another meal and planning for it, knowing that your supply is limited. You sacrifice today knowing that tomorrow will probably come.

"But this plague is different. If you do not slather a neighborhood in goods and food, in medicine and healing, how can you know for sure that you can save it? If you must neglect the slice of bread tomorrow for the one today, are you guilty of any crime?" He shook his head again, more definite this time. "Your resources are finite, your time and energy even more so. You must sacrifice, somewhere, or the entire city will go unbuttered."

"But the people!" I managed to gasp, my throat constricting painfully.

"The people had many chances to save themselves," he answered me, shaking his head as I looked at him curiously. "I don't mean by any kind of faith-building, though I'm sure that would have saved them from my coming as well." Belial smiled sadly. "They could have stepped forward to volunteer themselves, their goods, even their prayers. They could have moved to help one another... humanity should be like that. We should live by others' happiness, not their misery, for God's sake!" He crossed himself, pale fingers flashing north, south, east, west in fervent devotion. It was, perhaps, the most zealous thing he had done in recent memory.

"The Kingdom of God is in all men," I responded softly, the words coming unbidden to me from somewhere in the back of my mind.

"St Luke," smiled Belial, the expression more hopeful this time. He reached out to touch me on the shoulder. Weeks ago, I might have shuddered at the thought of him laying hands on me, but here and now I felt nothing but warmth, support from an enemy-turned-ally who wanted the same victory as I. "For a man who claims to be so removed from God, you know His word almost as easily as I do."

I met his gaze, surprised at how bright his dark pupils seemed right now. "My parents were the religious ones. Not zealously so, maybe, but they made sure we read the mysteries and could debate theology well enough to suit visiting clergymen who occasionally stayed with us."

"You told me that your parents died when you were young," he said cautiously, his eyes narrowing as he appeared to plunder his memories to confirm the fact.

"Indulge an eight-year old in enough books, and something is bound to stick," I tried to joke, but humor failed to make an appearance in my voice. "I never finished the Bible. My parents died of the wasting sickness before I did."

"And you turned away from God in grief," he finished for me, waiting for me to nod before answering with one of his own. "You have given your life to helping other people, Dietrich. The only crime you are guilty of is believing everyone can be saved, or perhaps should be saved."

"He's right, little brother," interrupted Sophie from the doorway, his arms folded to ward off a growing chill in the room. Belial gave a slight bow of deference as she came further into the war room, a servant appearing behind her with an armful of wood, slipping around the three of us to putter about the fireplace. I heard the scrapping of a poker as the houseman prodded the weak fire into a semblance of heat, listened to the crackle and crunch as he added more wood for the fire to devour. "You've always been a little too hard on yourself."

"If not me, then who?" I asked.

But she didn't answer me immediately, turning instead to Belial. "Belial, can you please go check the hospital near the Graben?"

I half rose, trying to escape another deep conversation, but Belial gently pushed me back into my seat, the movement powerful but restrained. "I'll handle this, Dietrich. I'll let you know what I find." With another bow, he slipped from the chamber and outside.

"For the record," I said petulantly, "You said I could be the one who ran this side of our efforts."

"And you are, little brother. But you would have told him the same thing after I told you about some reports in the area about sightings of plague doctors." Her head tilted to one side. "Have you heard what the city is calling them now?"

"Angels of Death," I said, nodding slowly, letting the matter of Belial's dismissal drop. "I am surprised that the people accept what we've said so easily."

Her lips shrugged. "They are scared and in need of a leader. Besides, they know who is controlling food and medicine."

I winced in the implied rebuke. "I just spoke to Belial about this. I really don't need to go over it again. Besides, I would have thought you would be pleased to be overseeing all of this." I let my hands sweep in every direction. "If we survive, you'll have gained a whole new web of informants and allies."

She ignored the accusation. "What's actually bothering you, little brother? It's not this whole neighborhood business. You've done things you're not proud of your whole life, and you've still never tortured yourself like this before."

"Sure about that?" I said petulantly. "Like I told Belial, I'm single-handedly responsible for so many deaths that I'm pretty sure I've ruined the family name."

So content on brooding, I missed her quick step forwards, not realizing she had closed the distance until her hand snuck out to punch me ungently on my arm. "Snap out of the self-pity. Brooding might make other women go wild, but it makes me feel like slapping the snot out of you." A darkly humorous grin appeared. "Actually, go ahead... Wallow in the pity. That felt pretty good."

My face burned from embarrassment, I held my hands up in surrender – and to ward off another blow. "Did you have to hit so hard?"

"Yes, actually," she responded. "You can be unbearably dense sometimes. I had to be sure I could cut through the self-doubt and get through your thick skull. Quite a feat some days." She backed away – thankfully – and sat across from me. "Now... what's wrong? Usually when you get this morose, it lasts a day or two and then you put things back in the proper perspective and carry on. Why not this time?"

I worked my jaw around before taking a sip of my tea, my skin still feeling like it was being pricked by a thousand tiny needles. "He made me a deal."

"Who did? Michel?" she asked, waiting for a nod before expectantly asking, "And...?"

I told her, "Forty people of my choice will be saved from the plague. They will not be touched by the disease now or again, or I roll the dice and they may die."

"He just offered that?" she said skeptically. "Forty people get to live? In a city of thousands?" Her eyes narrowed. "In exchange for what?"

"Me." I tried to keep my tone light, but the look of dismay that blossomed on her face told me I failed. My voice growing more somber, I tried to explain. "Michel wants me to join his doctrine."

"His band of mass murderers, you mean," she countered. "His merry, little troupe of anarchists. His den of –"

I knifed one hand across to cut her off. "Enough. I've been wrestling with it enough without you piling on."

Sophie's arms flew open, sarcasm dripping in every syllable.

"Enough?! Well, forgive me if I 'pile on' too much for you right now! What an idiotic notion to want to keep my little brother around for a few years longer yet. Forgive me if I get a little emotional. How could you possibly even consider this... deal?" she asked scornfully. "It's a deal with the Devil!"

"The Devil? It's not like you to take note of a power higher than yourself," I quipped.

Her eyes flashed dangerously, though they softened soon after in fatigue. "I've seen an awful lot these last weeks, Dietrich. Katarina almost died, you have been beaten to a pulp more than once, Belial, Michel, so many of our friends and associates..." She massaged her nose, her eyes closing as she sagged back against her chair. "I have worked my entire adult life to control and manipulate, to create something that would outlast both of us and protect Katarina and Freddie for their lives, maybe even their own children as well."

She waved vaguely towards the window. "Look out there now... In a few months, over a decade of work is gone. My business contacts are dead or fled, my network diseased or being bled dry of all usefulness. I have seen everything I have worked toward rot and fade because of the machinations of a madman and his disciples."

I opened my mouth to respond, but it was her turn to wave me to silence. "There are costs I will accept as being beyond my control. The loss of power, position – that's the way of the world and nobility. The sun rises and sets on everyone. But what I will not accept is the trade of an innocent man, a *good* man, to save a drop in the bucket."

"Even when it could save the entire family? Our friends?" I asked rhetorically, unable to keep silent any longer. "I could ensure that our loved ones are untouched, and at the cost of what? My freedom?"

"You have no way of knowing that Michel could even guarantee that," Sophie spat. "What has he done but lie and deceive since he's arrived here?"

I shrugged. "He told me that he healed Katarina as a show of good faith."

"Belial did that," claimed Sophie, "not Michel. That was the work of human hands and not some divine intervention. Besides, if Michel is some all-powerful being, why would he need you? If you aren't a good man, why would he make this deal to you and you alone?"

I was forced to concede the point, my mouth twisting in thoughtfulness. "Ok, I see your point there, but – "

"But nothing," Sophie interrupted. "Do you really want to be the lackey of a madman?"

"No, but... If it saved you and the children? If it saved Abraham and Sarah and Wilderich and Max? Wouldn't that be worth it?"

"Would it?"

"I... don't know," I admitted. "It would be enough for me to know that you are all safe, even if it is only from the plague." A new thought dawned on me, unpleasant perhaps but enough to shatter the gloom I had labored underneath these last days. "That's it, isn't it?" I wondered aloud, my head tilted to the side as I looked at Michel's offer with a fresh perspective. Sophie merely raised an eyebrow, clearly unable to read my mind, but unwilling to admit it aloud. Nevertheless, the look of bemused confusion on her face was enough to draw a painful chuckle from me. "You're right, Soph," I congratulated.

"Of course, I am, but about which part?" I could see her weariness tentatively fading, as if my sudden good mood was enough to infuse her with fresh energy.

But my mind was beginning to rush in all manner of directions now, and I was unwilling to backtrack. "Why did you ask Belial to go to the hospital near Graben? What happened over there?"

I watched Sophie's eyes narrow, her gaze peering as deeply as she dared to plumb my thoughts, but she relented, shaking her head in disbelief. "With you stuck here, I would have thought you would already know why."

"Could we skip the big sister criticism?" Despite my inability to completely contain my annoyance, I managed to keep my tone almost civil. "I've been busy trying to track down Michel and his people. Can you just tell me?"

"Despite our best efforts, our physicians have been struggling to maintain any measure of success against the plague there. I sent Belial to see if he could see anything different about the plague there as opposed to other hospitals."

"What do you mean, that we've been struggling?" I asked.

"We've been failing more there than anywhere else. It's to the point that I would suggest we consider closing the hospital and shifting our resources elsewhere."

"No," I responded reflexively. "Even if the rest of the city dies, that hospital remains open."

"Anywhere else and you'd have closed the site weeks ago. Why keep this one?"

"It's the heart of the city," I replied simply.

"Are symbols really that important right now?" asked Sophie.

"Now more than ever. Can you imagine what would happen if the people heard that Stephansdom was lost to the plague? Even if you aren't remotely religious, your own heart would die a little: the spiritual and literal center of the city, dead and buried under the weight of disease! Anyone who has stayed would lose all hope. And, because of that," I continued, getting slowly to my feet, gritting my teeth against the sore pain of my healing ribs, "I need to go to see what it's going on with this hospital as well. If nothing else, I need to see if I can help, relieve the burden of suffering there."

I had expected Sophie to stop me, but instead she nodded slowly, whether in acceptance or understanding I couldn't say. If anything, she looked resigned to my decision, though I couldn't tell for sure from her downcast expression. "I remember Father asking me to watch over you when we were children: I ask the same thing of Katarina and Freddie. For a long time, I was able to do that. To watch over you, to finance your education and keep you lodged here on the estate... Even if I wasn't able to protect your innocence completely, I clung to the knowledge that you always had a safe place to return at the end of the day, that despite everything I could give you a place to retreat to."

Her face rose to smile grimly at me. "It's part of the reason I fought so hard to keep this entire conspiracy out of your hands. It's part of the reason I tried so hard to hate Belial and the evil he brought into our lives."

"Without him, Katarina may not have made it," I admonished.

She nodded. "True, but let me sermonize a little. Sometimes little brothers are idiots." I let the barb slide off, seeing in the comment the same tough love that all siblings bestowed on one another. It was curious, actually, to see the change that had come over Sophie these last weeks. My entire life, my older sister had been the dominant force for the family, a *grande dame* in everything but her age, solid and immutable against every twist of fate or stumbling block placed before her.

The plague had torn away that façade, and for the first time in my life I had seen the tattered remnant of vulnerability that still somehow remained, scared and cold, underneath the calm that I had known my entire life. And while the first expression of it caught me off guard, stunning me that it existed at all, I felt nothing if not closer to her for the way she had striven each day to remain strong.

I turned to go, so intent on my rumination that her next admission caught me by surprise. "Forgive me for doing what I thought I had to do to save you from... all of this. I believed that if I had to dirty my hands to keep you clean, then it was worth it. If I had to dominate you in the fight against this plague to keep you innocent, then it was worth it. Even if I had to shoot Belial to save my children - and to save your belief that all people were worth saving - then it was worth it."

She got up from her chair to come over and hug me. Her arms were as thin as they always were, but I could feel the desperate strength in her fierce embrace, as if anything lighter would see me swept away by the world. "Sophie, you're hurting me a little bit." I saw small tears on her cheeks as I slowly managed to extricate myself from her hold, beads that she struggled to hide in quick dabs against her sleeves.

I saw her open her mouth, as if there was more yet she wanted to say, but she settled for a gentle, motherly kiss on my cheek. "Hurry and you might yet catch up to Belial."

I opened my own mouth, but words seemed tawdry and inconsequential. I settled for my own kiss on her forehead, gave her as tight a squeeze as I could, then left the manor house behind.

XXXVI

A Profaned Hospital

Catching up to Belial was difficult, but thankfully not impossible, the reformed cultist kneeling by the side of the road just outside the city's walls.

"Praying?" I asked without preamble, knowing that his preternatural senses had likely heard me coming from dozens of meters off.

"Healing?" he asked without looking over, the single word drawing a smile from me. Poor as the attempted humor was, that he had even tried spoke of his successful, if ever continuing, rehabilitation. "One moment, please, Dietrich."

I was overcome by a mad impulse to join him, my recent attempted religiosity almost enough to send me to my knees, but to pray next to Belial almost felt like sacrilege, my own stumbling words a far cry from his intense devotion. So I kept my hands apart and my words to myself, waiting as the thinner man finished his heavenly conversation.

Eventually he finished, rising to his feet with the same inhuman grace he had shown when our paths had first crossed. I couldn't help but feel a shiver down my spine at the economically fluid movement. "So you escaped Sarah?"

"There is a time to heal, and a time to go on despite the need to heal,"

I quipped, butchering some biblical passage half-remembered. "Sophie knows I'm along. What did she tell you about the hospital at Graben?"

Belial's shoulders lifted slightly as we turned to walk inside. "What you heard is what I know."

"Liar," I accused, smiling to soften the blow.

A small smirk crossed his own face. "Maybe only slightly. I have gone there before." The good humor left him, a pained cloud drifting over his face in its place. "You may find yourself... unsettled."

"Why?"

"The plague is different here. Even I have not seen such potent death before, and I have caused no small amount of it myself." His eyes might have watered then, contrition calling forth tears over the shameful actions of the past, but he cleared it from his face quickly, leaning close as if to ensure secrecy remained between the two of us. "Many of the bodies are, I've heard, corrupted by the Mark of Sin."

"The bite marks, you mean?" The Mark of Sin. There was little rhyme or reason behind their incidence, the two angry welts appearing at random on the dead and dying throughout the city Another time, another place I might have laughed at the inanity of the name, hearing in it the overblown imagination of a frightened child, but I heard it whispered far too many times, the title synonymous with a visit from Michel and his 'Angels of Death'. The people shrank from any location even a single mark was reported, common sense seeing them flee like cockroaches before a bright light. "Why haven't I been told about this before?"

Belial shrugged. "You were healing." I scowled, the expression drawing a gentle, amused smile from him. "Besides, we didn't hear of it from the monks until a few days ago."

He knew I knew he was lying, but I let the matter drop, my mind more focused on questions than arguing over the need to keep me in the dark. I felt my companion look at me in surprise, apparently unready for my lack of follow-up, but he said nothing to disturb the relative silence that joined us for the rest of our walk into the center of the city.

Perhaps relative silence was the wrong term for our journey: only our steps made any noise, the only other perceivable sound a light crackling from somewhere out to the west where the gravediggers and corpse-collectors lit their funeral pyres. Where weeks before I would have seen my progress impeded by scores of pedestrians, I now only needed to step over or around the most-recently dead, their last vestiges of life strangled by the black death. Where I would have been forced to slide cautiously past carts and their wares, I instead clutched a hand-kerchief to my face to stave off the rotted, festering waste of mush that had once been food.

Worse yet, the closer to city center we came, the less noise I heard, even the crackling of the crisping dead fading as the wind decided to whisper elsewhere. The realization was an unwelcome one, my eyebrows furrowing as I strained to hear anything of the hospital. I could see Stephensdom over the tops of the nearby houses. *Surely*, I should be able to hear something by now.

But there was nothing. I looked at Belial, seeing an equal amount of disquiet on his face. "Anything?" I asked.

Suspicion lay heavy on his brow. "No." I saw his head twist one way and then the other, the once-cultist reaching as desperately as I did to hear something. "I can normally hear the monks administering to the sick," he commented. "By now, I can normally hear their prayers as they change bandages. Something's wrong. I smell blood."

"Obviously," I said unhelpfully, pulling my pistol from its place at my belt, my other hand testing the pull of the knife at my waist. I had grabbed both on my way from the house absent-mindedly, part of me uncomfortable with the thought of bringing any weapons into the city on such a fact-finding mission. Now I was grateful for them.

Satisfied that my knife's sheath would not bind against the blade at all, I stopped a moment to twist the pistol back and forth, examining the weapon for any signs of disrepair or decay. My ribs grumbled as my last experience with the pistol came to mind; I was determined to not repeat my experience.

I loaded the powder and ball first, carefully ramming the charge home before I pulled the crank from my pocket. Slotting it around the peg, I twisted slowly, trying to still my mind from asking too many questions over the silence that otherwise reigned supreme. I heard a final click, the wheel pulled tightly into position. Keeping my finger away from the trigger, I stowed the crank, nodding readiness to Belial.

We slunk to one side of the street, moving slowly in an effort to prevent our steps from echoing against the cobblestones. A shiver skittered down my spine as we neared the building, an odd chill arising from nowhere to freeze my body and gnaw at my resolution. It would be so easy to turn around and return to the estate, to gather more forces before finding out the reason behind the blanketing silence so close to the hospital.

It seemed my feelings bled into my face, because Belial reached out to steady me, the delicate warmth of his strong grip reassuringly insistent. "Are you ok, Dietrich? I can always go on alone if you are unwell." It was the closest he would come to warning me off, I could see that, but I also saw concern in his face. Forcing my weakness from me as best I could, I shook my head firmly. If he was going on, so would I.

He led the way around the last corner, sliding from one shadow to the other like a pale specter. Even knowing what such sinuousness had cost him, I was momentarily jealous at the ease of his movement, though the feeling passed quickly. Taking a final breath before, I swung my pistol up before I leapt around the corner.

As with so many of the other hospitals, my sister's people had erected the temporary structures in the middle of the street, few laborers willing to venture into the plague-ridden houses on either side of the street. Barely cloth and rotting timber, the small tent village was rude but functional, its workers able to flit from one fabricked chamber to another with little more than a few steps as they ministered to the sickened lame. Anywhere else, Belial and I would have been met by a brace of brave guards, gruffly challenged for our presence and sent to the appropriate location for care or delivery of supplies. Here, I had actually placed over a dozen armed men of the watch, unwilling to see the important site violated in any way.

Despite this, the sight that greeted us was a far cry from such civility. The tents were shredded, the walls rent by clutching hands, the timbers shattered and broken like the toys of a wasteful child, shards of wood flung about like matchsticks caught in a gale.

Worse than this were the bodies that were strewn about the site, each dead face poisoned by the same heart-wrenching mix of terror, hatred, and trauma. I tried to keep my eyes from meeting all of the sightless stares, but one after another they bored into me, their unnatural ends bellowing silently out in pain and accusation. I tried to find a place in the hospital free of their presence, but everywhere I looked I saw nothing but more death and blithe destruction.

Once, for an instant, I thought I managed a moment of peace when my eyes were drawn to a pile of discarded bandages on the ground, but I was denied even that much peace, my eyes and gently probing hands discovering that the blood-soaked bandages contained a grisly, bitten trophy underneath. My stomach emptied itself afterwards, my innards as empty as my heart felt now.

I saw Belial cross himself. "How could I ever think to have given myself over to this madness?" he whispered. "This is not God's will. This... this is insanity."

I found myself hard-pressed to disagree, every response shriveling on my tongue. So I said nothing, unwilling to desecrate the scene with an empty platitude. Instead, I reached out a hand to Belial, trying with all my might to be the rock he had so recently offered to be.

He seemed to appreciate the gesture, a withered smile vainly trying to tease his lips as he pretended stoicism. I could see his pain, though I still said nothing, knowing that there was nothing I could say to lift his spirits.

So instead I stood with him quietly, and bitterly drank in the scene.

XXXVII

A Bestowed Mercy

I could not say how long we looked about the dead: an instant, an hour, I doubt any God above might have known.

At length we managed control over our bodies again, the well of our determination once more plundered for the will to continue in the face of such barbarism. Moving gingerly among the fallen, we did our best to tug the more complete bodies into rough rows, uncaring that most of these were rife with plague sign. The tents we left alone, the broken timber and small mountains of bandages, too. After seeing the grisly remains that had lain beneath one of those cloth hills, I was unwilling to touch or see another.

Besides, we had more than enough dead to examine without exploring the bloody piles.

Forcing emotion aside, I saw that Belial's comment before had been accurate: It didn't seem to matter how many bodies I examined, I found the same two angry marks on each wasted pectoral, the so-called Mark of Sin calling each corpse its own.

"Why here?" I asked sometime after the thirteenth corpse. "Why this hospital and nowhere else?" I forced myself to look around to see what possible significance I could find in the area.

"You've said yourself, Dietrich," answered Belial. "This area is important symbolically, if nothing else. Without Stephansdom, where is the center of the city?"

"The Hofburg?" I ventured.

"Long since fled," was the response. "You were right before. The Emperor is the head of the city, but Stephansdom is its heart. Without the mind, the heart still beats. Without the heart, though... the body withers."

"But this kind of attack hit the most guarded of these locations!" I countered. "Why hit this one alone and not any of the others? We would have been overwhelmed by any spread in the other districts." I felt my voice rise in frustrated anger, my vented emotion reverberating from the houses on either side of the street.

In the silence that followed, I heard a gentle sob, something so muffled that, at first thought, I thought that I was imagining it. But when Belial froze as well, I looked about for its source. My gaze alit on one of the untouched bandage piles that shook despite an absence of any wind, the heaped cloth juddering in time with the soft, sad sound.

'Survivor?" I mouthed over to Belial, his only response a bemused shrug. I looked about for my pistol, retrieving it from where I had lain it when we had first explored the dead. Holding it at arm's length, I crept toward the pile, unwilling to unearth the secrets within it but equally unwilling to let whatever lay beneath lie unmolested.

Long seconds passed as we slunk over, more as we positioned ourselves on either side of the bloody bandages. The sobbing had stopped, whoever or whatever remained underneath once more in control of his or herself. I nodded to Belial, taking a step back as he swept armfuls of bandages aside, revealing a wretched, pathetically weeping man underneath.

He was no holy man, that much was obvious from his lengthy hair. Though I had interacted with few of the Trinitarian monks during their time in Vienna, I had seen enough of them to know that there were all artificially bald, their scalps as poor in hair as they were in their money pouches. And the revealed man was also absent any robes, his dress rugged but serviceable. "You were part of the guard here, weren't you?" I asked irritably, unable to completely quash the cocktail of anguished frustration that I still felt in my chest. "What in God's name happened?"

The supine man shook as if he suffered from palsy, his lips twisting as if he wanted to answer my question. But something prevented any sound from coming forth, his speech fleeing as surely as his nerves to hide somewhere else more sane, more safe. Before his arms hid his eyes in terrified shame, I saw the aftereffects of acute shock plastered in every crease of his face. We would get nothing out of him, I realized. The trauma of whatever had happened had stolen every one of his senses from him save survival.

Belial did not share my pessimism, it seemed, kneeling by the man and pulling the guard's head towards his breast. The man didn't resist, instead throwing his arms around the thin man's neck with a ferocity that surprised me. Belial jerked at the response, but accepted the motion with no complaint, instead leaning forward to whisper in the man's ear something that I couldn't make out. I thought he had managed to calm the man, for the guard relaxed slightly, but fresh sobs erupted afterwards and the revealed man clung to Belial tightly once more.

I wanted to turn away, to give the two a moment of privacy, but what lay before me was the most innocent vignette of the otherwise ruined hospital. Regardless, I did my best to allow Belial a moment to attempt to calm the man, scrutinizing the rest of the guard in the meantime. He was unarmed: I saw an empty sheathe on side of his waist that spoke of a missing knife. He should also have carried a club as well as a jury-rigged spear, though I was hard pressed to find either of those in the ruination around me.

And he was wounded, I realized now, deep gashes in his side that colored the bandages around him scarlet. Lower on his body, half-hidden, I saw at least one leg bent the wrong way. Adding in the set of claw marks I had seen on his face before it had been buried in Belial's chest, I was astounded. The man wasn't a broken lunatic: it was a miracle that he was even as sensible as he was. Given that we had heard nothing as we approached the hospital, the guard had been wounded some time ago and had, until our arrival, been alone with his pain and suffering for hours.

"Dietrich?" Belial interrupted my quiet wonderment. I knelt next to him, looking down as the wounded guard extricated himself from my ally's shoulder. The converted cultist nodded in encouragement. "Tell him what you told me."

The man's face still shook, dry riverbeds on his cheeks where he must have cried out his last tears, but at long last I heard his voice. "Lord," he whispered, his voice choked with pain. Despite all that must have happened to him, he raised his knuckles slowly to his forehead in respect, ingrained social graces somehow still remembered in the wake of recent history. "It was a massacre."

"What was?" I asked, laying aside my pistol again and trying to stem the gelatinous gush of life ebbing from the guard's side with the swept aside bandages.

"They came last night... the Angels of Death were here." I felt my face twist in unconscious hatred, but I forced myself to nod in acknowledgement, silently wishing the man would continue. I watched his Adam's apple bob, a dry tongue flickering out in a vain attempt to moisten his cracked lips. Looking about, I retrieved a discarded skin of some kind of liquid, moistening the man's mouth. His eyes went grey and distant, but he went on after nodding a vague thanks. "It was quiet. The monks were changing the bandages this morning when they came."

Belial looked at me curiously. "Bandaging the infected sites allows the flesh a chance to heal and prevents further affliction," I supplied. "I don't know how it works but it may have to do with keeping the areas dry and preventing mold."

"Tobias and I were on this side of the camp. Heard noise and yells behind us. Watched them tear tents apart, throw men aside as if they were light as feathers! I tried to stop them. I swear by Jesus, I did. Broke my spear off in one when they tried to attack me, but it did nothing. Nothing! He just laughed and threw me into a wall. I wanted to go for help, to help the others, but my legs stopped working... so I crawled into

these bandages. One of the last monks tipped more of them on me..."
The guard coughed, the effort of so many words winding him for a moment.

Remembering my own encounters with Michel's brethren – Belial included – I nodded sympathetically. "Why did they attack?" I asked. "Did they say anything?"

"I don't know." The man shook his head, the movement clearly painful as his expression twisted into a rictus of pain. "No, they..." His voice fell while his brow furrowed, his memory plundered for the barest scrap of information. "Wait... they kept bellowing a single word."

"What was it?" I hissed desperately. I could see the man fading, his wounds so severe that he had nothing to look forward to except a hopeless life as a cripple later or a slow, witheringly painful death now.

He clutched at my arm, his grip equally desperate. "Lord, promise me something first." Nodding immediately, I was ready to grant him the man anything he wanted. He deserved no less for his bravery. "Kill me."

I recoiled. "You do not want me to save your life, to heal you at all?" I asked as much as pled my question. "Surely there are those who would miss you?" I glossed over his dire prognosis, but I remained unwilling to actively kill a wounded man.

He smiled sadly, his eyes somehow managing to focus on my face at last. "They are dead, all of them. As is anyone else I knew. All gone. I see it in your face, Lord. If I live, I have no life. If I die, at least I'll see them again."

I felt tears gather at the edges of my eyes, the simple sentiment heartbreakingly pure. I couldn't even argue with his logic; the city had become a necropolis, untold thousands dead and more yet to die. Even though I remained resolute to outlast the plague, I continued to have something to live for, my family, friends still on this side of heaven. But this guard had no such ties.

I nodded once, unwilling to vow openly that I would violate every tenant of medicine and murder an unarmed man.

The sadness in his face faded into peace, the creases on his face disappearing so quickly I half-thought he was recovering his youth some-how. "Vergilius," he said slowly. "They kept speaking about Vergilius."

"You're sure?" I confirmed, waiting for his nod before trying to re-assure him with a pat on his shoulder, regretting it when he hissed in pain. "I'm sorry," I apologized.

"Not your fault, Lord. You've tried to do good by us, I know. Without you, we would have had no chance." I tried to shake his praise away, but he rejected my attempt. "*Es wird alles gut sein,* Lord. I may be dead, but as long as you fight the sickness, Wien will, too."

I know he meant his words as a balm for my soul, but they merely made my heart heavier and that much more reluctant to pull the trigger. But a promise was a promise so I nodded my thanks, standing slowly and backing away so I might be sure of my shot. Belial pulled the guard close one final time, more whispering flowing from one man to the other before he gently laid his down and made the sign of the cross.

The wounded man closed his eyes as I took aim. I closed mine after drawing a bead on his head, unwilling to see the effect of my own hand-iwork.

My finger twitched, and thunder rumbled in response.

XXXVIII

A Fleeting Chance

"They were all dead?" asked Sophie.

I nodded dumbly. "The hospital was torn apart. Supplies are gone or ruined. Bite marks on most of the dead, though who was already infected and who was bitten was impossible to say on anyone but the monks. The guards were completely torn apart, almost as if their being there meant nothing at all." I didn't mention my assisted suicide, not wanting to burden my sister with the blood that already lay on my hands.

"And that was our most fortified location," muttered Abraham off to one side, his words echoing my thoughts earlier that day. Belial and I had done our best to police the fallen, including the brave watchman, lining them off to one side of the street out of the returning wind.

The rest of the impromptu hospital we let lie. There was little left that we could salvage as it was, and I felt more compelled to return with the dire news.

"And we have no idea why they attacked that particular location?" asked Sarah. This was the first meeting she had attended since Katarina had fallen sick: her presence confirmed my niece's recovery, a bright moment of victory in an otherwise dark day of loss.

Belial shook his head, responding before I could manage an answer. "No, unfortunately." That he felt confident enough to speak in front of the other original members of our conspiracy was almost as much a victory in my mind as Katarina's returned health. "A survivor we discovered in the ruin commented that each of the... attackers yelled only a single thing as they tore through the camp."

Wilderich's brow wrinkled in confusion. "A survivor? I thought all of those poor souls were dead?"

I felt my face flush in shame, but Belial removed the need for any answer. "He... expired soon after we got there, Wilderich." It was curious to me that someone with such reverence referred to the bishop with such familiarity, but nothing about Belial's transformation had been remotely normal, so I held my tongue. The older man seemed to be completely unbothered by it, though Max did bristle slightly from his place at Wilderich's elbow.

Regardless, I coughed to move the conversation along as surreptitiously as possible, not wanting to linger on that particular line of questioning. "He told us that they barely spoke as they pillaged the site, but he heard a word used in the rare times they did speak."

"What word?" asked my sister, leaning forward on the table.

"Vergilius."

"And Belial, you don't know that means?" When the thin man shrugged, she made a face turned to the *apotheker* and his wife. "I certainly have no idea what that is... Sarah, Abraham? Any idea?"

But the Jews were as confused as her. "I don't know what that is, Sophie, sorry. Definitely not Hebrew," commented one, the other nodding soft agreement.

"Bishop?"

The bishop, however, fidgeted with one of his shirt sleeves. I tried to catch his eyes, but they were both staring at the table, flickering back and forth as if the holy man was reading some book that only he could see. "Wilderich?" I asked, seeing Max flinch again at my usage of the bishop's Christian name.

The older man started, his eyes jolting to me. "Sorry, I was trying to remember any texts that may have used the word Vergilius. The name itself is Latinate, meaning 'he who watches.' Some scholars think that is where we get the term vigil." I grinned as he looked about the table and saw the mixture of confusion and boredom that was reflected his way. His fidgeting hand dropped from his sleeve as if Wilderich finally remembered where he was, folding itself in with its opposite partner. "There *was* a Saint Vergilius back in the darker ages of the Church..." His gaze grew distant again, though a wistful expression touched his face. "Bit of a rebel against the Holy Church's teachings, but Pope Gregory IX canonized him all the same. Thirteenth century, if I remember correctly."

"Not exactly the most applicable information," commented Sophie wryly. "Anything else?"

"Well, he died in Salzburg, if that means anything," offered Wilderich. It didn't, but I joined Sophie in nodding sagely.

"I'm not sure that it does, but thank you anyway, excellency," said Sophie. "But I somehow doubt that Michel would be here if his endgame lay elsewhere."

The bishop was undeterred. "Understandable... Well, there is a chapel in Vienna by that name."

I seized on the idea. "That sounds more our quarry. Where is it?"

Wilderich looked back at me, confused. "Under the Magdalen-skapelle. Forgive me, but I thought you already knew. You were standing on it when you came to see me for the first time months ago."

"Strange," I mused, idly rubbing at my ribs. "I thought Magdalen-skapelle was the only structure there."

Max interjected. "No, the chapel has been there since the early 13th century, when the duke back then was hoping to make Vienna an episcopal see. He failed, but not before trying to build several holy sites, including Virgilskapelle."

All sound at the table stopped, all of us lost for words at Max's response. Had the mood been brighter yet, I imagine I may have laughed out loud at the madness of it all. If I didn't know any better, I would have thought we had stumbled into a comedic drama. As it was, I barely managed a stammered "Max?"

He blushed a deeper crimson than I had before, though his response was tinged by a wounded dignity I had never heard in him before. "I've spent my share of nights watching the city from Stephansdom, Dietrich. Do you think Bishop Wilderich and I just pray all night together?"

"No, but..." I shook my head. "Doesn't matter. Why didn't you say so before?"

"No one asked me," he said bluntly. I managed to look contrite, but my oldest friend ignored my apparent discomfort. "One thing I don't understand is why they would want anything to do with the chapel... It's so tiny."

"True," agreed Wilderich.

"How small?" I asked. "Smaller than Magdalenskapelle?"

"Much," affirmed the bishop. Looking about the war room, I could see his eyes mentally calculating some point of reference. "I wanted to give you an idea using the dining room as a starting point, but it's a little bigger," he said apologetically. "Imagine this half of the house's ground floor? Maybe as tall as the first floor?" he suggested. "With a couple of naves off to the sides."

"You're right," I said. "Even if we assume that Michel only has a small group of followers, why would he want such a small space?" I looked about the table, but few met my gaze with anything other than a shrug of loss or outright refusal to meet my eyes.

Something nagged at the back of my mind, as half-remembered as a dream but yet somehow pertinent. "Belial, when you first... arrived, you raved something about 'Virgil's seat'." He shook his head helplessly. "You recall anything about that? What that might mean?"

I watched his mouth work in several directions without producing any sound. "To tell the truth, I remember very little of that time here in the city."

I nodded, understanding the mind's need to put up walls to protect itself any way possible from history: the guard's face ghosted into my mind, his calm resignation forced out only after a second's effort. "How about before? Did Michel ever mention his plot here?"

"I was told only to 'seek out a sinful city and to spread the divine touch of the sickness to test their faith.'" His face grew rueful. "But I had heard from the others that every city's testing was capped by a final service at a place of the Lord. A final requiem for the faithful and faithless alike before the doctrine left to go elsewhere."

I digested this new piece of information for a moment. "Michel does not strike me as a man who would give himself in to a half-hearted celebration. Vergilius Chapel strikes me as too obvious a place to do anything."

Max cut in again. "Besides, where did we last see one of them." He pointed over at Belial. "Where did we see the last one? In Stephansdom!"

Belial seized on the momentum now. "True... Like I said, Dietrich, it is the heart of the city. The Master is a man of symbolism."

Sarah and Abraham concurred from their side of the table; my sister nodded definitively from where she sat on the other end of the table.

"It would make sense as to why they would destroy the hospital nearby." I held up a finger. "But Wilderich, your friend has been there still, hasn't he? Holding services for the last few holdouts in the area?"

"No," he responded. "They were driven out from there a short time ago."

"By Michel's people?"

"No, by the smell," he said his nose wrinkling. "So many have died and gone unburned that the stench of death permeated every stone of Stephansdom herself. I was told that the catacombs beneath reeked so fully of desolation that even the Hapsburg relics are left unlit, in direct opposition to the Emperor's will."

To be honest, I didn't give a fig about the Emperor's will and, thus, didn't much mind if dead rulers were kept in darkness. But after all the monetary assistance we had received from the Empress Elenore, I did my best to look as dismayed as the others at the table. It was more dismaying – though also morbidly interesting, I thought – that the stench of death had become so powerful that the holiest site in the city had become somehow unclean by its touch.

I suppressed a shiver of macabre fascination. Strange, perhaps, to feel any kind of elation after the devastation this morning, but I felt like we were finally within striking distance of Michel, of all his vile brethren, of the heart of the plague itself! Even the soreness in my ribs wouldn't depress me.

Judging by the curiously confused faces of the others, I imagine some small measure of the queer joy I felt had escaped. I tried to reassure them, an unwitting smile on my face. "I'm sorry, but I can't help but feel like we are, after so long, close to destroying the darkness from Vienna."

I saw cautious optimism tug at the edges of each expression, a measure of the tension we all felt relieved by my blind positivity though Sophie, as I might have expected, was less sanguine. "I'm not sure how you can say that, little brother. We just lost so many this morning, and you're pleased about it?"

"Yes, but think about it. We've been chasing our tails for weeks! We didn't have a clue, but Michel has finally tipped his hand!" In that moment, my optimism was as infectious as the plague, though still my sister resisted my thinking, her head still shaking in denial. I gently pounded one hand into the other. "Sophie, he's given us what we need to find him."

She remained nonplussed. "We haven't even decided where he is –"

"Of course we have," I interrupted. "He tipped his hand by destroying the hospital this morning."

"So he's where, then?" Sophie crossed her arms and leaned away from the table. Though she seemed resolutely resistant, I knew she could see my logic and was merely playing devil's advocate. Helpful given the stakes, but I felt more than a little irritation. We had had so little to celebrate and she was trying to undermine the air of good humor that threatened to lighten the war room. "I'm willing to concede he is operating from the center of the city. It just makes sense, and allows him to be where he needs to be to spread the plague where necessary. But tell me... which is it? Vergilius or Stephansdom?"

"The latter," interjected Wilderich, his eyes rising from where they had fallen on the table. My mouth open to respond, I stopped, willing to let someone else apply the pressure. The bishop folded his hands as if he was ready to pray, but he kept his words earthly, though his tone was sober and somber. "Like you've both said, Michel is a canny man. He let us believe he was our ally for so long that we let him learn whatever he desired from us."

He got up from his seat, his hands remaining in front for now, but he began to pace, the air of the teacher about him. "The chapel is the obvious choice. It has the name, the history. It is isolated, hidden underneath Magdalenskapelle, a place I have not been for quite some time, may God forgive me." The bishop crossed himself gently. "It would be the perfect base of operations. And besides... Dietrich, you once mentioned that he called the city Vindabona – the old Latin name for the city. Given the relative history of the chapel over that of Stephansdom, on the face of it everything would and should point to supposing his..." Wilderich's hands wind milled in the air for a moment. "...headquarters would be posted there."

Sophie looked exasperated a moment. "And I thought I was the one playing spoiler in this argument. Bishop, you're making my argument for me."

But the older smiled kindly, wagging a finger gently. "Not so, baroness. Like I said, Michel is a smart man. We can imagine he spent a long time scouting the city before dispatching Belial into our company." I was grateful for his gentle phrasing; now was the time for solidarity and I regretted my own choice of words earlier. "Whether or not he is, as some believe, more than human, we cannot think that he knows the city any less well than we do.

"He knows that I am aware of the city's history. He knows of Max and Dietrich and Abraham and their roles in the city. We gave him ample opportunity to learn that. Whether or not we heard this last tidbit of information from that brave survivor Belial and Dietrich uncovered this morning, he must know that all our conclusion would eventually realize Virgilskapelle as his base of operations." He snapped his fingers, his climax reached. "So why would he pick it? No, like you said, Baroness, he wants to be in the middle of the city. He wants a holy place to profane even as he professes Christian values. And what better place to desecrate than the see of the city? He'll choose Stephansdom."

"Plus there is the name to consider," cut in Max. His sudden intellectual depth revealed, Max added in his two cents to the conversation. "I've stood in the towers of Stephansdom often enough to know that the entire city is under its watch. How many times have we learned of a fire because of what the cathedral sees? Before the plague, how many times a night do we patrol past the cathedral. It sees everything; it *watches* everything in Vienna."

The nods were more vigorous now, even Sophie's defensive posture softening as one by one each of the conspiracy was pulled onboard with my theory. "I think you are all giving Michel too much credit, but if worst comes to worst, at least they are across from each other." My sister pursed her lips. "Have you considered what to do if and when we find them? Would you try to heal them somehow, Dietrich? Ask them gently to leave the city?"

I didn't answer immediately, Sophie's question dampening my enthusiasm slightly. My sister raised an eyebrow in expectation, calmly sitting and waiting for my answer. She expected my answer to be one of softness and innocence, of mercy and peace. And, for so long, she might have been right.

But the last months had been a cruel reminder of the darkness that laid within a man's breast. Having seen my own darkness released more than a few times, I knew that no open palm could be offered, not to those who had tried for so long to destroy my family and my city.

And I so wished to say that I could change them, that I could heal them. I wanted to point towards Belial as proof that all of Michel's brethren could be rehabilitated and turned from the dark path on which they now walked. But past the desires to save and to heal, past the hope that evil might be turned to good somehow, I saw the truth of the conflict. To save Vienna from the plague and Michel and his doctrine, the infection needed to be cut from the city.

Michel and all his brethren would need to die. As surely as he stood ready to destroy everything we loved, we needed to be as ready to destroy him and his beloved creations. In doing so I would be turning away from my oath to heal and grow, desecrating that last piece of myself as surely as the plague has ruined my city. But I had desecrated many things in weeks past: what was one more broken oath in the name of the greater good?

"They die," I said simply.

XXXIX

‿❧

A Throw of Dice

Dramatic as my words were, they were easier said than done. The next days saw the estate turned into an armed camp, the last dregs of the nearly-gone city watch marshalling in the area before the manor house. My old home out back was turned into an impromptu armory, my sister spending the last of our coin to beg, salvage, or make whatever we could to arm our slowly gathering militia. The bitter lessons of the wrecked hospital fresh on our minds, we prepared our citizen soldiers as best we could.

The longer spears with which we had armed all hospital guards were shortened into rough darts, their former length worthless even in the great expanse of the cathedral. I was under no illusions that our best chance was in keeping distance between our watch and Michel's cultists. Having faced off with Belial and Kalb – and come out the worse for wear on both occasions – to allow them inside arm's reach would be the worst mistake possible.

For those who were quicker mentally, we trained a handful in the use of pistols and muskets, making sure that the latter were also given bayonets for when order broke down. Max and I paired these men off with larger companions, driving home the hard lesson time and again that teamwork would increase their chances of survival. At first this lesson was disregarded, at least until I released Belial on them. Those there were more than a few new bruises by the end of the experience, but we had the rough beginnings of brotherhood between fighting pairs and quartets.

Our confrontation with Michel and the others would test whether or not these burgeoning bonds would mean anything.

When I was able to pull myself away from this task, I was assailed by dozens of others. Many of the watchmen had come to the estate with their families. Bonded as they were to the success of our assault, wives and elders alike all came forward for a task. I delegated as many as I dared to come along with us, sure that we would need healers when the time. Others I pushed to provision or walk the streets in place of the training men: we needed to maintain the façade that we were still flush with resources.

In truth we were anything but, the scores of thousands dead and ill consuming voraciously any stores the Empress' money had allowed us to stockpile. Despite this, I worked with every last man, woman, and child to ensure that our fiction was maintained. I wanted Michel to still see us as a strong and vital force, to inflate our strength and numbers. Even if he didn't, even if he saw through our ruse as his people saw the gray hair of the patrolling men and women, I hoped that maybe he would be surprised by the violence of our attack.

It was a long, vain hope, but as optimistic as I was during those days leading up to the attack, I knew our preparations for what they were: a long wager, thrown against the weighted dice of a cunning opponent. I was under no illusion that all of our toiling and struggle came to this single balancing point. We were poised between heaven and hell, and I desired to see neither of them.

I found my optimism wane slightly as news filtered back from our substitute watchmen and women: with our funds running low, supplies had also begun to ebb, and the plague was once more in ascendance. Our efforts, in recent weeks effective at staving off the worst of the disease, now seemed to wither in the face of a resurgent wave of death.

Even districts thought cleaned and clear of the contagion began to report fresh contamination. The fires of the dead outside the city grew once more.

It was evil news received too soon. I had known that the plague would return – Michel's presence alone assured that. But I had hoped for a few weeks to prepare, not the handful of days that now seemed available before we were overrun with the dead for a final time. I had hoped to coincide our attack on Michel with the feast day of St Elizabeth of Hungary, but that would be impossible under the circumstances. (Though I doubt I could have cared less for the specific date of the attack, I was aware of the effect striking on a feast day of a woman who healed the sick.)

Now it seemed our attack was doomed to coincide with All Hallows Eve. One didn't have to be a genius to pick up on any dark symbolism nor its effect on more religious minds. It was bad enough that Michel and his ilk had taken on their status of fallen angels, this latest sign inciting several of our more fearful men to sneak away as soon as word of our timetable escaped. I wanted to wait a little longer, but that had become impossible.

No, as much as I despised the timetable, we needed to strike soon before the last of our strength had faded.

The day of the attack came grayly, though the sun managed to break through the clouds that had buried the city so long in gloom just after noon. Tired as I was, I dragged myself outside to bask in the weak warmth, some piece of me reassured by the vague heat that managed to remain in the face of a chilly breeze.

My chest still pained me, and while I could easily handle a pistol or musket as well as I ever could, more vigorous action left me struggling to stand, hacking and wheezing until Max or Belial would heave me back to my feet. The others tried to comfort me in the face of my invalidity, reassuring me that our cause was better served with me directing the assault than becoming embroiled in it, but I felt guilty nonetheless.

I closed my eyes, letting my senses drift away in my next soft breath, focusing on nothing else than the soft sound of my heart and the eternal moment between its beating.

One hand rose, confusion reigning in my mind as my fingers touched my forehead, my chest, and then both shoulders. The feeling only deepened as my knees buckled, my hands clasping one another in a weary desire for support, falling limply upon my bent legs.

I prayed then, words leaving my lips even before my mind could conceive of their very existence. I prayed for deliverance, for peace, for victory, for every empty notion that my mortal mind might wish to come to pass. I prayed for the safety of my family, that my niece and nephew might never know the touch of sickness again. I prayed for the retreat of the darkness that had so driven the city to the very edge of oblivion. I prayed that my vain hope would outshine a man who claimed to carry out a divinely ordained plan. I prayed for quiet and for peace and for healing. I prayed until I could think of nothing else to pray for, my entire body shaking, uttering plea after plea, only falling still when quivering lips sealed themselves out of exhaustion.

In the true silence that followed, I listened vainly for something, anything that might indicate that I had been heard, that my vain empty entreaty might have meant something to a God whose existence I had doubted for so long. For a moment, I thought that I had been heard, the pain in my body stolen away for the first time since its wounding. But there was nothing but stillness, my only companion in those moments the whisper of the wind, the breeze fading to an insidious hideous hiss.

Stones crunched at my side, the sound delicate enough that I knew that my moment of introspection was about to end but not so harsh as to destroy the momentary peace the morning had given me. Leaning forward, I pushed myself to my feet, my breath ragged but steady enough that I was able to meet Belial from my heels and not my knees.

"Praying?" he asked, the single word reminding me of our exchange days before, the day we had found the ruined hospital.

"Healing," I replied, a wan smile on my lips. He scrutinized me, up and down, peering into my soul in his knowing way that had become no less unsettling since we had met.

"You do not need to come tonight, Dietrich," he said, cautious concern on his face. "We can carry out the plan without you. You should stay here and rest."

"I've never felt better," I countered, the lie slipping from me easily. I moved through a short footwork routine, injecting as much energy as I could without giving myself over to a coughing fit. "I've already promised Sophie that I will keep out of the fray as best as I'm able. Trust me, I'm aware that I wouldn't last five minutes fighting your former friends up close and personal." I saw his face wince as I painted him in with those who remained solidly in Michel's grip. "But I need to go. Can you imagine me sitting here in the dining room and simply waiting for news? No, we have only gotten so far as we have because I have not allowed myself to become divorced from events on the ground."

"Even when you should have given yourself more space and time apart from them, yes." He nodded slowly, still skeptical but willing to place trust in me one more time. "The others won't like it any more than I do."

"I know," I replied, turning to lead the way back into the manor house. "But if Sophie has agreed to it, the others will, too. As it is, I've heard Wilderich wants to play his own part later."

Again the slow nod. "I am even less comfortable with him going than you."

"And you don't object to him?"

The ex-cultist shrugged. "Max has promised to keep him safe. I have promised the same." His eyes stole a glance in my direction. "Can you imagine a city without him?"

"No" I admitted. "But, then, I couldn't imagine Vienna without any of you at this point. Yet, there is a very good chance that some of all, maybe even all of us die tonight to save it."

"You won't die," he promised me. "Even if I need to lay my life down in exchange, I swear you'll see tomorrow." I didn't see any point to contradicting him, so I let the matter drop, the two of us finishing our walk in silence. Crossing the threshold inside, I mumbled something about needing to attend to some final preparations. He accepted my lie for what it was, disappearing into another part of the house.

Though it had begun as a lie, I found my time taken up by minutiae, ensuring everyone was armed and fed, meeting with each man under my command and going over their role in our assault. I was determined that every last one of Michel's murderers would be caught tonight: even letting one escape would be to allow the plague a fresh chance to infect again.

It was dusk before I was finished, my empty stomach reminding me that, though I had made sure everyone else had eaten, I had yet to do so. I remedied that with a trip to the kitchen, quickly consuming two bowls of stew that finally stilled my grumbling body. Though I knew it only would take a moment's exertion to cause me to feel differently, I felt almost whole then, though the fleeting feeling flew away to be replaced by trepidation.

I did my best to banish it from me, setting my bowl in the wash basin for the house staff and going upstairs to my room for what might prove to be the final time. Switching out my jacket and shirt for something far more appropriately rugged, I noticed myself in the full-length looking glass on one side of my room. To tell the truth I barely recognized the specter reflecting back towards me, but I managed to still the gasp smothered deep in my chest, my eyes entranced by the flesh-spare face that glowered back at me.

I confess that I have never truly considered myself an attractive man – barely middling, if I am exceedingly brutal about my appearance – yet I was unready to see what had happened to my body over the course of the last months. My gentle belly, gained over too many days poring over books and not enough exercise, was long gone. Yes, part of it remained obscured by the confining bandages, but I could see the hint of ribs above the strips of cloth.

The rest of my body was similarly wasted, but it was my face that haunted me most. I had long cultivated a faint whisper of a moustache, my only nod to rakishness in an otherwise bookish lifestyle. The moustache had spread as surely as the plague, hairs sprouting in irregular patches across skin that had become tinged by an unsettling greyness. I might have pretended that it was only a trick of the fading light, that the dying day had gathered the world's color back into it, but then I noticed my eyes.

Once a bright blue, they had frozen over, icing in response to the horrors of the recent past. I had seen the same dead-eyed expression in Belial's face, the same lost innocence. I tried and failed to suppress the shudder that coursed through me, the involuntary reaction drawing a subsequent wince as my ribs reminded me of their existence.

I tore my gaze from the haunted revenant in the looking glass, pulling on a fine undershirt and then a brace of shirts made of rougher, coarse fabric. I grimaced as my arms stretched painfully over my head, tugging on my ribs as the scratching fabric abraded my skin, but I hoped that the general toughness and layering might protect me from any close encounters I might have with Michel or the other Angels.

I called for a servant to help me with settling cross-belts across my chest, the wooden flasks dangling from it rattling as they cackled in anticipation. I would need these to reload my musket after each shot. Indeed, I had practiced as hard as any of the citizenry these last days, though my skill level was far and away superior to anything they had attained.

I added a belt around my waist as well, dangling a short blade off one hip even as I thrust a powder horn and pistol by the other. I had wanted to carry more than this, but the weight of each added weapon slowed me down and promised to steal away my energy, so I had compromised, contenting myself with a mere three weapons.

I dismissed the servant, thanking him for his help now and service throughout his life, my unexpected gratitude drawing a deep blush from the man. Picking up my hat from where I had laid it on the bed, I settled it on my head, exhaling softly to cleanse the clinging doubt from my mind as best I could.

I chanced one last look at the looking glass, if for no other reason than to admire the militant aspect of the entire ensemble. My face was as haunted as it was before, though my expression had lost some of its soullessness, subtle determination instead hunkered down in the face of the time to come. I saw my reflection nod at me, reality and its double committed to the course in a final grim reminder of its stakes. Nodding back, I turned on my heel and left the looking glass and myself behind without another word, unwilling to waste any energy on the shell of a man.

I still had no idea as I crossed the threshold to the exterior of the estate, past the shot-riddled target straw-men on the improvised firing range, past the poles nicked and abraded by endless thrusts and jabs. I had no idea as I climbed the steps of the wooden stage that looked out over several score of torches. And as I looked out over the faces of the bravest sons and daughters of Vienna I will ever know, I realized that I could only say one thing.

Nothing.

My mouth was already opening, though, no sound coming out as I instead gaped like a fish. I didn't know how to inspire this group any more than I knew how to fly, my heart rushing in fear as words continued to fail me. I saw the expectation in each eye slowly turn to doubt as I stood, like a statue, on the review platform.

I'll never know from where he came, because I never saw him as I arrived, but I felt Belial's touch on my shoulder. "Dietrich," he whispered. "May I speak?" Nodding dumbly, I retreated from my place at center stage, doing my best to look dignified.

But the crowd's eyes were already on Belial, more than one looking confused at this relatively unknown figure before them. For his part, the ex-cultist didn't look remotely concerned about his position, instead crossing himself and bowing his head slightly, his face somber. "There are many of you who stand here now because you are afraid of what is to come. And you are right to fear it – those we go to fight are beyond your wildest nightmares. They are quick and strong, fierce and cunning, equal parts man and fallen angel."

He paced slightly, his back straightening as the merest whisper of cast-off nobility returned to him. "How do I know all this, you might ask, and you would be right to do so." His face twisted into a parody of a smile, grinning but absent any pride or prejudice. "I know because I was once one of them." A wave of grumbling and whispers swept the crowd, the torches swaying uneasily as the men holding them tried to digest the revelation that one of the enemy was so close.

Belial pretended to not notice. "But I am that monster no longer. I am a changed man, saved by the actions of this man here." He reached back to point one slender finger at me, though his face remained turned away, fixated as he was on the crowd. "I have turned my back on the actions of my past, prepared to bleed and die so that the city might live."

His arms spread wide like a father welcoming his children. "But why? Why should I ask you to lay down your life in the name of the city and its survival? Haven't so many others fled? Why should you die for the benefit of other men?" There was another wave of grumbling here, but this was expected, even welcomed by Belial. "Yes, those who have fled may benefit from your sacrifice, but that you have stayed, here and now, shows you for what you are: children of faith."

I was in awe as Belial held the assembly in the palm of his hand. I could see the rapt attention, how every soul bent itself fully to hear his next whispered proclamation. For a moment, I realized how fortunate I was to have crossed his path when I did; I could see in him an inner drive that I had only seen in his former mentor, a will that could be harnessed for good or ill that would surpass all obstacles. In that moment, I felt my determination fire and redouble, determined to not fall short next to the pure example of leadership being shown here.

But he was not finished, fervor filling every word. "I say children because we are more than just Christian. We are Jew and Muslim, Catholic and Orthodox. We are rich and poor, noble and humble. We have come together, blind to the divisions that had previously separated us, every soul bent to the achievement of a single, final goal." I smiled as his words matched my unspoken thought. "I say faith because we have not come together in the face of any profession of holy commandment, much as that may appeal to us now. We have come together to defend the basic goodness that we have seen in every action and sacrifice over these last weeks. My heart is as heavy as yours, weary under the weight of such trial, but we are here! We have leaned on each other and come out to win through the torment!"

I heard rumbles of assent now from the crowd, could feel the energy that built sympathetically. The torches burned brighter, the darkness retreating in the face of such humanity. And still Belial was not done. "God once said to Lot that he would spare a city that had even one good man in it. And while Lot was unable to find a single good man, I see before me everything he might have hoped to find as he searched. I have seen every godly virtue on display: peace, patience, kindness, gentleness. I have seen the way we have come together.

"And it is because of this that I am so sure of our inevitable victory! I know that when Dietrich gives the order to march, we go armored in faith. Not in faith of God or life everlasting but faith in the bravery of the man who stands to our left and to our right! Remember that as we march and as we fight, we are not fighting for our city, or our health, or our families." He stopped pacing, his eyes turning towards each of us on the platform before turning back out to the assembled crowd. His next words were mere whispers, but I heard them as clearly as if he had shouted them from the tallest hills outside the city.

"We fight for each other."

My throat ached as it roared in response to the beautiful words, though I couldn't hear it as it vanished beneath the eruption of human emotion that flew from every throat. I watched tears stream from more than one set of cheeks as brave men wept at the chance to even be present here and now. Bishop Wilderich stepped forward, ready to lead the faithful in prayer. His eyes were as alight as anyone's, but none had time for prayer, all eyes returning to me, every assembled soul aching to be let loose to hunt out infernal quarry.

With the flames roaring and the people shouting, I gave a single, wordless wave with my arm.

And Vienna marched out to war.

XL

⊙◈⊚

A Virgil's Seat

I was aware only of moments as we marched into the city, our entire procession quickstepping our way towards our fate with a pace that would shame even an Imperial regiment of foot. I dimly recall one of the musketeers keeping time, his booming bass voice shattering the silence of the night as our feet cadenced against the ground. The torches cracked in response, their hissing snap reminding all of their end should the attack fail in the next minutes.

Yet no one in the band needed any reminder, a fierce song ringing out from the one or two veterans who had fought and beaten the plague in the last months. Few sang at first, the lyrics crude and uncivilized beyond all measure, but by the time we reached the plaza in front of Stephansdom, every voice bellowed the refrain throatily. Even the women cheered from their place at the rear of the column. Had we needed to merely win through by the power of our joined voices, we might have beaten back hell.

Stephansdom herself was less impressed.

The cathedral glowered in vicious quiet, every silent stone balefully gazing at the irreverent display. Our song died a slow death as rational-

332

ity resumed its cynical control over every man and woman in our militia. This was not some tavern brawl we were headed towards. This was life or death, not only for us but for everything we knew.

I know my steps faltered then, and judging by the muttered curses and oaths, I imagine I was not alone. Remembering Belial's words from only minutes before, I called out to those around for courage, pulling the men into their groups and pairs, forming everyone up roughly around the entrance of the cathedral. Wilderich, Max, and the others, seeing my example, called for order, for a weapons check, for anything that could settle the minds of the men around them.

But we were overshadowed as the bell atop the cathedral pealed, each mournful clang causing all to jump at the suddenness of the sound. "Take heart!" I cried, my shouts echoed by the braver among the group, our groups held together only by sheer will and hope. "Remember what you fight for!"

The bell tolled thirteen times before we were able to regain control of the assembly, our nerves already on edge by the frigid reception. Not that I expected to find Michel's men in the streets begging for death, but I had expected more than a ringing bell as a response to our march. We had done little to mask our approach, after all.

At least the bell's call had confirmed for me what we had taken so long to conclude: Michel and his cult were inside.

I tried to chivvy the most nervous forward, making a show of pulling out and preparing my pistol and musket. Belial called for the bravest among them to follow him inside. Seeing his example, I cheered, "For Vienna!"

The call was repeated weakly by several others around me, but more besides picked up the cry until the plaza rang once more with bravery. We rushed from the darkness towards the cathedral, javelins and swords raised, firearms at the ready, the city's faithful pouring over the threshold of the cathedral like a wave.

We ran like fools into an interior illuminated by thousands of candles, the darkness of without banished for a light so bright I momentarily forgot that the day had already died. Votive candelabras lined every wall, their racks gleaming in the fiery light of hundreds of lit wicks. Each pew was flanked by more candles, the dripping wax plummeting to the floor in gelatinous tears. Even the chandeliers overhead were lit, the lit tallow towers conspiring to make it seem as if fiery comets were crashing down inside the cathedral. No matter where the eye looked, there was fire and flame, the entire scene hauntingly beautiful in its perverted religiosity.

Which made the double handful of kneeling figures at the far side of the cathedral that much more unsettling, the lone moments of shadow promising nothing but violence as they huddled in silent prayer. They didn't react at all to our entrance, their heads remaining bowed and away. Pointing to Belial and Max, I watched our small army filter out to the sides, tight knots of men huddling together for the merest hint of safety.

Risking a quick look, I gave quick thanks that the women had stayed hidden.

"And so the Unclean have returned." I turned about to see Kalb come out of a door about halfway up the sanctuary. "I am surprised that you have even deigned to return to taint holy ground. As it is, we have already begun the final cleansing of the city, my friends." Never before had the title 'friend' been used with such contempt.

I struggled to find my own voice; again, Belial stepped in to speak for me. "Kalb, we need not fight. Please, listen. Michel has corrupted our purpose. We are not creatures of God if we murder his entire creation!"

But his former ally merely grinned darkly. "You, worthless one, I think I will take to Michel after we've finished with your... rabble. But the rest?" My head twitched to the side at his words. Take him to Michel? Wasn't the head of the serpent here, too?

My heart fell with my face. We were in the wrong location.

I think my confusion showed because Kalb's face twisted, all humanity flying from him until there was only a rictus of impassioned pain remaining behind. "Brothers and sisters?" he called. "The impure of this pit of vipers come to us to be tested by God. How should we act to their coming?"

The shapes by the altar rose, turning about until we were faced not with long black cloaks but beaked faces, each soulless countenance enough to unman the bravest soldier.

I heard a frantic prayer from Wilderich. "Lord, please forgive the violence we do in your house," he began, though I shouted orders over top of anything else he had to say.

Our knots of fighting men jostled one another, admirably shuffling forward until a rough row of muskets, pistols, and javelins bristled towards the enemy. "Aim!" I called, not wanting to fire until the dark figures had begun their attack, knowing that a fearful man would most likely fire high. I wanted to wait until the cultists were closer. It was a terrible risk. All it would take was a single, terrified finger to twitch and our volley would be thrown away.

On any earthly opponent, our threat of violence might have checked their approach, maybe even encouraged them to surrender. But not one of the dark figures gave so much as a moment's hesitation, each stalking forward like a wolf on the hunt, their hands reaching out to the side as they advanced in perfect silence.

No, not perfect silence. They were hissing in anticipation, the serpent's sound unsettling on a primeval level.

"Max," I called softly, careful not to make too much noise. If I shouted, someone would fire for sure, and I still needed everyone to wait just a handful of seconds longer.

My friend padded over to me, hunkering down slightly to ensure we remained out of the line of fire. "What's going on?"

"We're in the wrong place," I said flatly, cutting off his outburst with a knifing hand. "It doesn't matter. We're in the wrong place, and I need to go across the way to the chapel where he is."

"How do you know-"

"No time, but I know we're not getting out of here for free. Once it starts, I'm going to sneak away, maybe with a handful and-"

"Not without me," he grumbled.

336 - K. AVARD

"I need you here. These men will follow you, here. Please... stay." My eyes were as pleading as my voice, for his face stretched into a tight-lipped grimace before he nodded. We both knew that I wouldn't be taking anyone with me: every last body would be needed here. If I was lucky, I would be able to count on Belial, but I already saw his expression fixated on Kalb.

I would be on my own.

Further thought was stolen away as I realized with a start that only a few dozen paces separated our forces. Raising my musket first and cocking it, I shouted the order so many had been waiting for. "Fire!"

If a single shot was thunder to my ears, then the crash that followed sounded like the end of the world as musket and pistol bellowed together, hurling their deadly ammunition down to crash into pale flesh and masked faces. I reeled, unsteady, as my other senses struggled to compensate for my sudden deafness. Several of the cloaked figures had gone down, thrashing against the stones of the floor. One or two more had taken flesh wounds, their masks broken or knocked askew by a particularly well-aimed shot.

But far too many had missed, the painful effect of their inaccuracy seen in exploded candles and pockmarked stones. I shouted, or at least believe that I shouted, for pistols and javelins, but could not tell if any heard me. The dark figures still on their fight opened their own mouths to cry something, their stalk abandoned for a sprinting run that closed the remaining distance all too quickly.

Holy ground was quickly baptised in the blood of both sides, cartwheeling arms and legs clashing with flashing musket stocks and javelins. I watched as dark shadows threw themselves headlong into knots of brave volunteers, hurling bodies aside with all the care of a petulant child. Sometimes a body would rise to fight again, bloodied but unbroken, hurling musket shot and javelins as well as curses. But too many lay where they fell, rolling back and forth in pain.

I know that I should have fled at the outset of the fight: Michel had to be accosted, but I found myself awestruck at the countless moments of heroism which played out before my eyes. I watched one volunteer, flung aside to ignite on a fallen candelabra, rise completely aflame to hurl himself into the back of a dark shadow over two of his wounded comrades, beating the shape with flashing hands until the shape retreated. Utterly exhausted, the man fell once more, never to rise with all his strength gone.

Another man, alone with a cultist on either side, whirled back and forth, his body flowing between every attack until it seemed he, too, was as inhuman as his opponents, melting away from each of their attacks. I did what I could to help him, firing my pistol into the back of one of Michel's men, the momentary distraction enough to allow my comrade to batter the other away.

Wilderich was in the thick of the melee, the old portly man out of his element but hurling wild swings and prayers in every direction. Max, glued as he was to the holy man's side, turned away attack after attack that would have hit the bishop, commands flying from him for support, for encouragement. Belial was where I expected him to be, face to face with his once-brother Kalb, the two throwing such tremendous blows at one another, I half expected that those nearby would be knocked over by their force.

Everywhere I turned, I saw volumes of bravery that would never be written down. More than half of my men were down or wounded, each dark cultist brought down only after the greatest sacrifice. There were more than a handful of women now fighting, having taken up arms while others tried to tend to the fallen. Though the battle was slowly turning in our favor, the cost would be high. Too high.

Max caught me in a momentary respite, roaring, "Go!" Our eyes locked for an instant, we shared a nod that spoke of decades of brotherhood. I knew that it broke him that I needed to go on alone, that he needed to stay here. But there was no other way. He was needed here.

I was not.

I retreated from the fighting, past the healers who cried out to find out where I was off to, why I was running from the battle. I ignored them, busying myself with my weapons. My sword remained where it hung at my side, undrawn and unblooded, but I took the time to reload my musket and pistol. Knowing who and what I was about to encounter, having both loaded meant little, though the action was, if nothing else, reassuring. Picking up a discarded torch from the ground, I jogged into the small chapel across the plaza.

Magdalenskapelle was the polar opposite of Stephansdom. Where noise and cacophony reigned in the cathedral, the chapel was as silent as death. Where illumination still flared in the cathedral, the former was clad only in midnight, a lone candle lit longingly by a stone staircase that led, I suspected, to the Vergilius chapel below. I crept slowly towards the stone steps, my eyes flitting this way and that as I plundered every shadow for a sign of Michel, my ears listening for even the barest hint of sound.

I had barely arrived beside the candle when I heard the old, kindly voice call up from below. "Dietrich, please do come in. I wondered if you would ever show. I certainly hope Kalb didn't hold you up too much in the cathedral."

XLI

⚮

A Last Meeting

All pretense of surprise gone, I made my pistol safe, pushing it back into my belt, uncocking the spring to prevent any self-inflicted wound. I kept my musket and torch in front of me, both hands so tightly fixed to the pieces of wood, I thought I might break them then and there. Fine, though. At least it would be harder for Michel to see my nerves for the frayed things they were.

My unease faded for a moment as I descended the stairs unmolested, completely undisturbed by hidden assassins and ambushes. Given what my comrades were enduring across the plaza, I felt guilty, ashamed that I was not paying my own price in blood and sweat the way that they were.

Michel's voice drifted up to me, irritatingly kind. "Come, come. I've been waiting for quite a while, and I don't think your friends have forever."

I knew he was trying to bait me, trying to tempt me to a rash charge. He would be waiting by the door frame as I rushed through, ready to attack from the shadows. I slowed my pace further; hopefully, he would get annoyed and charge up the stairs. In the tight confines, I would have the advantage. But eternity came and went, and Michel didn't show his

face. Nearly to the foot of the staircase, I peeked around the last corner
to look into the chapel for the first time.

I understood Wilderich's earlier comments about its size; it seemed
small, even compared to the older churches like Rupertkirche by the
river – I doubted that I could have even fit my small army inside its
walls. On the wall opposite, there was a small altar, smaller than even
that of the chapel overhead, serviceable and rude, but no less holy for
it. There was no other furniture there, save a table and two chairs with
a single, low-burning candle. Michel sat in one of these, the architect of
so much death and misery calm and greeting me with a gentle smile and
a wave. "Please, sit."

I took a single step in before I saw that we were not alone, shivering
as hundreds of sightless eyes pierced me with their unblinking stare. My
torchlight reflected off each fleshless face, I nearly fled from the sight
of seeing so many thousands of bones stacked like cordwood. Here, a
small tower of ownerless hands waved in an impossible breeze. Opposite them, feet tapped irritably, as if bored as they – and the rest of the
ossuary around me – waited for their promised eternal rest.

Michel looked about, completely undisturbed by his surroundings.
"I used to not understand the need to strip the flesh from the bones of
the dead. For the Lord says, 'he that believeth in Me shall not perish,
but have eternal life.'" His lips pursed, the mask of the apparently frail
scholar in place. "Since God made me his messenger, I suppose I understand the need for the living to beautify the dead. I mean, given the
state of Sin and Infidelity you exist in, only the dead seem to manage
any kind of pure life."

I was chilled by the blithe dismissal in his words, the ice bitterly cutting the words of my own response. "Pure life? Considering how much
you cause them to suffer, I doubt that any of your victims would think
you for returning them to any kind of 'purity.'"

He merely shrugged, pointing to a wall sconce. "Please, hang your
torch. I would not want your own light to go out ahead of its time. And
then, please, sit. I insist." His voice promised violence if I did not follow
his instruction perfectly. I did as he asked, setting the torch in a ring

on the wall and returning to the table, sliding out the other chair and sitting opposite, careful to keep myself out of easy arms-reach. Michel didn't comment, a snake's smile his only response, as if he read my mind and was amused by what he saw. When I didn't speak, he apologized, "Forgive me for the misdirect. I needed to ensure that we were left alone for this last conversation."

The cold within me melted as I thought of the innocent blood being shed inside of the cathedral. "Will you apologize, too, for my ribs, or for the thousands of dead? Will you apologize for the killing of monks, even if they worked to keep your taint from ravaging their flesh?"

He scoffed. "Don't be so dramatic, Dietrich. Of course not. All this death has had its purpose."

"To cleanse the city of the impure. I remember our last 'last conversation,'" I commented bitterly. "I thought that you and I would never meet again. Those were your words, weren't they? Isn't that false witness a sin? Does this mean the plague will attack you now, too?"

Another sound escaped him, something between a sigh of frustration and pity. "My body has been afflicted by plague for a long time before you and will be afflicted by it a long time after you. Having the honor of being God's messenger does not come without cost, of course."

"So far that cost seems to have been shockingly light," I observed cynically.

"Compared to what others have lost, yes. I suppose that's true," he allowed cryptically. "But then, your lives are short and brutally cold. You stumble about in the darkness with God's light above you. But rather than moving at all towards the fire, you hunker in the night and bellow about the vileness of its chill." His lips pursed, the utter lack of concern stoking my anger again. "Might I ask you a question?"

I chewed on my tongue. "In exchange for one of my own? Fine." His head tilted slightly as if he had been somehow caught off guard by the condition, though the amused look on his face told the truth of it: he not only expected it, he had wanted me to name it. When he said nothing for long seconds, I snapped irritably. "What is it? People are dying outside across the plaza while we sit talking about nothing!"

My outburst did nothing to unsettle him, though his tone did, at least, fade into something more contrite. "If they die, it is because it is God's will that they die. Forgive me, though. This is the last time our paths will cross, and I would not waste the opportunity with an idiotic question." Lapsing into silence, I watched his eyes burrow into me once more. Yet, when all the times before I had felt nothing but discomfort at his scrutiny, an odd peace settled over me now. There were no secrets within me any longer. My soul had been laid bare over the last months.

At long last, Michel leaned forward, he finally asked, "How are you an agnostic?"

I would have scoffed at the question had his voice not come to me so innocently lost. The vulnerability unmanned me, confused me. Michel had maintained to be ancient, timeless, yet here he acted like a little boy lost in a sea of illogic. "I don't understand. You want to know why I don't fall to my knees and beg a higher power for peace, love, and happiness?"

Years fell from my enemy's face, dark wisdom replaced by childlike earnestness. "Yes. Don't you understand that all you are comes from God? How can you profess to not believe in something so obvious about the world?"

I shrugged. "Easily, I suppose. You paint this picture of God as all-knowing and all-knowable, but you don't see the division here, in the churches and in the streets. As a child, I heard that to love others as yourself was to know God, but I grew up seeing blind hatred, dismissal, rejection of anyone who was not immediately a comrade in arms. Look at yourself..." I suggested, one hand lifting to indicate his entire body. "You claim to be of God and for God, but you reject any kind of non-Christian. Where I, at least, have the good grace to see them as a collection of flesh and bone, you see only where their prayers are levied."

The words poured from me, falling to rest upon Michel's ears. "Yahweh, Jehovah, Allah, Elohim. If any or all of them exist, does that change the nature of man? No. If an evil man prays to God while a good man believes only in himself, does that make the evil man more holy or worthy of good fortune? No. I have seen priests bless and curse based on blind prejudice and, though those men can be won over, though their preconceptions can be changed given enough time, why and how should I believe in any master they serve if he – or she – allows them the hatred to live that way?"

Michel stared at me with wide, vacant eyes. Was he listening or had my irreverence eliminated any interest he had in my thoughts? "Besides," I allowed bitterly. "I have prayed more in the last weeks than I have in my entire life. I have turned my back on science in the hope that my blind faith would see the plague destroyed, the dying brought back to full life. I still doubt any higher power, but a man's heart should have room for more than one religion."

You might have heard a pin drop in the silence that followed, so deeply was Michel digesting my miniature sermon. And he was, I could see, his eyes flashing back and forth in the candlelight as if my words danced before him in a mad whirlwind only he could see.

But the silence was punctured by distant shots, the reminder of violence driving me to shake my head. "But I've answered your question, so I think it's time you answer mine... Why am I here, alone? Why are you here, alone, and not standing with the rest of your vile doctrine in the cathedral?"

Michel looked down, away from me, smoothing out an invisible crease in his obsidian robes. Though the action had nothing approaching shame at all, he did seem... uneasy, as if this meeting, though expected, had not been wholly desired. He recovered quickly, his face a mask as he answered. "Like I said, I wished to speak to you, Dietrich. And you desired to speak with me." His face became a spare, sad smile when I snorted, his brow furrowing in delicate, aged confusion. "Or am I wrong?"

"No, but you put it so delicately. You have no conception of the loss that I, that we, have endured. You do not know the fear or the terror that you and yours have brought to the city, do not know how many bodies we have burned, the tears we have shed..." I felt my own hot tears form. "If you are as divine as you pretend, then you know nothing of loss."

Part of me had hoped that Michel would be infuriated. And perhaps he was, his next words taut with careful restraint as he wagged a single finger slowly in front of my face. "Before you go further, remember that your rabble is killing my sons and daughters as we speak. I have lost far more than you will ever know." The waving finger stopped to point at my weapons. "But if you feel differently, by all means... shoot me."

I nearly did, mastering my emotion only after a moment of effort. But I would lose any confrontation between us, especially this close to him. Instead I asked, "So how does our story end? Your followers might kill everyone that had come here tonight to stop you, but what will that prove? That you are willing to slaughter anyone who passes your ridiculous test of faith? You realize that for every body you make tonight, I'll simply raise another three. We'll keep coming, whittling away at you, until you are each as dead as we are."

It was false bravado, my ego desperately scribbling cheque after cheque that would remain uninvested. The sad smile reappeared again on Michel's face. "That is very possible, Dietrich. Very possible, indeed." His expression grew wistful. "I like you Dietrich. Even when you struggle and scrape, you do it with a fervor that reminds me of me when I first was given this task of testing. Even your attack! It was a gamble, and one that still might succeed, at least in depriving me of followers for now, but you did it knowing the odds were long, nigh on impossible. And why? Because you love this city more than your own welfare."

It must have been a trick of the light, for his face softened further, the fury and hatred and zeal disappearing, replaced by... respect perhaps. He went on. "I was furious when you turned down my offer for protection of your family. In exchange for an eternity of servitude, is the peace of forty not enough?" He got up, the simple action enough for my hands to fly to my pistol and sword reflexively, anticipating an attack.

Michel chuckled, the sound echoed by the hundreds of jawless skulls that glared on from their place in the naves of the chapel. He waved his hands for calm. "Please, I did not bring you here to cause you harm."

"But you are willing to kill others in my place so we are not interrupted? Couldn't you have simply sent a letter for us to speak?" I flippantly objected.

My insolence seemed to only encourage him further, his booming laughter echoing in the small space until it rivaled the volley fired in the cathedral before. I felt my own ire grow as his good humor clashed with my bitterness over the spilled blood in Stephansdom. "After my last departure, I doubted you would show. A failing on my part," he apologized. "But we are here, now, and the price of our meeting is being paid, in full, by us both." He moved to one of the piles of bones, one hand reaching out to stroke the bare bones. My skin crawled as I imagined the victim of his touch, some nameless citizen of Vienna who would die in history an irrelevant footnote. "Do you understand why I wanted to speak to you yet?"

"No."

He waited for me to go on, vaguely disappointed when I did not. "I wanted to speak to you to offer you a new deal."

"No," I repeated.

Curiosity now. "But you haven't yet heard my offer?"

"No," I said a third time. "You have had your chance to make peace and have spat on it, time and again. I would sooner kill myself then serve myself up on a platter for your amusement."

"Not even if I guaranteed the survival of everyone in the city?" he asked, his eyes twinkling as my jaw dropped. "Even then, you would not want to listen to my deal?"

"After all of it, you would just... walk away?" I managed to say, stunned. "Why now? You have killed nearly everyone in the city."

Michel looked bored, as if he were disgusted by my obstinacy. "So cynical, even when I offer whoever remains salvation." His mouth shrugged, lips frowning momentarily. "You've said yourself, everyone who is tainted by sin is dead or dying. Those who will die will die. Those who know God's love will not." His continued blithe disregard for life nearly had me reach for my sidearms again, but he went on without concern. "You might think me a monster, but I have done exactly what I set out to do: I have tested the city and returned those found wanting to God's side for judgement. Sometimes my hand has been forced into a regrettable action – such as the attack on your physicians, but then you were not paying attention to the breadcrumbs I was leaving. But I offer this... peace now not for my sake, but for yours."

I felt my expression sour as he mentioned the ruined hospital, the memory of the murdered dead still painfully fresh. "At what cost?" I asked, expecting a higher price to be paid than simply my indentured servitude.

"No cost," he said.

I nearly flew to my feet. "Nothing? Salvation out of the goodness of your heart then, I suppose?"

He shook his head. "No, but then how could I expect you to see that you have held up your side of the bargain already? Your devotion and love, your desire to see life triumph over death, good over 'evil,' however you define it – you have given me your servitude. Or given it to God, more accurately." One hand rose slowly to forestall any reply. "You have done everything the Bible would ask of you. You have protected those who have harmed you. You, a quiet agnostic, have prayed, not for yourself but for every piece of creation around you, ready to sacrifice everything for the peace of others. What are you if not a servant of God?"

"A physician," I said. "Science and Christianity are hardly compatible."

He conceded the point with a tilt of his head. "Both are religions, though one is more heavenly than the other, as one depends on the work of heretics."

"I know, but then Christians have done enough to persecute those 'heretics,' haven't they?" I interjected.

He ignored my barb. "Regardless, you have held up your side of the bargain, even if that was only done ignorantly. Besides," he continued. "I would never accept you into my service. I take only the broken and the ill. You, for all your flaws, are too pure a soul to be cleansed in my service."

With every syllable, it was as if he begged for me to shatter our fragile peace, but I saw the offer for what it was: a return to normality. No, not normality, I realized. The city had been wounded far too deeply for that. But it would mean an end to the death, an end to the terror. He stopped his pacing, staring at me expectantly. "Well?"

"Fine, but under one condition," I said.

"Yes?" he allowed indulgently.

"When you leave, you never return. If another man, woman, or child dies of the plague, I will hunt you and your kind to the ends of the earth and destroy you."

The chamber echoed with his laughter again. Even the skulls of the dead cackled from their resting place. "You could try, Dietrich. You could try. And who knows? Perhaps you might even succeed." His face became grave then. "I go where God's will sends me. I would love to promise peace, but I cannot. What I will allow is that when God would send me here, I will intercede on your behalf, out of respect."

It was the best that I could manage, I realized. "Fine. But if our meeting here tonight has been baptized in blood, then our peace should be sealed in it, too."

"I have no doubt that you have promised to destroy every last sign of me and mine in the city. And I tell you," he said, his tone rich with perfect knowledge, "this will not happen. Let me go, in peace, and live out your days in relative happiness. Leave behind this hatred. You are too good of a man to take this last kind of petty revenge."

He backed away from me as I rose to my feet, his voice rising as my pistol came up as well. "Please, Dietrich. I would not want to harm you, but I promise you I will if you do not allow me to leave untouched. Do not break this last oath, in the name of God."

I warred with myself, a part of me begging me to put down my arms, another screaming silently for me to pull the trigger. I thought of the peace so newly made: pulling the trigger would likely wound it almost until death, and I had broken far more than one oath in the last weeks. What was one more? Wasn't it better to do no harm and allow Michel to leave than to endanger our tenuous treaty? If any higher power existed, surely it would be better, more heavenly, to turn the other cheek.

But I am just a man, flawed and broken. If there was any higher power, it would understand.

Lightning flashed underground, thunder roaring one final time.

XLII

A Sounding Bell

I knelt by his side, my hands cradling his head with an affection that I thought impossible. I had nearly flown to his side, rushing to gently lower him to the ground. I noticed finally that my torch had gone out by the door, having burnt itself into nothing during our conversation. But for the burning candle on the table, we would have been alone in the darkness with the dead.

Michel smiled at me benevolently, cherubic indulgence in every crease of his face. "I imagine you think our treaty is shattered," he whispered slowly. When I nodded, he shook his head softly. "No, I will hold to my side of the bargain. You have your peace... and my forgiveness."

The candle on the table guttered, the flame flickering in time with his slowing pulse. "I would have thought that you would be angry," I said, regret coloring my words.

He shook his head. "I return to God, to tell him that the city of Wien is in the hands of a righteous man." The pressure in my hands diminished, Michel's body seeming to fade beneath my touch even as I cradled his head. It was as if he was composed of nothing but fierce faith and shadow, his fierce conviction his last tie to the world.

The burning wick flickered again. Over the last echoes of thunder, I heard the cathedral bell sound. Again and again it pealed, the dead mourned by the few who lived, the wounded city tentatively celebrating the new peace sealed in sacrifice, sweat, and blood. To say the plague was over would be premature, but to say that light finally gleamed in the dark soothed my soul.

I looked down to see the last light die in Michel's eyes die, his body fading to nothing even as the candle whispered one last time before fading into darkness, leaving me alone in the dark with the dead. I gave him a moment of silence, but only one because I had oaths to keep to those who I could yet help.

And then I left, leaving the dead to their slumber as I went to heal the living.

About the Author

Though he has devoured books of all genres for years, *First, Do No Harm* is **Kurt Avard's** first step into the world of writing his own. When not reading books - or penning his own - he enjoys traveling to learn of new peoples, foods, cultures, and the stories that arrive with them. Though he remains only an occasional user of social media, he can be found both on Facebook and Twitter at theRealKAvard.

9 781735 408903